Marion Zimmer Bradley's Fantasy Worlds

Edited by
Marion Zimmer Bradley & Rachel E. Holmen

The Marion Zimmer Bradley Literary Works Trust
PO Box 193473
San Francisco, CA 94119
www.mzbworks.com

Copyright © 1998 Marion Zimmer Bradley Literary Works Trust
Cover photo copyright © 2012 by Dave Ruffle
All rights reserved.

ISBN: 1-938185-29-3
ISBN-13: 978-1-938185-29-8

CONTENTS

Introduction: The Wild Panhandle   1
   by Marion Zimmer Bradley

Introduction: Literary Offspring   3
   by Rachel E. Holmen

Lizzie Fair and the Dragon of Heart's Desire   4
   by Rosemary Edghill

Toyen   27
   by Cynthia McQuillin

Eyes of Moonlight, Tears of Stone   43
   by Robin Wayne Bailey

The Border Women   62
   by Paul Edwin Zimmer

Warrior Without a Heart   117
   by Jessie D. Eaker

Totem Night   132
   by Deborah J. Ross

Raven's Blade   141
   by Raul S. Reyes

When Coyote Came to Town   158
   by Diana L. Paxson

Earth's Song   171
   by Laura J. Underwood

Ingredients *by Lawrence Watt-Evans*	183
Lost Moon *by India Edghill*	193
Rehabilitation *by Syne Mitchell*	209
The Accursed Villa *by Cynthia L. Ward*	220
As Three to One *by Dorothy J. Heydt*	235
The High Altar *by Dave Smeds*	251
One Drink Before You Go *by Michael Spence*	263
Washerwoman *by Steven Piziks*	267
Change-Child *by Elisabeth Waters*	276
The White Falcon *by Heather Rose Jones*	279

INTRODUCTION: THE WILD PANHANDLE

by Marion Zimmer Bradley

When I first got into this business, the space behind my ears was what we used to call in those days, badly in need of a towel. I had never done any editing—nor did I know anyone in the publishing business. They used to say in those days something about, "It doesn't matter what talent you have, it's all in who you know." Well, I didn't know a soul; I was out in the wilds of Texas and I didn't know anybody! After I had been writing in the field for a while, I got to know everybody; but I started out as probably the most innocent and naive youngster possible, stuck in the outback—and believe me, in those days the Texas panhandle was really pretty wild. I still remember that I spent several years marooned with a baby and no car—the houses had indoor plumbing but not much else; I washed all my diapers by hand—we didn't even have a washing machine! (They were pretty crude then anyhow, compared to the ones now, which do everything but sort the clothes.) And sometimes, in that sandstorm country, I'd just get the diapers on the clothesline, and a sandstorm would blow up, making all the diapers so stiff with sand that I'd have to wash them all over again.

Well, I survived (somewhat battered, but I survived) and became a writer because I wanted a job where I need not leave my baby with someone whose market value was even less than mine—in those days, an ignorant or illiterate girl right out of the cotton fields—and I had no salable skills. Writing, at least in those days, was a job for those with no other skills. And I couldn't even type. My first several books were written on an old manual machine by the same hunt-and peck method I still use on my big computer. Well, I managed somehow to start selling, mostly with the help of my first editor, Don Wollheim, who was my first publisher and who virtually created the field of science fiction/fantasy as we know it now. These days, as an editor myself, I know how an editor can value anyone who can turn out consistently printable work.

It was Wollheim, too, after he had left Ace and formed his own company, DAW, who started me off as an editor; in one very real sense, he is responsible for the fact that there is such an editor as MZB—and who gave a great many of the present writers in the field their first chances. That's one reason why we have this volume today; wherever Don may be now in the afterlife, I hope he knows how much we love and remember him.

—MZB

INTRODUCTION: LITERARY OFFSPRING

by Rachel E. Holmen

You know about Marion. MISTS. SWORD AND SORCERESS anthologies. Darkover books.

But you may not know Marion as the literary "mother" of dozens of daughters, and not a few sons as well. Fandom, and the roots that many SF and fantasy writers have in fandom, has always meant a lot to Marion. Characters in her novel THE CATCH TRAP were based on members of her "fannish family" during the fifties. She feels at times that she is herself the literary daughter of C.L. Moore. In her anthologies and her quarterly magazine, in workshops at countless conventions, she has encouraged, corrected, and guided many people in the early steps of their writing careers.

We asked some of those writers to contribute stories to this volume. Not everyone we asked could send us anything, but I think the stories that we have gathered here will amuse and entertain you. (And I should tell you, we saved some of the best stories for last.)

You'll find, as you read the introductions to these stories, that the writers form a linked community as each other's readers, researchers, and advisors. Many of them became friends before they were writers. The friendships continued, at earlier Fantasy Worlds Festivals and other conventions, by phone and fanzine and letter and e-mail and electronic roundtable, as careers began and developed. Those careers were often spurred by sales to Marion's magazine or one of her anthology projects. Literary aunts and uncles such as Madeleine L'Engle, and Don and Elsie Wollheim nurtured Marion and her growing flock of protégées; some, such as Diana L. Paxson and Mercedes Lackey, nurture their own successors now, following Marion's example.

I hope you'll enjoy this book, and come away with affection for the writers who form part of Marion Zimmer Bradley's extended family.

—REH.

LIZZIE FAIR AND THE DRAGON OF HEART'S DESIRE

by Rosemary Edghill

Rosemary Edghill and her sister India (who also has a story in this volume) share dwelling and work space in upstate New York, where their combined libraries threaten to collapse the floor under them and their cats. "It's a good thing we live on the ground floor."

She has published a spate of Regency novels including TURKISH DELIGHT and FLEETING FANCY from St. Martin's; detective novels featuring Bast, a Witch: SPEAK DAGGERS TO HER, BOOK OF MOONS, and THE BOWL OF NIGHT; and a fantasy series including THE SWORD OF MAIDEN'S TEARS—which kept me up till 1:30 a.m. on a work night, THE CUP OF MORNING SHADOWS, and THE CLOAK OF NIGHT AND DAGGERS. She has had stories published in Marion Zimmer Bradley's FANTASY Magazine, Dragon Magazine, *and* SWORD AND SORCERESS VIII.

The tale you're about to read is so visual, you will immediately found yourself mentally designing Lizzie's red leather jacket and wanting to master watercolor techniques just so you can paint the oily sheen of Nimrod Wildfire's dark wings.

Her name was Elizabeth Amanda Fairchild. She was born, twenty-nine years before, in a part of the country where it was inevitable that sooner or later everyone came to New York. So she did, and became versed in the shifts and diversions of that strange country, and found that the tree-lined streets of her childhood had given her one marketable skill.

Lizzie Fair, Queen of the Rolling Messengers. For $9.25 an hour and no benefits, she skated the streets of Manhattan with knapsack and portfolio, brave and gaudy in leather and crash-pads, carrying contracts and manuscripts, bills, artwork, torts and retorts, film and photos and video cassettes from here to there. She wore a beeper. She knew where every working pay phone was in midtown Manhattan.

Lizzie Fair lived in the East Village, in a one-room walk-up on the same street where the Hell's Angels had their New York headquarters; the neighborhood, if not quiet, was safe.

Then one day she met Nimrod Wildfire.

She was skating down Broadway just south of 57th Street a little after noon on June 23rd. She had on a red leather jacket and a backpack full of tapes from CBS West, and was rolling hard and fast for Rockefeller Center when she saw the wacko.

In Lizzie's world, all the inmates of the world's largest open-air lunatic asylum were to a degree crazy unless they happened to skate for a living, but the wacko had them all beat.

He had dark skin, curly hair, a large ruby stud in his left ear, and perfect teeth. He was wearing a grey silk Armani-or-knockoff and looked like a slumming Tong hitman. He was standing smack in the middle of Broadway and rubbernecking as if he'd never seen a city before. Traffic beeped enthusiastically at him and didn't swerve at all.

For an instant they stared into each other's eyes as she skated past, and Lizzie had the spooky feeling she'd suddenly become an actor in whatever mind-theater Wacko was staging. Then she was around a corner and going cross-town.

Too much nose-candy, thought Lizzie with disinterested sympathy. She dropped off her tapes at Black Rock, but the lobby phones were all—as usual—busy and she couldn't call in. She skated down a few blocks to a coffee shop where the phone was usually free and ordered coffee and a bagel to go. The Lightfleet dispatcher was reeling off pick-up addresses in her ear when Wacko walked in. He was looking for someone and Lizzie knew in her heart of hearts who it was. She scribbled furiously in her dispatch book, pretending she didn't.

"Go up to 72nd and pick up a *what?* Vanya, do you think I—"

"I'm looking for a maid," Wacko said in her free ear.

"So call an agency," she said, out of the corner of her mouth. She looked at him sideways. His eyes flashed the false metallic leaf-gold of custom-colored contact lenses. Crazy *and* rich; a winning combo. "No, not you, Vanya. Okay, okay, I got it."

"A *mortal* maid," said Wacko, insistently.

"Look, will you just go back to Mars, Chuck?" Lizzie hung up the phone and gave him the full benefit of her attention for a moment, knowing it was almost certainly a mistake.

"My name is Nimrod Wildfire," said Wacko, who seemed to like being sneered at by rolling messengers. "I need a mortal maid."

Lizzie slithered around him and over to the cash register, revising her opinion of his sanity several degrees downward. She thrust $2.25 at the cute counterman, grabbed her bag, and skated out through the revolving door before Wacko could make up his mind to touch her.

It isn't easy to skate through a revolving door. But Lizzie was the best.

Up to Seventy-second. Down to Forty-first. Her calves ached, her back hurt, and she was starting to think longingly of quitting time.

She also suspected she was losing her mind.

She was the fastest thing in Manhattan. Faster than a pedestrian, much faster than a car, and only she and Uncle Vanya Hernandez knew where she was going. So why was she seeing Wacko everywhere she went?

"I am on a quest."

Lizzie spun on her skates and toe-stopped. There stood Wacko, just as weird and immaculate as he'd been four hours ago.

"Why me?" she demanded—not of him exactly, but he took it that way.

"I am Nimrod Wildfire. I have been sent to find a mortal maid and bring her to the Court of Phaerie. I have chosen you," Wacko said, just as if it made sense.

Half the art of being witty—and *alive*—was knowing when to leave the conversation. Lizzie let herself roll backward, picked up speed, zipped down the incline of a pass-through garage, and was gone. She spent the next sixteen blocks trying to think of what she should have used for a parting line, and the next several after that congratulating herself on her narrow escape. Then, like a proper urban primitive, she concentrated on forgetting about it entirely. By the time she reached Lightfleet's offices below Houston, she'd nearly succeeded.

She handed in her book, signed her time-card, exchanged skates for sneaks, spandex for denim, and a wet t-shirt for a dry one. She slung her ditty-bag over her shoulder and headed for home.

It was still daylight on East 8th Street, though the sun was mostly below the level of the tall buildings to the west. Nimrod Wildfire was waiting for her on the steps of her building.

"Look," she said, checking out her escape routes and the presence or absence of any Hell's Angels around the clubhouse down the street. *"What do you want?"*

"Mortal maid, I want you to go with me to the Phaerie Court," Nimrod said, just as if he'd been waiting to be asked.

"Sure. I'll do that. Now—" She'd turned to go back up the street, but the street wasn't there. She'd agreed to go, after all.

Three winged fay by the door were teasing a leashed hippogriff while in the corner someone juggled golden apples. A unicorn looked languishingly into the eyes of a young blonde girl with stars in her hair, and a pair of golden snakes slithered noisily around a stick held by a man in a white dress.

Lizzie Fair was at the Phaerie Court. Everybody was talking at once. The din was numbing.

SonovaBITCH, thought Lizzie, staring around herself. She was still trying to sort her impressions into some kind of order when Nimrod Wildfire dragged her toward the throne where the emperor and his consort sat.

"I have brought the mortal maid who comes of her own choice, without trickery," Nimrod announced.

Everyone in the room stopped talking at once. Oberon leaned forward.

"Did she really?" His Imperial Majesty Oberon, Lord Emperor of Phaerie and all the Lands Beyond the Morning, asked breathlessly. "Freely and of her own will?" His mad eyes gleamed and Lizzie recoiled, dragging back on Nimrod's grip.

"I did *not!* I'm *not* here of my own will and he *didn't* ask me to come here and he *tricked* me!"

There was complete and utter silence in Oberon's Court. "Too bad," said Titania at last. "I imagine that means you lose your forfeit, Prince Nimrod."

It occurred to Lizzie that no matter how much she didn't want to be here she might have been better off keeping her mouth shut.

"She agreed to come!" Nimrod protested. "And she is a maid, pure and untouched. Do you know how hard it is to—"

"What's your name, mortal maid?" asked Oberon kindly, and despite herself Lizzie took two steps forward, toward those drowning-pool eyes.

"Li—Elizabeth. Elizabeth Amanda Fairchild," she said dutifully, and groped for a suitable honorific.

The Court, which had been getting noisier, fell violently silent again.

"You brought a *Maid Elizabeth* to *Our Court!*" The Lord of Phaerie expanded like an exotic tropical fish until even the unicorn took notice. "A maid—a *virgin maid Elizabeth*—" he sputtered.

I'll leave if you like, thought Lizzie loudly.

"This is monstrous! Unthinkable! Impertinent! Nimrod Wildfire, you are banished! Yes! *Banished!*" Oberon roared.

"Until the next time," said Titania, just loud enough to he heard. "Leave this court and never—eh?"

Oberon turned to glare at his wife, and Lizzie took the opportunity to steal a glance at Nimrod, but Nimrod wasn't there. In his place stood a ...thing. A black, huge, leopard-tiger-some-sort-of-shimmering-fabulous-nightmare-beast, that somehow still looked like Nimrod.

And looked *at* her. Lizzie Fair emitted a thin distressed squawk and stumbled backward.

"But if we banish Prince Nimrod, what then shall we do with you?" Oberon said, speaking to Lizzie while glaring at Titania. "What shall we do with this mortal maid?" he asked his Court. There were a couple of suggestions, but fortunately Lizzie couldn't quite hear them.

"I'm not what you want. And I don't want to be here. Send me home," she said desperately.

It was the wrong thing to say again.

"Home. Yes, home is best. We will send you home, Mortal Maid Elizabeth—if you will do us a trifling small service first."

"What?" asked Lizzie, because she didn't seem to have any choice.

"Prince Nimrod, as you know, is banished from our sight. Go to the garden at the westernmost end of the world; find his heart, and restore it to him. Do that and he may return to Us—and you may go."

"No!" The dark wild-thing crouched beside Lizzie and hissed. "That isn't fair!"

"Of course it isn't fair," said Titania sympathetically, "but it's his Court and he can do as he likes—isn't that right, dear?" Oberon, Lord of Phaerie, beamed upon his Queen Consort.

"—and Prince Nimrod can do just as *he* likes," Titania finished happily. "If you don't want to come back, dear boy, you needn't, you know."

"Of course he wants to come back!" Oberon interrupted argumentatively. "Everyone wants to be here—that's why it's the Court!"

"Just as you say, dear," Titania said. Oberon's brow furled. "If—" Lizzie began, and Nimrod pounced upon her.

There was a moon shining over the valley. Its light was the pure blue of a robin's egg, and it shone so brightly that the seas and craters of its surface, if any, were invisible. Trees and hills were forced by moonglow into black-and-white, and a light breeze was heavy with the scent of lilies. It took Lizzie a moment to realize she was no longer indoors.

"I'll give you one piece of advice, Maid Elizabeth—though I don't know why I bother. Never question Their Majesties—and don't argue with them, either. It never helps."

"Yah!" said Lizzie, whirling around to face him. She watched in horrified fascination as Nimrod's muzzle blunted, flattened, and became a lion's mask to match the lion's body. "You're still here!" she added inanely.

The lion-thing folded black wings across its back and lashed its tufted tail. "As are you, Maid Elizabeth. If you ever mean to go back to the World of Iron, you had better not tarry here after the moon has set." The winged lion curled its tail over its back and prowled away.

"Hey! Nimsey!"

After a minute, Lizzie followed. Where else did she have to be, after all?

Nimrod Wildfire's heart was hidden somewhere in a garden at the westernmost edge of the Lands Beyond The Morning; to get home again she had only to find and return it to him. It wasn't that difficult for someone who'd grown up on Andrew Lang's collections of fairy tales to figure out.

Of course, Nimrod Wildfire had no desire for the return of the heart he had given up in exchange for power. But he could not get rid of her, and Lizzie Fair was stubbornly certain of what she wanted.

At least, she thought she was.

"Maiden's tears and maiden's hair; maiden's glance and maiden's touch; these are the charms that work her will; these are the powers in the blood—" Lizzie sang, only slightly off-key, a song that had been popular in the last town they'd gone through. She'd lost track of the places she'd been, looking for the garden at the edge of the world.

"Will you stop singing, Elizabeth?" Nimrod snarled. His body shimmered: fur to scales to feathers and back again, following some pattern she couldn't quite grasp. Like any Phaerie, Nimrod was fond of music; her inept singing annoyed him, which was why she did it.

"Why? It's a beautiful day; we've got our health—and I think this is probably it, Nimsey.

"Don't call me Nimsey, Elizabeth," Nimrod snarled. Antlers branched and withered; paws became hooves, became claws, became hands. Beautiful or not, she preferred not to look at him for very long.

"Then don't call me 'Elizabeth'. And since there's no place like this place anywhere around the place, this must be the place."

The walled garden stood in the center of the road. The garden wall was circular; a dust-pale roofless tower, and high enough so that standing in front of the gate you could not see over it. The doors set in the garden wall looked harder than the stone. Grillwork set into the door allowed sight of what lay beyond—if you were tall enough.

Nimrod padded past her, and reared, and stretched; his talons whittled bright curls from the wood and his wings spread like sudden thunder to balance him.

"You're right. It's a garden," he said, sitting down again. The wings folded into sleek, smooth hide and vanished.

"Great." *I want to go home.* "So all we have to do to get your heart back is get in there, Nimsey."

"I am not going in there," Nimrod pointed out with deceptive reasonableness.

"Why not?"

The great black unicorn looked haughtily away. Mane as fine as a woman's hair streamed silken in the sun.

Of course. I'm the one who wants his heart—not him. "Would you stop doing that for a while? I'm trying to think."

The black stag regarded her with grave interest.

Lizzie exhaled a short sharp breath and turned back to the doors.

There were no door-knockers, or door-handles; she put her hand against the bare wood.

Both doors swung inward.

Sorcery, or someone's watching, because Nimsey leaned on these things and they didn't move. The thought went no further, because then Lizzie saw the garden.

Tall trees in fruit and flower and leaf; low bushes and no two alike; beds of flowers, the tall ones standing up like spears out of a sea of bloom and the inward stones of the wall obscured by the growth of every sort of thing that climbed. At her feet there began a narrow path of smooth white sand, bordered at the edges by round black river stones.

The perfume of the garden struck her like a soft moving wall. The sky became more blue, the sunlight split into a squandered hoarding of color and sound and scent; she was drunken and giddy on rare atmospheres—

"What did you think you were *doing?*" Nimrod glared down at her, blessedly human for once.

She was sitting on the ground, the heat from the stones of the garden wall soaking into her back. He'd dragged her away from the door before she fell through it.

"*'The sedge is withered by the lake/And no birds sing'*," Lizzie explained reasonably. She shook her head in self-reproach and took a deep breath. "The garden—" she tried again, and looked at Nimrod. But there wasn't any point in explaining, so she scraped spine and elbows levering herself to her feet and went back to the garden gate to take another look. Nimrod's heart was somewhere in this garden, and all she had to do was find it. Lizzie took a step forward.

But she couldn't.

She could not walk into the garden any more than she could force herself to plunge her arm into a vat of molten metal. Nothing she could feel was constraining her. But she could not go in.

Then she saw the inscription. It had been covered by the doors before; it was written on the inside of the archway in large ornate letters widely spaced and embellished with carven foliage.

"Nothing pure can enter here."

And that was just terrific. That was just great. Because purity had gotten her into this mess: a mortal maid—untouched and untampered with, virginal and pure.

"Son of a *bitch,*" said Lizzie Fair. She stared at the inscription in incredulous exasperation.

"Well?" Nimrod snapped, and in a moment even Lizzie thought it was funny. *He thinks I can get in there. His heart's in there, and that I'm going to get it.*

"Oh, never mind, will you?" she snarled back.

"Aren't you going in?" Tired of humanity, Nimrod Wildfire shaded himself with leathery wings and coiled serpentine in the dust.

"No, I'm not going in."

"Why not?"

"Because I can't."

"And why not, little mortal maid?"

"Because," Lizzie said shortly.

The gunmetal-black coils unwound. The serpent went to inspect the open gateway. Sun flashed off the iridescent grey-blue softness under its jaw as the long reptilian head twisted itself on the supple neck to look.

"'Nothing pure'?" said Nimrod in incredulous amusement. "Nothing *pure?*" The cockatrice flung itself down in the dust, its jeweled sides heaving in frantic amusement. "Oh, my poor dear little mortal *maid!*" it wailed.

Lizzie set her jaw. What was it about virginity that these people found so god-damned funny? She walked forward deliberately, and planted both sneakered feet on one outflung leathery wing. Nimrod stopped writhing and looked at her.

"I'm happy you're happy," Lizzie said poisonously. "I'm happy that you're happy that we're going to be out here—*together*—looking for your heart for ever and ever. Because neither of us can go back anywhere until you've got it, and it's in there, and I can't go in there. So we're just going to have to keep going. So enjoy."

Nimrod had become very still as she spoke. A delicate tail-tip slid around her ankle and coiled up her leg.

"It's not actually impossible for you to enter the garden, little mortal maid..." he said seductively.

Despite common sense—that he couldn't mean what he sounded as if he did, because of all creatures, Nimrod Wildfire least wanted her to succeed—Lizzie yelped and sprang backward. She tripped over the rest of his tail and fell flat on her back.

"...but it's unlikely," the manticore finished. Delicately it rolled to its feet, beating feathery wings to shed the dust. "Shall we go on?"

That they really were at the edge of the world was proven when, passing the garden walls and heading onward, they found themselves walking back the way they'd come, passing the same fields and milestones they'd passed that morning.

"You know it's in there. Your heart. In that garden. It's what Oberon sent me for. You can't go back without it."

"But I don't want it. And you can't enter there, Lizzie Fair." Oh, he was smug, having won. He'd kept the same form for nearly an hour in token of his triumph.

"I'm not complaining, Nimsey," she said mendaciously. "I just want to know what you're going to do with the rest of your life." *And I want to go home, not that it matters to you.*

Nimrod didn't answer, not even to complain about being called 'Nimsey'. Maybe he'd change his mind? She'd *seen* flying pigs here, so it was possible.

But she couldn't count on it. Maybe there was another way in? Some way to trick the gate?

No. She thought she knew what would happen if she could cheat her way into the garden. How would it feel to drown in a vat of acid?

Lizzie shuddered, cold in the warm spring sun.

"Are you quite well, Elizabeth?"

She looked at the manticore, surprised. He'd almost sounded concerned.

"Great, fine, terrific. God, I hate this place."

"There's an inn."

They'd passed it that morning: a bizarre little gingerbread cottage that seemed whittled out of one giant tree stump. She'd thought then that the sign hanging over the door was a good omen: The Inn of Heart's Desire. Nimrod turned in between the gateposts, spreading a wing wide to sweep her in ahead of him.

It was bigger inside than it looked outside. The dark angel stood beside her and made its requirements known.

"Two of your best rooms. And a parlor. And wine."

"What, Maid Elizabeth, no smiles? Now that your quest is done I shall show you wonders—you may be valiant or adored as you choose! Tomorrow morning we shall take the road and find..." He spread both arms and wings in an extravagant Shakespearean gesture.

The golden goblet in her hand was filled with strong red wine, and Lizzie gazed out over tiny sunny fields and the broad white road that led to only one place—the garden that held Nimrod Wildfire's heart. She set down her cup.

"Don't you care?" she said.

But he didn't, not without a heart to care with. She hadn't expected Nimrod's help to recover the thing, of course, and she'd been sure the finding of it would be dangerous, maybe even fatal. But to know right where it was, and to know, with a fair and pleasant certainty, that she would never be able to reach it...

"Oh, banishment." For some reason Nimrod would not meet her eyes. "All the best people have been banished—why, Prince Amador of the Glass Castle was gone for centuries for calling His Majesty a—well, another time, perhaps." Nimrod looked around a bit nervously, as if someone might he watching.

"Sure," said Lizzie, around the tight lump in her throat. She either got into that garden to search for his heart, or she wandered through interlocking fantasies forever. And the only way to get into the garden was to become—in the literal-minded definition these people had—impure. Period. Make love to Nimrod, and then the garden would let her in. He'd implied as much, and he should know.

"So you just want me to give up, is that it?" she said.

"Maid Elizabeth, you did try—and it was a good try. But now you have failed, and you will have to be sensible," the angel said, trying to look sorry.

"Sensible?" Lizzie jerked to her feet. "You—" Words failed her, as decisively as if someone had thrown a switch. She threw her half-full cup at the wall, and the wine sprayed in a pattern of many-feathered wings.

"Maid Elizabeth..." Nimrod smiled uncertainly, as if he, too, were suddenly at a loss for easy words.

"Leave me alone. I hate you. Go away. I don't want to be adored. I don't want to see wonders. I want to go *home*—don't you understand that? Don't you have a home?"

She had not cried since she had come to Phaerie; now the aching unshed weight of all those unused tears threatened to burst forth at once—and the worst thing was, Nimrod would almost certainly find the spectacle funny.

She turned away—to go somewhere, anywhere—and Nimrod put his hands on her shoulders.

"Leave me alone, damn you," she said hoarsely.

"Elizabeth. Lizzie Fair—" Nimrod sounded plaintively puzzled, as if he could not understand why she would turn on him this way.

It was almost kindness. It was, at least, neutrality. She turned into the angel's embrace, and it folded its wings about her. Tears spilled down her face and splashed against his skin.

"No." Nimrod sounded frightened, as if the next words he spoke were dragged from him unwillingly. "Don't cry, mortal maid—I cannot bear your tears."

Tough, Lizzie thought, and cried harder. She didn't care if what Nimrod said was true or not, not when she was never going to get to go home, never, never, *never...*

"I will do anything that you desire if only you will dry your tears," Nimrod said frantically. "I beg you, mortal maid—don't cry."

Maiden's tears and maiden's hair; maiden's glance and maiden's touch...

"I want to go home and you won't let me!" Lizzie sobbed unthinkingly.

The setting moon shining yellow-gold through the window reminded her it was time to go. Her body ached with the effort it took to keep from crying; she thought she'd be happy, having won, and wasn't sure why she wasn't. Some French wacko had said that after love all things are sad, but this wasn't love, so why was she grieving?

Carefully she slipped from beneath the warm embracing canopy of Nimrod's wing. If she cried, she'd wake him, and he'd find some way to keep her from doing what she had to do.

T-shirt and jeans, and her sneakers gripped fiercely in one shaking hand, Lizzie Fair eased open the door and crept quietly down the stairs.

The sun had risen by the time she reached the garden. She went up to the gates, and they opened. It had worked. *It was worth it then,* she told herself, knowing that wasn't why she'd done it.

All around her the garden woke to the day. It was marvelous enough to steal away the heartsickness she guarded like a treasure; marvelous enough to suspend thought. Fruits fell from the trees into her hands as she passed; she'd forgotten herself enough to be hungry, and was nearly thoughtless enough to eat one.

Then she saw the apple tree.

She'd thought for one transported moment that it was Nimrod; the blinding metallic flash. But it was only the sun, rising high enough to strike sparks from the crystalline fruit of the tallest tree in the garden.

For all its size, the bark was the smooth close-knit grey she associated with apple trees, and the gleaming rose-gold fruit clustered on the lower branches looked more like apples than they did like anything else. But somewhere, in that green crown so perilously far from the ground, was something that gleamed unnaturally gold, as hot and bright as a dragon's heart.

She began to climb. It was hard until she reached the first branches, then easy for a while, then hard again as the trunk tapered and the branches became delicate. Every move became a figure in a formal dance, and the tree, her partner, bowed in glib responsiveness. A few feet away the apple hung, robed in shimmering air and dazzling as the star it had resembled from the ground. She could feel the heat from here. The leaves surrounding it were mockingly fresh and green, but the fruit itself flaunted its sorcerous origin and burned bright and hot and glassy.

This apple was Nimrod's heart. All she had to do was pluck it.

Nervously Lizzie licked her lips and rubbed dry fingertips together. The apple looked hot. It radiated heat. Touching it would be like touching red-hot steel.

She looked down. A mistake. Tiny and perfect and far away, a doll's garden sparkled at the foot of the tree. The top of the wall was a hammered silver circlet small enough to wear around her head.

Sweat ran down Lizzie's face. *Pick it. Just pick it. It can't be too bad. And then it'll be over.*

She gulped against the bile that rose in the back of her throat, and pulled her T-shirt out of her jeans to make a pocket to catch it in. Then she reached for the dragon's heart.

For an instant it seemed chill and hard as glass, but it wouldn't come free of the twig and as she gripped it tighter the hot caustic burn pain came. She tried to swear and moaned instead and pulled and the infinitely-bending twig followed after and it wouldn't come free. Black dots danced in a blood-red haze before her eyes and every heartbeat resounded like a hammer-blow.

Then the stem broke. The apple clung to her hand for one sticky sickening instant before dropping free into her shirt. She clutched the pocket against her with her arm before she realized what she was doing, but the apple wasn't hot now, only warm.

Her hand throbbed with tender agony; stiff, swollen, and cooked. Pain made her reckless instead of cautious; there was a swift sliding descent with the apple tucked cool against her skin. All the garden's paths were straight now; the way to the gate was smooth and simple.

And Nimrod was waiting for her in the gateway.

He still wore angelic form: the vaulting wings like a living cloak. With an effort she kept herself from searching his face for a tenderness she knew she would not find. Straight and flat-footed, Lizzie walked back to the arched gate and through.

"I got in. I found it." The golden apple of the sun. The dragon's heart. "So take it." It was quite cold now. "It's yours. Take it." *Give it to him. Give it to him and be free.* She held the apple out to him in her right hand.

"You're hurt," he said, and reached for the other hand, the empty burned one. She let him think, for a moment, that she would let him touch her, and then thrust the hard cold surface of the golden apple into his hands.

He recoiled as his fingers touched it, but it was too late.

"Mortal girl, don't you know what you've done?" he cried. His heart flared brightly in his hands, and Lizzie, dazzled, thought she saw gems and flowers and beating wings. A wind blew up, flinging her against him, and all summer was in his skin as he sheltered her with his wings.

No, I don't know what I've done; I don't; I don't—

Then darkness, and hot perfume, and a music she had heard before.

"Welcome back, little mortal. Are you ready to claim your prize?"

Once again Lizzie Fair and Nimrod Wildfire stood side-by-side before the throne of Phaerie, as if they had never left—or so she thought until she looked at Nimrod.

Not human nor angel, nor leopard, serpent, nightmare beast, or any other of Nimrod's protean forms was beside her now. Now a dragon crouched beside her on the jeweled paving, tail lashing and wings tight-furled, and snarled its displeasure through long white fangs.

"I do so hate melodrama," Titania observed disinterestedly, and the dragon subsided into an inky coil of savage misery. With difficulty Lizzie looked away—she wanted to comfort him, even though she didn't think he'd appreciate it. Was he in pain? Was this what having his heart back did for Nimrod?

If she had known this would happen she would never have forced him to take it back. It wasn't fair, nothing about this was fair—why should she have had to hurt him just to go home? "Well, girl? Will you claim your prize?"

She looked at Oberon. "I want to go home," she said, and realized the moment the words left her mouth that it wasn't the truth any longer.

"Elizabeth—*NO!*" The dragon started frantically up out of its crouch, lunging for her and being held back by unseen hands.

Oberon and his hellcourt roared with laughter, and Lizzie Fair knew with sinking horror that she'd made the last mistake she would ever be allowed to make. Something cold and nasty touched her; she closed her eyes in reflex and reality slid out from under her feet.

And then she was home.

Lizzie opened her eyes cautiously and looked around. She knew this place. She knew where she was. Home—a little town two hours west of Cleveland, Ohio; the tree-lined street where she'd been born, in front of the white frame house that stood slightly crooked on its lot in honor of being the oldest house on the street. Her parents still lived here. Home.

Or they had lived here. The windows of the house were boarded up, the yard full of dead weeds and trash. The clean white paint had faded to grey, and there was iridescent graffiti covering the battered and forsaken realtor's sign. No one had lived here for a long time.

Lizzie made a small sound of terror in her throat. All the houses on the street looked as bad as her own, some worse.

And then I awoke and found me on the cold hill side...

One night in Elf Hill equaled seven years in the world of mortal man, so the ballads said. She'd been questing from the Court of Phaerie how long? A month? Six weeks? How many years did that work out to? Had her parents died thinking she was dead before them?

"Damn you, Oberon. How long has it been? How *long?*"

She clenched her hands into useless fists and the burn-skin on her left hand sloughed beneath her nails. Pain shocked her calm, and she forced her fingers open so she could take a look. It was a bad burn, and it hurt. Broken blisters oozed bloody fluid, proof that her adventure hadn't been some interesting new kind of delusion, at least. She had to find some way to bandage it.

After an hour of walking through the thick summer heat Lizzie reached a completely automated drugstore. She still had her wallet, and her money—if not her Visa—was still good; the AutoMart sold her a colorless gel that set rubbery-hard in seconds and stopped the pain. The AutoMart purported to sell Love, too, but she didn't have the nerve to find out what it meant.

She received her change in greasy lightweight coins; the receipt had today's date on it—she looked, and wished she hadn't. June 23, 2028. Thirty-two years had passed—one year for each day she had spent in Phaerie.

On sober consideration, she wished it had been longer. Did anyone still remember her?

Her parents—if they were still alive.

She needed a phone.

The AutoMart had something called a "Netphon"—it looked more like a computer than a phone, with a keyboard of unfamiliar symbols stenciled on large brightly-colored buttons. In a burst of social continuity it had been vandalized, but netphons were as common as telephones had once been, and eventually she found one that worked. It took cash, though not happily, and gave her an address for Robert/Amanda Fairchild in Cleveland Metro.

So this is what the future looks like.

Lizzie Fair was a New Yorker; she had always lived in the future. Twenty-first century Cleveland Metro was her New York of thirty years ago—a little bigger, a little shabbier, just as weird. She could survive here—at least for an afternoon.

Couldn't she?

She stood across the street from Cortlandt Ark and stared at the guards, the doors, the advertisements proclaiming that the future was now. (Or, more precisely, "Futur: Real!") Cortlandt Ark was a mostly self-contained world 109 stories high. It wasn't even the tallest building in Cleveland.

If she had never met Nimrod Wildfire she would be sixty-two this year. Cleveland Metro would seem quaint and homey to her New-York-accustomed eye instead of looking like a bizarre road-show version of the Big Apple. She would greet her parents without a second thought.

What could she say now? *"Hi Mom, hi Dad—I'm home from Elfland?"* They'd mourned and buried their only daughter years ago; their little Lizzie had gone to the big bad city and become a statistic. Was it fair to come back now? She might not even be able to convince them that she *was* their daughter. She'd looked in a mirror at the AutoMart. She hadn't aged a day.

She tried to hate Nimrod for doing this to her, but it wasn't his fault. Oberon was the one who had chosen to place her here and now instead of where she belonged. Just because he could and because she hadn't been specific enough about what she asked for.

Be careful what you ask for, Lizzie Fair—you may get it. Maybe Mom and Dad could help her. She could always wash dishes. She'd manage.

But her life had been all future-dreams until she'd met Nimrod Wildfire—dreams of fame, recognition, career; of the things she would do someday. And now 'someday' was here, stripped of future and dreams, and it was hard to remember why becoming a professional photographer had ever seemed so important. She'd given Nimrod Wildfire back his heart, but she'd given him hers as well, and now when the knowledge was of no earthly use she knew it.

Oberon had been crueler than she'd thought.

She looked across the street again, and noticed the guards were watching her suspiciously. Lizzie walked away. She had to go in, of course. But not now. In an hour—she'd go see them in an hour.

She found a bench a few blocks away from Cortlandt Ark and sat down. The molded concrete was searingly hot through her jeans. She had seventeen dollars and forty-two cents left to her name and it was time to be realistic.

Just what did she have to live for, exactly?

Career? She couldn't imagine one she could care about now. Love? She'd been so obsessed with getting home, with getting her own way, with *winning,* that she hadn't stopped to think—about what she was doing to him, about what she was doing to herself. She'd only realized she'd found her own true love when it was too late.

Too late. We are too soon old and too late smart. The old saying was half right, anyway.

Lizzie got up, slowly. Time to go. Time to try and meet her parents, and see how her life would be without Nimrod Wildfire. *Men have died, and worms have eaten them, but not for love.* Someday she'd even believe it.

He was a black and glittering paradigm of midnight ecstasy; a fulgent paraclete all dark gunmetal flanges and skirling curves, with the raw June sunlight star-lensed across each dragonscale in flaming pinpoints.

He was *here.*

"Elizabeth?" said the dragon, uncoiling itself a little in the shadow of a parked truck. "Lizzie Fair?"

He'd come back for her. As if he loved her. As if he cared.

"Nimsey?" She stopped in the middle of the sidewalk when she saw him, hating herself for hoping. He uncoiled himself further, slipping out from beneath the truck. The sun shining through his wings made them run with rainbows.

"I came as soon as I could. Are you all right?"

"What are you doing here?" she asked, trying to keep her voice even.

"I came for you."

Guilt made her angry. It was too much, that he should have followed her back into the world just to play cruel games—and what other reason could he have?

"Well goody for me," she said bitterly, "I don't know how I'd get along without you." He didn't love her. How could he, even with a heart, after what she'd done to him? "You'd better hurry up and turn into something else, though, Nimsey; they'll be out here with nets, even in the twenty-first century."

He looked away, the sun sliding down the starry column of his neck. "I can't."

The flat statement stopped her as nothing else could. Had he come to her for help? It was probably just one more refinement of Oberon's joke, but she couldn't keep herself from reacting.

"What... What's wrong?" She looked around quickly, but they were still safe from detection. "Nimrod? What did Oberon do to you?" Fear for him made her chest hurt, as if her own heart were burning.

"Nothing. Oberon did nothing. I have found my heart now, Elizabeth, that is all."

The heart that he'd surrendered to Oberon for freedom and power—the heart she had forced him to take back. The freedom he had been given she knew: freedom, literally, to be heartless.

"This is my true self, Elizabeth, as I truly am." And the power...? Illusion. "Does my form repulse you?"

Trust a Prince of Phaerie to ask damnfool irrelevant questions at the worst times. "But what are you *doing* here, damn it?" She was going to start crying in just a minute; that would make him leave, all right, after what had happened the last time. And then she'd never see him again.

"I came for you. I told you. You gave me back my heart; I will give it to you now, if you'll have it. Do you love me, Lizzie Fair?"

She put her hands up to cover her face; the dragon folded her into cool, cinnamon-scented wings. She pillowed her hot aching face against the smooth tiled sculpture of his throat and clung to him, gulping back her sobs, knowing she'd given him his answer beyond any hope of deception.

"Hear me, Lizzie Fair: There is a palace in the mountains beyond the morning made for all delight. It is built of pearl and gold and jade, and I have waited a hundred mortal lifetimes to inhabit it. Let me bring you there and make you my queen; I want no one else. If you love me as I do you, let me undo the wrong that Oberon has done you—"

He'd told her never to question Oberon, once. But any child in the nursery could have reminded Nimrod that it was even more important not to mention him at all.

For the third and last time Lizzie Fair stood before the throne of His Imperial Majesty Oberon, Lord Emperor of Phaerie and all the Lands Beyond the Morning, and this time the Great Hall was deserted, the feasting tables gone. The throne itself was empty, and she was alone in the echoing twilight vault. Nimrod Wildfire was nowhere in sight.

"Nimrod?" Lizzie's voice sounded small and scared in the echoing emptiness, but she was frightened more for Nimrod than herself. The things Oberon could do to mortal humans were limited, she'd realized, awful though they were.

"Nimrod?" She looked around the empty hall.

"Oh, he's here, all right. Right through that door, in fact. But there's something else you have to do first."

Lizzie turned back and saw Queen Titania standing in her own private moonlight, all feathers and pearls like the Erté version of a Las Vegas showgirl. A changeling stood beside her, staggering beneath the weight of an enormous covered tray. Lizzie could see the door Titania had mentioned behind the throne, black and barred and even more impassable than the garden gates had been.

"Do?" said Lizzie blankly.

"Before you see him. Or, perhaps, instead of seeing him. It's up to you, of course," Titania said agreeably.

Lizzie stared at the Phaerie empress, every sense screaming peril. Titania sighed, and tapped her rouged lip with one perfect lacquered nail.

"Oh come now, girl! Prince Nimrod leads him a merry chase, but how long do you think you have before Oberon comes looking for you? He prefers his own inspirations, you know; not that he won't think this is amusing enough—but only after it's been done."

Lizzie'd had enough of Oberon's inspirations to prefer those of his queen. And perhaps Titania would be kinder.

"What do I have to do?" she said warily.

"Choose," said Titania, lifting the cover of the tray.

The dark room grew darker. The light blazed down on two objects of otherworldly device nestled in white velvet. A blood-red apple, candy-lacquer-gem-incarnadine, so red you expected it to shout with it. Red apple—Big Apple—New York. *Home.*

Home to the instant she'd left, or where was the choice? Home to her own time, her own place, her own life. Home without a single footstep out of place.

And the rose; perfect bud caught in the instant of opening, the petals velvet-black and the stem hot green, as if even here the hot ripe sun of summer shone down on it. Nimrod. Her love.

Choose one and give up the other forever—Nimrod would not be let to come to her a third time.

Her hand hovered, indecisive. Go home, and Nimrod would never know how much she'd wanted to stay. Stay with her dragon prince, and her parents would never know what had happened to her. Love or Duty?

"Please, if I—Can't I just talk to him? It isn't fair—"

"No one said we were fair," said Titania with cool amusement.

The apple and the rose. Choose.

Oh, god, I'm SORRY—she thought desperately—and grabbed the rose.

Like dawn breaking, the rose's petals flushed from black to white as it opened. Lizzie stared at it, stupefied, stunned with choosing.

"Go, then," Titania said austerely.

Clutching the rose, Lizzie walked slowly toward the door.

In the mountains beyond the morning there is a palace with walls of pearl and gold and jade, and inside its walls it is always summer.

Lizzie stepped through the doorway and stood blinded. She looked around. She was surrounded by white alabaster and apricot light, and against that splendor she felt grubby and opaque. She stepped forward, and everything stayed the same. Real.

But where was Nimrod?

"Nimsey?" Lizzie whispered, afraid to say it out loud. Her home or her love—Titania had promised, so that must mean Nimrod was safe from Oberon, too. If she'd been tricked, it was not in the heartless, literal fashion of the Phaerie Court.

But what if Nimrod had changed his mind?

After a period of fruitless wandering through the empty palace Lizzie came to a door that led to a garden. She opened it, wary of gardens but curious nonetheless. The lawn glittered like leaves of white opal; Lizzie took a cautious step forward and found that for all its strangeness it yielded grasslike beneath her sneakers like the lawns of home.

This was her home, now: Beauty forevermore a guest in the Beast's castle of her own free will. She looked around, weary to numbness—had it only been this morning that she'd gone to steal Nimrod's heart?—and saw that the milk-pale lawn swept down to a bank of pearly roses on crystalline stems that climbed the pale stone of the wall. The wall led the eye inexorably to the silvery sweep of sky, and when she looked into the sky, she could see the sweep of great wings. Her lover was coming home to her.

He landed with a great flexing of talons and a gust of captured wind from beneath his wings, a creature as dark as the garden was light. When she was sure he'd stopped, Lizzie flung herself against him. Dragonsilk wings wrapped her around and she felt the inhuman flex of muscle beneath his mailed skin as Nimrod pressed her close.

"My Elizabeth," the dragon said. "Lizzie Fair. You came back."

"I didn't have—" *much choice,* her mind finished for her, but that wasn't true—there *had* been a choice—she had chosen this and given up her home. She held Nimrod tighter to blot out the thought that her parents would never know what had happened to her.

I could have been hit by a car. It's just the same. But then at least they would have known. There would not be the grinding years of waiting while hope slowly faded.

"Are you sorry?" Nimrod asked uncertainly.

"No," said Lizzie, knowing it was almost true, "I just wish my folks could know what'd happened to me, you know?"

The dragon regarded her with faint puzzlement in his jeweled golden eyes. "Why not go and tell them, then? One return to mortal lands for the mortal bride is permitted, you know. Even Their Majesties cannot deny me that."

"Now?" said Lizzie eagerly. Titania had lied about her choices after all—in the way the Phaerie do, by implication. "Could we go now?" Her words were slightly muffled against the lapidary armor of Nimrod's neck.

"Now," Nimrod Wildfire agreed, and swept his wings about her tightly.

The white frame house was bright and clean again, lit rosy and warm behind its shades and curtains. It was Halloween night—there were carved pumpkins nailed to the gateposts, wedged in the fork of the tree in the yard, guarding the porch with their fiery yellow smiles. Lizzie shivered. The T-shirt and jeans of a hot New York summer didn't belong in a late October evening.

"How long do I...?" she asked.

The darkness beside her stirred. "One hour. You'd better go." Nimrod settled back into the shadows, his golden eyes glowing. And god help any trick-or-treaters that came this way.

"Yes." Her sneakers squeaked on the concrete as she took a step toward the house. One hour.

Across the yard, up the steps. Knock. The mortal bride, home out of Phaerie on All Hallows Eve to visit the loved ones left behind.

"Mom? Dad? It's me. Lizzie. I've come home to visit."

TOYEN

by Cynthia McQuillin

I first met Cindy at the Fantasy Worlds Festival in 1980—know this because it was the first SF convention I ever attended, and because I still have a tape of a bardic circle held there which features Cindy singing a number of her exquisitely-polished songs. Anyone who can pack an entire story into three or four verses as neatly as she can is a natural short-story writer, and it was no surprise to me when I started running across her fiction as well. I can't claim that we really became friends until later, when she moved to the Bay Area, but at that point I think it was inevitable. And several years ago, while I was working for MZB's FANTASY Magazine, I had the delightful experience of being in the same writer's circle as Cindy. I must confess that the writers who really impress me are not the ones who toss off something entertaining in a single draft without half paying attention—I like the ones who know why this works and that doesn't, who can identify the strong and weak points in a story, and who can articulate that knowledge so that others can understand. Cindy is one of these. And whether she's applying that ability to her own stories or to other people's, the results are masterful.
— *Heather Rose Jones*

Tien Mai Li paused from her afternoon's labors to stretch and wipe the sweat from her face with the edge of her sleeve. Her thick straight black hair had come undone and her back ached from bending to cut the long flat grass that grew along the lake shore. But the grass, along with the thin supple young bamboo she had been lucky enough to find, were needed to repair the woven walls of the house she shared with her grandfather, and to make or mend a multitude of other things.

Though she had gathered only half as much as she would have liked, Mai Li saw that the sun had turned the surface of the lake into a golden mirror, signaling the onset of sundown. It was time to start dinner.

"Late again. Grandfather will not be pleased," she chided herself with a put-upon sigh as she cleaned, then carefully sheathed, the short curved blade she used to cut the tough bamboo stalks and lake grass. Her grandfather, the wood-carver Tien Lu Chen, was the very soul of punctuality and dedication, and though he was in all other respects the best, most tolerant of guardians, he hated the delay of a meal more than anything.

Tying her harvest into a neat bundle, Mai Li hoisted the load onto her back and set off down the winding path toward home. But after a few minutes of walking, she paused to look about in annoyance. The path was clearly marked and the light still good, so how could she have lost her way? Yet she must have done just that, for she was in completely unfamiliar surroundings.

Instead of the grasses, ferns and occasional willow that edged the lake, dense forbidding thickets of dark-leafed trees surrounded her in every direction and the light, which had been clear and warm only a moment before, shimmered and dimmed as though she were underwater.

Startled by these inexplicable changes, she turned back the way she had come, certain she must have turned in the wrong direction without realizing it. The path would take her back to the lake and, if need be, she could follow the shore north to find her way home. But the faster she went the more uncertain she became. She stumbled into a clearing, just as she feared the light would fail completely.

Laying her bundle on the ground, she sat down to rest for a moment on the large flat rock which stood before a small oak tree in the center of the strangely smooth barren piece of ground.

"How very odd," she murmured as she glanced around the clearing's edge. Thick white mist began rising from the floor of the wood, obscuring the trees and the path which had brought her there.

Alarmed, Mai Li jumped up and turned to run back the way she had come. But she could find no trace of the path. The wall of mist thickened as she watched, roiling ominously so that she shrank from touching it.

"What shall I do?" she gasped, heart pounding like a frightened deer's.

"Tien Mai Li, whatever is the matter?" a soft voice called from behind, freezing Mai Li in her tracks. It was a young woman's voice, gentle and soothing, and yet...

"I seem to have lost my way," she quietly replied, trying to disguise the fear that had gripped her. The compulsion to turn and see who spoke was nearly overwhelming, but her grandfather's friend, the wisewoman Chan Lin Ming, had warned her often enough that spirits lurked in the woods. She had never believed the old woman...until now.

"How is it possible that you are lost, Mai Li? You know these woods so well." The stranger's murmuring tone seemed to hold a hint of mockery even as it lulled, and by the sound she had moved several steps nearer.

Mai Li trembled, near to tears—another moment and the stranger would be close enough to touch her.

"Twilight came so suddenly and a mist has risen..." Mai Li hedged, moving slowly around the edge of the clearing in the direction she thought she had entered from. "I was confused by a trick of the light."

"If you are lost, then you must allow me to help you find your way. You have only to turn and give me your hand so I may lead you."

"Your offer is kind, but I'm sure to find my own way once I'm on the path again," she insisted, still refusing to turn. To look upon a spirit, Chan Lin Ming had said, was to give it form and power.

"As you say, Mai Li. But surely you will not wish to forget the bounty you gathered so painstakingly."

"No, indeed!" she cried. Thinking only of how angry Grandfather must be with her already, Mai Li turned to retrieve her bundle, but stopped short to stare in amazement at the largest, reddest fox she had ever seen.

Eyes the cool creamy green of imperial jade returned her startled gaze with an imperious unblinking stare. The next thing Mai Li knew she was falling headlong through a swirl of chaotic brightness. Inhumanly wild and beautiful voices murmured, yammered and soothed her all at once, while tiny demon claws snatched at her, tearing away first her robes then her hair and flesh. She gave one last helpless cry of despair before her senses were plunged into darkness.

It seemed to Mai Li that she had lain in the darkness for a very long time, but she had no sense of time as a mortal woman might measure it. And though the place she now occupied was empty of light, there were sensations—touch came first, then smell and hearing. But everything was wrong; her senses were heightened almost painfully and her body felt itchy all over, stiff and strange.

At last the whiny singsong sound that was calling her inexorably back to consciousness sorted itself into the familiar pattern of a song Mai Li herself had often sung while working. The voice she heard seemed to be her own and yet when she opened her mouth only a plaintive little yelp came out.

Fully awake at last, she sat up, looking cautiously around to find herself in the same clearing once her new eyes adjusted. It seemed only a little later now than it had been when she started home, but it was hard to tell; as with her sense of touch and hearing, everything she saw was subtly altered. There were no colors, only varying shades of gray; but the images she saw were sharper, her focus shifted more quickly than that of a human eye, and every little movement caught her attention.

"The exchange is complete, Tien Mai Li," she heard her own voice saying. "I am most grateful for your foolishness, and wish you as much joy in your new life as you may find, but the hour grows late and I must be on my way."

Wait! Who are you and why have you done this? Mai Li demanded, leaping to her feet. But only a series of whines and barks issued from her mouth. Nevertheless, the creature who now wore her body seemed to understand.

"I am the Fox Maiden, Toyen," she replied. Cocking her head to one side, she stooped to gaze once more into Mai Li's eyes. A slightly predatory smile crept over her lips as she said, "I have taken your body because I desire to meddle in your world; it is my nature. You possessed great beauty, Mai Li, but did not cherish it nor appreciate the uses to which such beauty may be put. I do. I shall use this tender flesh to enthrall powerful and wealthy men, and with their help I shall spread chaos throughout the mortal world."

What of me? Mai Li plaintively whined, holding out one delicate black paw to touch the hem of Toyen's robe.

"In time you will forget you were ever human and become the creature you appear to be. A fox's life can be a difficult and dangerous one, but I doubt you will find it worse than the one I have taken you from, and perhaps you will be happy when your memory has gone. For now keep to the forest and do not follow me, or it will go ill for you."

Toyen stood up and strode out of the clearing, which had once more become simply open ground in the midst of a normal-seeming wood.

Afraid of what Toyen might do if she followed—for clearly the Fox Maiden was a powerful sorceress—yet fearing what might become of her grandfather, Mai Li hesitated for a moment before taking up the track.

Her newly heightened senses made it unnecessary to follow closely, and Toyen seemed to have only the limited senses of Mai Li's own body, so she was able to avoid detection. Hoping there might be some way to undo the Fox Maiden's spell, Mai Li took careful note of all she saw.

By the time she reached home, Mai Li had begun to take a certain pride in her newfound skills, but what she witnessed upon her arrival nearly broke her heart.

Hurrying up to the porch, Toyen called out in a pitiful voice that she had lost her way in the forest and humbly begged forgiveness for her tardiness. When Tien Lu Chen appeared, the usual look of chiding displeasure hardening his features, Toyen laid the bundle of grass and bamboo at his feet and, with the most obsequious manner and contrite expression, bowed deeply, begging pardon for delaying his meal by her carelessness.

Toyen's speech was so very pretty and so very clever that instead of scolding her as he would have Mai Li, who seemed always compelled to utter some impertinence even when she knew herself to be in the wrong, he petted her, assuring her all was forgiven this time and adding that he would spread the grasses to dry while she started dinner so as not to delay it further.

Grandfather! Mai Li cried, the sting of betrayal overriding good sense. But of course all he heard was the yipping of a fox.

"Horrid creature!" Toyen cried, upon spotting Mai Li crouched in the brush near the goat pen.

"What ails you, child?" Lu Chen demanded, a disconcerted frown crossing his features. "It is only a fox."

"Oh, drive it away, Grandfather," Toyen pleaded, throwing a stone which Mai Li easily dodged. "It will get in among the chickens and kill them, then we shall have no eggs."

"If it will make you easier," he replied, striking at his unfortunate granddaughter with a length of bamboo as he chased her from the yard. Mai Li hesitated just long enough to see Toyen's sly, triumphant smile before she fled into the brush, yelping in dismay.

When full dark had fallen Mai Li returned to her grandfather's house, and dug a small hole beneath the brush near his workroom to curl up in for the night. But she was too stiff and miserable and hungry to sleep. She had managed to catch and kill a small rat, but had been unable to bring herself to eat it.

When the rumbling in her belly grew too loud to ignore she crept back into the yard, having half a mind to steal one of the chickens as Toyen had suggested. At least that would be familiar meat, if raw. Besides it would serve Grandfather right for not seeing through Toyen's deception.

How could he mistake that simpering creature for me? she sniffed. But as she circled the henhouse the birds made nervous clucking sounds. The noise would undoubtedly wake Grandfather if she tried to take one, Mai Li decided, and she didn't have the heart to be driven from her own yard twice in the same night.

Tired and dejected, she crawled under the house and lay down beneath her grandfather's room with a heartfelt sigh. At least her fur was thick and warm and there had been plenty of fresh water to quench her thirst.

Head sinking heavily onto her paws, Mai Li surrendered to the exhaustion which had stalked her all evening, allowing it to drag her into feral dream-tableaux of death and moonlight set in dark tangled thickets. But the familiar sound of her grandfather's snores and mutters penetrated even her deepest dreams, awakening in her an overwhelming desire to speak to him.

Imperceptibly the world shifted and she started up seeming to rise out of herself through the floorboards above.

She found herself standing in Grandfather's room once more in human form, though unclothed. Softly, she came to the edge of his bed and sank down on her knees beside it, reaching her hand to waken him, but her fingers passed unheeded through his flesh. She too felt nothing.

Dismayed, she urgently whispered, "Grandfather, wake up. I must speak to you and my time is short!"

"W— what," he mumbled peevishly, blinking blearily as his eyes opened at last. Startled to see his granddaughter kneeling naked in the moonlight, he sat up ready to demand an explanation. But Mai Li silenced him with a gesture.

"Please," she whispered. "Toyen sleeps, we must not wake her."

"Toyen? I do not understand you, girl. What is this nonsense?"

"Please, Grandfather, listen to me," she whispered, hushing him again. "Today when I followed the path home through the woods, I became lost in the haunted wood. I know that Chan Lin Ming has warned me never to go down the southern shore of the lake," she was quick to add when she saw his expression. "But the grass was so lush and there was a new stand of bamboo just ripe for stripping—"

"—and it was not very far," he concluded with a sigh. "But then you went farther than you knew."

She nodded contritely, lowering her eyes.

"I have become the fox you drove from the yard this evening and Toyen, who was the fox, wears my body. Oh, Grandfather, what can I do?" Despair made her voice shrill.

Panic gripped her at the creaking of a floor board, far too near. Then Toyen's voice drifted sleepily down the narrow hallway.

"Is all well, Grandfather?"

"I must go," Mai Li whispered before she fled. "But I will come again."

The soft pad of footsteps down the hall alerted Tien Lu Chen to the Fox Maiden's approach and he lay down once more, pretending she had startled him from sleep when she held the lantern up.

"What is it, Granddaughter?" he peevishly demanded. "Why do you trouble my slumber?"

"I heard a cry and feared for your safety," Toyen said, the sweetest tones of concern and affection coloring her words and softening her expression. "But I see now that all is well, so I may rest easy. But why did you cry out?"

Gazing into her eyes, which oddly seemed to have taken on the tint and texture of jade, Lu Chen felt a nearly overwhelming urge to relate to her the strange waking-dream she had interrupted; but, remembering Mai Li's words, he did not.

"A nightmare. Yes, that is what it must have been. I cannot seem to remember," he muttered, stifling a yawn. "But I have much to do tomorrow and need my sleep, so you had best leave me to it, child."

Suspicions allayed, Toyen demurely lowered her eyes, kowtowing as was customary to show proper respect, and withdrew without further protest. This more than anything convinced Lu Chen of the truth of his dream. Mai Li was a headstrong, artless girl, not given to flattery or guile, and she most certainly did not have green eyes!

Why had he not seen the truth before? *This Toyen's magic must he great indeed*, he decided. *It is time to visit to my old friend, Chan Lin Ming. She will surely know what must be done.*

The next morning, after Lu Chen had eaten the cold fishcake and rice which Toyen had set out for his breakfast, instead of going to his workroom as he usually did, he prepared to go out. Seeing this, Toyen's eyes darkened with dismay.

"It is too blustery a day for a journey, Grandfather. You had better stay inside and finish your carvings," she quietly urged as she cleared the dishes away. "The Moon Festival is less than a month away and we have need of many things for the house. A little extra money would be useful, do you not think?"

"There is wisdom in your words, my child," Lu Chen replied, giving her an indulgent smile. "But you see, that is why I must go. I have used up the special dye I need to tint the ink for the inscriptions. You know the priest will not bless them if I do not use the proper ink. Chan Lin Ming lives only a short way around the lake on the other side and will certainly have what I require; that is hardly a journey at all. I shall easily return before lunch."

"As you say, Grandfather." Toyen lowered her eyes and bowed. "I shall prepare something hearty to warm you after so long a walk."

"You make me out to be an old man," he laughed. "Now go be a good girl and finish your chores while I am away, then you can help me mix the ink and inscribe the carvings I have completed when I return."

The Fox Maiden's influence had grown considerably in a very short time, Lu Chen noted uneasily as he gathered his journey bag and coat. Already he was beginning to doubt the reality of Mai Li's visitation the night before, and it had taken all his resolve to resist the Fox Maiden's desire to stop him from leaving.

Keeping his pace unhurried and his face a mask of unconcern. Lu Chen turned onto the path which would take him around the northern edge of the lake. He could feel Toyen's gaze upon him as he went.

When he was well down the path and out of sight, he paused, glancing quickly over his shoulder to see if she had followed. She had not, but a rustle near the edge of the path drew his eyes back to it. The large red fox he had seen the night before stepped out of the underbrush to seat itself demurely in the center of the path and raise one delicate paw in a plaintive gesture. The creature's eyes met his squarely, a determined look fixed within.

They were not the animal eyes he expected, but the onyx black eyes of his own beloved granddaughter.

"Mai Li," he murmured, going down upon his knees. "It is true then. What a calamity! But never fear, Lin Ming will know how to advise me; I seek her aid now. Toyen is suspicious and I do not trust her; keep watch on the house while I am gone."

The fox gave a yip of assent, then brushed her muzzle across his outstretched hand and disappeared back into the brush.

Chan Lin Ming listened thoughtfully to Lu Chen's tale, with much nodding and tongue-clucking. Then. after an unbearably long silence, she said, "This Toyen is a sorceress, Lu Chen, not like the fox-sprites which sometimes possess young girls during the onset of their woman's cycles. Such are capricious, playful spirits, no brighter than any fox and so easily dealt with. The entity which has enspelled Mai Li is powerful and dangerous and, I fear, far beyond my poor abilities, dear friend. I am only an old woman who prepares of herb teas and ointments, after all."

"I know better, Lin Ming," he said quietly, begging with his eyes, where his pride would not allow the words. "You are a holy woman, you sing the spirits in your trance and animals come to your calling; this I have seen and more."

"Be that as it may, Lu Chen," she firmly replied, "I have no power over such as she. Whatever is to be done to free Mai Li, you and she must do."

"But how do we know what to do if you will not tell me?" Lu Chen demanded, exasperation creeping into his tone.

"Mai Li must tell you that herself," said Lin Ming, straining leaves from the tea as she carefully poured the steaming liquid into two simple earthenware bowls.

"If Mai Li knew what to do, she would have told me." He accepted the bowl she offered, with a nod of thanks. "She was near to despair when we spoke last night, I assure you."

"I do not doubt your sincerity, Lu Chen, or that of your granddaughter, but perhaps she does not know she possesses the answer and so must be told." Lin Ming paused to gaze thoughtfully into the now-empty earthenware teapot that sat on the table between them before continuing. "Think how it is when you have a newly fired pot. Does not the tea taste of the clay until the pot is tempered with use?"

"Yes, but I do not see—"

Lin Ming raised a hand to silence him.

"Just as the tea may absorb the essence of the pot, so Mai Li's spirit may absorb some of Toyen's knowledge from the memory her body possesses."

"Ahhh," said Lu Chen, nodding. "You are wise, indeed, Chan Lin Ming."

Lu Chen was returning down the homeward path just before midday with a sack full of dyes and heart full of hope, when Mai Li stepped once more onto the path.

Settling himself on the ground to rest, he related all that Lin Ming had said, watching Mai Li's face as he spoke to make sure she understood him.

When he finished she cocked her head as if considering his words; then, giving a hopeful little bark, she nodded.

"Good," he said upon seeing this. "Now listen to me. Do you remember the meditations you learned at the temple in Hano before I came to claim you?"

She nodded gravely.

"You must find a quiet place where you can meditate undisturbed." He lifted her muzzle so he could look directly into her eyes. "It is most important that you open yourself completely and let your thoughts fly free. Your mind must be as an unstained cloth ready to absorb the dye of Toyen's memories."

Mai Li gave a sudden yelp and pulled free of his hold. The way her eyes rolled in fright told him all he needed to know.

"I understand, Mai Li," he said, gathering her to him in a reassuring embrace. Her fur was plush and soft, and he couldn't help but appreciate its texture even as he was revolted by the thought of his granddaughter's spirit trapped in the body of a beast.

"How you tremble, my little one; but all will be well if you are strong of heart and will. If you cannot overcome your fear and surrender yourself to the fox, you will never accomplish your purpose. Then you will become the fox in truth. The longer you wait, the more difficult it will become to find Mai Li again. Do you understand?"

She nodded once more, then lowered her head with a sigh. The look in her eyes tore Lu Chen's heart—fear and despair were so plainly written there. If foxes could weep, he had no doubt her cheeks would have streamed. But even as he watched she put her fear and weakness away; a look of resolve replaced all but the faintest shadow of fear.

"You are a good, brave girl, Mai Li," he murmured. "I know you will succeed and return to me, my own dear granddaughter, once more!"

He hugged her again before rising to brush the dust from his robe, then said, "Come to me tonight as you did before, then we shall see what can be accomplished."

That night when Mai Li slipped into his room Lu Chen came wide awake without a sound, sitting up immediately to quietly demand what she had learned.

"I did as you said, Grandfather," she murmured, "though it was a very hard thing to do and I was more frightened than I have ever been."

"Tell me, child," he anxiously whispered, noticing that her dream-form was somehow less human than it had appeared on the previous night. Her face was distorted, her features sharper, more foxlike, and her limbs seemed misshapen in some subtle way. He longed to touch her, but there was no physical comfort he could give her now.

"I became the fox," she blurted. Her eyes bespoke the depth of her anguish and shame, but her voice remained calm, almost empty. "At first I only knew and felt what the animal knew and felt. I acted as the animal must act, on instinct and with ruthless abandon. But I will not speak of that."

A shudder ran through her and her eyes darkened as she remembered how hunger had driven her to feed at last. But after a moment or so she regained enough composure to continue.

"In time, I became aware of other thoughts, other feelings, achieving a kind of understanding that reached beyond the physical world. I saw... No, I can't speak of what I saw then. Only, I became more than I have ever been, a part of the wholeness of being. And when I reached this center of being, I understood."

"You have found the answer, then?"

She nodded.

"Tell me what we must do, child, and quickly."

"You must rise before dawn to catch Toyen unaware." Mai Li's eyes were hard and grave as she spoke. "Bind her arms tightly, and gag her quickly. In human form she has lost much of her magic, but her tongue remains a deadly weapon."

"That I have discovered." He nodded. "Go on."

"Once she is secured, you must bring her to the clearing where she enspelled me. You will also need a bowl, a jug of goat's milk, another length of rope, and the hatchet."

He frowned at that, but said only, "How will I find this place?"

"I will guide you. Now listen well. When you enter the clearing you'll see an oak. A large flat rock sits before it like an altar. You must tie Toyen to the tree, and when she is securely bound, place a howl of milk on the stone along with the mice I will bring.

"When this is done, sit down on the ground across the stone from Toyen and pray. It will be some time before anything happens, but if we are lucky hunger may be her undoing. Though she is a spirit, she is still an animal ruled by animal needs, as I well discovered."

Mai Li's words were quiet, but her eyes darkened once more and her fingers clenched in distress.

"As time passes she will know hunger and thirst, while there, within easy reach if she were but free, will lie the means of satisfying both. If she is young enough or self-indulgent enough, she will be overcome by the wants of her body, entering her fox form once more to gratify those wants and casting me back into my own body. I shall then be myself again, so long she does not bespell me with her eyes once more."

"How shall I know when this happens?" he asked.

"I, in fox form, shall lie beside Toyen while you watch and pray. I too will fast, but since I am a woman and not an animal, I will be able to master my body as she may not. Watch the fox carefully; if she tries to eat or drink, or to leave the clearing, you will know the exchange has been made."

"I understand," he said. "Then what?"

"Cut me free and get me back onto the path as fast as you can, and do not under any circumstances let me look at the fox."

"What if I should meet her gaze? Will she not trap me as she did you?"

"Never fear, Grandfather," Mai Li replied with a tight, grim little smile. "Like her lesser cousins, Toyen's power to possess is limited to virgin maids on the brink of womanhood, and only those foolish enough to enter her enchanted wood as I did."

"And if she does not succumb to her hunger?" he demanded, meeting her gaze squarely.

"If she is still in possession of my body come sunset," Mai Li coldly said, "then you must take the hatchet and cut off her head."

"No!" Lu Chen softly cried. "I cannot!"

"Then all is lost, Grandfather," Mai Li quietly replied, "for I shall be the fox anyway, and Toyen shall be loose to wreak havoc on the world."

"Very well, child, I will do what I must," he promised, his tone and expression those of a beaten man.

"Everything depends upon it, Grandfather. Do not fail me," she whispered, then vanished through the floorboards.

It had been easy enough to catch Toyen as she slept, but binding her had been harder than Lu Chen had expected. Though Mai Li was only a girl, light-boned and small of stature, Toyen fought like a beast when roused, and he received several bites and scratches before he had her securely bound and gagged. Nor had it been an easy task to get her to the clearing, for she wriggled and plunged at nearly every step.

By the time he had her tied to the tree and had laid out the offering of milk on the rock altar next to the three plump mice Mai Li had brought, he was all but worn out.

The long hours passed slowly, and as morning wore on into the drowsy stillness of late afternoon it was all Lu Chen could do to keep from dozing. The woods and the clearing itself seemed made for just such employment: the dim, almost fluid quality of the light; the lulling sound of water lapping along the unseen lake shore; and the soft monotonous drone of insects.

"What?" He started groggily awake as Mai Li nipped his arm for the third time, this time far harder than before. Stricken with a pang of guilt at having dozed off yet again, he sat up and stretched, looking around the empty glade for what seemed like the hundredth time.

Panic gripped him as he saw how dark it had grown in the surrounding trees. The late afternoon was fading quickly into dusk as it often did this time of the year, but he tried not to see it. The day was nearly gone and Toyen had not stirred the entire time, not once. Fear gripped his throat making it ache as he tried not to think about what he must surely now be called upon to do.

He turned at last to look at Mai Li. She had not returned to lie beside Toyen as she had before, but sat before him with a demanding stare. When he remained stubbornly still, she gave an impatient yelp and glanced meaningfully towards the oak where their captive waited, green eyes burning with triumph and hatred as she peered at them over the gag of wadded cloth Lu Chen had used to stop her mouth.

There was no doubt in his mind that he was a dead man if Toyen were ever loosed.

His heart became a leaden weight, as he slowly rose, stretching his legs and stamping his feet to get the circulation moving his bones ached after sitting so long on the cool hard-packed ground. With a final tearful look a Mai Li, he picked up the hatchet from where it lay on the stone, and gave it a practice swing before turning to face Toyen.

The blade was sharp and deadly. The handle as he hefted it fit comfortably in his hand, which was callused from its long familiar use of that tool, now to become a weapon.

Yes, he thought, hardening his heart to the task, *for Mai Li I can do this.* It would be no different from cutting away dead wood.

Toyen watched his ponderous approach with unwavering defiance. The force of her will beat against him like palpable waves of heat, but still he went on, step by torturous step. Mai Li had come forward also, to crouch at his feet. Her progress had been as slow and reluctant as his, for all she had urged him to this.

He gave her one last haunted look, then raised the hatchet to strike. But as he did, time seemed to telescope, making seconds into hours as the dark finely-honed blade began its fatal descent. Sometime in-between, the defiance in Toyen's eyes had been replaced by pure human terror. And there was something else..but it was so hard to think.

The fox, Grandfather, look at the fox! Mai Li's voice was screaming deep within his mind.

As one waking from a dream, he turned the blade aside just in time, glancing around the clearing in fearful confusion. Then he saw it. The fox was on the altar stone lapping ravenously at the milk he had placed there. Understanding slowly dawned and he turned back to the helpless girl. Mai Li's black eyes stared anxiously into his own as she struggled frantically against her bonds.

He cut her free as quickly as he could. Then, gathering her still bound and gagged into his arms, he hauled her back to the path, not stopping to untie her until he had her safely home.

"Is it truly you, Mai Li?" he panted, as he stripped away her bonds and unstopped her mouth.

"Somewhat the worse for wear, grandfather, but yes it is I, Mai Li," she hoarsely replied, massaging her wrists and then her mouth with careful fingers. "I must have water, I am so very thirsty. And by the look of things you could do with a cup yourself."

"Yes, yes, I believe you are correct," he replied, sinking wearily down at the table. Amazed at the strength and stamina he had demonstrated in carrying Mai Li so far—a not an inconsiderable feat for a man of forty-eight—he drank thirstily from the cup she poured him from the kitchen jar. Refusing the plate of sweetened beancakes she had also brought, he sat back with a sigh to watch her consume one after another of the sticky cakes with good appetite.

Her manners were less elegant than the false Mai Li's had been, and he had often wished they were better; but remembering Toyen's ravenous attack on the food they had left in the clearing, he thought it likely he would never chide his granddaughter for her manners again.

"I am pleased beyond measure that you are returned safely to me, Mai Li," he said when she had finished. "But I do not completely understand how this miracle was accomplished."

"It was simple enough," she said, setting the empty plate and cup aside. "When Toyen believed you were going to cut off her head, she fled my body for the safety of the fox's. Thankfully she was overwhelmed by hunger as I had planned, or we never could have escaped. That clearing is the wellspring of her power."

"Will she not seek vengeance?" he murmured, a look of alarm transforming his features.

"No doubt she will wish to," Mai Li calmly replied. "But in fox form she is bound to her clearing and cannot stray far. As long as we stay out of that section of the woods we will be safe enough."

A slight frown creased Lu Chen's still slightly flushed face at the look of amused superiority that had crept into Mai Li's expression. She had always been a headstrong child, but this was new, as was the calm self-assurance with which she spoke.

Regret filled his eyes as he realized that though he had saved her from Toyen, he had somehow lost her just the same. Seeing this, Mai Li's smile vanished and she lowered her eyes.

"This is what you had planned all along, isn't it?" he said, at last.

"I would have preferred the other way. But having become Toyen, after a fashion, I knew nothing else would work."

"You could have told me!" he blurted, more hurt than angry. "Can you even guess at the depth of my despair? And what if I had not stopped in time?"

"I never meant to cause you pain, Grandfather, please believe me." Her eyes welled with unshed tears, but her voice was unyieldingly reasonable. "There was no other way. If you hadn't believed you were really going to do it, Toyen would have read the truth in your eyes. It *was* the only way."

"And what will you do now?" he asked, reading one more unwanted truth in his granddaughter's unwavering gaze. "You are nearly a woman, but I doubt I would easily find a husband for so willful a maiden, especially one with such knowledge as you possess."

"I believe you are right, Grandfather," Mai Li said, a familiar impudent smile spreading slowly from her lips to her eyes. "So I have decided to apprentice myself to Chan Lin Ming, if she will have me. I have developed a taste for such learning, and the talent to use it, it would seem."

"The Gods help us all," Lu Chen murmured, shaking his head in mock dismay, "but I believe you also are correct, my impudent granddaughter." And thereafter, no more needed to be said, on that subject at least.

EYES OF MOONLIGHT, TEARS OF STONE

by Robin Wayne Bailey

Robin Wayne Bailey is the author of eleven novels, including SHADOWDANCE from White Wolf Books and the highly successful BROTHERS OF THE DRAGON series from Roc Books. His short fiction has appeared in numerous anthologies and magazines, including the THIEVES WORLD volumes and Marion Zimmer Bradley's SWORD AND SORCERESS series. His newest novel is SWORDS AGAINST THE SHADOWLAND, the first in a trio of works that feature Fritz Leiber's famous characters, Fafhrd and the Gray Mouser.

He lives in Kansas City, Missouri, where he organized a very successful Nebula banquet for SFWA members last year—a labor of love for the community of SF authors. I remembered an earlier Nebula weekend, and an evening when Robin demonstrated graceful dance steps on the deck of the Queen Mary, when I read his novel SHADOWDANCE. The novel featured a protagonist who could dance—who must dance—every night lest he lose the ability to use his legs at all; but he had to dance in secret, for anyone who watched him would act on their darkest desires. But Robin wasn't his protagonist; the main desire I felt was for the ability to move as lightly as Robin did, tapdancing up and down the stairs as if were floating.

This story is not about dance, but it's still about darkness. I bought an art book once about sketching, and noticed that its title in Spanish was "Sol y Sombra"—sun and shade. The setting of Robin's story, in a tenement without electricity, and on city streets at night, is dark—literally—but, as in any good fantasy, the story speaks of the light as well. Sol y Sombra indeed.
    —REH

"Isaac," Alice whispered through the fear that choked her, "please come down."

Twelve-year-old Isaac didn't reply. Unmoving, he perched on the edge of the low wall that bordered the rooftop, balanced on his toes, his fingertips barely touching the old brick between his feet. A black, blistering abyss of concrete yawned below. He stared into it, unblinking, birdlike in the night, seeming not to breathe.

Only minutes before, chancing to look up as she parked her old Toyota at the curb, Alice had seen him. In the dusky evening gloom, the moon had flashed on something, perhaps his tee-shirt, drawing her attention. Her heart still hammered from her frantic run up treacherous stairwells.

Summoning her courage, she dropped her battered purse and scarred leather briefcase, trying to ignore the dried piles of pigeon shit and the rotting tarpaper that crackled underfoot. The old boards groaned with every shift of her considerable weight; for a moment her knees jellied. She hated heights, and she hated her job with Child Protective Services. Yet she fixed her gaze on Isaac's small, rounded back and curly head, determined to lunge for him if he tried to jump.

Alice forced calm into her voice. "That's no place for you, Isaac. What are you doing?"

This time he answered. "Thinkin'. I like to come up here alone and sit"—he turned his head slowly to the right and left "with my friends."

On either side of him, a pair of granite-carved gargoyles rose from the cornice. Massive hunched shoulders and misshapen heads leaned away from the roof, loomed over the abyss. Alice had never really noticed them from the street. Up close, in the rapidly darkening night, they looked like devils.

"Those monsters?" she rasped, hugging herself against a chill October wind that swept across the crumbling tenement rooftops. She thrust her fist against her mouth. That wasn't a smart thing to say. To talk Isaac off that wall she had to win his trust. If he called those things his friends...

Isaac gave a sad little laugh, interrupting her racing thoughts, as he slid safely down to the rooftop without further coaxing. He reached out his small arm and stroked the winged back of the rightmost creature. The moonlight burned upon its pitted and weathered form, igniting a streak of white spray-paint, old graffiti, where some tagger had marked its spine.

The peculiar lunar glow also turned livid the bruises on Isaac's alabaster skin as he pointed beyond the roof to the next building. In a dimly lit window behind yellowed, half-drawn shades a pair of shadows, one larger than the other, struggled. Alice guessed suddenly that Isaac had been watching those shadows for some time.

"Don't you got eyes, Miss Carpenter?" Isaac murmured. "The monsters are all out there." He paused, his gaze on the tableau in the window. "The Preacher's beatin' his woman again," he said. He continued to stroke the gargoyle, to pet it with an unnatural, yet fascinating affection. "Beats her ever' night."

Alice thought to creep up on him now, to snatch him back from the wall and hold him hard with all her might. Yet her own fear of that edge rooted her to the spot where she stood.

"You listen real careful," he continued softly, "you can hear the whore workin' her trade in the alley below. An' gunshots comin' like firecrackers from two blocks over on Maple Street. An' sirens all the time, but far away." Once more he paused, and Alice thought she saw his thin frame shiver. "Sometimes you can hear the slide of that ol' needle pushin' easy into someone's arm from right underneath us." He threw his arms around the gargoyle and leaned his head against it. "Ain't no kinda music, Miss Carpenter."

Just a child, she thought, but he spoke like an old man with a world-weariness, and his words cut slices from her heart. Despite her fear, she crossed the roof and put a hand on his shoulder, tried to hug him close. He resisted that stubbornly and backed off a step.

"All I hear," she whispered, "is a little boy crying inside. I know what you're feeling, Isaac. I grew up in a place just as bad as this. I got out, and I'll get you out somehow."

He turned away. "Too late," he said, and the coldness in his voice chilled Alice Carpenter more than the October wind. "I don't cry no more. I've turned to stone, too, inside where it counts. Like my friends here." He stared out past the grotesque statues and down into the blackness of Lichmere Street where a thin fog began to crawl. Alice allowed her gaze to follow his.

The vertigo came like a wave, sweeping over her senses. The nearer buildings began to bend and fold on themselves; the world became a carousel. The wind pushed against her back. For a black instant, she felt herself falling.

Then she was clutching at the wall with both hands, kneeling on the dirty tarpaper, shaking uncontrollably. Isaac stood over her, his face stark with concern. He offered her a hand, and she put her darker one in his.

"Let's go downstairs, Isaac," she said weakly. "Please."

She let him help her up, and gathering her purse and her battered briefcase with its shoulder strap, they moved toward a rusted iron door and a stairway. The knees of Alice's stockings were ruined, her skirt soiled. She felt like a fool for fainting like that. But ten stories—ten stories! At the doorway, with one foot on a metal stair, she forced herself to look back. She wet her lips nervously.

The pair of gargoyles, their broad winged shoulders to her, sat as if in judgment over the city. She hadn't observed before the flakes of mica embedded in the granite catching the moonlight. How they glimmered! The effect was eerie, yet beautiful.

"I tell 'em things I can't tell no one else," Isaac said, his gaze following her own. "Sometimes they talk back."

He looked up at Alice with eyes large and liquid and shining, child's eyes alight with secrets and secret laughter. Then, too rapidly, sorrow filled those eyes again and drowned the light. He took her hand once more and, producing a tiny squeezable flashlight from his pocket, led the way down.

Dante at twelve years old, she thought, and the Livermore Hotel was a kind of hell. Property of an unknown owner who'd abandoned it years ago, it was home now to anyone who crawled in off the street. The tough ones or the wily ones, the long-term tenants, had staked out rooms for themselves. The weak and hapless ones camped on rough pallets of rags and newspapers in the hallways for one night or two before moving on.

The corridors smelled of urine and vomit, of bad wine and crack smoke. Electric light sockets, ripped from the crumbling ceilings, dangled bare and empty from frayed cords. In the glow of Isaac's flashlight, they looked like snakes lunging down to bite the faces of fools who passed beneath them.

The upper floors were empty tonight—too many stairs for the drunks and bag-people to climb. From behind a closed door on the eighth, however, wafted the pungent, tell-tale odor of heroin cooking.

On the seventh floor, a weak board creaked under Alice Carpenter's foot. Halfway down the corridor, a door—charred at the bottom as if someone had once tried to burn their way in opened an inch. A bony face peered out. Eyes hungry for many things settled on Alice's purse, then on Alice herself.

Alice and Isaac had to pass him to reach the next cascade of stairs, but the boy hesitated, his light centering squarely on the blocking figure as he moved into their path. The man's feet were bare, the old chinos and undershirt he wore filthy. He clenched one hand into a fist.

Alice Carpenter reached into her purse. Her gaze never leaving the bony-faced man, she curled her fingers around the grip of a .38 revolver and exposed just a bit of the grip. It meant her job if her bosses ever learned she carried it. But the man noted the weapon. He slid wordlessly back into his room, and a lock snicked shut.

On the sixth floor near the stairway was the door to the pair of rooms that made Isaac's home. He pushed it open; Alice followed him inside. A pair of flickering candles and a neon sign from across the street provided the only illumination. She winced at the smell, and a barely controlled anger surged inside her. That a child should have to live like this!

Someone had knocked a hole in the wall to the next room. That second outer door, she knew, was barricaded with old boards and nails. A scarred chest of drawers stood propped against it as further security. All the furniture was strictly curbside discount. The faint light fell upon a mattress on the bare floor. A woman who slept there.

Slept, of course, was a charitable term.

"Tiffany?" Alice whispered to Isaac's mother. A little louder she repeated, "Tiffany?"

The woman on the mattress stirred. One eye opened and tried to focus. Tiffany Graham struggled to her hands and knees with a little groan, then crawled to where the mattress met the wall beneath the window. She settled down again, her back to the paint-chipped plaster, drew her knees up and wrapped her arms around them.

She looked like a child herself, all bone, skin, no meat or muscle on her. Her hair was shiny with oil, in need of washing, as was the thin slip she wore. Confusion filled her darkly ringed eyes. She passed a hand over her face and stared at Alice with a squint. "Miss Carpenter?" she said at last. Her voice was a tiny flower of sound that opened slowly and hinted at a beauty long faded. "What you doin' here?" Her gaze wandered around the dingy room. "I didn't have time to straighten up...."

Alice's stern gaze swept the room, looking for signs of drugs or paraphernalia. Just a pipe or a needle, so much as a roach clip or a rubber tube—any evidence her superiors couldn't ignore and she'd have legal grounds to take Isaac out of this hell-hole. She could have him in a foster home by morning if her division administrator would just sign off on the damn papers.

"I'm authorized to make these spot-checks," Alice interrupted, "as a condition of Isaac's probation."

Tiffany's head jerked up; panic flooded her eyes. "He's been a good boy, Miss Carpenter. He's not gonna get in any more trouble. I'm lookin' after him, I swear!"

Only a month before, Isaac had broken into a grocery store late at night and walked out with a sackload of canned goods and candy bars right into the arms of the police. A disinterested judge with more serious crimes on his docket had shown leniency for a first-time offense.

Leniency? Alice ground her teeth in frustration. What kind of leniency was it to send a kid back to this?

"Show me your arms, Tiffany," Alice demanded.

Meekly obedient, the young mother extended her arms, wrists up. Small, fresh prick-marks and the mottled bruises of tracks days older told Tiffany's whole life story. "I'm clean," she lied stupidly.

Alice Carpenter bit back a harsh response. Instead, she let go a long sigh and tried to push down her indignation. "Do you have any food here, Tiffany?" she inquired in a gentler tone. "Have you and Isaac eaten anything today?"

She asked more questions; Tiffany became less and less responsive, finally closing her eyes and slumping sideways into the corner to lean there like a rag doll. Alice watched her, wondering if she should call an ambulance. But Tiffany breathed regularly without effort.

A smothering quiet filled the room. In the weak flicker of the candles, Alice Carpenter looked at her own arms and felt again the waves of shame and guilt that came at moments like this. Beneath the sleeves of her white blouse and her Kmart brand suit jacket, she could feel the fine needle scars that would never quite disappear on her own flesh.

She had spent most of her teen years just like Tiffany, stretched on her back in one shooting gallery after another, trading sex for drugs, living from one fix to another any way she could. Oh, she knew Tiffany well—she had been Tiffany.

But she'd gotten pregnant. In a charity hospital she'd held her poor addict-born baby and felt it die in her arms. From that tragedy, she had found the strength to clean herself up and begin the long crawl to a real life.

Alice stepped to the window and stared out at the desolate cityscape. A familiar, hard anger grew in her again. There was the enemy—the miles of unfeeling concrete, the uncaring darkness, all its heartless denizens. She knew its pock-marked face; she knew the seductive power in those nighted stone canyons, the allure it held for some.

"Woman," she whispered to Tiffany, "don't let it take a tragedy to open your eyes."

She adjusted her briefcase's strap and hugged her purse as if they were the symbols that separated her from her old life. Her lips drew into a grim line as she moved about the dirty space. Turning over a wrinkled magazine on the kitchen counter, she riffled its pages. Next, she popped open the door of the battered refrigerator. Its shelves held a few canned items, a box of cereal, half a loaf of bread, nothing that required electricity to cool.

Shaking her head, she prepared to leave, but first she bent near the hole in the wall and peered into the next room—Isaac's room. Nothing there but another crummy mattress and blanket. Not even a pillow. No toys. No books or games. No posters over the bed. Nothing to indicate the room belonged to a little boy.

For an instant she despised Tiffany. Yet there were too many Tiffanys in the world to hate them all; better to try to help them. At least the ones that would accept help.

But where did that leave Isaac? On his rooftop, perhaps, or down in the bleak streets, for there was no sign of him now.

Alice closed the door softly behind her as she stepped into the corridor. There, she hesitated, suddenly nervous. Without Isaac's little flashlight to guide her, she felt her way through the darkness toward the stairway. Earlier, she had raced through these black corridors as fast as her plump body allowed, propelled by her concern for a child in danger. Now, she crept forward, her eyes barely adjusting to the faintest trickle of violet light that seeped through a window at the rearmost end of the corridor, and when a board loudly creaked underfoot, she froze, trembling.

Chiding herself, squaring her shoulders, Alice drew a deep breath. With one hand against the wall, she groped her way to the stairs, found the cool, wooden banister, and prepared to descend.

Out of the blackness, a voice spoke. "Saviors and angels, Alice Carpenter," it murmured. "All fall down."

Alice's hand tightened on the rail. "Who's there?" she whispered, her pulse quickening.

A match flared, causing her to squeeze her eyes shut momentarily against unexpected brilliance. When she opened them again, a flickering glow illumined the haggard, stubbled face of a man who sat on the top step of the flight just above her. His cheeks were hollow, his look gaunt. *AIDS,* Alice thought, trying to meet his gaze. Intense eyes reflected the match's glimmering light.

"The times they are a-changin'," he said, "and the millennium approaches." The match's flame diminished as he spoke. The circle of radiance around his face grew smaller and smaller. "Some will be lost, but some will be saved, Alice. Hold on to that." The match died and darkness swathed his final words.

Alice's hand clenched and unclenched on the smooth banister. She waited in uncertainty for another match to strike, for another word, maybe an attack. She felt for the gun in her purse. Then she realized, *He knew my name!*

"Who are you?" she demanded. No answer came. Another gentler thought occurred to her. Summoning her courage, she moved to the bottom stair. "Are you sick?" Still no answer. The first step creaked under her weight as she dared to ascend. "Mister, you there?"

A chill shivered through her as she climbed halfway up and stopped. She didn't need to go farther to know she was alone. Without so much as a creak or groan from the old stairs to tell it, the man had gone. And yet she felt some gaze upon her, some presence close by—too close.

With a gasp, she spun about, swinging one arm up to ward off an anticipated grab. Her heel caught in the few remaining threads of carpeting. Briefcase and purse further unbalanced her; shoulder straps tangled her right arm and wrist. She shot out her left hand, awkwardly managing to catch the banister before she tumbled.

The sound of her ragged breathing echoed in the darkness. Her heart hammered. She stared toward the far end of the hallway toward a grime-smeared window, the source of the violet light. Someone moved there, briefly eclipsing that light.

A slow fire ignited behind Alice's narrowed eyes. She didn't like games, or people who played them, nor would she be intimidated. Adjusting her clothes, shouldering her belongings again, she descended the stairs with a firm tread, not pausing or looking back until she reached the Livermore's lobby.

There she slowed her pace again. A trio of half-melted candles burned on the scarred surface of what was once the front desk. A few more candles burned here and there. In that pathetic light, she set a deliberate course for the front doors.

Dust and filth covered the Livermore's once-beautiful marble floors. Beer cans, liquor bottles, discarded needles and empty crack vials lay scattered at random among scraps of old newspapers and paper bags. Battered chairs and broken couches, some left from the hotel's closing, others dragged in from the curbs, were situated in the darkened corners.

Sullen eyes watched her from those chairs and couches, but no one made a move toward her. The neighborhood regulars knew Alice and left her alone. The danger came from drifters who saw a plump, middle-aged black lady in a place like this as an easy mark, or from shooters too stoned to remember that she sometimes helped their children. So she watched as she made her way across the lobby, nodding to those she knew, receiving a nod or two in return.

The doors groaned as she pushed them open. Plywood boards had long ago replaced the window glass in the heavy metal frames. Inside and out, they were marred with graffiti. On the sidewalk finally, she paused to draw breath, feeling the oppressive weight of the Livermore Hotel lift from her soul. Without quite knowing why, she gazed up.

The gargoyles on the rooftop seemed to be staring at her. The moonlight caught the chips of mica in their eyes, filled them with a glittering that she perceived impossibly all the way down on the sidewalk. Backing up slowly, the better to observe this phenomenon, she tried to shake the queer feeling the things were actually watching her.

Abruptly, she bumped into the fender of her beat-up '78 Toyota parked at the curb. Easing around the front of the car, she prepared to open the driver's door. Her hand hesitated on the handle. As if a cloud had passed over the moon, the light faded from the gargoyles' eyes. Yet the moon shone down full and bright over Lichmere Street. Alice Carpenter frowned in puzzlement. Tearing her gaze from the stone creatures, she surveyed her surroundings.

At the far end of the block, limned by the amber glow of a lonely streetlight, Isaac stood between a pair of tall black men. Alice recognized one of them—a man called the Preacher. For a price he could show you heaven, all right. But the way to his heaven was through a syringe or a crack pipe. As she watched, Isaac accepted a package and disappeared around the corner. The two men lingered a moment more, then merged into the darkness.

Alice swallowed and forced herself to remain calm. When she opened the car door, the interior light flickered dimly on, then off, as she slid behind the steering wheel and closed the door again. Starting the ignition, she eased the car forward, glided past the streetlight, spied no sign of the two men—or Isaac.

Past the next corner she went, then a block northward. Tired to the bone, her thoughts roiling, Alice pulled over to the curb again, leaned her head on the steering wheel and cried. Her sobs shook the small car. Tears streamed down her face, smearing her mascara and the cheap rouge she wore.

When the tears ended, she sat back, took a tissue from her purse, and dabbed at her face. *Why do I let it hurt me?* she asked herself. Her job was pointless, futile. *I can't save any of them. Why do I try?*

She knew too well what had just gone down on that corner. Isaac was running drugs. Her sweet child, the one she had hoped to rescue, was the Preacher's delivery boy.

She recalled the first time she'd seen Isaac, a frail little boy, eyes big and scared, in a police station's holding room. Her heart had gone out to him at once. This one, she had promised herself, this one she would save. This time she'd make a difference.

Isaac was a runner.

She blinked back new tears and resolved to cry no more. In the quiet privacy of her car, she weighed those words, felt their numbing power, whispered them over and over—they tasted bitter on her tongue.

Thrusting open her car door, she got out, desperate for fresh air. She wasn't a woman given to dreaming, but as she leaned on door, she wondered suddenly what it would be like to leave the city, go someplace far away where the air was truly fresh, where nothing could hurt her anymore.

St. Anne's Episcopal Church stood across the street. A shallow flight of broken concrete steps led up to massive, arched doors. Alice stared toward that gothic facade, recalling a service she had once attended there. She had enjoyed that service, the minister's reassuring voice, the choir, the sweet ringing of the Sunday morning bells.

She no longer went to church. Now she laughed with a silent resentment at the idea of a kindly all-wise old man who would reach his hand down to the poor and unfortunate and lift them up to something better. She had given up prayer—she had stopped asking for miracles that never came.

Measuring the empty place in her heart where her faith once had been, she crossed the street suddenly and stood at the foot of the broken stairs. She did, in fact, see one miracle on this godforsaken night—stained-glass windows that, in a neighborhood like this, remained intact. A mad rage rushed through her as she thought of Isaac and all the people who bought into the pious lies and worthless promises spewed from the pulpits of such churches. Temples of lies! Bending, she scooped up a small chunk of concrete and flung it, intent on smashing one of the stained glass panes. "That for your miracles!" she cried.

Her arm had lost its youthful strength. The stone arched, falling short of the window. It clattered against the wooden doors, rebounded, skipped a few times on the broken sidewalk. For a moment, all was silence.

Then a sound jarred the night, so sudden it made her jump. It came again, and a third time. The bells! St. Anne's bells! But they never rang at night! Her heart pounding, she stared upward, seeking St. Anne's bell tower.

Something else caught her eye. Along the peaked rooftops, crouched in the shadows of taller buildings, three watchful gargoyles sat as if in judgment of her deed. The bells continued to ring.

Jaw agape, Alice spun about. Except for herself, the street remained empty. The tenements that loomed above her remained dark. No one raised a window to peer out; no door opened. Nor, she realized, was there any light from the church, not from the tower, nor the rectory, nor from any of the stained-glass windows.

Her hands clenched into fists, and she prepared to run back to her car. Instead, she found herself turning once more, seeking in the darkness the barely perceived shapes of those monstrous statues. "Stop!" she shouted, clapping her hands over her ears.

The bells stopped.

A drop of rain splattered on Alice's brow. One by one, droplets kissed the black pavement around her feet. The street began to gleam with wetness. The tower began to gleam. The gargoyles began to gleam and glimmer.

Alice struggled to control herself. Wiping a hand over her face, she turned away from the church, got calmly back into her car, closed and locked the door. Too tired to think, she fastened her seat belt and resolved to dismiss the whole experience. Nothing made any sense anymore. As she let go a sigh, she started the motor and headed for home.

The insistent ringing of bells frightened Alice Carpenter. In that strange state halfway between sleep and wakefulness, she dreamed she was back at St. Anne's. The streets were writhing under her feet, and she was falling, falling helplessly toward a church door that gaped like a black maw.

And the gargoyles sat watching, like judges....

The ringing persisted. Struggling up from the dream, she forced open her eyes. For a disorienting moment, she didn't know where she was. Slowly the details of her unkempt little apartment asserted themselves. She thrust out one hand and fumbled for the phone. "...'lo?"

A voice spoke thinly from the receiver. "Miss Carpenter? It's me, Tiffany."

Alice sat up and rubbed her eyes. Balancing the receiver with one hand, she reached for the bedside clock and turned it to see the digital face—half past midnight.

"Miss Carpenter..." Tiffany hesitated. Her voice was more than apologetic. It was a shy and frightened thing, more a kitten's mewl than a voice. She began again. "Miss Carpenter, I know you been good to Isaac and me, keepin' him out of trouble an' all." She paused again. "I think he's in some trouble again. Bad trouble this time."

Alice came completely awake. She flung back the covers and switched on her bedside lamp. "Where are you calling from, Tiffany?"

"Liquor store on Fifth an' Grand," Tiffany answered. Then, she began to gush. "The Preacher came up to our rooms lookin' for Isaac, but I heard 'im comin' an' locked the door, so he kicked it in, but it didn't matter, 'cause Isaac wasn't there."

Alice's eyes narrowed as she rose from the bed. "Did he hurt you,

Tiffany?" she asked. "Did he touch you?"

Tiffany's voice rose a notch toward hysteria. "That don't matter, Miss Carpenter. Isaac's all that matters. You got to help him. I don't know who else to call but you!"

Alice juggled the phone while she slipped out of her night dress. "Where's Isaac now, Tiffany?"

"I swear I don't know, Miss Carpenter, I don't." Tiffany stopped talking suddenly. Then in a quieter voice, "You gonna take him away from me, Miss Carpenter? He's all I got. Please don't take him away from me! I'll get clean, I will, I promise!"

Promise, indeed, Alice thought harshly. If she had a dime for every time she'd heard a junkie make a promise, she could feed the world Thanksgiving dinner. "You stay right where you are, Tiffany. I'll pick you up. Don't leave that store, you hear me?"

When Tiffany agreed, Alice hung up the phone. Hurriedly, she pulled on slacks and a blouse, shoes, and snatched up her purse. At the door, before leaving, she paused at her answering machine, hit the memo button, and recorded a message, dictating where she was going and why. Then she flew out the door. *Social worker to the rescue,* she thought bitterly. She needed a mask and an Indian companion.

Dressed in jeans and a too-tight shirt, Tiffany was waiting nervously by the pay phone just outside the door at Big Papa's Liquors. She wrung her hands and hugged herself as Alice drove up and parked, and Alice regarded her sternly. Whether Tiffany was anxious about Isaac or just needed her latest fix, Alice couldn't tell. She ushered the young mother into the passenger's seat and got back in the car.

Her fingers dug into Tiffany's bony arm. "Did you know Isaac was running for the Preacher?" she demanded.

Tiffany's eyes widened with surprise, then flared with anger. She wrenched Alice's hand away. "If he was doin' that," she hissed, "makin' that kind of money, would I be peddlin' my ass up an' down this block all day an' livin' like we do? Isaac wouldn't do that. I don't let him go nowhere near no drugs."

It was a rare moment of honesty for Tiffany. The shock of it stung Alice like a slap. "Well, he's fooled us both, then. I saw him take a package from the Preacher."

Tiffany looked stricken. She put her face in her hands and hung her head as the tears came. "Oh, my God," she muttered. "What have I done? What have I done?"

"It's what we have to do now," Alice said, shaking her head. "If the Preacher's after him, it's for no small thing. We've got to get to him first." She bit her lip, and her gaze settled on the pay phone. She fumbled in her purse for a quarter. "Stay here," she told Tiffany as she opened and closed the door.

Snatching up the phone, she shoved the quarter in its slot and hit 911. When the dispatcher at the other end answered, she wasted no time. "Send a car down to the Livermore Hotel on Lichmere," she instructed. "Tell them to shake the Preacher tonight. Shake him hard, and something interesting will fall out of his pockets."

She slammed the phone down on its hook. Forgetting to collect her quarter when the operator returned it, she got back into her car. Tiffany had stopped crying. "Let's go get Isaac," Alice said.

The little Toyota shuddered as she threw it into gear and pulled out onto Fifth Street. Another block over was Lichmere. Swinging onto that, she headed west three blocks to the hotel. Parking at the curb, she switched off the ignition.

A pair of men loitered outside the hotel doors. She didn't recognize them. They had a seedier, meaner look than even she was used to. A bagman sat against a wall, guarding his cart. Another man sat nearby, hunkered over a brown paper bag containing a quart of beer.

Alice had never been down here so late. Still, there was no turning back. Reaching across Tiffany, she popped open the glove compartment and extracted a slender flashlight. Then, clutching her purse tightly, she got out of the car. Tiffany followed.

Moving swiftly, ignoring the men by the doors, Alice shoved through the plywood panels and into the hotel's lobby. Flicking on the flashlight, she froze.

Someone growled to shut off the light. She barely heard. Instead she played the beam around. The lobby floor was covered with people, some trying to sleep, some just passed out. Leaning against a column, an old black man hugged his knees, rocked himself, and hummed "Amazing Grace" ever so softly. A young white boy, no more than fifteen years old, rose quickly from his bed on a pile of newspapers to regard her with steely and murderous eyes.

Alice gathered her resolve. "Have any of you seen Isaac?" she called boldly. "Tiffany's little boy?"

No one responded. Behind them, the doors opened, and the pair of toughs from outside entered. For a moment, their eyes settled on Alice's purse, but then they were looking past her to the staircase.

Alice whirled, directing her flashlight. The gaunt man with the intense eyes and the AIDS-thinned face stood on the first step. He said nothing, but the toughs seemed to lose some of their attitude as they slunk off into a corner. Tiffany moved toward the stairs, eclipsing the beam. Alice cursed, but when the light lit up the stairs again, the man was gone—just as before.

She chewed her lip, then hurried after Tiffany, taking the steps as fast as her plump body allowed, driven by a renewed sense of urgency. When they reached the sixth floor, she was quite out of breath. With no thought but for her son, Tiffany left Alice on the landing and dashed ahead into her rooms.

Her sudden scream, truncated by a harsh slap and a grumbled command, reverberated in the corridor.

The Preacher was waiting for them—or rather, waiting for Isaac! A second short scream followed another sharp blow. Alice charged into the room. "You leave that child alone!" she shouted, shaking a fist.

But the Preacher wasn't alone. As she pushed into the room, hands clamped on her shoulders, flung her off-balance. She hit the wall hard, her head knocking loose a chunk of old plaster. Sagging to the floor, she caught sight of a shadowy figure—the second man she'd seen earlier under that streetlight. She tried to crawl away from him. He kicked her in the stomach, knocking the wind from her, and she collapsed.

The Preacher's deep voice seemed to come from under water as he slapped Tiffany again. "Your boy's been skimmin' me, woman," he said. "I seen you leave, so we come back to search around a little, an' guess what we find pushed way back under your little bastard's mattress?" He waved a handful of bills under her nose.

Alice could barely breathe, but she spat out words. "I called the police!"

The Preacher smiled patiently at Alice. "I know the police around these parts," he said. "An' it'll be twenty-thirty minutes 'fore any of 'em show up. You trust me on this."

"Plenty o' time," said the second man smugly.

"Plenty of time," the Preacher echoed.

"You got your money!" Tiffany shouted. "Now just get out!"

The Preacher slapped her again. Tiffany spun about like a doll under the force of the blow. Her heel caught on the mattress she slept on, and she fell. "Got the principal back," the Preacher said with mocking gentleness. "Now we got to collect the interest." He reached for his belt buckle and began loosening it.

Alice watched him through blurred eyes, pain giving way to anger, and that to a mindless hysteria that surged up from her own repressed memories and experiences. With a shriek, she flew up from the floor. With flailing arms, she attacked the Preacher while he was still tangled in his pants, hitting him again and again, scratching and kicking, holding back nothing. Like a maddened bird protecting its young, she beat and clawed him.

The second man grabbed her. A blow came from somewhere and set her ears to ringing. *The bells!* she thought crazily, *the bells!* She flung up her arms, striking out at both men, and found herself spinning across the room. The refrigerator came up too suddenly.

A loud *boom!* sounded. At first, she thought it was her head hitting hard metal. Then it repeated—six hard, loud blasts of thunder. On the floor again, she forced one elbow under her and lifted her head.

Isaac stood just inside the doorway. In his hand, he clutched a smoking gun—the .38 he had taken from her purse, which lay near his feet. Like a small stone statue, he stood there, unmoving, unblinking, while the blue gunpowder vapor curled about his form.

The Preacher's shadowy pal lay dead in the middle of the room, blood pouring from his head, from his side, from one hand.

A bullet's impact had smashed the Preacher against a wall, and he sat sunk down against the baseboard. Blood poured from his upper chest. Yet his eyes fixed on Isaac. With a grunt, clutching his wound, he rose to his feet.

Isaac woke from his trance. The empty gun fell from his hand. Turning, he ran into the hallway, his footfalls making a loud noise. The Preacher shambled after in pursuit.

Drawing a painful breath, Alice rose to her knees. Her flashlight lay in a corner under a table, its beam trained grotesquely on the dead man's bloody face. She snatched it up. The gun was of no use now.

Tiffany had retreated to the farthest corner of her mattress, where, hugging her knees, she crouched against the wall, wide-eyed with shock. "Come on!" Alice cried as she lurched toward the door. "Isaac's heading for the roof!"

Tiffany made no move, just whimpered and stared at the body on her floor.

Cursing, Alice ran into the hallway and up the steps. She gave no thought to the old, rotting carpet and crumbling wood under her feet, to the banister that threatened to give way under her weight. She ran as fast as her body allowed, thinking only of the boy and the monster that pursued him.

She burst through the final door onto the roof. Taller buildings loomed like black monoliths over the Livermore, and neon burned holes in the night. The wind whipped suddenly at her, and overhead the full moon shone down. She froze in mid-step, realizing where she was, as her old fear of heights rose up like a barrier.

Isaac crouched against the low wall between his beloved gargoyles. Despite his wound, the Preacher moved upon him with a single-minded purpose. Catching the front of Isaac's thin shirt, he lifted the boy, who for the first time emitted a child's shrill cry. Moonlight sparkled on tears that sprang from his eyes.

Alice matched his cry with her own. Her fear melted in the heat of her need to save her child! She lunged at the Preacher, pummeling him again, forcing him to release his grip on Isaac. Dropping the boy, he turned on her, and still she lashed out with hysterical fury.

Suddenly, her feet left the rooftop. She felt the cold stone wall under her sharply arched back. The moon whirled, and the monolithic buildings danced wildly. For a moment, she caught a glimpse of a gargoyle face—*such a misshapen thing of sadness and grief* she thought crazily.

Then she was out in space, the cold air whistling about her, snatching her hair, her clothes. The wind, the wind!—The wail of sirens somewhere across the city trumpeted her fall, and the echo of her own scream sliced the heart of night.

Thrown over the edge, she fell, she fell! The neon lights and pieces of darkness and fragments of memories jumbled and tumbled like chips in a kaleidoscope—the needles in her veins, her baby in her arms. The babies! The babies all lost and dead!

And now she was falling. The thought flashed through her mind.

At last, an end to trying, to failing.

But what of Isaac? Must he be lost, too? Through her screaming, she cried, "Oh God! Save Isaac!" But the rush of wind drowned her words, and a black wave swept over her senses.

Then from the heart of that blackness, a mighty shape, dimly glimpsed as if through veils of consciousness, surged down upon her; *Death,* she thought, *death with clawed hands, with the gentleness of an angel, with a warming presence that closed about her.* A new wind from impossible pinions blew upon her face as she felt herself borne up.

Someone shook her. Alice opened her eyes and looked around in a panic, her heart hammering. She lay on the sidewalk, unharmed, and a gaunt man with intense and familiar eyes bent over her. "The times, they are a-changin'," he said, and he rolled his eyes toward the rooftop.

Alice didn't question how she had gotten on the ground or why she was not dead. All she thought about was Isaac. Clambering to her feet, she ran back into the Livermore, once more up the stairs, driving herself against all her bruises and injuries. Outside, she heard sirens, the police arriving at last.

On the roof again, she found a shocking tableau. The moon spotlighted a bloody form—the Preacher. He'd threaten no one else, destroy no more lives with his poison. His flesh lay in neat scarlet ribbons about him; his exposed ribs shimmered wetly.

Sobbing, Tiffany curled against the low wall where the gargoyles loomed. She held her arms stiffly before her, palms up, a disbelieving look mingling with pain and grief. The countless needle tracks on her arms were all open again, and they oozed a milky fluid that dripped onto the tarpaper. Every ounce of filth she had ever poured into her body now poured back out.

Alice knelt beside Tiffany and threw her own arms around the girl. She didn't understand it, any of it. Yet here, she knew, was the miracle she had always hoped for.

"Where's Isaac?" she whispered, rocking Tiffany gently, fervently.

"They came alive," Tiffany said, her wild-eyed gaze seeking Alice's face. "They came alive! One saved you, and the other saved Isaac from the Preacher!" She looked toward the still form in the center of the roof, and the words choked in her throat. "I ran up here in time to see it all!"

Alice clutched the young woman's shoulder. "But Isaac?" she whispered. "Where's our precious boy?"

A pair of policemen rushed through the door onto the rooftop, their guns drawn, their faces unfamiliar. Down below, sirens sang, and the shouting voices of men echoed upward.

"Where no one can hurt him anymore, Alice," came Tiffany's awed whisper. "Where no one can hurt him!"

More police achieved the rooftop now, and hands reached to help Alice and Tiffany. Alice shook them off. She stared at the pair of gargoyles. No longer a pair, she saw. They were three now, one smaller than the others, one sheltered protectively under the wing of the largest.

She began to cry softly, wondering if she were in shock for feeling no horror. Near the door, a ragged man stood, his hair thinned from illness, his body emaciated. Yet his eyes shone with fire. The police seemed to ignore him, if indeed they saw him at all.

Someone set a blanket around her shoulders. Someone else tried to ask her questions. She would answer them all as best she could in time. But now, she turned slowly, scanning the sky, noting the rooftops, and she saw as she had never seen all the gargoyles nested in the shadows, on the cornices, in half-hidden places, gathering, watching, waiting like...

...guardians.

She drew Tiffany closer and hugged her tight. The girl held up her arms. Together, they watched as the tiny track-marks healed and faded away completely. Then Tiffany's head nestled into Alice's shoulder. *Here at last,* Alice thought, *is one saved child.*

She looked around for the gaunt man. There was no sign of him, but now she saw a fourth gargoyle where only three had been.

In the distance, St. Anne's bells began to ring.

THE BORDER WOMEN

by Paul Edwin Zimmer

My brother Paul Edwin Zimmer followed me into the business of writing—and I've always been as proud of him as if he were my own child. My older son David has chosen to write, but he is not as devoted to the field of commercial writing as I am; and while he has never said so, I suspect he tends to share the view of those who affect to look down on "commercial" writing; while I cheerfully share the belief of no less a person than Charles Dickens, who felt that writing for money was not at all beneath his dignity but actually made a very good living at it, although he is now regarded as a "classic" writer—taught in colleges and so forth. Who knows, maybe someday I will be too.

Paul was enough younger than I that for a time in his childhood he probably did not know the difference between "Mommy"—our mother—and "Mimi"—me, his older sister. It's always surprising when somebody you've carried around on one arm as an infant grows up to be both articulate and knowledgeable; it's one of the joys of motherhood and I knew it first with Paul. We were, however, very unlike; his work rested on very different principles than mine. I found that he had a particular kind of strength I didn't; to write action scenes which used combat, martial arts and the like, as a way of delineating character. This was how we first came to collaborate, first on the combat scenes in my novel SPELL-SWORD, then on the book which was basically his idea, HUNTERS OF THE RED MOON. HUNTERS and its sequel THE SURVIVORS exploited his strengths and, I think, mine. The first of these was published under my name as I had at that time a good record of sales; the second managed to include Paul's byline. After which he went on to write the basically horror-oriented DARK BORDER novels.

Our methods of working were as unlike as our faces—and Paul and I were basically not much alike for brother and sister, though oddly, we both looked like our father. Paul was a night person; I was a day person. At about four in the morning I would always get up to write; my best work has always been done by getting up before my kids were awake and working—I sleep very badly, and if I want to sleep at all, have to get to bed early. If I wake up after midnight, my sleep is basically over. Paul has always been a night worker; even on the farm he couldn't get up in time to milk the cows—natch, he didn't like the farm. So, while we were collaborating, I'd get up at three or so, go up to find Paul finishing up his "day's" work, and we'd talk about the book; then I'd wish him a "good *night", and he'd go down to bed, and I'd go home to get my kids off to school. It worked and we have the books to prove it.*

Paul died very suddenly, very young; he was hardly fifty—proof, if required, that only the good die young. He should have outlived me by many years. His last work was this story, which I bring here in his memory, with love.
—MZB

Sumitri looked through fretted silver screens, toward Shadow. Twin Suns were setting: pitiless light flared on miles of poisoned grey dust. The looping swathes of ruined land were like scars burned on her own body.

Beyond the green fringe of fields, harsh land stretched south, to the smothering pall that had killed her babies, and still tried to wither her thin body, as it had withered the skeletal trees she could glimpse just across the Border.

A hen cackled over an egg. Emptiness gnawed her belly. *Raw fish again,* she reminded herself, trying not to think about food. Footsteps echoed in terrible emptiness. Even when the men had been home, Giripor had always seemed too large for its scant garrison. Now, with only six women and their children, the lonely corridors seemed to stretch away forever...

Men waste their lives in foolish games, she thought, *while women do the work that keeps the world alive.*

It was an old saying on the Border, but she felt its truth more keenly now, with the men away in this *stupid* war, not even fighting to save the Land, but fighting other men....

A door banged. The loud clatter of feet woke one of the babies in the room below, and its wail brought milk surging to her breast.

Pirru, she thought, and started to jump up to go to him, but then, remembering she was on guard, forced herself back to the window. There were others to answer that cry....

It couldn't be Pirru. The wail was too shrill. It must be little Kisa, or Diti, or maybe Kullu.

Rainbow light flooded through the western window, but south was only the darkness of the Shadow, except where the Hastur-Tower of Srarcis stood, a slim stalk of dim light. East, the sky was clear blue above the Stassian Mountains.

Juvali's voice rose above the baby's wails, singing one of the world-old nonsense songs for children....

Ommeny, O-ommeny Pam-mi-on!
Father, tell me why Are there two suns? Instead of one?

The familiar rhyme soothed her. She had sung it to so many babies, over the years.... Mother Gayatri said that that rhyme must go back thousands of years, to the first men that Hastur had brought into the World....

Ommeny, Ommeny,
Truth is one!

Clamoring feet came booming up the stairs, and she heard the shrill echoes of boyish voices, and Taravi's voice, trying to hush them. Juvali's singing stopped as she hissed at them. The baby cried on, unheeding.

The clatter grew louder. Startled chickens ran around the room; then fluttered up, squawking, onto piled sacks. Sumitri glanced up as the two boys burst into the room.

No, not boys, she reminded herself, turning back, *they are men now....* Perhaps the only men she or her sister-wives would see—or sleep with—for years.... Vikram was thirteen, Uttaro twelve. They were the men of the house, now, left behind to guard women and Land.... Taravi, taller than either, was at their heels.

"Hurry, now!" Vikram exclaimed. "It's nearly dark!" Something heavy scraped across the floor.

"What are you doing?" Taravi's disapproving voice cut in. "That Troll will be out again, as soon as it's dark!" Vikram said. "This time, we'll be ready for him!"

Glancing quickly from the window, Sumitri saw him balanced atop an ancient chest, lifting one of the heavy crossbows down from the wall.

"When he comes we will have a clear shot at him, before—"
"Hurry!" Uttaro exclaimed. "Vikram! Hurry! It's nearly dark now! There go the Suns!"

Vikram handed the bow to Uttaro, then, jumping down, pushed the chest over under the second of the three crossbows. For three nights now, a Troll had moaned about the castle wall, smelling their lonely cow, and had twice tried to pound with ponderous fists through the thick stone that shielded the stable. Sumitri almost welcomed it: the Border had been unnaturally quiet for two months now. Mother Gayatri in all her seventy-some years could remember no such extended period of peace.

Outside, sunset began to fade, and beyond the Stassian Mountains in the east, the blue deepened. The Hastur-Tower glowed somberly, and now she glimpsed a distant light, like a dim star, far in the west, at the base of the Shadow—the next Hastur-Tower, forty miles away.

Taravi was helping Uttaro wind the windlass that cocked the powerful steel bow. Vikram was trying to maintain his superiority as he strained against the crank of the other. Sumitri almost got up to help, then turned back, with a secret smile. She wondered if even the massive steel strings of the crossbows would drive a missile far into a Troll's stone-hard flesh. Behind her she heard Vikram and Uttaro arguing whether to use iron or silver bolts.

Then their feet were pounding the stairs again, while women's voices protested. Her breasts ached. She still nursed Pirru, even though Mother Gayatri said he was too old, and she helped nurse little Kullu and Diti sometimes...

The Troll roared. It could not be coming all this way from the Shadow, she thought. It was too close. It must have a cave to hide in during the day. If the men had still been home, she could have told them, and they would have hunted until they found it.... The Troll roared again, louder. She heard a door slam, and shrill boys' voices. Then something moved below, and looking down, she saw the boys running onto the parapet.

They had stopped to pull on their armor, even though they had promised Mother Gayatri not to leave the parapet. Uttaro looked like a comical beetle in the loose flapping corselet of bones sewn with leather, and the flaring flaps of lacquered wood that hung from his helmet. Vikram was magnificent in his cuirass of lacquered bone. She could not see his face, but she could picture the great dark eyes—like Sajan's—alive with boyish excitement.

Light faded from the sky. The Troll moaned, nearer, and she saw Uttaro point, and heard his voice echo from stone. Vikram leaned to look, then both laid crossbows across the wall. She saw Uttaro's shoulder jerk as the heavy bow kicked. The Troll roared in anger and pain. She saw Uttaro jump up and down in glee, as Vikram tensed to shoot.

She blinked as bright light glared in her eyes.

The Hastur-Tower burned bright as sunlight, and a crackling curtain of flame flared on either side. Need-fire leaped from the west, from tower to tower, all along the Border.

Her hand fumbled for the rope beside her, as she choked back a scream. As her fist clenched on the cord she saw Vikram's bow loosed, and the Troll's angry bellow was drowned in the deep tone of the bell. She saw them stiffen, but now she was using the bell-rope to haul herself to her feet, and throw her whole weight onto it, willing the bell to ring louder—louder! She felt threads pop in her shoulder-seam.

Between peal and peal of the bell she heard the sudden clamor of feet. Both hands clutched the bell-rope as it lifted her from the floor. She felt the seam tear at her shoulder. Twisting, she looked down through the grille and saw the two boys stark against the wall of blue and yellow flame that was now the entire sky.

"Hurry!" she screamed, her voice drowned in the boom of the bell.

Uttaro had drawn his sword, and Vikram was trying to fumble another bolt into the crossbow—but they were standing still, staring at the vast wall of Need-fire, when they should be running.... She sensed as much as saw something like a spinning puff of vapor dart down onto the wall. She let go the rope and dropped to the floor. Below, mist curdled and condensed into a human shape.

Mother Gayatri and Juvali burst through the door, children in their arms. The other women followed.

"*Quick, the* crossbow!" Sumitri shrieked, as the bell's peal died. "It's their only hope."

Taravi set Pirru on the floor and leaped to the top of the chest. Pirru, startled, let out a frightened wail, but his mother whirled back to the window, pinching the flesh of her arm in her teeth to choke back useless screams.

Uttaro slashed at the tall pale figure that had come from the mist, and Vikram, throwing down the useless, half-wound crossbow, pulled his sword halfway from its sheath. Behind them, a second pillar of mist collapsed into human form, and leaped onto Vikram's back as Sumitri jerked her arm down and screamed. Behind her, Taravi and Maitriyi were winding back the crossbow.

Uttaro looked up as she screamed, and the other figure in a sudden blur gripped his sword arm. The white face came down on his throat.

Sumitri felt nails tear her cheeks, and screamed again before she realized they were her own.

Maitriyi pushed her out of the way, and fitted the head of the quarrel carefully through the silver grille before taking aim. The great bow sang. The vampire that held Uttaro jerked and staggered, but did not fall.

Maitriyi jerked frantically at the windlass on the bow, and Sumitri joined her hand to the other woman's, and between them they jerked the heavy crank around and around, jerking the strong string back, slowly bending massive steel.

"Another bolt!" Maitriyi gasped. Taravi held one out.

"Wait!" Mother Gayatri closed her frail old hand around Taravi's.

"But—the boys—!" Taravi began, but the older woman shook her head.

"Too late now! They've both been bitten. All we can do is recover their bodies when daylight comes—if we can—" Only for a second the old woman's voice broke. "I know it's hard. Do you think I've never been through it?"

Sumitri straightened, letting go of the crank. Her teeth were pressed tight together; her nails dug into her palms.

"If there is a dawn...." Sumitri wanted to shout at the old woman, but her voice came weak and shaken, and all her muscles trembled. "Look outside! Suppose dawn never comes?"

Through the silver grille the veil of the Need-fire was torn with black, gaping rifts. The tower flared and flickered and flared again. The chickens' squawking and the children's crying in the room behind them, seemed to rise and fall in eerie rhythm with the flicker of the light.

"If the tower breaks—" Taravi said, barely breathing, "then—"

"Then we will do whatever we must," the old woman said, her voice sharp. "Remember from whose blood you come! Maitriyi!" She pushed Taravi's arm forward, the bolt still gripped in both their hands. "Load the crossbow, then give it to me, and go help Juvali lay the fire. Taravi, go and check the warding on the windows. Sumitri—"

"But even if the Suns do rise tomorrow," Sumitri broke in, her voice oddly weak and shrill, "that won't help us! *They* won't go away. They'll just go inside, out of the sunlight. They'll be all over the castle, waiting for us to come down!"

"But we've got to go down," Maitriyi said, her hands frozen on the windlass. "We have to get their bodies, before—" Her voice rasped to a whisper, tears running down her face. Uttaro had been her son.

"That is why we must waste no more bolts," Mother Gayatri answered, her voice firm. "They are our most reliable weapons. And we must recover the other bows, if we can. But we *must* save the boys, even if there is no sunrise, and bring them for the Warrior's Bride."

Sumitri felt her mouth burst open by a sharp bark that was like a laugh, but a laugh more painful than tears.

"The Warrior's Bride!" she said, her voice bitter. "The Warrior's Bride likes them young, doesn't she?" And in that moment she hated the Earth, the child-devouring Mother of All: womb and tomb, the Eater of Men, the Warrior's Bride; breast and cradle and grave in one.

"There is no need to talk like that!" There was pity in the piercing dark eyes in Mother Gayatri's wrinkled old face, but her voice was sharp. "Until the Dark Things came, men had only such foolish little wars as this one of Hansio's, wars against other men, to keep them from living as long as women. Some men never went to war at all, but lived long, peaceful lives, tilling the soil or selling goods, just as men do away from the Border now—those farmers and merchants that you scorn as cowards!" The old woman had straightened as she spoke and her voice was clear above the wailing children and the panicked, fluttering chickens. Then, exhausted, she seemed to shrink into herself, shoulders slumping.

"Earth must be fed," she went on, "but do not blame the Earth for the Dark Things, or for what men do to themselves."

Sumitri's eyes stung with sudden tears, and she turned away, wiping at them furiously. Then she felt the other woman's hand—thin and bony, but amazingly strong—clasp her shoulder.

"It is no shame to weep, child. The Land is watered with tears. But Pirru is crying. Go to him."

The room was filled with wailing children. Juvali cradled little Diti and Bini to her swollen breasts, crooning softly, while Kajioni tried helplessly to console Pirru and Kairi.

Sumitri ran to them, and Kajioni was glad to let Pirru go and hug Kairi more tightly, while Sumitri pressed her son's rigid, kicking, little body in her arms, rocking him back and forth, feeling more threads pop in the shoulder-seam of her robe. She began to croon, wordlessly, along with Juvali...

Suddenly she remembered the words that went to that tune...

How many rode home from the battle?
How many died in the fight?
How many came back strapped to their saddles?
And how many still haunt the night?

"Juvali! *No! Not that* song!" She burst into a storm of weeping, while Juvali stared dumbly, and Pirru, who had begun to relax in her arms, screamed and kicked out violently, straightening his legs and leaning backward over her arms, so roughly that he almost banged his head on the floor.

She felt her shoulder suddenly bare, as the seam tore out entirely, and silk slithered over the skin of her back. She rocked to the side, to keep the stick-stiff, bony body across her knees as she pulled her arm free from the cloth, and then bent, to push her nipple against the screaming mouth, and braced herself. He bit, as she had known he would, and for a moment she wondered if he had bitten through.

Slowly she felt the boy relax, and the pain ease. Even then, she was not sure whether he was drinking milk or blood.

"Did anyone shut the trap door?" Mother Gayatri asked. One of the dim figures working at the hearths jumped up, and the dull boom of falling metal made Pirru jerk in Sumitri's arms, biting hard. A bolt grated loudly.

"There!" Taravi said, in the dark. "It is shut."

The room was lit by the dim glow of warding jewels. As Pirru's whimpers stilled, Sumitri could hear wood clank and clatter as Taravi and Maitriyi worked, back-to-back, laying wood in the two hearths that faced each other on either side of the trap door. In the alcove beyond, the dim light of a single moon poured through the screened arrow-slit that was their only window to the north.

Steel scratched flint: sparks leaped. Maitriyi's face appeared, cheeks puffed as she blew. A thin thread of flame flared. Maitriyi's face vanished again. A painted face glared out of ancient plaster, and in a blink was gone. Gold threads twinkled gaily in the rich brocade of Maitriyi's ancient gown, and Maitriyi's hand rose holding a flaming splinter, her skin gold in its light.

Taravi's darker hand took it. Kindling flared up in the other hearth. Taravi's robe flashed bright green under the soot-blackened arch. Sumitri's scars tingled, as she remembered age-dried cloth burning on her skin...

The alcove was floored with brick and stone, and the threshold was like a rough stone trough, filled now with wood.

Sumitri saw Mother Gayatri slump wearily onto a bale, the heavy crossbow laid across her lap. The old woman fumbled for a moment in the breast of her robe, then drew out a small box, either of incised leather or carven wood. She opened it, and something rattled and clattered as she reached inside.

Pirru squirmed, and Sumitri lowered him gently to the floor. He was sound asleep now, and she became aware of exhaustion that pulled at her own eyelids.

Mother Gayatri drew out a clattering string of large wooden heads. With a sudden chill, Sumitri realised that the old woman was putting on her funeral jewelry, priceless beads of carved cedar and sandalwood that she had hoarded to burn with on the pyre.

Taravi's voice snarled a sudden curse. Mother Gayatri looked up.

"Taravi!" she shouted. "No! Your sword is too broad!"

At the west window the younger woman was standing with the heavy sword drawn back. Through the silver grille, firelight flared on a bone-white face.

"You will break the grille! Then they can get through! Stand aside!"

The old woman hobbled across the room, wooden heads swinging against the tight-gripped crossbow.

At the window, she set the arrow's point carefully through the mesh. The warding-pattern of the jewels above the window flared with Need-fire, and sparks flickered along the silver.

Sumitri saw the white face writhe as the heavy iron stake shot through the gap, never touching silver, and drove through the vampire's heart, hurling it into darkness.

A sleepy chicken clucked atop a pile of grain-sacks. Mother Gayatri handed the bow to Taravi, and limped slowly back to where she had left the wooden box. Taravi put another bolt into the crossbow, and began to wind it back.

"There's another one at the east window!" Maitriyi whispered. "And another at the south," said Mother Gayatri calmly, putting on the dangling wooden earrings.

Taravi finished winding the crossbow and ran to the east window, but as she reached it, the figure vanished. Turning, she darted to the south window where two faces could be seen. But they vanished as she lifted the crossbow. Mother Gayatri laughed.

"They know we have teeth now," she said. "You won't catch another one that way!"

Taravi turned, baffled, back to the west window—and now five white faces clustered there, staring between the meshes. And now it was the same at every window. Even in the arrow-slit beyond the fire, white faces peered.

"What shall we do?!" Kajioni cried. "They are all around us, Mother Gayatri, what shall we do?"

"Don't look at them," the old woman answered. Then, rising, wooden bracelets clicking at her wrists, "Sumitri, dear, you've torn your dress! And all of us could use some patching, I think! Come along, we have sewing to do!"

She limped briskly to one of the trunks, heaved a small sack of dried spices off the top, set some cooking pans down carefully, and examined her find with bright black eyes.

"Yes, this will do nicely, I think." She smiled, cheerfully. "Taravi! Sumitri! Drag this over there, where there'll be plenty of light."

White faces clustered at the windows, while the women tugged the heavy chest toward the fire. Mother Gayatri bustled around the room, ferreting out homemade candles and old, cheap candlesticks.

She lit one of the candles at the fire, and set it down beside the old wood-and-leather chest as she struggled to undo the buckles that held it closed. She threw back the lid. A faint sweetness rose from flat, neatly-folded cloth. Oiled silks and ancient, richly embroidered brocades: gold threads twinkled as the candle moved.

The women gathered around, while red, hungry eyes glared from each window. Sumitri stood bare to the waist, with the top parts of her robe hanging down over the belt. Looking down, she saw the print of Pirru's little teeth in the flesh around her nipple, but no blood.

"Oh! The old wedding dress! This should fit you, dear," Mother Gayatri said. "I remember my grandmother wearing it, and she was about your size."

She pulled a folded cloth from the chest, and unfurled it to reveal age-faded red and saffron silk, that flamed with golden thread. A wedding dress, the color of the sacred fire. But holes showed in the worn old cloth, and Mother Gayatri shook her head sadly.

"Each time it is harder to find anything to mend, or even to mend with. But there is a little new cloth."

Sumitri recognized the roll of cheap red cloth that Mother Gayatri lifted from the chest, and felt her cheeks flush with sudden blood. She pulled her arm across her bare breasts, even though she knew that those watching looked only at her throat.

"What cheap cloth!" exclaimed Taravi, looking down her nose. Her family in the north was wealthy.

"I call that cloth dearly bought!" Sumitri snapped, before she could stop herself. Then, blushing, she looked away. A dead face leered at her through the window, licking pale lips with a worm-white tongue.

"What do you mean by that?" Taravi said, in a pettish tone, disregarding the glares of the others.

"Taravi..." Mother Gayatri warned.

"Well, it's not fair!" Taravi complained. "If she says something like that, she ought to explain it!"

"You don't understand!" Kajioni began, blushing furiously, and stammering. "The merchant..." Withering under Mother Gayatri's ominous glare, she bit her lip and fell silent.

"You're right, I don't understand!" Taravi shrilled. "The merchant *what?* Did she sleep with him to get the cloth?"

"Yes!" sobbed Kajioni, and Sumitri laughed.

"Oh, *Bini!* Little Sister, you're making it worse!" She turned to face them, still laughing, and let her arm fall away from her breasts. "You make it sound much worse than it was." She met Taravi's eyes as she spoke. "This was a few years before you came. The Royal Gift that year was very small."

She remembered that Taravi came from the northern part of Mahavara, where the land was fat, far enough from the Border that calves were almost always born alive, and there was grass to feed them, and grain safe to eat, and Night Things were rare and easily hunted down.

"I don't know if you can understand what that means, this near the Border. The raids had been very bad that year. A demon had wiped out acres of fields. Our men had been fighting constantly, and weapons had to be replaced. We had to buy lances and arrows, even a sword. The money was very low: it was months before harvest—and a thin harvest it would be, we knew.

"Maitriyi was just pregnant with Kairi, and Juvali with Kurru, and I was pregnant myself—" She stopped then, and closed her eyes a moment. That had been one of the ones that had not lived. For a moment she hated Taravi for making her remember that.

"So we needed rice badly, when the man from the Supplier's Guild came," she went on. "I'd had my eye on this bolt of cloth, but I knew we couldn't afford it.

"But the—the merchant—was trying to cheat us. He knew we needed rice, so he raised the price...." She looked at Taravi steadily. "All the money we had wouldn't buy enough rice to last through pregnancy. You know what that means?"

Taravi nodded, all brashness gone. The Massadessan rice was the only grain that could be counted on to be safe from the ergots that blew across the Dark Border.

"We tried to barter, but everything really precious had been bartered away years ago. At last, we gathered around him in despair. 'What can we give you?' one of us asked, and then...." she hesitated, and bit her lip.

"He smiled, and—and said, *give you the whole ten bags if she—*' and he pointed at me—'*if she spends the night with me. Well, why not?*' he said, '*Everybody knows you Borderwomen sleep with every penniless adventurer that bungles by! So why not me?*'

"Mother Gayatri was ready to kill him—!"

"You *should* have!" Taravi exclaimed. "*I* would have! What stopped you from just sticking a knife in him?"

"The King's Justice," Sumitri answered, "and the Supplier's Guild."

"But—surely—the King would pardon you!" Taravi said passionately. "After an insult like that—"

"The King's Justice," said Sumitri, "*might*—just might—have pardoned the killing, if we had sent the rice and everything else back to the Supplier's Guild, to prove our honesty and purity of purpose. We needed that rice! That would have been theft *and* murder. But whatever the King's judgment, the Supplier's Guild would never have forgiven us, and would never have sent another man here. Then we would have starved. All of us, not just me."

"So how was he?" Taravi asked, impudently, ignoring Mother Gayatri's angry glare.

"Fat. Greasy. Astonishingly clumsy and ignorant for so old a man. It was over very quickly. But I made him throw in the cloth."

"And so then he went home to spread the story through all the—"

"No!" Sumitri shook her head, sure that all could see her struggling to restrain the terrible, triumphant smile that sought to lift the corners of her mouth. "Oh, no," she said again, "No. He rose late; traveled slowly, and was still outside, unable to reach shelter, when night came. He's out *there,* somewhere, now."

She closed her eyes, suddenly afraid to look up and see the merchant's smirking face at the window....

"Oh, Sister!"Taravi squealed and suddenly Sumitri felt herself snatched up against the big-boned girl's body. "I'm so sorry! I didn't mean to—to hurt you, to—"

"Hush, Little Sister..." Taravi's arms were tight around Sumitri's slender frame, and she had to struggle to get one arm around to pat the other's back awkwardly.

"Can we go on with our sewing, now?" Mother Gayatri asked, sweetly. Juvali laughed. Taravi let go, and Sumitri saw milk on the frayed brocade of the other girl's dress.

"Sumitri, dear, can you thread this needle for me?" Mother Gayatri's scissors had been busy, Sumitri saw; the old woman was surrounded by carefully shaped patches of the cheap red cloth. "My eyes aren't what they used to be, and in this light—Maitriyi, why don't you grind up some spices for us? We haven't had a real fire to cook over for such a long time!"

They had been eating raw fish from the castle ponds since the rains started: the thought of cooked food was a thrill of sensual craving strong enough to banish the numbness of fear. She hoped Mother Gayatri was still strong enough to do the cooking herself. Only Taravi had had much experience cooking with fire instead of focused sunlight—and Mother Gayatri's cooking was better. She remembered times when the Border had flared, but there had been no attack upon Giripor—or, at least, no members of their little family had been lost—which remained in the mind chiefly as occasions of feasting and delight.

She wet the end of the thread with her lips, and held the needle up to the firelight. Her eyes were better than Mother Gayatri's, but in this light it hardly mattered. Beyond the needle, the firelight was rosy on the swelling of Juvali's belly. She had pulled off her robe to sit naked by the fire, feeding it bits of wood and the dried cow-dung that Taravi's kin in the north had sent to augment their slender stocks of fuel.

She felt a sharp pang of envy. Juvali's husband was still alive: two of three children had lived, and now she was eating rice again. Tears of self-pity blurred her eyes as she pushed the thread at the needle. Blinking, she felt, rather than saw, the thread quivering as it slid through the eye of the needles, and with practiced motion pulled the thread through and looped it.

The gold thread of Taravi's green robe glittered in the firelight as she brought more wood from the larger pile in the center of the room—the pile they would light when there was no hope...

"Taravi!" Mother Gayatri's voice was sharp. "You'll set yourself afire! What are you thinking of, girl?! Take off your robe before it catches!"

Sumitri tied off the ends of the thread and handed the needle to the older woman, seeing the green robe flutter to the floor, and the dark hollows of the big girl's ribs. Mother Gayatri's needle was busy. Sumitri had to thread it for her twice more before Mother Gayatri gathered up her sewing kit and climbed painfully to her feet.

"There! Now, Sumitri, dear, just slip this on—take off the old one first."

Sumitri took the dagger and the light woman's sword out of her sash, and laid them on the trunk, ready to hand, then undid the knot and let the old robe drop to the floor. The room was quite warm, now. Mother Gayatri laid the new robe across her shoulders, and Sumitri slipped her arms into the sleeves, and folded the ancient, heavy cloth about her. It smelled musty and strange, sweet with herbs that had been packed with it, so long ago...

She wondered if Kairi and Biti and Kisa and Diti, when they grew up—if they lived to grow up—would wear the same ancient cloth—patched and mended more—or if things would improve, and they would be able to buy new cloth—or if, as she had heard they did in some of the older Border countries, they would be forced to live without clothing altogether, with only belts to hold weapons.

Flame-colored cloth. A bridal dress, to burn in, she thought, and a line from some old romantic song ran through her mind: *"To lie by his side in the fire; burnt bones blending with bone..."*

With a touch of wild longing she thought of old stories that ended with lovers uniting in death; with wives leaping onto a dead husband's funeral pyre. In real life, a woman had to live, for the sake of the children and the Land. All the Border country was a land of widows.

Sajan had been fourteen when they had married. He had lived to be almost twenty. That was longer than most men. Vikram would have married next year, if he had lived. And he had looked so much like his older brother—like Sajan. He had been like him in bed, too—her eyes filled with tears.

She remembered the terrible flame and smoke of Sajan's funeral pyre, while old songs sang in her mind—

"Sumitri!" Mother Gayatri said. "Are you listening? Wake up!"

"I'm sorry, Mother Gayatri." She blinked down at the older woman, trying to blink the tears from her eyes...

"Turn this way a little, child," the old woman said, soothingly. "I need to get at this shoulder-seam. The threads are all rotten, but if I strengthen it with new thread, and then put this patch across it, it should hold for a few years, at least. The new thread will tear through the old cloth, eventually." She sighed. "If only we could afford new cloth!"

He voice stilled, as she concentrated on her tiny stitches, and Sumitri could hear the steady skirr of stone on stone as Maitriyi ground the spices for their meal.

"As soon as I finish this seam," the old woman said, after a moment, "I'm cooking Juvali up a nice pot of rice, only—" She paused a moment, and then went on, defiantly, in a louder voice: "Only I'll cook up a little extra, and add it to the meal, so that we can *all* have some!"

Sumitri, shocked and startled, shivered at the sinfulness of it. Rice—if you weren't pregnant, rice was a forbidden luxury, but once you were—then it was life itself; the only safe food. You usually got to have a little each cycle, when there were men around—while you weren't sure. Mother Gayatri, of course, would not have been allowed any since her courses stopped...

With a little chill, Sumitri realised that Mother Gayatri did not really expect them to live through this attack—that she expected that they, their enemies and the whole store of hoarded rice, would all go up together in one flame.

"Do you think that too—" the old woman blinked, "—too wicked of me, dear?"

"No!" Impulsively Sumitri reached out and hugged the older woman. There was a sharp prick, and she jerked back. The needle was still in the old woman's hand. Sumitri laughed.

"Ouch! My skin doesn't—"

Suddenly whatever she was saying was driven from her mind by the frantic raucous squawking of panic-stricken chickens from the floor below. Mouth dry, Sumitri listened to the fluttering and battering that mingled with the frightened cackling. Now the handful of chickens that had gotten up the stairway was awake; adding their own sleepy cackling to the clamor below.

She heard flapping wings, and fought the urge to scream. A chicken flapped heavily from one pile of feed-bags to another. The wooden floor under her felt suddenly very frail. She remembered stories about vampires finding entrance through the tiniest cracks. But this room had been designed to be a last refuge, after the rest of the keep had fallen. They had put silver powder between boards carefully shaped to fit.

"Are the spices ground, Maitriyi?" Mother Gayatri's voice was shockingly cheerful, without a quaver of fear, and only an unusual loudness to hint at strain.

"I—I—" Maitriyi's voice trembled a moment, then, "Almost, Mother." The scraping of the mortar began again.

"Good, dear. I'm hungry. Keep the fire up, children." There was only the faintest hint of forced cheerfulness in her voice. "Now where did we put that rice?" For a moment the cheery clatter of pans banging together drowned flapping and screeching from below. Sumitri took a deep breath, struggling to calm herself.

"Here, Mother Gayatri. I'll help." She heard the strain in her voice, but perhaps the others would not. They had to keep their spirits up somehow. Silence led to terror.

Juvali and Taravi were piling more wood in the stone trough between the hearths. The entire alcove was a stone platform that could turn into a single huge fireplace at need. She got water for Mother Gayatri to cook the rice in, and they carried the long-handled pan to the fire and set it on the metal frame that Maitriyi dragged over. Sumitri was glad to doff the thick robe; the room was definitely too warm. Mother Gayatri began to pull off her own robe—

"Gayatri!" The hoarse whisper came from the eastern window. *"You are old, Gayatri! Why did you not stay young, like me?"*

Sumitri saw the old woman flinch, and start to draw the ancient brocade back around her bent figure. Sumitri recognized the face at the window. She had seen it peering through windows before, prowling around the battlements when the Border was aflame. And she had seen the old portrait, from half a century before, of the young man Gayatri had married.

She ran to Mother Gayatri and threw her arms protectively around the old women's hunched shoulders.

"Never mind—" Mother Gayatri gasped, "Pay them no mind—don't let them—never let it bother you.." Her eyes still blinded with tears, the old woman let the robe drop, and naked but for her funeral jewelry, tottered toward the fire.

The chorus of dusty murmurs—dry, croaking voices, rasping with long thirst—swelled. Sumitri tried hard not to listen.

Hearing the tones of the beloved dead among the traitors' voices was one of the hardest things. She thought she heard the merchant's sniggering, but did not look to see. But there were others she knew were out there; her cousin Hirajio, and her brothers Kejar and Netajio... All her family from Adripor.

And the worst fear was of seeing someone you thought still alive; of seeing Jal or Narain or Tanaj, or any of those who had ridden off two months ago, full of bright hopes of adventure.

Juvali screamed.

Sumitri saw her pointing upward at the arch: caught a brief glimpse of something moving—

"No, you don't!"Taravi shouted. Her long man's sword flashed in the firelight as she leaped, striking up at the crawling shape. A tiny black thing fell from the arch. A bat, spreading its wings. But as it fell, it changed and blurred: and it was a human skeleton that lay on its back in the fire, writhing and screaming in the flames. It started to heave itself onto its feet, but Taravi's sword crashed through the breastbone, scattering ribs. A great gout of blood burst from the broken rib-cage; caught fire in midair, and burned like a flaming fountain. And the bones lay still.

"There are more of them in there!" Juvali shouted.

"More wood!" cried Taravi. "Fill the alcove! More wood! *Quick!'*

Sumitri handed Mother Gayatri the crossbow, and turning, ran back to the central pile. Maitriyi and Kajioni were already there, loading their arms with the largest pieces of wood. Sumitri joined them. Twice she pinched her breast between two pieces of wood, and once felt a splinter near her nipple, but there was no time for pain now. Kairi also had come and was picking up wood as well as she could. Maitriyi was back for a second load.

The air was burning her throat as she threw wood over the burning skeleton, out into space above the trap door that covered the stair. The flames were leaping up, turning the alcove into one gigantic hearth.

What had seemed another puff of smoke suddenly condensed and fell: a loud wailing rose and another burning skeleton reeled in the fire, screaming. It staggered toward them, flame sputtering about each bone, bony hands clawing, trying to break free from the fire into the room.

Taravi's heavy sword met it at the fire's edge with a sweeping stroke that hurled the skull in flaming splinters back into the alcove. The other bones stood reeling, clawing the air, until the broadsword smashed into the ribs, burning blood fountained, and the bones fell. That they did not burn like ordinary bones was readily apparent to women who had burned lovers, husbands and children, and were all too familiar with the slow crumbling of ordinary bone.

Taravi leaned on her sword, breathing heated air hoarsely. Maitriyi and Kajioni came staggering back, and heaped immense loads of precious fuel over piles of burning bone. Mother Gayatri held the crossbow, and they all stared, expecting another burning skeleton to run screaming out of the fire at any moment. The flames danced and leaped.

Mother Gayatri, with a little exclamation, pushed the crossbow into Sumitri's hands and pulled the long-handled pot from the fire. Steam was pouring out, and it bubbled violently.

"Curse them! That can't be all of them," Taravi gasped. "Did we do it? They can't hold out against the fire this long, can they? We must have killed them all!"

"The rest probably got out through the arrow-slit." said Juvali. There was a sort of crude silver grille pushed into the arrow-slit, but they had known for a long time that it was probably not enough.

Sumitri held the crossbow steady, peering into the flames, but her eyes flew to the arrow-slit, hoping Juvali was right: hoping they were gone.

She imagined the iron-plated door glowing cherry-red in the darkness below. There was a fine, blazing heap of wood on top of it now.

"We *did it,* curse them!" Taravi whooped, exultantly. "We killed them! I couldn't have done it with those silly little knitting-needles you call women's swords."

"You wouldn't have been able to do it if the fire hadn't slowed them down," answered Maitriyi. "You don't know how fast they are. You haven't been here long enough."

It was an old argument, and Sumitri was thoroughly sick of it. Taravi, bigger and stronger than the rest of them, insisted on carrying a heavier sword. That was sensible enough. But she felt they should all use heavier swords. But at least their quarreling voices drowned out those *other* voices, the hoarse murmurs from outside..

"Hey, Pretty Tits, over here!"

That voice! Startled, she looked up, and saw the merchant's sneering face peering through the west window. The gross, heavily jowled face was dead white, now, and the eyes were no longer black. They were red—blood-red—rose-red—sunset-red—It was all so hopeless! What were they struggling for? Why did it matter? They could not win. Even if they did escape this time, it was only to go back to the same dull, miserable existence..dead friends and dead children..never enough food, or enough money..fields fed by the ashes of the dead...

The great red eyes filled her vision. The crossbow had fallen from her hands. As in a dream, she felt her feet moving, but she remained suspended in red mist, in the dull hopelessness of life.. She heard shouting, but it made no difference, nothing mattered...

Something gripped her shoulder, pulling her back—back to what? She felt herself being shaken, but the red mist did not move. A sudden sharp pain made her close her eyes. Her head rocked. *"Sumitri!"A* sharp slap across her face, and then another. She reeled, blinking.

"Sumitri!" It was Taravi's voice, and another—Mother Gayatri's—joined, and another slap across her face made her head

swim. She blinked, and gasped out, "Please...please..." Blinking, she saw Taravi's face, and then another slap stung her cheek and knocked her head back...

"Stop! Why are you hitting me? Stop it!"

Suddenly the other girl jerked her forward, and Taravi's warm flesh pressed against her face...

"You mustn't look at them, dear." Mother Gayatri's voice came as though from far away. Other sounds too—children screaming, chickens squawking...

Pirru! That was Pirru crying! She pushed free from Taravi, and suddenly Pirru, hysterical, was in her arms.

Other children were crying, the screaming skeletons had waked them. She pressed Pirru close and pushed her breast into his mouth, then winced from the pain as his teeth closed on her nipple again. Mother Gayatri was right. He was too old. Suddenly his teeth let go and he sat up in her lap and touched her smarting cheek gently.

"Mommy?" His huge eyes blinked at her. "Mommy hurt?" "Hurt Mommy." She took his hand to her aching nipple. "Bite Mommy. Hurt."

"No." He said, and touched her cheek again. "Auntie hurt Mommy."

"Auntie hurt Mommy," she agreed. "Baby hurt Mommy. Poor Mommy!"

"Poor Mommy," He lay back and took her nipple into his mouth a little more gently, and sucked.

She closed her eyes... *mustn't look at them,* Mother Gayatri had said. Well, of course not! She knew you must never let one catch your eyes. She knew better than that! She would never...

"Hey, Pretty Tits, let me have some of that! I'll suck you like you've never been sucked before...!"

She quailed, closing her eyes, suddenly remembering that corpse-pale face, and bright red eyes.

She *had* looked. She knew better, but she had looked, and the next she remembered was Taravi slapping and shaking her. No wonder! She curled protectively around Pirru, frightened and miserable. What had Taravi stopped her from doing?

She looked down at her wrists in sudden panic, wondering for a moment if they had stopped her in time; if she could have been bitten and infected...

But there were no marks of teeth, only the long-healed straight scars from the time she had tried to end it all years before, when her first baby had been born dead—Sajan's baby. She curled herself more tightly around Pirru and began to cry, her whole body racked by great shuddering sobs.

Pirru stopped sucking and began to struggle. She held him tightly, terrified. What was happening? He shook his head violently from side to side, until her breast worked from his mouth.

"Mommy!" he wailed. "Can't *breathe!*"

"There, there, darling." She tried to hug him tighter, then loosened her grip, as his words penetrated.

A powerful scent of cooking rice flooded her senses. Mother Gayatri had pulled the lid off the pot, and clouds of delicious steam filled the chamber. It was the same wonderful, forbidden aroma that Sumitri remembered pouring out of the big kitchens in Adripor, knowing, even as a child, that it was not for her. She saw Maitriyi lift the mortar over the pot, scraping finely-ground powder down in a dark rain. Mother Gayatri's little knife was flashing as she sliced something Sumitri could not see clearly into the pot. Pirru stopped wiggling, and was falling asleep. She envied him. If only she could sleep...

She stiffened as an arm went around her shoulder.

"How is it with you now, Little Sister?" It was Taravi's voice. "Are you better? How are you feeling now?"

"Hungry!" she answered, before she could stop herself. She mustn't complain. It only made everyone feel worse. Usually it was Taravi who complained.

"We're all hungry," said Taravi, with a little laugh. "But there'll be food soon enough—real food—cooked food—not that stinking raw fish! I was getting so sick of choking that down, day after day! But we'll have a real meal now!" Taravi's arm tightened around her, in a quick hug, and then she was gone.

Sumitri's head ached, and she could not think clearly. After so long keeping her mind from the thought of food, the smell of rice was unbearable. And it was all so hopeless! After years of self-denial, hoarding the rice and bearing their children and struggling to save the land, to have it all go up together in one flame...

Why had she been born into this miserable life, chained by her own pride to this barren, demon-haunted country? Some women, she knew, got away, escaped to the cities—escaped, penniless and homeless, to live by selling their bodies to men who despised them...like the man from the Supplier's Guild.

A wisp of smoke made her cough. The whole alcove was ablaze, the chimneys overloaded. Smoke must be pouring from the arrow-slit. If this lasted until daylight, the plume would be visible for miles, to show the trouble they were in...

But who was there to see it? Prince Hansio had stripped the men from the castles for miles around. The only ones to see would be women like themselves, cut off and surrounded. Only the Hasturs, the Immortals in the Towers would see, and although Sumitri had heard many stories about them, she had never seen one.

Her head ached. If she could only sleep! But if she went to sleep the fires would die, and then the traitors would wriggle through the arrow-slit and crawl across the ceiling to get them.

She must not sleep—she had to protect Pirru, Mother Gayatri and the rest. She must be ready to fight for them. If she could only take them all and run away...

She was a child again, in Adripor, but in the darkness outside the castle Night Things prowled and prowled, demon and traitors and trolls, while she went down long corridors from one room to another, searching for Pirru...

Suddenly something seized her shoulder, and she woke with a little scream.

"Sister! Sister!" It was Taravi's voice. "It's me! You were dreaming. Here. Eat." The smell of rice and spices, of anise and cinnamon and garlic, was so wonderful that her eyes filled with tears as she grabbed for the plate, sure she was still dreaming, and that the plate would be snatched away. She began to pinch up the food, and her mouth was flooded with sharp, glorious flavors. A terrified bass bawling broke out.

"Oh! The cow!" exclaimed Mother Gayatri, sitting up sharply. "The poor cow!"

Then all of them were silent, frozen, as the bellowing became more frenzied. They could all picture what was happening. The bawling suddenly cut off sharply. Sumitri closed her eyes; then opened them again and looked at the fire instead, trying not to see the gentle, fragrant, soft-eyed beast, that she or one of her sister-wives had milked each morning, bucking in frenzied terror under the weight of a dozen or more of the white-faced enemy.

"Curse the filthy traitors!" Taravi's knuckles were white on the hilt of her heavy sword. "I wish there was something we could *do!* "

"Build up the fire, dear," said Mother Gayatri, her voice carefully light and cheerful—and Sumitri guessed what an effort it must be for her, for the old woman had always loved her cows. Sumitri remembered how hard it had been for her, as advancing age had kept her from being able to manage the stair that led to the stable, so she could no longer milk... "It won't be long till dawn."

Sumitri forced herself to bring the handful of rice all the way to her mouth, and chew and swallow slowly. When the cow's first agonized bellow had reached her ears, she had stopped with her hand halfway to her open mouth. She suddenly realised that her stomach was, in fact, uncomfortably full, and that if she ate more she would be sick. She had, in a few moments, greedily gobbled up more food than she would normally have eaten in a week. She should get up, and help with the fire, and stand watch while others slept.

She leaned back against the warm grain-sacks. In a moment she could get up and do her share of the work. Pirru stirred a little, and she touched his cheek gently. He was so beautiful! The sacks were warm and soft and comfortable. In a moment she must get up....

"Sleep!"Taravi's voice, raised in outrage, woke her. "How can I sleep, with them out there, *waiting* for us to let our guard down, curse them!"

"Do you not trust me to keep watch?" Kajioni's voice was as sharp as the crack of a whip. Mother Gayatri's soft "I'm sure she didn't mean *that,* child—" was almost drowned in Taravi's: "It's not that! But I sleep better—" and Kajioni, protesting—"I am *not* a child!"

Sumitri's grit-glued eyes blinked open. She sat up and her stiff back told her she had slept for hours.

"—in the daytime, and I don't think any of us should be standing watch alone!" Taravi's voice emerged triumphant, like the crow of a trumpet. "Not with them, *whispering* at us!"

Turning, Sumitri rolled Pirru off her lap onto the warm grain-sacks. He stirred, but did not wake. She pushed herself up, staggered a moment, and then strode toward the quarrel and the fire.

"Go to bed, sister," she said, firmly. "I've slept. I'm rested now.

It's time I did my share." Taravi stiffened, eyes defiant, but Sumitri turned to the frail, bent figure beside her. "You too, Mother Gayatri!" she said, her voice fierce with protectiveness. "You need your sleep."

"Yes, dear," said Mother Gayatri, submissively. "You're quite right. But remember—all of you—we cannot sleep all day. Wake me—not at dawn, no—" she paused, thoughtfully—"a little before noon, I think. Noon will be—not safe, but as nearly safe as any time will be—to do what—we must."

She looked over at Maitriyi's sleeping form, sighed, and then walking to where she had left her robe, she wrapped it around her bent and withered body, while, from the window, the vampire murmured her name over and over.

Taravi's eyes were still defiant. Sumitri knew she was just waiting for her to speak, and rather than argue she turned to Kajioni, who was kneeling beside her two sleeping children.

"Little Sister, do you want me to get more wood?"

"Please do, Auntie," the younger girl said, sitting up. "Taravi, what are you waiting for? I won't be alone now! Go to bed!"

Taravi glared, and opened her mouth angrily, and then turned away, scooping up the green dress from the floor. She did not put it on, but carried it in her hand as she walked to one of the pillars that upheld the roof, and, draping the robe across her lap, she laid her naked sword gleaming on it, and sat with her back against the beam, staring silently into the fire. Sumitri sighed. She loved Taravi, but she was not Border-born.

Kajioni was adding more wood to the fire as Sumitri came up, but she rose and went to the pile for more, while Sumitri finished stacking her armload, carefully watching the soot-blacked ceiling. The heat of the fire dried the sweat from her skin, but she had to add more wood—if the flames were not high enough, the enemy would be able to maintain its bat-shape across the ceiling...

She lifted an armload of wood and threw it as hard as she could into the heart of the alcove, above the iron door. The heat was so intense that she felt the hair on her body frizzling and curling, and searing pain shot through tender areas of skin. She watched explosions of sparks shoot up to the stone ceiling. They would never get past *that!*

Maitriyi moaned in her sleep, and Kajioni, soft-footed, dashed to her mother's side and hovered over her, then went back for another armload of wood.

"Poor Mother!" signed Kajioni, "and poor Uttaro!" Wood clinked and chimed as she laid it on the pile. "At least Vikram's mother wasn't alive to—to *watch* while—" Her voice broke off in a choked sob.

"Sometimes I think that the dead," she went on, "—the *real* dead, the ones who die clean—are the lucky ones. Oh, Auntie, do you think it's true—what they say? That the real person the soul—is trapped in those—those things out there? Forced to—to be aware of everything the body is doing, but unable to stop? That they—suffer?"

True? Sumitri thought: *How do I know what is true?* She almost said it, but the look of appeal on the young girl's face tore her heart. She remembered when she had been fourteen, and all adults had appeared wise with mysterious secrets.

"No dear, surely not." *That would be too cruel.* She put into her voice a certainty she was far from feeling. "Even when a vampire gets them, the dead are truly dead, their spirits freed from the suffering of the flesh, until they can find rebirth. The evil spirit that re-animates the body only controls the flesh, and the real person goes free, to be born again in some far land—far away and green." She wished she could believe that.

"Hey, Pretty Tits," that voice was murmuring from the window, over and over. She had always believed in the other theory, and since she had learned of the merchant's fate, had almost prayed for it be true—but it was too cruel. Even for him.

"Oh, Auntie!" The awkward adolescent body pressed against her. She hugged Kajioni tightly. Her eyes filled.

"You must believe, my dear," she said, stroking the younger girl's long, black hair. "The soul goes free. You *must* believe that." If only she could believe it herself!

She imagined herself, out in the night, starving, hunting, waiting... Were those outside, she wondered, the bodies of all those who had died here in the last thousand years, since the fall of Rashnagar?

"Thank you, Auntie," Kajioni sobbed. "I couldn't bear to think of Vikram—and poor Uttaro too!—trapped out there in the dark! Vikram could be—could have been Diti's father—" Her voice lowered to a sobbing whisper. "I didn't want Mother to know. She—she was trying to have Vikram's baby herself I wouldn't want to—to hurt her—"

"I think—" Sumitri hesitated, then went on with an assurance she did not feel—"I think it will make her feel better, if you tell her, now."

"Poor Vikram. And Uttaro too—Oh, Auntie! To see them out there—even if their souls are free—I can't bear to think of them—like that." She waved at the white faces that clustered outside, and buried her face in Sumitri's shoulder. Sumitri patted the thin, bony back as if Kajioni were still the little girl she remembered.

"There, there, hush—they won't be out there..."

"Hey, Pretty Tits!" The merchant sniggered from the windows behind her. *"Why don't you hold me like that? I can—"*

"They won't be out there." She said. "We'll go down in the morning, and burn them—"

"Oh, Auntie." Kajioni shuddered violently. "How can I Mother will make me help with the pyre, with the Funeral Rites! Mother Gayatri will insist on it! I can't! I can't bear it. To watch the flames—to watch—I can't bear it—"

"None of us can bear it!" said Sumitri, sharply. "I couldn't bear it either! But I've had to bear it—again and again!" She gripped the thin shoulders, and pushed the girl from her. "Don't be like that! Remember the blood—" she saw the girl's face white and wet, and shook her, "—or else give up and go to the city, to live as a whore and a traitor, selling yourself to the sailors at the dockside and giving the money to the Guild-Master of the Panderer's Guild for food and rent!" She could hear shrill hysteria in her tones. "Selling yourself to sailors every night, knowing all the time that you've betrayed your kin and your blood—could you bear *that?!*'

Kajioni was weeping even more violently now. Over her sobs came a shrill, whining screech, not like anything from a throat of flesh and blood. A Demon. If the traitors that clustered outside had found a way to break the wards around the castle, so that cold, burning death could come flowing in, or others of the hordes of Night Things that swarmed on the plains below... The vampires were only the vanguard for the nightmare hosts that had burst out of the Shadow.

The murmuring stopped.

Was the room brighter? The south and west windows still flamed with Need-fire, a glowing blue curtain that ran across the long wall of Shadow. She turned towards the east window. No white faces clustered there. Was it lighter? It seemed a paler grey. She watched, holding the sobbing girl tight against her breast, and slowly saw the dark fading to the dim light that preceded dawn. A pale spark of gold lifted over the half-seen dark bulk of the mountains.

"Look!" she said. "It's nearly dawn. We've lived through the night." Inside her head a line from an old song sang in her mind:

And glad indeed was Young Pertap
To see the light of day!

Kajioni's head lifted from her shoulder, and they both stared at the paling eastern sky, where clusters of tiny moons hung golden in sunlight that rose from below.

Wings clapped among the grain-sacks. The two girls started apart, as the shrill thrilling cry of a rooster challenged the world. The rooster was alive, Sumitri thought, with a surge of irrational relief. He had flown up through the trap door before it had been shut. She had feared him trapped with the others in the room below.

Srarcis Tower still glared white-hot in the midst of flaming curtains of blue-violet Need-fire that stretched across the mountains in a great curve. A red-eyed bat wheeled outside the southern window, between her and that light, and she stumbled back a step as it dipped, turned and fluttered away. The plains that she had watched the night before swarmed with tiny fleeing figures, and she became aware of the faint sound of thousands of distant, wailing voices.

"They're all running away," she said, in wonder. "Back to the Shadow. It's dawn."

"Are they gone?" Kajioni whispered.

"Gone?" snorted Taravi's voice, loudly, behind them. "Gone? Not them, curse them! They'll be hiding somewhere out of the light, waiting for us to get careless!"

Turning, Sumitri saw her rising from the pillar where she had sat. She caught the heavy sword as it slipped from her lap, and rested its point on the floor as she stood. She was still naked, the green robe draped carelessly across her shoulder.

"Speaking of getting careless," said Sumitri, sharply, "aren't you supposed to be sleeping? You'll be a lot of use tomorrow!"

The cock crowed again as Taravi pulled the cloth from her

shoulder, and shifted her grip until she could shrug her free hand through one sleeve: then, switching her sword to the other hand, wrapped the robe around, and slid that hand through the other sleeve, before sinking back down against the pillar again, robe still open in front, laying the sword back against her knees.

"Starting to cool off again," she said. "Are you going to just let the fire die down now?"

"We can't get out until it does," Sumitri pointed out.

"Well, don't get careless," snapped Taravi. "They're just waiting, curse them!" She leaned back against the pillar and closed her eyes. Sumitri held her lips tightly closed. She loved Taravi dearly, but she was growing tired of being lectured by someone who, after all, had grown up miles from the Border.

The room was brighter now. The rooster crowed again. Sumitri searched for the robe that she had let fall; the flame-colored bridal robe that Mother Gayatri had mended for her. The fire had died down now, and though it was still warm by the alcove, a chill was growing in the corners of the room. The brief elation that had surged through her with the rooster's crow had faded, and now she felt only tired and miserable.

A wind began whistling through the fretted silver screen. She shivered: goose-bumps covered her skin. She found the flame colored robe, and put it on, moving closer to the fire. The fragile old silk was cold against her skin. She went closer to the fire and held the robe open, to let the heat warm the cold cloth. Then, wrapping it about her and belting it, she found a soft place on the sacking near Mother Gayatri, and laid herself down, bone weary.

Angry voices woke her—hours later, she guessed. The Twin Suns must be high above the roof. It must be noon, or nearly so. Taravi and Juvali were massaging Mother Gayatri's back. But Maitriyi stood glaring at Kajioni, and Kajioni was crying again. "But Mother, don't you understand? I can't! I can't bear it!"

"You *must* bear it!" Maitriyi answered, tight-lipped. "I'm ashamed of you! Your own brother! And I thought you were fond of Vikram!" Kajioni let out a wordless wail. Mother Gayatri pushed herself up, and hobbled over to put an arm around the girl's shoulders.

"There, there, dear. We all know how hard it is," she said gently.

"We'll be with you. We've all been through it. We'll be right there with you."

"But you don't—don't *understand.*"

"Quiet!" Mother Gayatri's voice was suddenly sharp, and Kajioni's voice stopped in mid-wail. "We *do* understand, child! All too well!" The old woman's eyes fixed on the adolescent's. Kajioni blinked and swallowed. "How many times to you think I've gone through it! If you think it's bad to watch your brother burn, how do you think it feels when it's your own baby? What do you think your mother is going through, right now? Do you think it's easy for her?" The girl's eyes fell, and Mother Gayatri went on, more gently. "We'll all be with you—nearly all of us, anyway. Juvali should stay inside with the babies. Taravi, you stay with her, and protect her—"

"No, curse you! I'm going out with you!" They all stared at Taravi, shocked. "You need protection more than she does. Those traitors will be waiting under the stairs, or behind one of the old screens, and you'll need something better than those silly knitting needles you call swords—I'd like to see you take off a vampire's head with one of those cursed things!"

"That's why you should stay with Juvali, dear—" Mother Gayatri began. "If we have a future, it—"

"I *said* I'm *going,* curse it! Let Kajioni stay and guard Juvali, if she's that—"

"Taravi!" Sumitri exclaimed.

"—cursed tender! Or let Sumitri stay—"

"Don't talk to Mother Gayatri like that!" Sumitri flared indignantly.

"Follow orders!" Maitriyi added. "And how dare you encourage my *filth*—my daughter that way!"

"I'm *going,"* Taravi shouted furiously, towering over Maitriyi and Sumitri. "What can you do to stop me? Is one of you going to hold me while the other drags Kajioni downstairs by her hair?"

"How *dare* you!" Maitriyi shrieked, and even Juvali, normally so calm, shook her head, and said, "Very rude! Who do you think you are!"

"You should be ashamed of yourself!" Sumitri snapped. "To talk to Mother Gayatri so!"

"Ashamed!" Taravi shouted. "I'd be ashamed to sit here safe while you walk into those cursed corridors with nothing but those silly—things."

"I've killed vampires with those 'knitting needles', as you call them," Mother Gayatri said, very quietly but very clearly.

Taravi stared. They all did.

"You put too much trust in that cleaver of yours," Mother Gayatri's little voice went on. "It's only plain steel. I have this—" She displayed a crystal dagger, that glowed with faint light. "And Maitriyi has the dagger with the silver inlay on the blade. We have this crossbow, and the other two are still lying out there. I looked. And when we go out, we'll all be wearing silver and carrying torches. You know how quick a vampire catches fire? Like that!"

She snapped her fingers. "Faster than dried hay. Faster than oil-soaked cloth! We're not helpless, Taravi."

"I'm still going!" said Taravi stubbornly.

Mother Gayatri drew a long breath, and then let it out slowly. "Whoever is going, we have to go now," she said. "We have no time for argument. We haven't even swept the ashes away from the trap door yet. Maitriyi, Sumitri—start clearing them away."

"I'll help," said Taravi.

"So will I," added Kajioni.

"Whoever is doing it, get at it now," the old woman said, sharply. "If we are not out of here soon, the rites will last past sunset, and the fire will be our only refuge. Hurry, clear the ashes away!"

*Fire will be our only refuge...*the line throbbed in Sumitri's head, as she kilted up her robe about her thighs and waded into the ashes. She cringed in memory from the flames, and remembered again how much Vikram had reminded her of Sajan in bed. If it came to that, she thought, she would take refuge in Vikram's pyre, and join him there as she had so longed to join Sajan.

The ashes were more than ankle deep, and there were still unburnt pieces of wood to stumble over. A hot coal seared her calf. She tried not to imagine what else might lie hidden in the ashes. The teeth, perhaps? She told herself firmly not to be a fool. The job was had enough without frightening herself with imagined terrors...

The ashes flew everywhere, of course, and no telling when or if she would ever be able to bathe again...

"Mother Gayatri!" Maitriyi's voice was shrill with anger. "You can't mean to let them get away with this! My slut of a daughter—"

"We have no time for this, Maitriyi!" The old woman's voice was sharp, but fell to an indistinct murmur.

It was grueling work. Kajioni was whining under her breath, and Taravi cursed continually. Sometimes the ash flew up in choking clouds, and they had to stop, coughing, until the finer dust settled and they could breathe again.

"...and if she's that much stronger than the rest of us," Mother Gayatri's voice rose, suddenly clear, "she can carry the extra firewood."

"I heard that!" Taravi shouted. "And I *will* too, curse you, and gladly!! Pfoo!" She coughed, and spat. "Cursed ashes get in *everything!*"

"Not," said Sumitri, in her sweetest tones, "in closed mouths."

At last the shape of the trap door appeared through the ashes. The iron was still hot to the touch. Kajioni shot back the bolt, gripping the handle, as though to raise the trap—

"Wait!" shouted Taravi. "They're just waiting down there, rot them!" She drew the heavy sword. "There's not enough light in that room to drive them out—"

"Mother Gayatri," Sumitri called, "we've uncovered the door."

"Thank you, dear," the gentle old woman's voice answered. "Come and clean up now."

Smudged and blackened they trudged out of the alcove, Taravi at the rear, sword in hand. Sumitri stared, amazed, to see ready basins of water, with homemade soap and scraps of rough cloth. Did they dare waste so much water on washing, with the Dark Things all around them?

They stripped, and made shift to wash the caked soot and ashes from their bodies, while Juvali and Maitriyi shook out the robes and beat them, to get as much of the soot out of the ancient silk as they could, without damaging the frail fabric.

Taravi kept her drawn sword close beside her as they scrubbed, and stood so that she could see into the alcove, peering suspiciously at the trap door. Sumitri, clean, felt much better, although the waste of their precious water supply still nagged her. Still, she thought, it was the rainy season, and the cisterns on the roofs were full. There was enough water here for a fairly long siege—far longer than they had any real hope of holding out, she suspected. Again, she wondered if Mother Gayatri really thought they had any hope of lasting until help came.

There was an egg apiece cooked for each of them, and while they ate and washed, Mother Gayatri had dug out a curiously wrought wooden box, and from it began to hand out silver rings and bracelets and necklace chains—odd pieces of ancient jewelry carefully hoarded for times like this, after all the more valuable jewelry had been sold.

Sumitri, when her turn came, found herself as excited as a child. Two massive rings weighted her right hand, a silver chain wrapped about her left. They would not save her by themselves, but they might help her hold off an attack long enough for help to come.

And then they were handing her a small bundle of wood, and she was sliding the rope over her head that would hold it securely at her back. She felt a small flurry of panic, and wished she had volunteered to stay with Juvali. Something was thrust into her hand, and looking, she saw one of the sharp wooden swords that they carved in the Kantara, the point dipped in pitch.

Mother Gayatri was calling her to come and light her torch. Sumitri staggered over to the tiny cooking fire on which Juvali had cooked their eggs, and thrust the point into the tiny flame.

Taravi was already at the trap door, burning torch in one hand, drawn sword in the other. Stooping, she heaved up the iron door, and thrust the blazing wooden sword-point into the opening.

She crouched there, peering into the room where Mother Gayatri usually slept, where they had all slept the last few weeks. The bundle of wood on Taravi's back, Sumitri noticed, really was twice as big as the others.

Taravi darted down the stairs, sword-torch stretched out in front of her, steel sword poised behind. Mother Gayatri followed, more slowly, then Maitriyi, heavy crossbow raised and ready. Then it was Sumitri's turn. That was the order Mother Gayatri had given them. It was her job to watch Maitriyi's back, and to keep watch behind.

A smell of burnt chicken feathers met her as she started down. She blinked, trying to adjust her eyes to the dimmer light. Daylight did penetrate here, but only barely. Dead chickens lay everywhere; headless, most of them; headless and drained. There were tears in Mother Gayatri's eyes at the mess in her room.

The stone steps were cold, but there were great burnt patches, where coals had fallen through the grate of the iron door, and set alight whatever might burn. At first Sumitri had to try to see around the flame of her own torch, but as the ceiling drew away she was able to raise it over her head, and then she could see the moving pattern of light and shadow below her. This floor was all one big room, unlike the floor below.

Sudden movement beside the stair made her heart lurch, but it was only Taravi, looking into a recess with her torch.

Torchlight moved confusingly. Taravi was sending shadows leaping, as she looked for enemies in every corner.

"They *were* here, rot them!" Taravi muttered. "They'll be hiding—somewhere.."

"Kajioni!" Mother Gayatri called. "Shut the trap door now!" A moment later they heard the clang of the trap falling above them, and the sound of the bolt.

So that was it: they were shut out now. Sumitri tried to fight off the despairing notion that she would never see the little room above again—or would see it only through the window, from outside. Poor Juvali, and Kajioni! How long could they hold out, alone, if the rest of them never came back?

Then they were trooping down the steps to the floor below. This floor, divided into smaller rooms, was more dangerous, for dark corridors, leading to other parts of the castle, ran off on every side, and she had no doubt that vampires had crept into them, hiding from the light. Sleeping, she hoped.

"Taravi!" Mother Gayatri called. "Don't get so far ahead. Stay where we can see you, and where Maitriyi can bring her crossbow to bear if you need help."

The familiar furnishings seemed incongruous. The floor was tiled, and the faded paintings on the walls—scenes from the triumphant march of Sakur the Sixth into Devonia—or Kraitar, or whatever it was called back then—flashed in and out, and seemed to move in the torchlight. Tiny red-turbaned soldiers, marching in ordered rows, appeared to mill in confusion. The battered old cabinet beneath that panel, covered with chipped and dented fragments of ancient sky and tree and mountain, crouched like some strange, blocky beast.

King Sakur swayed on his elephant, as Taravi's voice echoed, hawk-shrill, through the chamber and corridor—*"No, you don't, curse you!"*

Sumitri looked up. Torchlight whirled and dipped in the corridor ahead. Beyond Taravi's green dress she caught only a glimpse of a milk-white face. Taravi leaped, thrusting with her torch at the white-faced figure, lashing with firelit steel.

A sudden lurid orange glare filled the corridor, and a screaming pillar of fire staggered back. Black, greasy smoke rolled up: Taravi stood outlined against the smoky glare, erect and splendid, sword poised to strike again, if need be. The screaming died away.

"Got the cursed traitor!" Taravi's voice rang like a trumpet, echoing from the stone walls around them. "Did you see? He thought he could just step out and grab me, but I was ready for him! Did you see?"

"Yes, Taravi, we all saw," said Mother Gayatri, tiredly. "We're all very proud of you, Taravi. Can we go on now?" She hobbled into the corridor, leaning heavily on her stick, and Sumitri realised how long a walk this was for the old woman. She remembered, then, that she was supposed to be guarding the rear, not staring at Taravi, and thought at last to look behind.

Her heart lurched as red sparks glared out of the shadows.

She whirled, bringing up the torch, but the eyes vanished. She waited a moment, watching for any sign of movement, then hurried to catch up with Maitriyi, who had followed Mother Gayatri into the corridor.

She shivered as she passed the little heap of burning bones. Flames still burned fitfully on the tiled floor, but the walls were very close here, and she kept as near as she could to Maitriyi's back, and turned often to be sure they were not followed.

The door at last, and glaring sunlight and blue sky and cold wind. The boys lay where they had fallen. Maitriyi went rushing past Mother Gayatri and Taravi, to throw herself down, sobbing, by Uttaro's corpse. Mother Gayatri hobbled over to Vikram's body, and threw off the bundle she had carried. Taravi did the same, with her larger load; then, at a word from Mother Gayatri, went to gather more.

There was wood in plenty stacked under the little coned roofs that sheltered sentinels. Taravi came back lugging a huge log. Sumitri ran to help. Together they dragged out another, and settled down to that long, sad, horribly familiar business—building the pyres and dragging the bodies onto them.

Every exposed patch of skin showed the mark of fangs. Sumitri struggled to drive from her mind the image of each boy buried under a pile of the feasting dead.

She had been afraid that the wind would blow out the torches before they could get the wood arranged, but, though the flames flared out like bright flags in the wind, all the swords still flamed bravely as Maitriyi and Mother Gayatri thrust them deep into the kindling under the bodies.

Mother Gayatri's thin voice began the Funeral Chant, and Sumitri joined her -

'Man is but a vessel—" Maitriyi sobbed continuously, but now words formed in her wailing as she joined them—*"in which Immortal Fire burns."* Taravi's deeper voice joined theirs, and. Maitriyi's began to steady...

"Man is but a channel
In which Immortal Water runs.
Man is but a hollow
Through which Immortal wind breathes—" Maitriyi's voice caught and broke—

"But the bones must go back to the Earth—
Bone is a part of the Earth."

Sumitri's face was cold with tears. The lacquer of Vikram's armour caught, and as little sputterings raced over it, Sumitri closed her eyes convulsively, and tried to lose herself in the too-familiar words of the chant.

"Mother Earth rises, takes up shape..." She tried not to smell the horribly well-known odor of burning flesh. A blast of sudden heat dried the tears upon her face.

"Now for a time, Mother Earth has walked among us in the shapes of Uttaro and Vikram."

Her eyes opened, still wet, to the glare of flame and, above, the thick smoke—blowing away from them, down over the parapet, toward the Border. She looked higher. She did not want to look at the bodies in the flame—

"Mother, Earth Mother, You who walk in our shapes, We have loved you as Vikram and as Uttaro."

The Twin Suns were low, settling into the west. They would have little time to get back to the redoubt in the tower. Or else there would not be time, and she would have to lie down by Vikram after all, his pyre her only refuge.

Only little flickers of flame darted across the ebony wall of Shadow now: the Tower of Srarcis was a slim stalk of dim blue light. She wondered if the Immortal who dwelt there could see them.

Mother Gayatri's voice rose, alone.

"The warmth of Life to the fire!" Sumitri's voice joined the others in response; *"And the Soul returns to the Womb!"* As chant and response went on she watched the Suns sinking, and wondered if the Dweller in Srarcis could help them; if it knew their danger and their pain.

Men said that the Children of Hastur were shaped like men; that they dressed in blue, and had red hair more often than not.

"The bones into Mother Earth!" Gayatri called, and Sumitri, hearing Maitriyi's voice break and catch, threw her arms around her as she joined the response—*"And her child returns to Her womb!"*

She felt Maitriyi's body sag in her arms, shaken with convulsive sobbing—then Taravi's arms were around them both, supporting them.

Then the chant was finished, and Maitriyi leaning against her, sobbing, and the Twin Suns still clear above the horizon. Why not lie down with Vikram anyway, and get it over with? It would probably come to the same thing, in a few days. And even if they did come through this, there was only the same life awaiting them...

Then Mother Gayatri was pulling Maitriyi away from her, and pressing two crossbows into their hands. Taravi was holding a stick of wood into the fire, kindling a new torch from the pyre.

Mother Gayatri urged them towards the dark door of the tower, leaving the sacred fires burning to ward the castle. But could they climb to safety, Sumitri wondered, before the vampires woke to full power? Vampires mostly slept by day, and when awake were only walking corpses, awkward and vulnerable as the one Taravi had overcome so easily. But once their full powers came on them, at sundown, that was another story.

Mother Gayatri helped her wind the crossbow, and fit the bolt into place. Maitriyi's was already loaded, and so was Mother Gayatri's. That made three crossbows, and Taravi had her torch and the heavy sword...

At least the pyre was behind them now. The door stood open before them, with the dark corridor beyond. Sumitri blinked the tears from her eyes. She had to be able to see. The place would be crawling now, she was sure, with new-waked vampires still bound in human form; still vulnerable—but not for long. Taravi darted in ahead of them, while Mother Gayatri held her crossbow ready. Sumitri and Maitriyi, on either side of the old woman, did the same.

Fire blossomed inside as Taravi found an unlit torch in one of the wall sconces and lit it. Sumitri hesitated in the doorway, listening. Faint rustles echoed somewhere in the dimness ahead, and she pictured to herself the dead stirring in the corridors below.

"Inside!" Mother Gayatri shouted, and gestured for Sumitri and Maitriyi to precede her. Weapons raised, they obeyed. Sumitri wondered why they were not following the same order in which they had come down. Had she not protected their rear well enough? Shame mingled with relief at the thought.

But perhaps Mother Gayatri feared that she would slow them down. Perhaps she wished to move at her own pace. Or, perhaps, she felt that she was the most expendable, and should take the most dangerous position, giving the younger women the best chance of reaching the dubious safety of the top floor.

She heard the heavy door close behind them, and glanced back to see Mother Gayatri fasten the heavy bolt.

"Taravi!" Maitriyi shouted. "Watch out!" And even before Sumitri, whirling, saw the white-faced figure that lunged out of the door of the room where she had made love with Jal before he left, she heard the twang of the heavy string. She saw the dim shape stagger and fall, smashed from its feet by the force of the bolt: saw the second white face loom out of the darkness. But even as she brought her own crossbow up, Taravi leaped into the way, and wheeling steel mirrored torchlight, as the heavy sword drove into the vampire's neck and smashed it from its feet.

Joy and relief surged through Sumitri. The traitor was down. She heard Maitriyi's windlass turning, winding back the string of the heavy bow. Then the fallen vampire stirred, and lurched up. Its head hung at an odd angle, but it was still attached.

"*Die,* curse you!" Taravi shrieked, lashing out with the sword. Sumitri began to run. The vampire staggered back, but Taravi's sword seemed wedged in its shoulder.

Taravi brought the torch down on its head, and the hair burst into flame. Taravi wrenched her sword free as parched flesh caught, and the creature screamed, stumbled back, and blundered into another figure half-hidden in the shadows, and suddenly there were two screaming pillars of flame, lighting up the room behind them. Other shapes scattered away to either side.

"Rot you all!" Taravi shouted, and leaped toward the phantom figures, the heavy blade raised.

"Taravi!" Sumitri shouted, hearing Mother Gayatri's and Maitriyi's voices like echoes behind her. "Wait! Don't get too far ahead!"

The torch-lit sword whirled again, but this time the pale head leaped cleanly from the shoulder and spun to the ground.

"*Got* you!" Taravi shouted, continuing to run after the scattering figures. Sumitri ran, trying to keep Taravi in sight.

A figure moved towards Taravi's back, and Sumitri aimed, and tripped the release on the crossbow. She pulled a bolt from her belt as the figure reeled and fell, and began winding the winch to pull back the string and bend the massive steel spring of the bow...

A tall form loomed over her. Red eyes glared. Mouth dry, she felt for the hilt in her sash, knowing she could never get the short sword free in time.

With a crack like dry wood breaking, the figure staggered back, clutching at the short ugly peg jutting from its smashed chest. Dark blood came pumping out over the quarrel's end, and the dead thing swayed and fell. She heard running feet behind her. Torchlight grew brighter and with hysteric clarity she saw one of Pirru's dropped toys, a battered little statue of a horse, on the floor near the corpse's foot.

"Sister!" Maitriyi held her crossbow raised with one hand, while the other held the torch Taravi had lit. "Hurry! Set your bow!" Using both hands on the windlass, Sumitri finished drawing the bow, and dropped the bolt into the waiting slot.

She heard Mother Gayatri, breathing hard, coming up behind them, heard the ratchet clicking on her crossbow as she wound it. It had been Mother Gayatri, then, whose bolt had saved her.

"Die, blast you!" Taravi's voice echoed. Sumitri jerked her crossbow up. She saw the torch by the stair, and the blur of still-bright steel. A corpse burned on the floor: greasy black smoke rolled to hide most of the room.

Blinking, she tried to make sense of the confusion. She caught a brief glimpse of a gashed figure that stood swaying in the doorway at the stair's foot—the door that led out of the tower, and into the attic of the long building where Jal and Narain and the rest slept when the men were home—where she and her sister-wives slept with them.

"Guard my back!" she cried to the others, and rushed into that turmoil of glare and smoke.

She could not see to shoot. Taravi would be holding the stair like some hero out of old songs—like Sumitri's ancestor Karnarao of Adripor, or like Mother Gayatri's great-grandfather, Vanraj, who had held this very stair against a host of Night Things while his family fled into the redoubt.

"You won't get away that easily, rot you!" Taravi shouted.

Sumitri raced to the door, but stopped, and looked up the steps, half-expecting to see vampires clustered there, to stop their ascent—but as far as the flickering corpse-light reached, the steps were clear.

"Stand still, rot you!" Taravi's voice come echoing from the doorway. *'Die!"*

Sumitri set herself at the stair's foot, remembering old songs about Karnarao that she had not heard since childhood.

"Maitriyi! Mother Gayatri!" she shouted, and waved at them through the smoke. *"Hurry!"*

Was it sunset yet? Had the vampires regained their powers? She had to hold the stair. But she could not help glancing at the darkness behind the door, and then back across the floor. She glimpsed the others, moving slowly, back to back. In sudden resolve she sprang down from the stair, and looked through the door. She glimpsed torchlight, far down the corridor that ran to Jal's bedroom.

"Taravi!" she called. *"Come back!"*

She turned back to the stair's foot. If the vampires had gained their full power, they could be hiding as mist in the smoke.

"No you don't, curse you!" Taravi's voice came. Sumitri stepped up onto the lowest step, and set her back against the faded painting that covered the wall; watching the two women as they moved around the burning corpse.

"*Rot* you, you—" and suddenly Taravi's voice broke in an inarticulate scream. *"Help!"* Sumitri leaped from the stair, and rushed to the door.

She looked back, once, seeing Mother Gayatri and Maitriyi almost there. Then she dashed through the door, and down the familiar corridor, under the heavy beams that held up the roof. The torchlight seemed faint and far away. She ran towards it.

Metal glittered near the roof. The torch lay sputtering on the floor. Her throat closed on the scream she felt building there. She held the crossbow raised and ready as she ran, but there was no one. No white-faced lurkers to shoot. No Taravi. The air rising from the nearby stairwell reeked of blood and death.

Metal glittered in the low roof-beam. Edge deep-wedged in wood, Taravi's sword-hilt hung before her eyes. She reached with one hand, and tugged. It would not move.

At any moment they could come out of the dark. Yet she set the bow against the ground, leaned the stock against her hip, and gripped the hilt with both hands, working it back and forth.

"Taravi! Sumitri!" It was Maitriyi's voice. "Come back!"

The steel began to move, and suddenly the weight of the heavy sword was in her hands. She blinked, slid the sword into her sash and snatched up the crossbow. What had she been thinking of?

She snatched the torch up from the floor, seeing charred wood where it had lain, and turned to run. She heard thumps and rustling sounds from the floor below. She ran through the corridor that was part of her own home, down which she had walked hundreds of times, to make love, to soothe children. Maitriyi shouted again.

She saw Maitriyi peering through the doorway, torch raised. She dashed up, out of breath, saw Maitriyi lowering her crossbow, and realised how close she had come to getting a bolt through her heart.

"Sister!" Maitriyi said, then "—Taravi?"

"Gone—" she managed to croak. "Just gone. Only her sword—" Her voice failed.

Winded, panting, out of breath, she followed Maitriyi out the door, into the tower again. Everything blurred.

Mother Gayatri sat on the steps, very small and old and frightened, but the crossbow resting in her lap came up and was level.

Her whole face lighted with a smile as she saw them, a smile of relief that faded as she realised there were only two. She glanced back towards the door.

"Taravi?" she asked, soft-voiced. Maitriyi shook her head sadly. "Her sword was stuck in a beam—" Sumitri managed to gasp. "That—cleaver!" Mother Gayatri shook her head, and pressed her lips tightly together.

The corpse on the tiled floor had burnt down to a few glowing bones. Mother Gayatri climbed laboriously to her feet, and took Sumitri's arm. But who was supporting whom? Sumitri felt herself shaking all over. The roof-beams were drawing closer as they climbed. Then they were passing between the floors, into Mother Gayatri's room, all its usual neatness destroyed with chicken feathers and dead birds. The window to the west showed only a faint trace of color on the horizon.

A white face loomed suddenly out of the darkness. Sumitri screamed. Gayatri's crossbow snapped, and the face vanished, as the shape staggered back, and fell.

"Give me that!" Her crossbow was snatched from her hand. She blinked, confused. Now Mother Gayatri was pushing her own bow at her, and as she took it, the old woman seized the torch. "Here! Reload this! Hurry!"

They *were* hurrying, up cold stone steps, slippery with chicken feathers under bare feet.

"In Hastur's name, open up!" The iron door boomed as Mother Gayatri pounded and shouted. Suddenly the trap flew up, and a torch thrust flaming down; and beyond was Kajioni's face, pale and set and wet with tears, and the gleaming point of a woman's sword poised to stab.

Relief flooded Kajioni's face; she fell back and they scrambled up. Fires burned in the little hearths on each side: wood was stacked about the trap, ready to fire.

Kajioni threw herself into her mother's arms, and they wept together.

"Shut that!" said Mother Gayatri. The iron door boomed. Mother Gayatri leaned against the pile of wood. "Juvali, help me!" Wood began crashing, *boom—boom—boom*—on the iron door, echoing thunderously. Mother Gayatri tossed down her torch into the falling logs and she and Juvali continued to toss wood onto the trap.

"But Taravi—" said Juvali. "Where is Taravi?"

Falling wood drummed on the iron door. Sumitri staggered out of the alcove, and tried to sit down, but nearly cut herself on the long sharp sword thrust through her sash. She pulled it out and stared at it dully. Taravi's sword. How she hated the thing!

Why had she brought it back? It had killed Taravi. Why hadn't she been sensible, and left the stupid thing sticking in the beam?

Stupid and dangerous, to leave the torch scorching the floor, and lay the crossbow down to wrench with both hands when the air about her could have coagulated into bloodsucking death.

Pirru came running, and threw himself at her and hugged her, and she gave him her breast while Juvali and Kajioni helped Mother Gayatri out of the alcove, and the fire roared up behind them. The old woman looked terribly frail and pale and tired, and now she was lying down while Juvali went running to get something, and outside the windows it was dark, except for the white face that hung there, whispering, whispering.

"Come here, Pretty Tits, and give me some of that. Come on, I'm thirsty—so thirsty..."

She started to go to him, but Pirru was holding tightly and she was too tired to fight. She closed her eyes, sobbing, feeling Pirru draining her milk that could feed the world, and saw corpses burning on the tiled floor, and chased Taravi through long corridors that she recognised as ancient Adripor where she had played as a child; Adripor that was now under the Shadow, with all her sisters and brothers and cousins and uncles and aunts all hunting white-faced and red-eyed through the gloom, and Taravi was out there too, and she must find her, and give her the breast... So thirsty...

Sumitri woke. Kajioni's slim, forked figure stood naked before the fire burning in the alcove, standing guard, short sword in hand.

But who now could shatter the flaming skeletons if they came charging out of the flames? Taravi—oh *Taravi!* The dream had been true. Taravi was dead.

Her eyes opened wide, and she started to sit up. Pirru made a little sleepy sound of protest, but did not wake. His little arms gripped more tightly as he curled against her.

"Come on, Pretty Tits, wake up!" The dry, whispering voice scratched at the edge of her mind, and she shivered. Only Pirru and exhaustion had kept her from rising last night. She had been ready to press the flesh of her breast against the fretted screen...

Oh, *Taravi! Taravi*—dead now, doubtless, drained by a dozen mouths..The nightmare had been true. And it would never, ever end...

Why had Taravi not stayed in northern Mahavara, away from the Shadow, where grass was green and most children lived, and the

Night Things almost never reached? Pirru sighed, and she felt the little body relax. He rolled over on his back, and firelight picked out his little face, and the beautiful line of his throat. She rolled up to look down at him, enchanted by his wonderful beauty, lying there, so sweet and innocent, asleep.

Beyond the sleeping child's perfect face, she glimpsed Juvali's rounded curves against the firelight, next to Kajioni's angular, emaciated form. Kajioni's voice rose clear for a moment.

"Everything I love—dies—" The voice caught in a sob, and the two figures were one shape against the firelight.

And looking down at her child's perfect beauty, Sumitri's heart clenched.

If the worst happened, and they had to burn themselves in the tower to escape the Night Things, she would have to cut that perfect throat, to keep him from suffering in the flames. She almost screamed at the thought, and felt her nails claw her cheek. In the thousand years since the Dark Things had poured into Takkaria from the north, how many mothers had been forced to that terrible choice?

Fire is our only refuge... All those ancient, cruel traditions, the pride of her bloodline. Why had she never had the sense to run away? Being a whore in the city could be no worse than this! At least her babies would have lived, even if they grew up to be dockworkers and hired bullies for the guilds.

The old songs made it seem different, something heroic and noble, and thousands of women over the centuries must have made that terrible choice to save their children from the loveless half-life in the Shadow. She sat up, clenching her fists, nails driving into palms. She could not go on thinking like this. She could not bear it!

As she moved her fingers touched Taravi's sword, lying where she had dropped it. It was a part of all those proud, ancient traditions. All that ancient, heroic passion had brought Taravi to the Border, to marry into an impoverished Border family, and to die so uselessly, led into a trap by the dead, betrayed by her pride in this clumsy blade.

Taravi had thrown away the choice that Sumitri had never had. Passion for Sajan had brought her from Adripor, young and scarred by flame; but, born on the Border, she had had nowhere else to go. For a thousand years the Shadow had grown. And for a thousand years, her ancestors had fought to hold the land, armed with little more than naked courage.

Her heart lurched as she saw Mother Gayatri lying nearby, so pale and shrunken and still that, for a moment, she was sure that sorrow and the long climb had been too much for that brave old heart. But she saw the crumpled figure sigh, and knew that the old woman still breathed.

Kajioni and Juvali still clung together by the fire, and she could hear the girl sobbing and Juvali's low voice murmuring. Heat made her flesh cringe, as she felt the frail old silk drying against her body, and remembered the spark in her dress in Adripor; the fire that had scarred her arm and back and hip. She watched sparks fly up to the soot-dark ceiling, and wondered if bats crawled there.

"So you're awake at last?" Juvali said. "You've slept most of the night. There's hot water—help yourself to tea."

As the two girls separated, Kajioni turned away, dabbing at her eyes, trying to hide her tears. *It is no shame to weep,* Sumitri remembered Mother Gayatri saying, *the land is watered by tears.*

"Thank you for letting me sleep," she said, slipping out of her robe to pour herself tea.

"It's been quiet so far," said Juvali, "and—you all looked like you needed sleep."

That was true enough, thought Sumitri, sipping hot, bitter-tasting tea; listening to the rustle and roar of the fire, while vampires whispered from the windows.

"Have either of *you* slept?" she asked.

"I dozed a little while you were gone," Juvali answered, softly. "I am afraid Kajioni is very tired!"

Kajioni came up with an armload of wood, and dumped it rattling and thumping into the fire. Sparks shot high, and Sumitri cringed. She glanced up at the soot-crusted ceiling where the flying sparks struck and died. No bats crawled there.

"Kajioni, you should go to bed now," she started to say. "You need your—"

She paused, listening, suddenly aware of some subtle change. The vampires were whispering more loudly, with an undertone of excitement. She drained her tea.

"What is it?" Kajioni asked. Sumitri only shook her head.

The vampires' murmurs died. She donned her robe as she crossed the room to peer through the west window into the gloom of the court below. A sudden *boom* gonged through the night outside. Need-fire glared, flaring across the sky. She squinted against the glare, trying to see. The pyres atop the parapet had burnt down to a ruddy pile of coals. The brazen gong sounded again, and she saw the strong gates shudder, and near them a grisly throng gathered.

Her ears rang with monotonous chiming, as something beat against the gate. The vampire pack seethed. What were they doing? Were those spears they drove against the center of the gate, where the great doors joined?

Then, with a chill, she knew. They dared not touch the spell-guarded steel-and-silver bolt. But with sticks and spears and long poles, perhaps, they could hook the bolt, and open the gate to whatever drummed on the other side...

"What is it?" Maitriyi's sleepy voice asked, at her elbow.

"They are trying to force the gate," Mother Gayatri answered. "If there were men to defend it, they could never do it. This gate is stronger than the one they threw down in great-grandfather Vanraj's time. But I fear that this time, with no one to defend it, they will get it open."

Sumitri saw something moving against the bright curtain of Need-fire, something that soared and dipped high in the air above the gate.

"And—what if they do get the gate open, Mother Gayatri?" Kajioni's voice was shrill and scared. "What can we do then?"

"Then, my dear ones," the old voice hesitated a moment, then—"I am very much afraid that the other creatures who come in when the gate is opened will find a way to break into our redoubt—and then, fire will be our only refuge."

Sumitri's scars all tingled. Fire! To burn in the tower! Her nails drove into her palms as she thought of the children, remembering Pirru asleep beside her—so beautiful, with his head thrown back and the soft line of the throat that she would have to cut...

Black against the Border's Need-fire blaze, great wings swooped down to settle on the battlements above the gate. Dim light rising from the dying pyres turned the wings to a dirty yellow-white as the small body between them staggered off the crenellations on a pair of human-looking legs.

The wide wings furled. Sumitri thought the head looked like a skull until the pyre-light picked out the cruelly hooked bird's beak under the enormous golden eyes.

She stared at it in horror, feeling helpless. If only the men were here! Even with only part of Giripor's normal garrison they could drive off that winged thing, and keep the vampires away from the gate with torches and fire-arrows...

Fire-arrows! She was *not* helpless, after all!

Turning quickly, almost knocking Mother Gayatri down, she pushed her way through the crowding women, and ran to snatch up the crossbow she had left lying where she slept. She paid no heed to the shrill babble of protest behind her, her mind on the problem at hand. One of the silver-plated iron quarrels was still set in the slot—inexcusable carelessness, she thought: suppose Pirru or one of the other children had tripped the lever? It would have to do, there was no time to hunt for a wooden bolt. She found an old scrap of age-dried cloth, and began wrapping it around the shaft just behind the head.

"Fire-arrows!" said Mother Gayatri, who had studied her intently, while the other women had babbled questions. "Of course. Quick! Help her! Make more!"

With a rustle, they scattered, and when Sumitri looked up from her finished arrow they were all at work, nimble fingers flying. Maitriyi, a second arrow in her hand, was pulling a burning brand from the fire, following her to the window, to light the arrow. As soon as it kindled, before it flamed too high, she pushed the new-kindled point through one of the tiny holes in the silver fretwork, aiming down, into the thick of the pack by the gate.

String and steel spring sang: the flaming bolt flew. Taking the new bolt from Maitriyi, she stepped back to reload, as Mother Gayatri stepped in, kindling another arrow and sending it flaming into night. Juvali stood ready with the third bow, Kajioni with another bolt.

Intent on the whirling winch, Sumitri still heard the screams, and glimpsed the sudden flare in the court below. Mother Gayatri stepped back: Juvali stepped and sent another fire-arrow whirring. It was Sumitri's turn again, and through the window she saw flaming forms stagger and scream. The vampire pack had scattered from the gate to avoid those already aflame. Only two still pried with poles at the lock: she took aim at one of these. Both vanished before she could loose again.

The gates flew open... Through the sudden arch strode a monstrous form, like some huge statue hewn from stone: a Troll.

The jutting stump of a crossbow bolt in its neck told her that this was the beast that the boys had shot. Behind it a dozen dog-headed, human-sized forms loped, shouldering each other as they pushed through the gate. Behind marched an army of tiny twisted forms.

Her mouth was dry. She was still holding the loaded crossbow, the lit arrowhead still flickering. Not that it mattered now. She worked the flaming point carefully through one of the tiny, precisely measured openings in the fine silver mesh, sighted carefully, and loosed. A dog-headed shape fell, shrieking. Others swarmed over the body, biting and rending.

Atop the gate, wings unfurled with a snap, and the winged thing was in the air, growing larger and larger, as the beating wings drove straight towards her. The great wings filled the window. She stumbled back. The wings swerved and sheared away, but a dark blot tumbled on.

Silver buckled and bulged inward with a screech of stone on metal. Rock bounced away into the dark. Silver wires parted; tiny, precisely measured holes stretched...

She stared, mind numbed, at the rents in the silver, at the white fog that was already beginning to creep through.

Mother Gayatri's voice rose.

"Fire is our refuge!" The frail old woman's voice was suddenly strong, as she took the torch from Maitriyi's unresisting hand, and turning, hurled it into the heart of the heaped fuel. "Be strong, now! Remember, others have taken this road before you! Do not shame their memory! Gather the children. We haven't much time."

The fire from the torch began to lick the wood around it. The flesh of Sumitri's scars flinched, but worse than the fear of fire was knowing what she must do first.

Children were crying. She saw Pirru running towards her, and forced herself to smile as she held out her arms.

But how was she going to get the knife out of her sash and up to his throat? Behind the ear would be the quickest. But he must not see the knife, so there would be neither fear nor pain.

"Ashes are our bodies' end!" The frail old voice rose in the funeral chant. "Fire is our refuge, and the soul returns to the womb."

Other voices, faltering, joined hers, as she marched toward the pyre, singing. The white fog that seeped through the rents in the silver was rising in pillars. Fire ran along the thinner scraps of wood. Soon the whole pile would blaze. There was not much time. Sumitri pressed Pirru tight against her with one arm, while she groped for the knife in her sash.

Blue-white light flared, and a beam of brightness flashed from the southern window to the fire. Sumitri thought she saw a whirling ball of moonbeams roll down that beam, and hang above the flames.

White faces formed in pillars of fog. Her fingers closed on the hilt of her knife. Suddenly the fire lifted, draining from the wood, rising up in the form of a human figure—like those forming out of fog.

But it was not another vampire. Sumitri stared, uncomprehending, at the blue robe—the red hair—her mind still struggling to get the knife to her son's throat without him seeing...no fear...no pain.

"Wait!"

She could not tell whether that organ voice filled the air of the room or only her mind. The blue-robed figure balanced carefully atop the wood, and fire danced above upraised naked palms. It was not another vampire, but something that she barely dared to imagine. Wild hope ripped through her, and she almost dropped the half-drawn knife.

Suddenly the dancing flames above its palms concentrated into points of brilliance. A ray of intense light lanced from the right palm to the window and vampire screams were cut short. Blackened figures fell, and shattered into dust.

"Wait!" that organ voice throbbed. *"No need to burn! Your men are coming! The war is over. Your men will be coming home, with others to help them. From your west window you may see the fires behind which they stand and fight! They should be here in two days, no more! Live!"*

The point of light pulsed above its left palm, and suddenly a globe of intense flame flared out. Sumitri blinked, blinded, feeling in her flesh a strange, unaccustomed prickling. She heard screams from the building below, and the courtyard. The Troll roared once—and was suddenly still, the roar cut off.

Another pulse, another sphere of expanding brilliance. Blinded, the inside of her eyelids bright red, she felt heat this time as well as the strange tingling. From the courtyard as well as the floors below came a shrill chorus of wild screams, and the pounding of feet.

Sleepy chickens clucked.

"There should be nothing more to fear this night," the voice throbbed. Sumitri opened her eyes. The blue-robed figure was gone—

No! There he was, by the west window, running his hands over the buckled silver. Pirru struggled in her arms, and she set him down. He promptly sat, put his thumb in his mouth, and looked around with wide-eyed innocence.

The other women were staring as raptly as she at the red-haired man who stood at the window. A pale radiance like moonlight seemed to spread from his hands across the crumbled surface of the screen. Sumitri gasped. The twisted metal began to glow with a faint pink light. Blue sparks leaped between the broken ends of wires.

She stared at the long, slender hands that moved just above the surface of the screen. There was a curious shimmering about them. She blinked. The battered screen rippled. Broken wires moved, sparks leaping furiously as the ends drew closer touched—fused.

The screen was whole.

He looked up, and smiled. He beckoned, and Sumitri stumbled towards him. Mother Gayatri, too, was limping forward.

"That tiny light—" he pointed into the darkness above the castle wall—"is all you can see of the bonfires on the walls of Katikot behind which your returning army stands, fighting until dawn while the hordes of the Shadow try to drag them down. They fight all night, and travel all day, trying to get back to you. They only sleep at dawn and sunset..."

Her eager eyes followed his pointing finger. Beyond the corpse-lit courtyard, where some of the vampire bodies still smouldered, a black stretch of land lay at the foot of the great wall of Need-fire that stretched away, dwindling and vanishing far to the west. All that flat black space blazed with tiny flickering lights. Some, she knew, were other castles, where other women faced the same terror that she and her sister-wives faced here.

She stared at the tiny, flickering spark, and hope surged up.

"They are all there," he said, and now he spoke with his mouth, as other men speak. "Jal and Narain; Dumat, Tanaj and Tikrao. Only Tikrao is wounded, and that lightly—they were lucky, and came late to the battle."

"Who won?" asked Mother Gayatri.

"The Dark Things had more to gain than either side," the Hastur said. "But Prince Hansio was slain—" Mother Gayatri gave a sharp cry, and seemed to sink into herself "fighting against Istvan the Archer, and now Olonsos's son, Chondos, is firm on the throne, and sends his men to help his former foes. And so there are with them not only men of northern Mahapora, but others who, ten days ago, were enemies. Now all unite against the Dark."

"Then—my sons—" Mother Gayatri's voice trembled. "They will be here soon?"

"If they push on tomorrow—and I think they will—" said the Hastur, "they should be at your gates by sunset. But it is a steep and hard road from Kattikote, and they may have to fight their way through after dark—or camp and fight all night."

"Can you not help them?" Sumitri asked, and her tone was sharp.

"We help when and where we can." The Hastur turned to her, and his sad blue eyes met hers without flinching. "But often we cannot help, for we are fighting worse things on the far side of the Border. It was only because the attack had slackened that I was able to come here.

"My kin and I help when we can, but often we cannot. Be wary, even if your men are here to fight for you. I will strengthen the wards around the castle, but the Night Things will return."

And he was gone.

One of the women made a small strangled sound. But Sumitri, looking down, saw him reappear in the courtyard, near the gate. The gate swung shut. A white line of brightness flared. As she watched, the bright bolt stirred; slid; locked into place. He turned to look up at her, raised a hand as though in farewell—then vanished like a blown-out flame.

So they are real, she thought. Even though she had always known that there had to be some kind of intelligence controlling the towers, she had never—she realized—really believed the stories she had heard—that they had human form; or that they ever really aided ordinary people. She knew too many they had not helped. She thought bitterly of her own long-dead family. No Hastur had come to save them.

Yet this time they *had* come. Why? Why had they acted to stop this little group of women from leaping into the fire, when they had not moved to save Adripor?

She gazed out over the land, and the great cliff of flame that rose above it. Tiny moons wandered among cold stars overhead, and the black flat land below blazed with the tiny sparks of men's castles. Wildly shimmering flames flickered and wove across the Border, great bands of violet, rising miles into the air, leaping from tower to tower.

It was the Hasturs that maintained that vast barrier, she knew. Men said that when it flared up most brightly, it was holding back the attacks of the greater powers—and sometimes, she knew, it failed, and things like walking mountains of black fire came out of the Shadow, things that could blot out a castle or a city or an army in a moment.

We help when we can, the Hastur had said, *but often we cannot.* Was that why Adripor had fallen?

She could hear Mother Gayatri murmuring to herself, and turning, she saw tears running down the wrinkled old cheeks.

"Mother?" She stepped quickly to the old woman's side. "What—"

"I'm happy, child! My boys are coming home! And the castle will still be here for them—we almost burned it..." She buried her face in Sumitri's shoulder, and sobbed. Sumitri threw her arms around the frail shoulders and held her tightly, her mind awhirl as she stared out over the fire-dotted darkness at the foot of the wall of flame.

One of the babies whimpered. She twisted to look. It was not Pirru. He was sound asleep against a pile of old spice-bags, thumb still deep in his mouth.

"Did the—did he not say that we were safe?" Kajioni's voice spoke from somewhere behind them. "That there would be nothing to fear tonight?"

"He said to be wary," answered Juvali. "Let us build up the fire again before we go to sleep."

"It's almost dawn," Maitriyi commented, but even as she spoke she was gathering up wood from the pile.

Sumitri listened to the clatter of wood against wood, her arms tight around Mother Gayatri. After a moment the old woman patted her arm.

"Run along and help the others, dear. I'm crying with joy. I'm not unhappy."

"Yes, I see them! Oh yes, look!"

There was a smell of cooking food—of frying bread patties and of spices and of rice... Sumitri realised she was ravenous, and that her swollen breasts were achingly full.

"See—that must be Jal, there, on the red horse—"

"No—" That was Mother Gayatri's voice—"No, that is Jal on the black horse. I know my own son!"

There was laughter, and Maitriyi said, "I don't see how either of you think you could tell at this distance."

"I know my son!" said Mother Gayatri, quietly but with a firm dignity.

The excitement in the cooing voices drew Sumitri to the window. On the road below them tiny shapes were toiling, men on horseback, some gleaming in mailshirts, most in the blocky homemade Border armor. At the front fluttered a banner, whose familiar colors tugged at her heart-strings, even though it was still too far to see the device and know for sure it was *their* banner.

The Twin Suns were well to the west, now. She had slept away the morning and well past noon. All that day they watched distant men and horses growing while the Twin Suns settled toward the west, and Srarcis Tower glowed dimly against the great wall of the Shadow. There were more than twenty in the little group, and they remembered that the Hastur had said that others accompanied them.

They cooked a large meal, and watched at the window, and then, as the men they loved, with Jal, on the black horse, in the lead, toiled up the last slope, Mother Gayatri gasped.

"The gate! We must open the gate for them."

"I'll go, Mother Gayatri!" said Sumitri.

And quickly, before any could argue, she swept ashes from the iron grate and raced down through the devastated neatness of Mother Gayatri's room, past the tiled floor where they had fought, and down the last level, to the barn.

She caught a glimpse of their poor cow, stretched out with a great hole in its side. She turned her eyes away from that, and dashed into the courtyard—

And almost ran into the Troll.

She stopped, gasping, heart pounding—then realized that the great beast had turned to stone—probably the night before.

She went around the looming shape, toward the gate. Above the west wall, the sky was red. To the south, the Border was like a wall of black glass cutting away half the sky.

She reached the gate out of breath and sweating. Beyond, she heard the hammering of hooves. She heaved against the heavy bar, sliding it back in its well-worn grove, and pulled back against the portal even as she heard Jal's voice outside.

"Vikram! Uttaro! Open the—" There was a sudden pause, as he saw the gate already opening.

Then horses were thundering into the courtyard, too many horses, and Jal was reining the black horse around to where she stood behind the gate, and he threw himself from the saddle and rushed to her.

"Sumitri!" he exclaimed, shouting over the clamor of hooves and the shouting of other men. "What are you doing here? Where are Vikram and Uttaro? Are you—well? Safe?"

"No." She shook her head, and felt sudden tears sting her eyes. "Uttaro—Vikram—Taravi—all dead!"

"No!" Pain twisted his face. *"Taravi?* No..." He stared. All around them men were shouting, and feet pounded up the stairs to the ramparts. "And—my mother?" he asked.

She smiled at him. "She's been taking care of the rest of us," she said. "She's waiting to see you." *Desperate to see you,* she thought.

"Of course she is. Tell her I—I will be up as soon as I can." He caught her suddenly to his chest, and hugged her tightly. "At least you're still—safe!" He kissed her, and then turned away towards the ramparts. "Get that firewood lit, up there!"

She worked her way around the edge of the courtyard, filled now with bustling men and horses. Flames from the ramparts cast ruddy firelight over all. Then a brighter fire sprang up far to the south, as need-fire leaped up from Srarcis Tower, and the whole southern sky was ablaze.

She turned in at a little door that led into the old banqueting hall. She did not want to go through the stables, and see and smell the dead cow.

It was dark, but she quickly made her way up to the next level. Here windows gave plenty of light as she made her way through cluttered rooms. All the confusion outside was comforting. She and her sisters were no longer alone. There were men to defend them, a larger garrison than they had had in years...

"Sister!" a familiar voice called.

Taravi was beside her. For a moment it seemed perfectly

ordinary, and Sumitri stopped and smiled...

And froze, remembering.

She tried to step back, groping in her sash for the hilt of the slender sword, but Taravi's hand came down on Sumitri's wrist. "What, Sister? You can't be afraid of *me!*'

She smiled, and lips writhed up from growing fangs—if she screamed, Sumitri knew, no one would be able to hear her above the racket in the courtyard.

She had not warned Jal—she had told him Taravi was dead, but he had only half-believed her, and if he saw Taravi he would go running to her...

"Traitor!" she spat.

"What's to betray?" Taravi shrugged. "Carrying brat after squalling brat and watching them die? Making love to men, and then burning their bodies? Grubbing in garden-dirt? Eating raw fish all winter, and never enough of that?"

Hopelessness washed over her. All Taravi had said was true. She had said the same things herself. Taravi's eyes were no longer black, but paling, paling—soon they would be blood-red.

"Sumitri." Mother Gayatri's voice was gentle. "Step back, child. Step away."

Mother Gayatri! She had to protect her! She threw herself back, her hand half-dragging her useless sword from her sash despite the vise on her wrist.

She felt the heavy iron stake crash through Taravi's chest, pinning her against the wall.

Horrified, she saw Taravi pluck at the heavy shaft between her breasts, then go limp, as a single gout of dark blood pulsed out, then stopped. Sumitri fell on her knees, and buried her face in her shaking hands. She heard Mother Gayatri limp past her to the wall where Taravi hung.

"Poor dear," the frail voice said gently. "You rest now."

"Oh, Mother Gayatri!" Sumitri sobbed. "I can't bear it, I can't, I can't!"

"None of us can bear it, dear," the old woman said. "But we have to. People used to run away from the Dark Things, but the Shadow just grew, and then, there they were again. Men used to send their women away from the Border, but their widows had no children to carry on. No one can bear it, but we do."

And looking up, Sumitri saw in the old woman's face that humble resolve—to bear the unbearable, to endure and die when necessary, but never to yield—the indomitable spirit of the Border.

WARRIOR WITHOUT A HEART

by Jessie D. Eaker

This will be Jessie Eaker's first appearance outside of the SWORD AND SORCERESS anthologies. His other stories, "Name of the Demoness", "Staying Behind", "Blademistress", "Bad Luck and Curses", "The Needle and the Sword", and "To Live Forever" have appeared in SWORD AND SORCERESS 6, 7, 9, 11, 14, and 15.

He is male, despite the feminine spelling of his first name. Jessie, with an ie, is the Eaker family's traditional spelling and has been used for generations. And on top of that, his last name, Eaker, is pronounced like acre, as in a measurement of land. Admittedly this causes gender and phonetic confusion, but he is now at the age where confusion tends to be a way of life. (Well, I still get letters addressed to Mr. Marion Bradley, and then there are the folks who think my last name is Zimmerman. That's Bob Dylan's real last name, but it was never mine.)

Jessie and his wife Becki live in Richmond, Virginia. This past year has been especially busy for them, because for the first time, all their children are in school or college. Homework around the Eaker house can get pretty intense. This past year, they've also adopted an abandoned puppy that his son found. They named her "Lady" but so far she hasn't quite lived up to her name.
—MZB

The young sorceress approached.

Still as a stone, Renity crouched behind a clump of bushes close to the edge of the road. She scrutinized the surrounding forest with quick darting eyes, searching for the slightest hint that her presence might be noticed. But all seemed in place. The birds and small animals, having long since decided to ignore her, made their normal squawks, clicks, and grunts. And with the unusually warm spring breeze filling the air with the smell of fragrant flowers, her scent would be safely hidden. A fly buzzed by noisily and landed on her bare arm. Renity didn't dare move to shoo it away. It probed for sustenance, attempting to dig deep into her skin for moisture, but it flew away disappointed.

Then just for a moment, as the wildlife paused at the newcomer's approach, the wind stilled. Renity closed her eyes and listened closely to the footsteps: light and quick. Renity could tell the young sorceress was wearing sandals. But more importantly, she was alone.

The warrior opened her eyes and stared out through the eyeholes of her mask. Although her mistress had insisted she wear it, Renity could not see its purpose. Being made of straw, bark and horn, and shaped with long teeth and downward-pointed ears, it offered no protection as a helm might. She imagined most would consider it quite hideous. Only her deep green eyes were visible through the mask's eyeholes.

The bush partially obscured Renity's vision, so when the young sorceress came within sight, all she could catch was the white of her tunic and what appeared to be a scabbarded sword belted to her waist. But the details of her face were concealed.

Renity had not believed her mistress when she had been given this assignment. It seemed too easy. "Bring the young sorceress to me," she had said. "She will be alone and armed only with a sword. But do not underestimate her powers. Though undeveloped, they are considerable."

And with that, she had given Renity an amulet which made her immune to the sorceress's magic and undetectable by her other-sense.

As the young sorceress approached the ambush point, Renity tensed and prepared to pounce. The warrior gripped her wooden club tightly in her right hand. Her quarry's footfalls marked the timing...

Unexpectedly, the young sorceress stopped. Despite all of Renity's preparations, her quarry seemed to be searching her surroundings...seemed to sense that something was amiss. The sorceress turned on her heel and sprinted back down the road.

Faster than an eye blink, Renity was out from behind the bush and running after the young sorceress. As the long-legged warrior closed the distance, she noted that the woman's hair, bound in a tight braid, whipped her back with every step, beating her to faster speed. But its color...hair so white it was almost silver. She had seen hair like that only once before. So she wasn't surprised when the woman glanced back and Renity recognized the lift of her nose and her dark blue eyes. It was Neola, her best friend—or at least she had been when they had said their last tearful goodbye.

But that did not matter now. Renity raised her club to strike.

The young sorceress whirled, and with her sword leaping into her hand, parried Renity's downstroke, gouging deep cuts into the club. Renity was not surprised when the young sorceress shoved her back and struck several times in quick succession. Most sorceresses had no knowledge of swordplay, but Renity knew this one did. And in fact, had been quite good at it when they had trained together. Back then, Neola's sights had been set on becoming a warrior like her mother. Since her friend was now training as a sorceress, something in her life had changed. As something had changed for Renity.

The warrior picked up the tempo, using her club with the agility of a sword and raining down blows so fast the young sorceress could barely counter them. Step by step, Renity drove her back. Renity knew it would only be a few more moments before the young sorceress would tire.

But Renity was caught unaware as Neola broke from the pattern. She spun, ducked under Renity's swing, and wheeling her sword with all her might, came back around to knock the club from her Renity's hand. In quick follow-through, the young sorceress reared back and sank her blade into Renity's exposed chest...

Renity winced at the sudden pain, noting the way her flesh and bone parted around the blade, and how its steel chilled her chest. But no blood came out, nor did she fall. Renity simply gazed at her through the mask's eyeholes.

The young sorceress stared at her open-mouthed, her hand dropping from the sword's hilt as if burned.

Renity reached for the sword and slowly drew it out. She flung it to the side of the road and grabbed the young sorceress's tunic, drawing her closer. One punch to the side of her head and Neola, the young sorceress, her once-good friend, was knocked unconscious.

Not having a heart was quite an advantage.

Young Renity got up from her pallet inside the barracks and silently began to prepare her small bundle of belongings. Although the room was dark, the lanterns outside the window provided her with enough light to complete her task. She worked silently so as not to wake the other young apprentices. Most were about her age of fifteen summers.

"Where are you going?" whispered a wide-eyed Neola on the pallet next to hers. She propped herself up on one elbow.

Renity held up a finger to her lips and stepped over to her best friend. She put her mouth to her friend's ear. *"I've got to go home. Father died."*

Neola looked worried. "But why leave in the middle of the night? Surely, the commander will think you have deserted. Wouldn't it be better to wait until tomorrow?"

Renity shook her head. "The commander will order an escort plus supplies, and we won't leave for days! *I can't afford to wait. My mother, sister and brother have no other support."*

Neola looked at her with bright eyes. "You're really leaving, aren't you?"

Renity nodded.

Neola's eyes suddenly filled with tears. She hugged her close. "I'm going to miss you."

"I'll come back if I can."

"Can we still be friends?"

Renity smiled sadly. "Of course. We'll be friends forever..."

Renity was brought back to the present by a groan from her captive. She listened for it to repeat but the only sounds came from the pops and hisses of the small fire and the rejoicing of the frogs and crickets in the coming evening. There was barely enough light left on the horizon to illuminate the tall oaks guarding one side of their campsite. The young sorceress (Renity found it easier to think of her this way) had been unconscious since late afternoon. Renity must have hit her harder than she thought.

Sitting cross-legged and rigidly erect, Renity resumed her vigil. Above her, the stars began to gather for their nightly dance. She watched them appear by ones and twos until they filled the sky. At one time, she would have said they were beautiful jewels. But now she saw them with unbiased clarity as merely colored points of light. Suddenly, she felt an *emptiness* in her chest: a feeling she had come to associate with her missing heart. It usually happened when she remembered some emotion from her childhood, something she could no longer feel. She had heard of such ghost pains in veterans who had lost an arm or leg. Surely her pains were similar. Yet, it was a small price to pay for her superiority.

Renity adjusted her mask and looked back to her captive. She noticed a faint movement of her legs. Evidently, her captive was now feigning unconsciousness in an attempt to escape. Renity opened her mouth to warn her, but it was too late. The young sorceress leaped up and ran for the oak trees, realizing too late that her feet were tethered by a length of rope tied ankle to ankle. It drew up tight, jerking her feet from beneath her. She sprawled face-forward, scooping up a mouthful of dirt and nearly knocking the wind out of herself.

"Finally decided to get up, I see," Renity said, matter-of-factly. "I wondered how much longer you were going to pretend."

Spitting out dirt, Neola slowly pushed herself up and sat. Then she turned to examine her ankles and the tight knots holding the rope. She looked at Renity peculiarly, no doubt noticing how emotionless her voice sounded.

"Do not attempt to untie the ropes," Renity continued. "If you do, I will be forced to bind your hands also." The warrior reached in her pouch and pulled out a carefully-wrapped travel cake. "Here, take this. You must be hungry."

The young sorceress glanced at the offering in distaste and glared at her with fiery eyes.

"Go ahead," Renity said. "It is not poisoned. It would have been far easier to kill you than to take you captive."

The young sorceress lowered her gaze, trying to hide her eyes behind the wisps of hair which had pulled free of her braid. She stood and, mindful of the tether, stepped forward.

But Renity could tell that her gaze was fixed on the knife resting at her side, and just as she cleared the fire, the young sorceress lunged for it. Renity's hand shot out and grabbed her former friend by the throat, immediately halting her charge.

Shifting her weight and unfolding her legs, Renity stood in one fluid motion. The young sorceress pulled at her stone grip and made gurgling sounds.

She drew Neola up close to her face. "I have a potion in my bag which will put you to sleep for several days, but hauling you around would be quite an inconvenience. It would be preferable to have you carry your own weight...but not if I have to fight you every step of the way. You decide which way it will be."

Renity released her grip. The young sorceress stumbled and fell, landing on her backside. For just a moment, Renity again felt that emptiness in her chest. She pushed it aside.

Neola glared at her captor. "Who are you!" she croaked, rubbing her throat. "Why have you taken me prisoner?"

Renity shrugged. "My name is unimportant. And I captured you at the command of my mistress the Stone Sorceress. I do not really know what she wants, nor is it my place to question. But I suspect she wants to take your powers for herself." Renity picked up a stick and stirred the fire. "Some say she is a demoness."

"Then, you must be a demoness, too." Neola frowned. "You should be dead now. My sword was true."

Renity shook her head, the mask rattling from side to side. "No," she said. "I am as human as you...only better." The warrior stood and undid the ties on the front of her shirt. Pulling it open, she revealed the ugly scar running between her breasts. "You see, I have no heart. My mistress has removed my weak point. I feel no pain and I do not bleed. Emotion does not color my decisions." She closed her shirt. "I am the perfect warrior," she stated flatly.

Neola twisted her mouth in revulsion. "It also means you feel no love, no joy, no compassion. I hardly call *that* human!"

Renity threw the stick onto the fire where it quickly caught. "For a warrior...feelings are a liability."

The young sorceress glared at Renity with a smoldering rage. "Courage and loyalty are a warrior's best weapons. Without them, you are nothing."

Renity did not rise to the argument. "Believe what you will."

Neola, sensing this tack was fruitless, drew up her legs and laid her forehead on her knees. She sat that way for a long time. Renity had thought she had fallen asleep. Finally, she looked back up at Renity. "Why do you wear a mask? Your voice is...familiar. Are you hiding something from me?"

Renity paused before answering. "I wear this mask at my mistress's order, so you will have to ask her that question herself."

Neola studied the ground for a moment and then looked up at her curiously. "I don't know much about magic yet, but removing all of someone's heart is not possible. You would become as lifeless as a stone without some part it. Your mistress must have left some tiny piece of it intact."

Renity sat back down cross-legged. She did not immediately reply. "My mistress does not lie."

Neola leaned forward. "Your mistress had to leave part of it so you would remain loyal. Otherwise, you might kill her."

"My mistress does not lie," Renity repeated a little louder. The emptiness in her chest began to grow. It almost burned.

Neola leaned forward onto her hands and knees, her face coming closer. "Even with a piece of a heart, the laws of the Goddess Mother will gradually begin to exert themselves, slowly turning you to stone. It's only a matter of time before you die."

"My mistress does not lie!" Renity shouted. She backhanded Neola, sending her sprawling.

Neola slowly picked herself up and dabbed at the blood leaking from the corner of her lips. She turned to look at the warrior though the loose strands of her hair. "If your mistress doesn't lie, then why did you just get angry?"

Renity stared at her in silent contemplation, the burning in her chest gradually diminishing.

She didn't know.

For the next three days, Renity directed her captive through the forest along a barely discernible path. And each day, her spirited captive tried her best to escape; she was very resourceful—just like the younger version the warrior remembered. But she was no match for Renity's strength and quickness.

But as the attempts grew more daring, Renity reluctantly decided she had no choice but to tie her hands behind her back. In fact, she wondered why she had delayed so long. Could there be something to what the young sorceress had said? That a piece of her heart was still intact and had clouded her judgment? Renity resolved to speak to the Stone Sorceress about it.

On the fourth day, their path intersected a rough, but well-worn road, and they travelled down it. At about mid-afternoon, a mark in the dirt caught Renity's eye. She went down on one knee and examined the ground.

"What is it?" asked the young sorceress.

"Nothing," answered Renity, looking at the signs of a recent scuffle.

"I'm not blind," Neola spat. "I can see that there was a fight here. Looks like it happened just a short time ago."

Renity considered her for a moment before answering. "There is a group of bandits that haunts this section. I'm sure you know the kind. Once, they mistook me for easy prey and I was forced to reduce their numbers by a third." She rose and dusted off her hands. "I had hoped to avoid them this day." She placed her pouch on the ground and drew her sword. "Stay here while I see what lies ahead." She turned and walked down the road.

The young sorceress pulled on bound hands and nearly stumbled over her tethered ankles. "You're just going to leave me like this?"

Renity looked back. "Yes." She resumed walking down the road.

The warrior had only gone a little way when she heard voices. Male voices. She stood perfectly still and listened. The voices seemed to be coming from just off the road up ahead. She moved tentatively closer, using the brush beside the road for concealment. When she peered through it, she had her suspicions confirmed: it was the thieves. She and her prisoner would have to detour.

There was the barely audible snap of a twig behind her. Renity whirled with sword held ready, to find a sentry with a crude spear aimed right at her. He shouted and charged, the spear coming uncomfortably close to her face. Renity barely knocked the spear aside in time, but not before he caught the edge of her mask. It flew off. In counterstroke, she swiftly felled the man. But the others, having been alerted, broke from their camp and sprang after her.

Renity grabbed up her mask, not having time to put it back on, and sprinted down the road. She risked a look back and counted ten or twelve men chasing her. She wondered if she could outrun them. If they caught her, despite her strength and agility, they would overpower her.

She ran back towards her captive who was still standing defenseless in the middle of the road. She would be easy pickings for the horde running after her. She would have to free Neola so she could fend for herself.

"Run!" Renity shouted.

Neola's eyes grew large as they took in her naked face. *"Renity! It's you!"*

"Yes, you fool. Now *run!*"

Immediately the young sorceress turned and tried to run, careful not to trip over her tethered feet.

Renity scooped up her sack of belongings and quickly closed the distance to her captive. The warrior then deftly sliced the bonds on her hands and between her ankles while the sorceress was still moving. "Into the forest and run like you mean it," Renity shouted.

"This horde will not show mercy, but I think they'll be more interested in me."

Neola didn't argue but fled off the road and into the bushes. Renity glanced behind her and resumed running down the road. *I should take refuge in the forest,* she thought. *But I need to lead them away from Neola.*

Renity risked a look back. The one in the lead was close, but she appeared to be winning... Suddenly, her foot landed badly in a rut in the road. Her ankle turned and she fell. She picked herself up, but was immediately tackled from behind. She landed face-first, the rocks painfully scraping her face. Her pack, mask, and sword were knocked loose and sailed into a nearby bush. The man rolled off and rose to his feet, pulling a knife from his belt. Renity leaped up and, barehanded, faced him in a fighting crouch.

He feinted once, twice, then charged. She knocked the knife aside, but not before it struck her shoulder and ripped open her shirt. Surprisingly, it didn't sink in beyond her shirt. It instead scraped along a patch of hard skin. Renity was surprised at this. That patch had not been there just two days ago.

The surprised man jerked back, giving Renity an opening. She grabbed him around the throat and threw him aside. Renity then turned her attention on the advancing wave. Unarmed, it wasn't going to be much of a battle.

"HERE!" came an unexpected voice.

She looked to her right in time to see her sword arcing through the air towards her. A grinning Neola stood beside the road.

Renity plucked it out of the air and examined the weapon as if it were the first one she had seen. *Why had she done that?* But she quickly recovered and stepped towards her attackers. Neola had found the pack and she took up her own sword. She stood easily beside her.

The leader of their attackers urged his men to stop. Most did, but two foolish men came anyway. Renity and Neola made quick work of them. The rest of their numbers fled.

With the threat past, Renity turned to gaze at Neola. Neola nervously returned the gaze; she seemed close to tears. "Renity, what have they done to you? Your shoulder. Your face."

Renity gave her a puzzled look. "My face? What is wrong with my face?"

Neola stepped forward, took her left arm, and turned it towards her. "It looks like this. You have a patch running up the left side of your face."

Renity was surprised to see that a streak of skin, running up her arm, had turned hard and gray—like stone.

"Without a heart, you're becoming cold and inflexible." Neola shifted and squinted into the sun. "You're turning to stone."

Renity felt that emptiness in her chest. As if something wanted to stir.

Neola put a hand on Renity's shoulder. "Come with me back to Percillius. The Priestesses there can help you..."

"NO!"

Renity swung around and drove her fist into the side of the young sorceress's head. She fell back stunned. Renity quickly turned her on her belly and rebound her hands. "I told you not having a heart had advantages. I thank you for your assistance, but I feel no obligation to reward you."

She stepped back while an amazed Neola twisted to look at her.

Renity continued, "You are still my captive."

The night was quiet except for the sounds of frogs and crickets. Overhead the stars were clearly visible through the break in the trees, but in the southern sky, one could see dim flashes of light from a distant thunderstorm. Renity hoped it didn't rain. She didn't like rain.

Across from her, sitting on a fallen tree, Neola stared at their campfire. Her hair had finally come loose from her braid and now hung down in her face, hiding her eyes.

"Why did you do it, Renity?" asked Neola, continuing to stare at the fire. "Why did you have your heart ripped out?"

Renity was sitting cross-legged on the ground. She stirred uncomfortably and readjusted the mask. With her secret now out, she wasn't exactly sure why she still wore it. "After I left the guard, I went home to find men outside my mother's door demanding their silver. Apparently, Father had taken to borrowing here and there. When they left, she had only a rickety hut, her three children, and a meager plot of stone-filled land."

Renity sighed, feeling that old familiar emptiness in her chest. "For a year, I helped Mother wrestle our crops from the land, but it was a losing battle. I finally went looking for work to help my family. When I heard a certain sorceress was looking for a bodyguard, I immediately offered myself to her. She said I was too inexperienced. But if I were willing to have my heart removed and become the perfect warrior, she would consider me. I agreed immediately. My family received a handsome payment and I went with the Stone Sorceress."

Neola's head snapped up. "But you're not the perfect warrior! You're cold and unfeeling—nothing like the girl I once knew. And don't you see you're gradually turning to stone!"

Renity shrugged. "It does not matter. My heart is gone. And I must serve my mistress."

Neola came off her log and knelt before Renity. "But don't you see? It's not too late. Just from the way you're acting, I can tell she didn't remove all your heart! And it's trying to heal."

"The Stone Sorceress said..."

Neola shook her head. "When I was a child, my mother cut down a tree outside our home. She said she needed the wood and didn't like the vermin that lived inside it. All winter long I watched that dry lifeless stump. But when spring arrived, it came to life and sent out new shoots. I think your heart is trying to do the same. It's trying to send out new shoots. It's trying to regrow. All you need to do is try to *feel*."

Renity shook her head. The inside of her chest began to burn. She ignored it. "You are wrong."

Neola stood and stared at her for several moments. A sudden flash of lightning illuminated her face and made her eyes sparkle. "Am I?"

Neola hesitated at the threshold of the cave, reluctant to enter through the door-sized opening. Renity put a hand on her shoulder and gently urged her forward into its dark recesses. The warrior understood Neola's hesitation. Although she herself had been inside many times, one never got used to it.

As the outside light quickly vanished, torches, set high on the rock walls in iron holders, took over the illumination. But they burned with an unnatural flame, which flickered in hues of dull gray and radiated a harsh white light. It gave the surrounding walls a sickly look and caused ghostly shadows to stalk one's path.

They continued through the cave until it suddenly opened into a larger chamber with the finest construction Renity had ever seen. The room's curving rock walls had been smoothed to head height and, in places, carved with elegant designs. Plus the floor had been leveled and tiled with polished marble. More of the sickly lamps were spaced around the room, providing their ghostly illumination. And the room's echo made one think something was right behind one. The chamber had always reminded Renity more of a tomb than a dwelling.

The room's only flaw was a large ravine—wider than a person could jump—at the back of the chamber. From the cold air it breathed, and the absolute blackness within, the ravine appeared quite deep.

A waist-high slab of polished stone occupied the chamber's center. And on a raised platform behind it, on a throne of polished iron and inlaid jewels, sat a robed and hooded figure who, from the swell of her chest, appeared to be a woman. In her hand, she held a scepter which had a lifelike snake curling around its end. The hand which held it was that of a perfectly carved statue. Renity dropped to one knee before the throne. "Mistress, I have done as you asked. Here is the woman you requested."

"Good!" came the booming reply. The woman's face and hands were hidden within the dark recesses of her hood. "I have been anxiously awaiting your arrival. Place her on the slab."

Renity nodded deeply. "I will have to re-bind her hands in front of her." The warrior stood and drew a length of rope from her pack. She faced Neola. "Do not resist. It will go easier for you."

As Renity retied her hands, Neola leaned around her and spoke to the sorceress. "What are you going to do with me? Drink my blood or eat my flesh?"

The Stone Sorceress sighed. Painfully slow, she leaned forward and gradually stood. The sound of grating stone accompanied her every move. "Nothing so primitive. I am simply going to take your magic to replenish my own. As you can probably guess, I have exhausted mine and this body is badly in need of repair." She carefully stepped down from the dais. "Unfortunately, I must kill you to release it."

Renity looked up from tying Neola hands and straight into her friend's eyes. For just a moment, their gaze locked. "You don't have to do this," whispered Neola. "You can still change your mind."

Renity nodded, feeling that emptiness in her chest. "Yes, I could."

"Then let me go."

Renity shook her head. "I can't. I'm the perfect warrior now and I must obey." She promptly picked Neola up and placed her on the slab.

To her credit, Neola didn't struggle, but lay there calmly, gazing at her friend with wide, disbelieving eyes. Renity ripped open Neola's shirt and stepped to the opposite side of the slab so her mistress would not have to walk around.

Painfully slow, the Stone Sorceress stepped up to the slab. She reached up and pushed back her hood to reveal the stone likeness of a woman's head, complete with hair and eyebrows. Only this one's eyes moved. From within her sleeve, the Stone Sorceress produced a long, extremely sharp knife with an ornate hilt of gold and inlaid jewels. The blade was engraved with tiny skulls. Her mistress extended the knife on the flat of her hand.

"I need you to plunge this knife into her chest," said the voice from inside the hood. "As she dies, I will take in her magic."

Renity felt that twinge in her chest, only it was stronger, mildly burning. She slowly shook her head. "Mistress, I do not think I can do it well."

"It doesn't have to be done well, just done. Now do it!"

Renity dipped her head in submission and picked up the knife. Its blade seemed to vibrate with a power of its own.

Neola looked up at her with tears in her eyes. "Renity, I know you're still a good person inside...and I forgive you. I will travel to the Goddess with the thought that you are still my friend."

Renity's eyes were drawn to the pulse beating in Neola's neck. It was pulsating rapidly. Renity jerked her eyes back towards her target and centered on Neola's breastbone. Renity resisted the urge to place a hand on her own chest. The burning had continued and seemed to be growing worse. She raised the knife over her friend's chest.

"Hurry!" ordered the Stone Sorceress. "Strike now!" Closing her eyes, the sorceress raised her arms from the elbows and stretched them out over Neola. Renity could feel the magic building.

Neola continued to stare at Renity with her large wet eyes.

The warrior licked her lips, the pain in her own chest growing to unbearable proportions. She thought she was going to be sick. She raised her hand to her chest and rubbed her breastbone. And noticed something was missing. Something that should be hanging there, wasn't...

She looked down and saw that the necklace the Stone Sorceress had given her was gone. And probably had been since the fight with the thieves. Renity looked at her friend in disbelief. Neola could have used her powers against her at any time. Yet, she hadn't. "Why?" she mouthed to her friend.

"Because you're my friend," Neola whispered.

"Kill her, now!" yelled the Stone Sorceress.

And then suddenly Renity felt something approaching. Felt it as if it were coming from a great distance, like a sneeze that had been building, like an itch that begged to be scratched. The pain in her chest suddenly stopped and she heard...

Thump...thump.

She felt the warm rush of life course though her.

Thump...thump.

She felt the coldness flee from her fingers and toes.

Thump...thump

She felt a tear slowly slide down her cheek.

The Stone Sorceress's eyes flung open and locked with Renity's. She knew instantly what had happened. "No!" screamed the Stone Sorceress, shaking the chamber with her fury.

Renity immediately reached up and ripped off her mask. She leaned across and slammed it down on top of the sorceress's head. Her mistress staggered back heavily.

Renity pulled Neola off her side of the slab and used the sacrificial knife to cut her bonds. On the other side of the slab, she heard the mask hit the ground.

"Run!" she shouted. "I'll hold her off as long as I can."

Neola scrambled up and Renity rose to confront her former mistress. But as Neola ran towards the entrance, the Stone Sorceress raised her staff and tracked her path. A blast of light erupted from its end, sending Neola sprawling.

Renity gritted her teeth. She ran around the slab and grabbed the sorceress from behind, lifting her upwards with all her might, and began to carry her towards the ravine.

"Put me down!" commanded the sorceress, struggling weakly. She was too inflexible to resist.

"You stole my heart!" Renity yelled at her. "You told me that I would be the perfect warrior."

"You are perfect!" she yelled, her struggles becoming more violent as they neared the edge. "You're perfect just like me!"

Renity stopped just at the edge of the ravine and felt the cool air blowing in her face. "You're sadly mistaken," she said. "You're broken." She released the sorceress, who toppled towards the abyss. The cave shook with the sorceress's scream as she fell, but it ended abruptly at the bottom.

Renity turned and went over to her friend. Turning her over, she found Neola still breathing. Slowly her eyes fluttered open and locked on Renity. "The Stone Sorceress?" she whispered.

"Gone," said Renity.

Neola nodded weakly. "I'll be all right in a few moments. Just let me catch my breath." She smiled. "It's good to have you back."

Renity smiled back awkwardly. "It's good to be back... friend."

TOTEM NIGHT

by Deborah J. Ross

Deborah started writing stories in the 4th grade, some time around the Mesozoic Era, and kept on writing through degrees in biology and psychology, work as a bacteriologist, a librarian, and a preschool gym teacher. In between two children, a black belt in kung fu, and a chiropractic career, she's sold two novels and three dozen short stories. Her two novels from DAW are JAYDIUM and NORTHLIGHT Some recent/forthcoming short stories are "Transfusion" (Realms of Fantasy, 8/95), "Survival Skills" (SISTERS OF THE NIGHT, Warner), "Unmasking the Ancient Light" (ANCIENT ENCHANTRESSES, DAW), "Sing to Me of Love and Shadows" (RETURN TO AVALON , DAW), and "Goatgrass" (TALES FROM JABBA'S PALACE, Bantam Spectra). She lives in Los Angeles with her husband, two daughters, one physicist, and two cats. Raul, who visits her home occasionally when he travels south, tells me the meals there are wonderful, so she must be a good cook as well as a fine author.

   This story is about learning who you really are and trying not to be too surprised by the answer.
   —MZB

The night was darker than she expected. Darker and colder. Frostmist haloed the stars. As she pulled her sheepswool *ruach'* tight around her shoulders, Xiera wished, not for the first time, that she'd paid as much attention to her weaving as to her wizardry.

She had traveled, alone and unarmed, from Choa'tlexa at the edge of the Harvest Plains and into the barren mountains of Hua'tha's Curse. At the fifth setting of Choa'tl's Eye, she came across the circle of fallen stones. When she touched one, a spark crackled, stinging her hand. Her fingertips came away, covered in acrid dust. She sat crosslegged in the center of the circle and composed herself.

It will come, she reminded herself. *My totem will come to me.* Everything so far had been exactly as her teachers foretold, the journey to Hua'tha's Curse, the moonless night, this place of power.

Moments crept by, bleeding into one another. The earth shivered, so light a ripple that she might not have noticed if she hadn't been sitting so still. It was the third tremor that hour, each one raising it own false hope.

A speck of silver winked along the western ridge. Heartbeats followed one another. The mote of light elongated into a circle, quickly followed by the second moonlet.

"The Kiss of the Twins," a man's voice spoke from the night, velvet-smooth. Darkness masked his face, as coppery as her own. She'd never known a life without him, from her earliest memories of following, playing and fighting with him and his brothers, sleeping on the mounded carpets of the children's tent, curled together like puppies.

Only later, as her wizardry stirred and her body changed, so did Xiera's feelings for him, and his for her. She wept when the elders sent her to Choa'tlexa with its towers, stepped pyramidal temples and markets, as priests, traders, artisans and wizards bustled along the narrow stone streets. She wept again when Tl'al followed her three years later. His beauty burned as sharp as the sun, as did the answering fire within her. That was the last time she had wept, for wizardry kills tears.

"Tl'al! What are you doing here?"

His lips brushed hers, melting sweetness to fuel her rising irritation. She wanted him gone, to have this sacred time all to herself. Once this night was passed, once she was sealed to her totem, she could use her power to do as she wished.

"I'm supposed to be alone!"

"I just wanted to make sure—" another kiss, lips gliding over hers, "—that you wouldn't forget."

She couldn't breathe.

He said, "People come back from Totem Night *changed*."

Of course people came back changed. They came back wizards.

Summoning all the patience of her wizard's discipline, she pointed to the Twins. "Within the hour their paths will bring them so close, they will embrace. You must be safely gone by then."

"I know. Or the initiation will be spoiled." Tl'al sighed, repeating the words she'd said to him, the reason she must remain virgin for this night. "But no one knows if they really touch."

When she knew, by the quality of the silence, he had left, she turned her face once more to the heavens.

Moving in a solemn dance, the moonlets approached one another. Xiera's heart raced and she forgot Tl'al, forgot the cold, the hardness of the rocks, the emptiness in her stomach, the soreness of her feet. Forgot everything except the glow, brightening with every passing moment until the two orbs blurred into a single point of radiance. Her eyes watered with staring at it. As she rose to her feet, the *ruach'* fell away, leaving her naked except for a narrow silk belt, knotted according to her wizardry lineage, needing only this night for the final pattern.

A droplet of light separated from the fused moonlets, dipping and then rising, slowly growing in size. Xiera closed her eyes, praying to Choa'tl of the Harvest Sun and Her consort, the double-tongued serpent, Hu'atha. From the depths of her wizard's heart, she asked that her totem be wise and powerful... and just a little bit beautiful, too.

When she blinked, the light was almost upon her, hovering just beyond reach. The body of a plains deer it had, with a proud arched neck and flowing tail, rounded hooves and wings. Wings rippled in syncopated beats, three on each side, attached along the sharply ridged spine. Feathers glimmered, iridescent. The creature was unmistakably male.

He came lower. She saw the eyes, dark as a starless sky, and the single milky nub of a horn. Curved eyeteeth showed between its lips. The smell arising from his body reminded Xiera of wildflowers, of autumn honey, of blood.

Xiera sank to her knees. She had no idea anything could be so beautiful and so terrible. It was too late for flight or indecision, for she had prayed the creature into her heart. In all the centuries of wizard-lore, no one had ever been sent such a totem. She didn't know if such creatures had a name.

Then I will give you one. You will be mine, my beauty, my teacher, my guide. And I will be yours...

The beast drew nearer, head dipping, nostrils flaring to take in her scent. Breath flowed over her bare skin. Xiera tingled all over.

Fire sparked in the dark eyes. With a *whuff*! the creature's head shot up, turning, ears pricked. Muscles tightened beneath the silver-lit hide. Wings hesitated, then beat faster.

"It's all right..." Xiera said softly, glad that her voice did not betray the pounding in her chest. "Here, come here to me."

Ears swiveled in her direction. As if drawn by a lodestone, the creature approached her once more.

A sound like leather on wood, like willow branches breaking under a killer frost, shot through the stillness. With a scream, the beast threw himself backwards. The light from his body shifted from moony silver to Choa'tl's gold.

Xiera froze. Her eyes focused on the rope now tightening around the creature's throat. A second noose settled behind his ears and a third caught one forefoot. The beast reared and screamed again. Red streaks laced his hide. One of the ropes around his neck snapped clean through.

"Hoald heem!" came a voice, unmistakably female. The accent sounded like trader's *ling*.

The next moment, the creature fell heavily on its side.

"The rope, damn you!" the other woman yelled. "Are you blind?"

Xiera threw herself to her knees beside the creature, terrified that he would injure himself, break one of those impossibly slender legs, strangle on the ropes. With both hands, she stroked the taut, quivering neck. Immediately, the creature calmed.

"Be still, my beauty," she crooned, blessing any power that would listen for her steady voice. But she had no knife, no hand axe. Weapons were forbidden for the totem journey.

Too frantic to think straight, Xiera tugged at the knots with her bare hands. The coarse rope tore the skin on her fingers. The second neck rope, which had been slack, went tight.

"Ha!" The other woman stepped from behind the largest of the fallen stones. She was dressed outland style, all in leather, breeches tucked into scuffed, patched boots, and a jacket missing most of its metal studs. Her head had been shaved in stripes, now grown to a fuzz.

She pushed Xiera aside, with a few practiced movements bound the creature's foreleg to the opposite rear foot, and slipped a rope halter over his head. She knotted a strip of cloth over his eyes.

"*What have you done?*" Xiera cried. Her hands curled into fists, but she held herself back. She must spill no blood on Totem Night, least the wizardry in her veins turn to evil. "Let him go!"

"Let him go?" The woman put her hands on her hips, threw back her head, and laughed. "It's the luck of a lifetime, a big strong buck like him. Why, his balls alone will fetch a thousand, maybe more, in Rindar!"

"B—balls?"

"Balls, horn, liver. You did well, my girl, keeping him quiet for me. I thought I'd have a real fight on my hands." She jabbed the creature's flank with one boot. He thrashed once, then lay still, breathing heavily. "It'll take a bit for the potion in the blindfold to do its work. Then I can handle him without all these ropes and we'll be on our way."

Xiera's thoughts began to clear. "Where do you mean to take him?"

"Rindar," the other woman repeated, as if speaking to a simpleton. "The gentles there are crazy for any kind of strange meat, when all that really ails them is being too damned inbred. Me, I can't tell the difference between horsemeat, unicorn, or shoe leather. Give me a nice fat goose anytime."

Unicorn... The word rang like a bell. Xiera touched the mane, felt the strands like unspun wool. "I never knew unicorns had wings."

"What wings?"

The huntress unbuttoned her jacket and took out a wide-mouthed glass jar and a short, curved knife. Before Xiera could stop her, she set the inner edge of the knife against the base of the unicorn's horn and sliced it off.

The light from the unicorn's body vanished. He lay still, unprotesting. Only his breath, hesitant and shuddering, revealed that he still lived.

The huntress lifted the stoppered jar with an air of satisfaction. Within its murky red depths, a pale light glimmered. Xiera wondered what creature had given its blood to preserve the unicorn horn.

The other woman untied the unicorn's neck and legs, keeping a firm hold on the halter rope. When she removed the blindfold and slapped the end of one rope against its sides, the unicorn heaved himself to his feet and stood, legs splayed, head down. Eyes dimmed, as if unseeing.

"Pl— please!" Xiera stammered. By Choa'tl and Hu'atha and their thousand offspring, what could she do? Take on this armed outlander with her bare hands? "Name your price!"

"More money than you'll ever see!" The woman jerked on the halter rope. The unicorn took a single step forward and set its feet. "Balls! I'll have to drag him the whole way!"

"Then let me come with you." Xiera gathered up her *ruach'*. "To care for him. He'll come easy for me, less work for you."

At her words, the unicorn dipped his muzzle between her breasts. His breath swept over her, sweet and warm.

"I don't owe you any favors in return," the huntress said, her voice guarded.

"I don't care."

"You'll freeze your tits off."

"I don't care."

The huntress lowered her voice. "It won't make any difference in the end, you being there."

Xiera held her tongue. She *did* care.

They went on a little while, sliding and skittering down the trail, the huntress in front, the rope slack. Xiera kept her hand on the unicorn's neck.

Not far, tucked in a shadowed cleft of rock, they came to the huntress's camp. A strange beast, humped and three-horned, jerked awake at their approach. Tied to a fallen tree, the unicorn folded its legs and lowered itself to the ground beside the banked fire.

"We'll move out at first light. I hope you travel fast. You can wear my spare shirt and breeches. No so new, but they're clean."

Xiera shivered and pulled her *ruach'* more tightly around her. A garment of her own weaving was all that ritual allowed on Totem Night. Rather than being told again that she'd freeze her tits off if she refused, she asked, "Do you have a name?"

"Josselinda, that's what my mam gave me. Most folk call me Joss, when they call me anything. Suit yourself."

Xiera blinked in surprise. She knew by the signs in Joss's voice that she'd spoken her soul-name.

Joss squatted beside the log and leaned back. "You're such an innocent. You're thinking you can witch me by my name. Ha!" She closed her eyes and pretended to snore.

Xiera sank to her knees beside the unicorn. She rested her head against the creature's flank. Its warmth enveloped her. Joss was right and she was wrong. A soul-name carried power, but power which Xiera, so close to her totem and so far, could not wield. Yet.

Embers fell, rustling. Xiera's eyes flew open. For an instant, she thought she'd slept through the night, that the color misting across the sky heralded dawn. But the light was cold and blue, with no trace of Choa'tl's gold, and it quivered with the singing of the stars. She'd never dreamed such glory, such harmony. Her eyes caught a second source of radiance, the human body curled at her side, one slender hand entwined in her mane.

One foreleg and then the other, hindquarters beneath her, Xiera rose to her feet. Her nostrils flared, filled with the flowery pungency of virginity, the dying prayers of the tree whose embers faded in the firepit, the mute misery of the tri-horn, dreaming of lumbering free on the far high-desert, dreaming of rutting females, of *noa'chal* heavy with seed...

One scent drew her most of all, a soul-scent layered with pain and pride and soul-iron, complex like wine that had lain in the temple cellars for many seasons.

The light from girl's body died. On the other side of the camp, Joss scrambled upright and caught hold of the halter. The coarse rope bit into Xiera's tender nose. She *whuffled* in indignation.

"So you've still got spirit in you!" Another jerk.

Xiera spread her wings and fanned them to their full display before she remembered that Joss could not see them. Emotions surged through her—fury and pride and things she had no human names for. With the transformation, the drug had cleared from her unicorn's blood and already she could feel the nub of a new horn on her forehead.

Give in. Don't waste your strength. Xiera forced herself to lower her head, blowing as if even this small show of rebellion had left her exhausted.

As the girl stood up, Xiera sensed her fleeting confusion. She dipped her muzzle, caught the rush of hot blood to the girl's cheeks as she felt the moist warm breath across her uncovered breasts. The girl reached one hand to lightly stroke Xiera's arched neck.

"That's right," Joss said, breathing hard. "Keep him under control."

The huntress turned back to her place at the log, where she'd left her sword—

—and came up short as Tl'al pressed its tip to the base of her throat, the little cup where the collarbones met.

"Easy, boy," Joss said, a wary edge to her voice. "Just put the pig-sticker down."

In reply, Tl'al nicked her. Blood made a slender dark ribbon down her chest.

Xiera had seen Tl'al throw and truss a wild plains sheep, who were far less docile than Joss was now. It would take Joss hours to work free once he was done with her. All the while the unicorn-girl gazed at him with such wonder and such hunger...

They raced through the dark, Xiera leading the way. Her unicorn eyes saw colors she'd never known existed. Her unicorn muscles flexed powerfully, untiring, and her feet never slipped on the rock. The others followed the pearly beacon of her body.

When they slowed to draw breath, Tl'al talked in low, soothing tones to the girl, the girl he thought was Xiera.

By Hu'atha of the Double Tongues! Xiera had no idea how she was going to tell him that he was talking to a unicorn, a *male* unicorn. Once they were safe, she'd have to find some way to sort things out. That assumed she still could, once Totem Night had passed.

They came around a bend as the trail plunged toward the Harvest Plains. The very air here tasted different, warm and heavy, smelling of pollen-thick plainsgrass.

Home...

But not hers any longer. Instinctively, she knew that once she returned, she would become as dull and drowsy as any ordinary wingless, hornless beast.

She paused to think and let the humans rest. Choa'tlexa's lights glowed below them like bits of amber. Far behind, she sensed Joss free herself and gather her weapons, her ropes.

Tl'al had taken the unicorn-girl into his arms. Xiera remembered how it felt, her body melting against his, the sweet fire of his lips brushing hers, trailing down her neck, the answering fire within herself—

Within the unicorn-girl, too.

Acolytes returned from Totem Night *changed*. She had always assumed the change came from the initiation itself, the mystical bonding to one's totem. A dizzying thought struck her, that perhaps the spirit which now drew Tl'al into an even deeper embrace, was not at all that of a unicorn, but of an untried wizard just like herself—young, passionate, impatient, arrogant with her own wizardry.

Xiera pawed the ground, snorted. Shook her head, sending her mane flying.

Tl'al turned to watch her. His puzzled expression quickly faded as the unicorn-girl drew his hand beneath the *ruach'*. Tl'al tilted his pelvis and pressed against her. Xiera could feel his hardness, his strength, the rush of delirium in the girl's own body. The girl's eyes met Xiera's for an instant.

Xiera could not guess how long the girl had been held captive in this unicorn's body, waiting for the next virgin wizard to come searching on Totem Night. And how long would it take her to find another body?

On the dark mountain trails, Joss spurred her three-horned beast to the chase. Vibrations shivered through earth and air, heart and hoof and stone.

Unicorns came to the pure, the innocent, the maiden. Joss was hardly that, nor was she wizard-trained, but beneath that brassy exterior lay a host of other interesting possibilities. One could be innocent in many ways. Even a hardened heart must long for something. And Joss had so casually spoken her soul-name, secure in the belief that Xiera could not use it against her.

Of course, Joss would want to bind the unicorn and take him to Rindar to be slaughtered for the delicate palates of the gentles. That would only make the challenge more interesting.

Or she could disappear into the heights, lose herself in Hu'atha's Curse, remain a unicorn until Choa'tl closed Her Eye forever.

Being a mystical beast was all very well, but she hadn't trained as a wizard to spend eternity star-gazing. Besides, she owed Joss something.

Freeze my tits off, indeed!

Xiera tossed her head. Wings beat with slow, sure force her until her hooves barely touched the gritty earth. *Later*, she promised herself, when her horn had fully regrown.

But not, she thought as she eyed the entwined couple, too much later.

RAVEN'S BLADE

by Raul S. Reyes

Raul S. Reyes has worked for Marion Zimmer Bradley since 1987. It's a job more varied and hectic than his previous ones: Police Officer in Berkeley, CA, and accountant at the University of California/Berkeley. The latter, however, did serve him well the day one of Marion's children threatened to turn him into an accountant (I guess a frog wasn't original enough) and Raul just smiled and said, "I am an accountant."

Raul is also known for his interest in things non-Western (he collects Kimono). This interest often results in unusual settings for his stories. In addition he has an interest in architecture, especially the work of Frank Lloyd Wright. Other interests are the space program and science, shooting, ikebana, brush and ink Zen paintings, and history. He is an avid X-Files fan, which accounts for the photo on his web site—it was taken while he was in costume for an X-Files party.

Raul was part of a writing circle with Cynthia McQuillin and Heather Rose Jones. Their critiques helped hone his fine story "Raven", which was printed in Marion Zimmer Bradley's FANTASY Magazine*, issue 32.*

So far he has had only short stories published, ranging from fantasy to SF to mystery. In his spare time he is currently working on a pair of novels, one hard SF and the other fantasy. What he works on depends on what kind of a day it's been.
   —Elisabeth Waters

The sword was mounted in the old Tachi style, ornate in gold fittings and black lacquer. It supposedly housed the spirit of a *tengu*, a bird-faced demon. Some people believed that. Even more *said* they believed it. Reiko was one of the few who knew the truth, and the knowledge made a chill run down her spine. For a moment she hesitated, racking her mind for another alternative. But in truth there was no other way, and so she unrolled the ancient scroll slowly and carefully, so as not to damage the brittle paper. The writing on it was archaic, the ink faint and difficult to make out in the dim light of the temple lamps. Slowly, piecing out the words one by one, she began to chant.

The vessel tacked out of the fog and into the bay at dawn, dark against the rising sun that gave the land its name. The ship was dark of hull, and dark of sail, as if a part of the night had lingered on into the daylight. Men on shore looked on as it glided to anchor just offshore and some, more insightful than others, shivered. Tadeo gazed at the ship from his perch atop a rocky crag that overlooked the water and his hands moved under his kimono robe, fingering the prayer beads hidden there. *So she has done it*, he thought. The dice had been tossed. Now they would see how the game would be played out.

On board the vessel weathered and wiry crewmen furled the sail and dropped anchor, while others manned a long and narrow boat with a high bow and stern. When their lone passenger was on board they paddled ashore with powerful and rhythmic strokes, running the bow up on the sand with a final flurry of paddling. Their passenger jumped ashore and walked up to the village.

He was lean and dark, and left tracks on the sand that were no different from those of other men. Still they looked odd, spidery and birdlike, very much at odds with the build of the man who made them. His face was that of the foreigners from across the sea, but men had an impression of a nose that was even larger and more hooked than those of the seafaring merchants who sometimes visited their shores, and of eyes that were darker and more far-seeing than those of other men.

He was dressed like the rest of his crew in bearhide boots and soft dark leathers that protected him from the wind and driving mist, but the silk-clad nobles watching him did not feel the usual disregard for barbarian traders that was their wont. He moved gracefully, and was armed only with a flint dagger at his hip and a short wide-bladed spear with the head made of chipped obsidian, but something in him stayed the hands of the young warriors who waited among the small knot of men at the high water mark on the sand. Their swords, curved and deadly, were more than a match for his spear. But something told them they weren't....

The stranger stopped a few steps away from the small party awaiting him and sketched a small bow that was just short of discourteous.

"Honored Ones, this one is called Tanaksan, and has come long and far to trade with your village, and learn of your wisdom, of which we have heard."

"You are welcome here. We welcome honest traders and true seekers of wisdom. Our markets and our temples are open to those who seek honorable relations with us." That was from Tadeo, the Town Elder and Headman, who all had decided would speak for them. He was expendable if things went wrong, and easily overlooked if they went well.

"We bring cargo from across the sea. May we meet with your merchants to discuss trade?"

"Our merchants will be happy to discuss trade," the Headman replied. "They await you in the town. As for our teachers and sages, they are to be found in the temple just beyond the town gates." As if to underscore his words the distant booming sound of a massive bronze bell rolled down through the fog from the heights above the town.

"It seems to call me," the stranger said with a quick smile. "My Captain will meet with your merchants. May I visit your temple before I begin my business here?"

"I would not hamper a seeker of wisdom," the Headman said. Tanaksan nodded his thanks at that and walked past them toward the path that led past the town and up to the temple. Only Tadeo noted that the stranger had taken the proper path, even though it was not marked. He saw the stranger look back at him and wave. He nodded back, and received a smile in return. Then the stranger resumed his walk uphill to the temple with an easy gait that spoke of long familiarity with hills and mountains.

The temple stood in fog and mist near the top of the hill. Large and with many rooms, it was so well designed and fit so well against the mountainside that its true size was not readily apparent. Ancient pines protected it from the winter winds and shrouded it in shadow. Tanaksan walked up the steps and pushed open one of the thick wooden doors. A pair of lamps provided feeble illumination, but enough for him to make out the woman seated cross-legged at one end of a mat near the far wall. She sat facing away from him, and toward an alcove. A stand in it held a sword and a framed scroll. A slight smile touched his face as he saw them.

"You are amused?" she asked. Her voice was low and clear.

"Men make much of things," Tanaksan replied.

"But are you not also a collector of things? Shells, mirrors, and such?"

"You have heard of me," Tanaksan said.

"And you know much of me?" the woman asked. Abruptly she turned, seating herself properly on her heels, her knees close together under black and white silken robes. She motioned to a spot opposite her on the other end of the mat. Tanaksan left his spear on the floor near the door and approached, seating himself with an easy graceful movement. She noted he sat as she did, on his heels, knees together, as a sign of respect. She cautioned herself not to be swayed by that. He was a trickster, after all...

"This may amuse you," she began. The sudden glint in his eye stopped her attempt at light banter, and she changed course.

"There is a matter of deceit and trickery that afflicts our land." She looked at him, saw that he was listening courteously, and went on, more confident now.

"A year ago our Lord Takeda was wounded by an archer at the siege of a castle. He was taken home to his lands in the mountains of Kai. It is rumored that he died en route, and that his Clan, to fool his enemies and prevent them from taking advantage of his death, substituted an impostor, a man whom nature had favored with our Lord's visage. Under the guidance of the Clan's counselors and generals this man has played the role of our Lord Takeda." She looked at him again, saw him nod for her to go on, and continued. "A man from the Kai domains, who is known to me, claims knowledge and proof that our Lord was indeed killed."

"How would he know?" Tanaksan interrupted.

"He is an aide to the majordomo of the palace," Reiko replied, "and has worked with me before. He is Araki Mataemon, a great swordsman, and his duties take him to all the major cities of this land. He learns much."

"One of your spies," Tanaksan murmured. He smiled to see her blush under the rice powder that was the only make-up she wore. "Do not be upset," he went on. "I too have listened in on talk not meant for my ears, and looked on matters others thought hidden. Lord Takeda did well when he chose you to head one part of his net of spies." He looked around. "Many people visit a temple, and none would see anything out of the ordinary if a visitor paused to talk with the temple attendant. And the head of this temple would have the attendants of other nearby temples under her supervision. Frequent visits from them to you would also not attract undue attention. I'm sure they have much to tell you. I am impressed." She nodded her head at the compliment.

"Also," she added, "our Lord is noted for his piety. Not only has he endowed this temple, as well as others, but he has recently taken holy vows, and is a monk of the Cha'n sect."

"And yet he is still a warrior," Tanaksan said. He might have been amused.

"Araki Mataemon will arrive later this day," Reiko went on, ignoring his comment, "as part of a party from Kai. He will find time to visit the temple and pray for the souls of his ancestors. He does that twice a year."

"I may want to meet him."

"He will be staying at the Three Willow Inn. Tadeo is the owner. He is also the Town Headman."

"I have met him. Others higher in rank let him speak for them. That is unusual."

"These are unusual times," she said. "The land is in turmoil. Armies march from one end to the other. Battles flare up like wildfires in a dry season. Brothers turn on brothers. Sons turn on fathers. Town Headmen speak for nobles."

"Good times for a spy," he observed. With an easy motion he stood. "I will talk with you again later." In moments he was gone, and she turned to look at the sword. But now it was only a blade of steel, encased in wood and gold. No thoughts came to her, no insights or revelations. She dropped her gaze to her hands, and squeezed tightly on the prayer beads she held.

In town the commercial activities were in progress. Both sides had met on the street running the length of the shore. Tanaksan met with Similiuk, his Trader/Captain, the man in charge of the ship and crew.

"It goes well," Similiuk said in reply to Tanaksan's query. "They offer silks and steel knives, both of very high quality. And the lacquered boxes they produce. In return they want furs, amber, and Northern ivory." Tanaksan looked at the old man, still wiry and tough after many years. Two eye-teeth of the Snow-Tiger ringed his silver-gray topknot, a reminder of a wild youth who had long since learned caution. Few Trader/Captains lived long without a good measure of sense to temper their courage. Tanaksan smiled.

"I leave the trades in your able hands, Similiuk," he said. "I will meet with some men who come in later this day." Similiuk suddenly sobered, reminded of who his master was. He nodded in agreement. He would see to the trading. He wanted no part of the rest of their purpose in this land.

Tanaksan looked over at the haggling in the sand and smiled slightly. He liked trading, and the life of a trader. He walked over to join in the scene. Saanlian, a young man with a few trading voyages to the Southern lands, was examining the silks. He was looking disdainfully at the bolts of shimmering cloth.

"Maybe good for wrapping fish for the winter," he said when Tanaksan asked him about the goods. Tanaksan looked in his eyes and saw that his words and manner were for show. The silk was very good, and they would take home quite a few bolts of it. Saanlian was an astute trader, for all his youthful exuberance. In the corner of his eye Tanaksan saw Tadeo.

"Headman," he greeted. "After a long sea voyage we would rest on land. Is there some place here in town where my men and I can stay?" The man tore his eyes off the pelts before him. They were thick, soft, and dazzling, and vastly appealing for people in a wintry land.

"You may stay in my poor place," the Headman said with a deep bow. "It is the Three Willow Inn. I can offer only the poorest of hospitality, but we will do our best."

"I am sure it will be very good," Tanaksan replied. He picked up a handful of furs and gave them to the Headman, ignoring the winces of Saanlian and Similiuk. "I hope these will be a fair trade for food and lodging." The Headman struggled hard to keep his shock from showing. He took the furs with a very deep bow.

"More than fair. It is too much for my poor little inn. You will have the best." Suddenly he recalled the party that would arrive later in the day. His mind raced. He would have to evict some people from their rooms to make space, and forfeit the rent. But the furs would more than make up for it.

"Good," Tanaksan said, and turned away to return to his ship. Similiuk and Saanlian watched him go, privately relieved. He was prone to such extravagant gestures. They returned their thoughts to more restrained, and profitable, trading.

Evening came and the trading ended for the day. A skeleton crew stayed aboard to watch the ship and cargo while the rest of the crew followed Tanaksan into town. The townspeople peered from their windows and doors at the strangers. Traders from across the sea were no novelty, however rare, but they were still odd in their leathers and furs and bearhide boots. The merchant company stopped at a door adorned with an engraving of three willows. After a moment Tadeo came out and bowed low. Tanaksan responded with a courteous, if sketchy, bow.

"Welcome to my humble inn," Tadeo greeted them. "Please enter and make yourselves at ease." He turned and led them into the low-roofed interior.

He may have thought it humble, but to the men who followed him indoors it was a welcome change from the cold and wind-tossed sea. The odor of food being cooked caught their attention and promised surfeit later. The soft mats underfoot would have drawn their boots off even if the customs of the land did not require it. They left their boots, short spears, and heavy jackets in the spaces provided for them near the door and went in. They washed in tubs of hot water brought in from the kitchen and sank thankfully to the soft mats while attractive serving maidens hurried to bring trays of hot steaming food.

It was all good, if odd to their tastes. The rest looked to Tanaksan and Similiuk and followed their lead. The paired sticks provided for handling food were tricky at first, but sailors' hands, adept at knots, easily learned to use them. The savory food was an incentive. And there was a lot of it.

Soup in lacquered bowls came first, and it was hot and flavorful. Pickles came next, spicy and crunchy. The rice, bland and white, puzzled the sailors, but hunger is a good sauce, and they each ate a bowl. The hot noodles, with meat floating in the broth, were greeted with relish, as were the hot steaming rice buns with meat and vegetable fillings. Tadeo was pleased to see his cook's efforts so well received.

"A good meal!" Tanaksan exclaimed as the last of the dishes was taken away. Similiuk and the rest shouted agreement, filling the low room with praise. Tadeo beamed and bowed in thanks, mentally calculating the cost of the furs he had received in payment and seeing a good profit, even allowing for the sailors' appetites. He even considered keeping a pelt or two for himself, despite the sumptuary laws forbidding it. If the authorities couldn't see the lining of a winter kimono, would it matter...?

"Tadeo does make visitors welcome," a quiet voice said from the doorway. Everyone froze. Tanaksan and Similiuk looked over at the door to see who it was. Saanlian, with his hand near his dagger hilt, noted the newcomer wore two swords in his sash, and mentally calculated the distance to the spears in the hallway.

"That he does," Tanaksan agreed with no obvious change in his mood. "He does honor to your land with his hospitality. Will you join us in a drink to his cook?" For a moment there was no answer, then the Samurai shrugged and took out his long sword, leaving it at the door with his companions. In a moment he was sitting with them, and a terrified Tadeo was scurrying to bring warm bottles of sake for his assembled guests.

"I am Tanaksan, of the Haida. A trader with my own ship. This is Similiuk, my Captain, and Saanlian, his second in command."

"I am Miyagi Murahara, Vice Chancellor of the Takeda Clan." The man was short and stocky, with an air of quiet strength.

"I have heard of the Takeda Clan," Tanaksan said. Tadeo returned then with servants bearing trays of warmed bottles of sake, and small shallow cups to drink it from. The next few minutes were taken up with the ceremonies of drink. Saanlian made the mistake of thinking this new treat was like the mellow honey ale of his homeland, and provided everyone with some amusement as he gasped at the potent brew.

"We see few of your people in our land," Miyagi said at last, when the laughing had stopped.

"A loss, for both our peoples. Yours is a beautiful land."

"You have had good trading here?"

"Yes," Tanaksan replied. "Your people make many good things."

"Yes," Miyagi said slowly. "Have you seen our swords?" Saanlian and some of the other young men tensed at the mention of weapons, and the veiled threat. But Tanaksan and Similiuk stayed jovial and relaxed.

"I have seen them," Tanaksan replied. "They are the best in the world."

Miyagi seemed pleased at the compliment. "My sword," he gestured at the doorway, "is called 'Evening Breeze'."

Tanaksan looked over at it. "And my dagger is called 'After-dinner fart'," he said.

For a moment Miyagi appeared shocked at the crude jest, then saw the easy humor on Tanaksan's face and broke into laughter, laughter that was echoed by all present. After a few moments the laughter died down, leaving all in a good humor. Tanaksan gestured at the doorway, where "Evening Breeze" rested.

"A name that implies renown," he said.

"It is well known," Miyagi replied. "But there is a better-known blade not far from here in the Tennko-Ji Temple. It was forged long ago. One of several given to the temple to keep in honor of the gods. But that one has pride of place. It is called 'Kogarasu-Maru'. That means 'Little Raven'." The air in the room froze. Tanaksan and Miyagi locked eyes.

"I know of that blade," Tanaksan said. "And I have visited that temple earlier this day. It is most impressive."

"I must have arrived soon after you left," Miyagi said. "I prayed for a while there before coming on into town. The rest of our party had to wait for some of the Takeda officials who were delayed en route to the official residence. They follow at a distance, and will join us later, after stopping for their own devotions at the temple." Tanaksan nodded at that and took another sip of his drink.

"Have you been in our land before?" Miyagi asked. Tanaksan nodded slightly. A shadow of a smile ghosted across his face. Miyagi's lips pursed, then relaxed, as if a decision had been made. He straightened.

"The rest of our party may still be at the temple. Would you like to join me in meeting them there?"

"I would be honored," Tanaksan replied. They stood and left, stopping only to gather their jackets, boots, and weapons. Similiuk stayed to keep the sailors in hand, and Saanlian went with them as they went out of town and up the trail to the dark mountainside. The moon was almost full, and enough light managed to make its way through the fog to light their way. A silent knot of Samurai followed at a distance.

"These are difficult times," Miyagi said, echoing the words of the temple attendant. "Conflict weighs on our land, and lies and rumors are weapons of war." In the shadows he saw Tanaksan's head nod slightly in agreement. The temple appeared ahead of them, angular and dark against the moonlit fog. A small group of Samurai waited there. They turned to face the newcomers, hands drifting toward long sword hilts.

"We are Takeda Samurai," Miyagi called out. "Stand at ease." He stepped forward into the torchlight and the men at the temple door relaxed somewhat, two of them bowing in greeting.

"We are with Araki Mataemon, first aide to the Majordomo of the Lord Takeda," one of the guardian Samurai said. "He prays within for the souls of his ancestors."

"An honorable man," Miyagi replied. "I will join him, and pray for the souls of my ancestors."

"No need," a voice said from the shadows under the eaves. A man stepped forward from the half-open door. "I have finished, but allow me to join you in prayers for your ancestors and for the well-being of our Lord."

"Araki Mataemon!" Miyagi greeted. "We see too little of you!"

"My loss," Araki replied. "My duties take me far and often from our domains. It is good to breathe the mountain air and see our own lands." He bowed deeply to Miyagi and was rewarded with an equally deep bow in return. All the guards present were gratified by the obvious respect the two senior Samurai showed each other.

Miyagi turned to indicate Tanaksan with a nod. "Tanaksan, of the Haida, of the lands over the Eastern Sea, and Saanlian, also of the Haida."

"Honored," Araki said, with another deep bow. One that Tanaksan and Saanlian returned, although theirs were not as deep. Tanaksan and Araki regarded one another. Araki was stocky and strong-looking. Thrust in his sash were a pair of swords mounted in silver fittings and a blue lacquered scabbard. White rice powder adorned his face and scented oil mixed with black dye had been applied to the hair of his Samurai tonsure. So he was a dandy. But his obvious strength and the easy way he wore his swords belied any effeminacy.

"I also am honored," Tanaksan replied. "Please forgive me if I have interrupted your devotions."

"You have not," Araki said. Miyagi gave his fellow Samurai a questioning look.

"Araki-san, would you object if he joined us inside?"

"I would not," Araki answered, sensing something more than a simple courtesy invitation to a stranger. They left long swords and short spear in the alcove just inside the door and went on into the dimly lit interior. Saanlian stayed outside in the torch-lit mist with the other warriors.

Reiko was sitting before the takemono, the alcove holding the Kogarasu-Maru and its scroll. She raised her head at their entrance but did not look back. The three men sat properly on mats facing the alcove and Miyagi clapped loudly three times. Then he and Araki began their prayers. Tanaksan sat, quiet and respectful, while they did their devotions to the Gods of their land.

When they were through they all sat silent for a while. Tanaksan contemplated this temple. The smell of cedarwood reminded him of the cedarwood longhouses of his homeland. The sword resting in its stand in the alcove brought back other memories...

"The Lord of the Taira wants a sword of quality," the master swordsmith had said that Winter day so long ago, "and a sword befitting his position as defender of the land from the pirates of the Inland Sea."

"Who will join their ancestors no faster for all the extra work you will put into this blade." his visitor had said dryly. That day he had been dressed all in black buckskin, supple as shadow and dark as night. A shadow standing in shadows. The smith, who was more than a worker in steel, however skilled, was not fooled by appearances. He had wondered at the sudden and unexpected visit but had asked no questions.

"Truth," the smith chuckled. "Truth." He took two blanks of steel, one soft and one hard, and began to work. The necessary prayers and rites had been finished prior to the stranger's appearance, and now the steel working must be done.

Sparks flew, the forge flared, the hammers and tongs made a steady ringing sound, and slowly the steel blanks melded and grew into a slender curved blade.

"It is both old and new," the smith said, his eyes still on his work. "The sword has two edges, like swords of old. But the blade is curved in the new style. The Lord claims noble ancestry, and looks to a great future for his house."

"A blade to bridge the generations," the stranger remarked.

"Exactly," the smith agreed. He lifted the glowing blade from the forge to let it cool before coating it with his own secret mixture of clay, charcoal and powdered bone. When it dried he scraped it off in irregular waves along the edges. Another heating on the forge and the blade was ready to be tempered. But as he was about to sink the red-hot blade into the water his visitor spoke.

"Wait," he said, stepping out of the shadows. With a swift motion he drew a flint dagger and made a slash on his wrist letting several drops of blood fall into the water. Then he nodded for the smith to continue and stepped back into the shadows.

The smith sank the blade into the water, watching it draw the drops of blood toward it. He was not surprised. It was obviously a day for affairs beyond the ken of most men. He finished the tempering and was pleased with the result. But when he turned to look into the shadows his visitor was gone.

"An excellent blade!" the Taira Lord had exclaimed when he saw the gleaming arc of steel. "It needs a name befitting it!"

"I am honored that you think so," the smith had agreed. "And what will that name be?"

The Taira Lord thought for a moment. "I will call it 'Kogarasu-Maru'," he said. "'Little Raven'."

The smith nodded, not at all surprised...

"The rumors are true?" Miyagi was asking in a low voice.

"I had suspected for some time they were," Araki answered. "Our Lord dismissed his old masseur and retained a new one. He does not bathe in the communal baths as he once did. He sent away his concubines. And he is distant from old friends and retainers. Most think it due to his near death from that archer's arrow. Such events often change the behavior of even the bravest of men." He stopped to cast a quick glance at Tanaksan, as if asking a question. Miyagi motioned for him to go on.

"But last month I had a secret report for his ears only. I was alone with him in his chambers when he reached inside his robe to scratch his shoulder. For a moment I saw his bare left shoulder, the one wounded by the arrow. It was smooth and not at all scarred."

"I am surprised at his carelessness," Miyagi murmured.

"What I had to say was important, and may have distracted him," was Araki's response. Miyagi looked at him for a moment, then nodded in agreement.

"Yes," he said. "Even the most vigilant may make such a small mistake."

"Would not the Takeda councilors and generals have warned him that Lord Takeda had such a scar, and warned him against such careless acts?" Tanaksan asked.

"I would have thought so," Miyagi murmured in agreement. "It may have slipped his mind."

"They must be informed that the double made such an error," Reiko noted quietly, "so that he can be cautioned against repeating it."

"It would be a good idea," Miyagi agreed. "For now, we will all say nothing about it." He straightened. "We should go back to town," he noted. "Too long an absence will draw comment." All present agreed, and the men left.

Saanlian seemed to have gotten on well with the rest of the Samurai guards, and followed at a distance with them while Tanaksan and the two ranking Samurai walked ahead. Araki looked back for a moment to see how well the two groups were getting along, and that gave Tanaksan time for a few quick words with Miyagi, who nodded in agreement with them and sent one of his Samurai back to the temple with a message. Tanaksan nodded for Saanlian to join him. The rest continued on the path downhill.

Most of the crew had gone to bed. Tadeo was still awake, talking with Similiuk. A brazier sat on the floor nearby, the charcoal coals glowing a cheery red and providing some warmth to ward off the night's chill. They looked up when Tanaksan and the two Takeda retainers entered. Tadeo quickly bowed low, his forehead touching the mat.

"Sake," Miyagi told him. "Quickly." Tadeo scurried off to comply and the three sank to the mats in informal cross-legged position, the two Samurai setting their long swords by their sides. This late at night there was little need for full formality. Still, Similiuk noted the change, and also saw that Tanaksan had set his short spear at his side, easy to hand.

The innkeeper returned with the sake and then left, not really too anxious to hear more than was necessary. He was aware that people said his ears stuck out too much. But he knew when not to use them.

"I am impressed with your Lord's piety," Tanaksan ventured. "The temple is impressive. The spirits there watch over the land and keep it from harm. He does well by his people to see to their welfare."

"Our Lord is most pious," Miyagi agreed. "Would you not say so, Araki-san?"

"His piety is well known," Araki said, sipping from the shallow saucer-shaped cup.

"One hears that the sword, 'Kogarasu-Maru', is enchanted," Tanaksan went on. "And that one holding it can tell only the truth and act in the most honorable way. Is that so?"

"One hears that," Miyagi said mildly. He might have been amused. He sipped contentedly from his cup, and then refilled it. He offered refills to the other three and they accepted.

There was silence for a while as they all sat and drank contentedly of the fiery liquid. Soon there was a minor commotion at the door and they all turned to look.

Reiko was there, carrying a long bundle wrapped in silk brocade, with Saanlian right behind her and one of Miyagi's Samurai. Miyagi motioned them all to enter. They all sat courteously in a line opposite him and were served sake.

"We were discourteous," Miyagi said to Araki after everyone had taken a sip. "We left Tennko-Ji without letting our guest see Kogarasu-Maru. I have decided to correct that error." He motioned to Reiko, who carefully unwrapped the bundle to reveal the gold fittings and black lacquer of the legendary blade. "You are more familiar with proper protocol than I," Miyagi went on to his fellow Samurai. "Would you do the honor?"

"I would be pleased," Araki said. He accepted the proffered blade and held it in the crook of his arm, letting all see the workmanship of the scabbard and fittings. Then he gripped the scabbard near the sword guard and used his thumb to loosen the blade. He then drew it slowly, letting everyone see the gleaming steel as it eased out of the scabbard.

It was magnificent. It gleamed in the dim light as if it had a life of its own. The temper lines along both edges glistened like mother-of-pearl. The blade's curve was a carefully crafted arc of steel, deadly and efficient.

"Truly a work of art," Saanlian breathed. Araki nodded and held it before him, letting the light play over the surface.

"Has Lord Takeda ever seen Kogarasu-Maru?" Tanaksan asked.

"No, never," Miyagi replied, in a low quiet voice. Like everyone else he was absorbed in the blade.

"A shame that such a great warrior has not seen such a work of art as this blade," Tanaksan noted. "Perhaps he should."

"Yes," breathed Araki. "He should."

"You have a connection to the Spirit World?" Tanaksan asked, his voice low and lazy. Araki looked up, a flash of wariness in his eyes that was quickly masked.

"He would need to view it from the Spirit World," Tanaksan noted. "Is that not so, Araki Mataemon?" There was a sudden stillness in the room.

"Answer our guest, Araki," Miyagi admonished. "Do not be rude!" Only silence greeted his outburst. Those present tensed slightly, all aware of where swords and spears lay.

"He holds Kogarasu-Maru," Tanaksan noted. "He must tell the truth, and be honorable. Or so I hear. Is that not so, Araki?" More silence. Miyagi's hand moved ever so slowly toward his sword. Reiko had stopped breathing, her chest frozen in terror. Living all her life among Samurai she was always aware of how close death lay below the surface of civility and good manners.

"Or perhaps he is not Araki," Similiuk said in a low voice. "Paint often hides the identity of a well-known ship." A bead of sweat rolled down the brow of the man they had been calling Araki Mataemon. Slowly he set Kogarasu-Maru on the tatami mats. He looked up to see that Miyagi and his guard were both holding their swords in hand by their sides, although neither had drawn yet...

"Our Lord recently took vows," Miyagi said into the silence. "That is why he dismissed his concubines. Had you stopped at the Residence you would have learned that. But then your deception would have become known."

"People wondered if our Lord's place had been taken by a double," Reiko said in a low quiet voice. "But there is another double. You."

"You see him only once a year," Tanaksan said. "He thought it would be easy to fool you. This town and Tennko-Ji made a good place to start rumors and plant deceptions that would cause division and uncertainty in the Takeda clan. Araki's taste for decoration made it easy for someone with only a slight resemblance to Araki to pass for him. A clever plan."

"So who are you?" Miyagi asked. "A common ninja hired by our enemies?"

"I am no Ninja," the man before them hissed. "I am Samurai!"

"Then die like one!" Miyagi hissed back. "Not here! Outside." The man before them, whoever he was, faced the supreme moment of his life. Then with a smile, he calmed down. With a bow he bade them farewell and left the room, Miyagi's guard in his wake. Those left all bowed deeply, respectful of a brave man, whoever he was.

Silence gripped the room. Finally Miyagi spoke. "Kogarasu-Maru has found deception."

"No," Tanaksan said, his voice distant and odd. "It has only one power. To call me at need from my land. It was a simple trick that uncovered his deception. He spoke of the death of Lord Takeda when he sought to spread his deception, but his unguarded words showed he believed your Lord to be alive. When he thought his deception unmasked, my words about Kogarasu-Maru led him to believe that the sword held his fate."

"So it was just a trick," Reiko said.

"A good one," Tanaksan said, with just a note of pride in his voice. But a mournful note. Miyagi reached out, took Kogarasu-Maru in hand, and sheathed it. With a bow he gave it back to Reiko.

"Take it back to Tennko-Ji. It has served its purpose." She took it wordlessly and they sat and waited until Miyagi's guard returned to report on the honorable end of a brave Samurai. Then they all drank to his memory.

The next day the trading vessel lifted anchor and sailed out of the bay and East into the great ocean, with all but one of the crew aboard. Tadeo wondered why the ship's master remained on land. With Tanaksan and Miyagi he stood beside a newly dug grave.

"So our Lord lives," Tadeo said. "That is good news. People will be glad to hear that the tales of his death were all lies."

"Make sure you tell everyone you know," Miyagi told him. Tadeo looked at him, saw dismissal in Miyagi's eyes, and left quickly, leaving them alone by the grave.

"But it wasn't a lie," Tanaksan said. Miyagi looked at him suddenly, then nodded.

"That is truth," he said slowly. "Our Lord did die of his wound. A double has been taking his place. But time may be running out for the deception." He laughed, a bitter hollow sound. "An impostor told the truth, believing it to be a lie, and died nameless. Fine jokes the gods play on us!" He looked up at his companion but found himself alone. The sound of bird wings flapping raised his eyes to a raven perched on a cedar branch nearby. It looked at him keenly for a moment. Then with a sad cawing sound it took wing and followed the ship out into the fog-shrouded sea.

Author's Afterword: The sword in the story, "Kogarasu-Maru", really exists and actually did once belong to the Taira, a pirate-fighting clan active in Japan's Inland Sea. The name is usually translated as "Little Crow", but for obvious reasons I changed the translation slightly. It has an unusual design for a Japanese katana, and is described correctly in the story.

Takeda Shingen was an historical figure, and was wounded, by a musket, during a siege and reportedly died two years later. It was suspected that he had died soon after, and there were rumors of a double. Akira Kurosawa based a movie, *Kagemusha*, on that suspicion. Many stories have been written into that two-year period. This is another.

WHEN COYOTE CAME TO TOWN

by Diana L. Paxson

Diana Paxson has been known to say, when asked how she got started writing, to say that she "married into it."

What happened was rather funny; Diana, like myself, went to a highly literary college, and, like me, had been indoctrinated into the idea that unless you were Henry James, or someone like that, you shouldn't even try to write. They had tried to tell me that, but it didn't work because by the time I got to college—well into my thirties—I was already selling commercial fiction. No doubt my English professors would not have approved; but I didn't bother to ask them. Because, like such writers as Charles Dickens, I needed the money. I don't know which great writer said that only a fool ever wrote except for money (Dr. Johnson?), but I would rather emulate him than some literary snobs.

When Diana found out that I could write, I guess she figured that if I could do it, anybody could do it, and she was encouraged to try. When she married my adopted brother, she was at the stage of collecting rejection slips; I read one of her much-rejected stories and told her that if I ever edited anything, I'd buy it like a shot. And not too long after that I got a chance to edit my first anthology, and she hadn't sold it yet, and I bought it.

And the rest is history.
    —MZB

Diana comments that she started writing this post-Cataclysm, proto-Westria story during the speech at this year's SFWA banquet, and anyone who was there will understand.
    —Margaret Davis

Backstory: A tour of the Los Alamos research lab, and conversations with scientists who honored the creative inspiration they've found in SF & fantasy books, preceded the SFWA banquet.
    —REH

The old man came to town on the first hot day of summer, when the dust lay thick on the road and the cicadas sang in the ripening grass. A dull haze covered the great valley, veiling the mountains of the Sierra and the coastal hills so that the town seemed to float, disconnected from the world.

It was pretty well true.

The terrible times of the Cataclysm were past, and the Old Powers, having destroyed most of the works of man, didn't seem to care what we did in the space they had left to us. These days nothing ever happened here except when Captain Jack came with his men, and that was the kind of excitement, my father said, that we didn't need.

The stranger appeared at the edge of town, just outside Ben Nunez's wagon shop. Before the Cataclysm, the shop had been kept busy repairing the machines that broke down on the road. That was when Ma was a little girl and Ben a young man. Now he spent most of his time watching the road, waiting for business that never came.

Sometimes when Ma couldn't catch me for chores I would go down there and wander about, curling up in the dusty upholstery of the old cars and wondering about the people who used to sit there and the places they had traveled to. I guess we all spent a lot of time looking backward, and why not? There was nothing to look forward to that I could see.

I was perched on the hood of an old Cadillac, listening to Ben and his brother Will argue over their checkers game, when a shadow lengthened past the door. Then an old man came into view, leaned his staff against the wall, flipped up his shirt and started to piss on the ground.

"Hey! You can't do that here!" cried Ben.

The last yellow drops splattered in the dust. The old man turned, the brim of his hat shivering and his stringy grey hair lifting a little in the dry wind, replaced his clothing and grinned.

"You got anything to drink?"

"So you can piss it away?" asked Will.

"Gotta refuel—" the old man answered mildly, but his amber eyes gleamed.

Ben grunted. "I won't deny a man a drink of water." He reached for the big glass jug and offered it. The old man took the bottle, his long fingers caressing the smooth surface of the old glass. We watched, eyes widening, as the entire bottle went down.

When it was empty, the old man belched, wiped his mouth with the back of his hand, and handed it back. Ben started to replace the jug on its shelf and stopped, nostrils twitching. Even I could pick up the decidedly alcoholic odor coming from that direction, and though we had all seen the stranger empty the bottle, it looked half full. Ben took an experimental sip, raised one eyebrow, shut his mouth, and corked the jug once more.

Will leaned forward. "Where you from?"

The old man gestured vaguely back up the road.

"You came from Cow Town?" These days that's what people called the place that used to be Tracy.

The stranger brightened. "Some pretty girls up there. You got any pretty girls?"

Ben frowned. He had a daughter, born when he'd given up hope of more children after the big sickness. "Not for you—"

"That's all right. I'm not particular."

Will gave a snort of laughter. "The girls might be."

"You particular about work?" Ben asked then. "You better be willing to earn your keep if you plan to stay in this town."

The old man bared stained teeth in a grin. "What do you need?"

"The Widow Washington's pump don't work. Can you fix that?"

"A pump?" The stranger's hips twitched suggestively.

Will shook his head. "A water pump—" he said repressively. "And she'll pitch you out if you say a word out of line. In the old days she was the minister's wife, and she don't make allowances."

The stranger looked unconcerned. "Where's she at?" Like a thirsty plant revived by the water, his skin had plumped out, and he no longer seemed so old.

"I'll show you—" I got to my feet. The long yellow eyes slid towards me, though he must have known I was listening all along.

We started down the street. During the Cataclysm, earthquakes had opened cracks across the surface, and time and weather had widened them. Sometimes in the summer the men of the town would try to fill them with gravel, but each winter plants sprouted in the crevices, their tiny roots completing the work that the Cataclysm had begun. What had once been a four-lane road now had barely enough good surface for two wagons to pass. Some folks hated the weeds and would pull them out ruthlessly—the only action against the Green Powers they were now allowed. But others had a superstitious fear of even so small an act of rebellion.

"What do they call you, girl?"

"Marcie—" The old man's strides were longer than they seemed. I had to skip to keep up with him.

"Huh—" those yellow eyes considered me. "A name should mean somethin'. I'd name you 'Poppy' for yer bright hair."

"All right—" I lifted my braid, squinting as the red-gold strands caught the sun. "What do they call you?"

He gave a snort of amusement. "Oh, I got a lot of names. Sinkalip or Tsistu, some call me, or Manabozho. But some just say 'Old Man'."

I stared at him. "But what's your *real* name?"

"Oh—that's a secret. Think I'd tell just anyone? Anyhow, unless you figure it out for yourself it won't mean a thing." The amber eyes slitted with laughter.

For a few minutes we walked in silence. How about 'Rumpelstiltskin', I wondered, remembering one of my grandmother's tales. But that name came from another land. I looked at the stranger's long nose and yellow eyes and grinned.

"Think I'll call you Mr. Coyote—" I said, grinning as he stopped short, eyes wide.

"Now why'd you choose that name?"

"Why not?" I frowned, feeling an odd tingle, like you get on a day when the wind is high and anything you touch can shock you. "It suits you. We had an old dog that was part coyote—you remind me of him."

"Do I now? Well, that's all right then." He laughed again. "How many families in this town?" he added suddenly.

I hesitated, trying to reckon without using my fingers. Sometimes the old folks in town would try to get a school going, like they'd had when they were young, but there weren't many children left, and we couldn't see the point in learning about a world that didn't exist anymore.

"There's my family—Ma and Pa and my grandma and my brother Joe. Old Ben has a wife and a daughter, and Will lives with them. Then there's the Tomsons on Peachtree Lane—" I listed twenty more households before I got to the Widow Washington, who lived alone. "And of course there's folk from the Valley farms that come in on market day. I've seen near a hundred fifty people all at once in the square when Captain Jack came with his men."

And when he left, I remembered suddenly, there had been five less of us. I could still see the five still shapes on the ground, and old Ben's daughter crying 'cause the Captain had said he'd be back for her next year.

The old man snorted. "Last time I was here, this town had three thousand."

"You mean *Before*?"

"Before the Guardians came back, yeah—what, you still afraid of 'em?"

My parents had taught me not to name the Cataclysm aloud. In one year, the old folks said, the whole world had collapsed in earthquake, flood and fire, and when things calmed down at last, those humans that survived were at the mercy of the First People, the old powers of the Earth that now ruled the world. Nobody I knew called them Guardians.

I had never seen one, but Grandma told me once about the day the Trees came down from the hills and walked through the town. She said that grass pushed up through the side streets and vines twined around City Hall and tore it down. All the gas stations were leveled, too, and the mall where the market square was now, and the electrical plant at the edge of town. When the Powers finally went away, only a few buildings remained, and the only road with paving was the main street through the town.

"That happened when my mother was a little girl," I said, not answering his question. "You don't look that old."

"Oh, I'm older than I look!" he laughed.

I shook my head, figuring he was teasing me. Right then he didn't look old at all.

We walked past grass-covered mounds where houses once had lined the road. Here in town, everything useful had either burned or been scavenged long ago. The minister's house still stood beside the ruins of the church. The Green Powers had not killed humans directly—they said Reverend Washington had tried to defend his church and died when the roof fell on him. But the house had not been touched. Its paint was flaking, and the gate had been mended with rawhide thongs, but the flowerbeds that edged the walk were newly weeded, and the roses were in triumphant bloom.

I went up the creaking steps and knocked. "Hello—" After a moment the knob turned. "Miz Washington, I've brought a man to fix your pump."

The door opened wider, in the darkness a dark face appeared, framed by a halo of silver hair. I motioned to the stranger to follow me in. "This is, uh—Mr. Coyote. He just came to town."

For a moment she stared at him. Then she sat down again. Her Bible lay open on the table by the chair.

"I have seen the seven angels with the seven trumpets, and the army of locusts." She jabbed at the page with her forefinger. "Babylon is fallen, and the evil of the earth has been consumed by wind and water and fire. But where is the angel who will take up the Blessed into paradise? You've been other places—Has the angel come? Did God forget about us in this town?"

She leaned forward, peering at Mr. Coyote through her scratched glasses. I flushed with embarrassment.

For a moment he just stood there. Then he pointed to the bowl of flowers on the table. "Why you grow roses?"

Mrs. Washington blinked. "Because they are beautiful..."

Mr. Coyote nodded. "Then for you, the angel comes."

I wasn't quite sure what he meant by that, but it seemed to satisfy the old lady. The crazy look went out of her eyes; she closed the book and levered herself out of the chair.

"I can't pay you—" she went on in answer to his nod, then remembered that no one used money anymore.

"You feed me," he grinned, looking like a young man. In amazement I saw the stiffness leave her posture.

"You get the pump working again, child, and I'll do that. I'm too old to carry water from the creek anymore."

"Miz Washington has a great garden!" I put in, looking from one to the other. "Lots of things no one else can get to grow."

There was no doubt about it. This time the old woman smiled.

The next few days Ma kept me busy with chores. Everything we ate we had to grow or trade for, and there was always weeding, or carrying water from the well. It took a while for me to realize there might be another reason for keeping me close to home—it was getting towards the middle of the summer, when we would have enough crops harvested to make the town worth another visit from Captain Jack and his men.

The weather grew hotter. I heard that Mr. Coyote had finished fixing the widow's water pump and was still living there, sleeping in the toolshed and doing odd jobs for others in the town. Night by night, the moon grew like the gourds in our garden; her pale light lay across the Valley, nearly as bright as day. From the coastal hills came the faint wild music of the coyotes, and one night, when the moon was full, I thought I heard, so clearly it seemed to come from somewhere close by, another coyote howling his answer.

I opened my window and stuck my head out, but the sound seemed to move around, as if the animal was wandering the streets of the town. That seemed unlikely. These days we buried our garbage and scavenged the dump for materials that could be reused. Even a coyote wouldn't find much to interest him here. Eventually the concert ended. I went back to bed, but strange and shining forms continued to make music in my dreams.

Just before Midsummer, clouds gathered and lightning stalked across the Valley floor. That night it rained, and in the morning, when the puddles were beginning to steam in the sun, Captain Jack rode in. This year close to fifty men were behind him, hard-eyed and weathered, with wide-brimmed leather hats and jingling shirts of chain-mail. They made a brave show, but Ma whispered that they looked gaunt, as if the other places where they took tribute had let them down. That must be why they had shown up here so early in the year.

Not that they were about to admit it. They rode in pairs, the pennons on their lances fluttering bravely. Captain Jack himself was mounted on an Appaloosa mare. He had an old-fashioned shirt with military patches, like Ma said the soldiers used to wear in the days when there was still a real army, and he carried a rifle. His bugler blew a commanding call on a dented brass trumpet, and he waited for those who had not already come out of their houses to gather in the market square.

One of the men had a sheet of paper and was checking off people as they came in. I looked over and saw Will and Ben and his wife, but I began to get a sick feeling in my belly when I didn't see their daughter Jenny. Captain Jack had noticed her absence too. He was frowning.

"I make the tally one hundred and eleven, sir," said the clerk. "Same as last year."

"Not quite the same," answered the leader. "That man—" he

pointed at Mr. Coyote, who was standing with the Widow Washington, "is new, and the Nunez girl ain't here." His dark gaze fixed Ben. "Thought I told you I'd want to see her next time I came."

"My apologies, sir. Jenny's not feeling well," Ben said tightly.

"Well, that's too bad. But I'm sure she'll be well tomorrow."

He grinned mirthlessly. "Me an' my men work hard, protecting folks like you—seems only right we get a little rest and recreation when we come into town. You do understand..."

Ben's face flushed dangerously, but he nodded.

"You want entertainment?" a new voice brought the captain's head around. "I know lots of songs an' stories, make you laugh—"

It was Mr. Coyote, looking even older than the first time I saw him, his long nose jutting over his wispy grey beard.

Captain Jack stared at him, and if there was more amazement than amusement in his grunt, at least Ben had time to ease back out of sight among the crowd.

After the captain had finished making speeches, the crowd broke up to gather the stuff he'd asked for. My Pa talked about warlords and tribute, which seemed a fancy name for a few vegetables. He and Ma were still arguing about it when I managed to give them the slip and ran off to Ben's shop.

He was there with Will and some of the other men, and Jenny, in her usual blooming looks if she hadn't been so scared, and Mr. Coyote. I went over to Jenny, who hugged me hard, then pushed me away.

"You shouldn't be here, Marcie—"

"I'm Poppy now," I corrected. She stared at me as if she scarcely heard, then shook her head a little, her eyes evaluating my figure.

"Still flat as a boy," she muttered. "You're safe for a while, but I guess you're old enough to know. Do you understand what that man wants with me?"

"To take you away and make you work for him—" That much I had gathered from listening to my parents talk.

Jenny gave a snort of bitter laughter. "You might put it that way, but I wouldn't mind cleaning house and mending clothes and that sort of thing. He wants to have sex with me, like a dog does with a bitch in heat—does that make it clear?"

"And you don't want him to—" I added, nodding wisely.

"I want to get married to a man I can love, though goodness knows where I'll find one."

The men's voices were rising, a bitter, ugly sound. They pointed to the old tools, discussing ways to use them as weapons. Ben's face flushed when he talked about how the chisel would sink into the captain's belly, but even I could see how likely it was that Ben's blood would feed the earth instead.

"I can't run away," Jenny whispered. "They have horses, and they know every inch of the land. My father can't fight him. Rather than let Captain Jack kill my family, I'll be his whore."

"No, no, you don't want a dogfight—" another voice cut through the babble and I recognized Mr. Coyote's drawl. "You want to have a *party*..."

I could see jaws dropping all around the room. Mr. Coyote showed his teeth in a grin.

"Right now, this captain expects trouble. You act all nice tomorrow when you bring the food. Tell him yer grateful for his protection. The women gotta bake some cakes, and you bring out the beer."

"We don't have very much—" said Mr. Tomson. Every summer there were always arguments about whether we could spare any of the grain for booze.

"Don't worry," said Mr. Coyote. "There'll be enough. Trust me..."

Ben and Will traded glances, and I knew they were remembering the day the stranger had arrived.

"I believe you—" said Ben, choosing his words carefully. I suppressed a giggle. I wouldn't have trusted that old man as far as I could throw him just now.

"But what about me?" asked Jenny.

Mr. Coyote looked her up and down appreciatively. "You come. Put on pretty clothes, act happy to see him. But you don't go away with him, oh no—" Again he grinned. "Trust me."

The men got to work gathering supplies, with a look in their eyes that set sick flutters going in my belly. Whatever Mr. Coyote had in mind had better work, because if it didn't the men, even my Pa, were going to fight for sure. Nobody knew if Captain Jack still had ammunition for that gun, but there was no doubt that his men kept their lances sharp. I didn't want to see my father's blood soaking into the earth of the square.

By nightfall, the square was as full of folk as I'd ever seen it. Good smells of cooking food made me breathe deep. Despite the tension, there was a festive feel to the air. The Tomsons had even donated one of their pigs—in addition to the one they had to give Captain Jack, that is. I still didn't know what Mr. Coyote was planning, but I could see what he was doing. In the center of the square he was directing the men who were building a bonfire. He must have gone to the hills for the wood himself—I didn't know anyone else who would dare. At least it was all deadwood, so we wouldn't have the Tree folk marching down to take their revenge.

The men Captain Jack had left on guard grinned broadly as he came marching back again. Even the captain's sour look softened a bit as he took it all in. He brightened still further when the Nunez clan arrived with Jenny in tow, wearing an old party dress of her mother's, with her lips reddened and a bow in her hair.

He said something to one of his men, and presently Jenny was being escorted to the table they had set up for him and given a chair by his side. He put his arm around her and she stiffened, gazing at Mr. Coyote in appeal. He grinned back at her and trotted over, carrying a tray with a jug and glasses. That proved an effective distraction, and from the captain's expression, I guessed the beer was better than he had expected.

As the evening progressed, he certainly drank a lot of it. So did his men. I wouldn't have thought there was that much beer in the town, but whenever a bottle was emptied, Mr. Coyote would take it away and return with another that was full. By the time all the food had been served some of Captain Jack's riders were already stretched on the ground, snoring. The captain himself pawed at Jenny when he wasn't drinking, but there were too many distractions for him to give her his full attention.

As the evening went on, it seemed to me that even our folks were having a good time. Miz Washington had on a purple dress I'd never seen her wear before and a red rose in her hair. The Nunez brothers still stood stiff and watchful on the sidelines, but Joe Tomson had got out his guitar, and some of the others were backing him with a catch-all jug band. Mr. Coyote had got a drum from somewhere, and pretty soon people began to dance.

In the confusion, I didn't notice when he handed the drum over to Will Nunez and disappeared. By this time, Captain Jack was drunk enough so that the beer was no longer his first priority, drunk enough so that Jenny could still fend him off without too much difficulty, though his fumblings were getting more persistent. I got my courage up enough to sidle over and distract him with silly questions—there was never a man born, my Ma used to say, who didn't like to boast about his deeds.

"You be glad you got Captain Jack t' take care o' you—" he said, patting Jenny's hair. "There's other gangs would torch this town and take the women without askin'. But I figure that's like eatin' all yer seed corn. Way I see it, we keep the others offa you all and you feed us, unnerstan?"

Jenny and I nodded. It wasn't feeding him that we objected to. He might be more thoughtful than most, but he was still a predator.

He was halfway through a meandering account of a fight with one of those other bunches of "protectors" when light blazed suddenly on the other side of the square. About time, I thought, peering under my hand to see who was carrying the torches. I'd been wondering when Mr. Coyote was going to light the fire.

But it wasn't Mr. Coyote. All I could make out through the radiance was the flutter of a flowered skirt I didn't think I'd ever seen before. I looked around the square. All the women in town were accounted for. From the back I saw a tangle of ginger hair crowned by a wreath of roses. Who on earth was this woman who was carrying the torches, hips swinging rhythmically as she danced around the fire?

Will had picked up the beat, and the other musicians followed. Three times the fire-bringer circled the heap of wood. By this time people were clapping out the rhythm and stamping so hard the earth shook and the glasses rattled against the jug. Then, with a howl of triumph, she threw the torches. They arced towards the wood like lightning, and exploded in a pillar of flame.

Captain Jack jerked back, swearing. The fire-bearer turned, and I glimpsed a long nose and glowing eyes in a brown face that looked oddly familiar, though I knew I had never seen this woman before.

Whoever she was, even I could see that she was what men called 'sexy'. Her hips swayed with each step, and big breasts made the flowers printed on the cloth of her dress flutter as she moved. Every male within view, including the men of our town, sat up, tongue lolling, as she came towards us.

"Hi there, big boy," she said in a throaty voice. "Whatcha doin' with those little girls? What you need is a *real* woman—come on an' dance with me!"

She leaned forward, chucking Captain Jack under the chin, and my senses swam in the wave of rose perfume. Jenny was so stunned I had to pull her out of the way as he lurched to his feet and stumbled after the strange woman towards the fire.

If the music had been lively before, it was crazy now, and everyone was dancing. Even Miz Washington was hopping around with Will Nunez, and Ben had his wife by the hand. Jenny twirled alone, hair flying, and I jiggled in place, trying to keep an eye on her and still see what was going on by the fire.

Captain Jack was grunting with effort, sweat rolling down his face as he tried to get a hold on his partner. She certainly touched *him* enough, with a kiss here and a brush of hip or breast there, but every time he tried to hug her she managed to slide away. Everyone else was too excited to notice, but it made me laugh. Maybe that's why I was the only one who saw what happened when he managed to grab her at last.

For a minute it looked like he had a good armful of woman. Then she dissolved in a shower of sparks. The flowered dress and the roses slithered through Captain Jack's grasp, and the sparks solidified into a new shape, four-legged and furry, with a long nose and glowing yellow eyes.

For a minute I just stared. Then I grabbed the rifle that the captain had left leaning against his chair. "Look everybody! Captain Jack is tryin' to make love to a *dog*!"

It was a pretty good yell. The music stopped. Everything stopped except for Captain Jack, who was still clutching at his furry partner, whimpering. But it wasn't, as I had first guessed, a dog. What squirmed out of his grasp was unmistakably a coyote, and male at that, who looked back at us for a moment, tongue lolling insolently, then trotted across the square and disappeared.

Everyone saw it, and everyone heard in their heads the familiar voice of Mr. Coyote—

"Well I've made a fool of him—the rest is up to you!"

There was a moment of amazement, and then we all began to

laugh.

After that night, Captain Jack was never the same. One or two of his men tried to give trouble, and a couple ran off, but our men were the top dogs now. Ben Nunez took the rifle, and he was the one who made the deal with the riders, to keep them fed if they would work with us and help build a meeting hall with a wall around it that will defend us all if others should come. After a while people started calling him our head man. It's a job he seems to do pretty well.

Last year Jenny got married to one of the riders, a young one, and I stood up with her. The other men are beginning to pay attention to me, now, but none of them interest me. I've always had the feeling I was waiting for something, and last night I found out why.

The moon was full, and the coyotes were singing on the hill. I couldn't sleep, and I went for a walk at the edge of town. Just past the old wagon shop I saw a whirl of sparks in the grass. But there was no fire, and no wind. It got solid, and in another minute it was a coyote, yellow eyes glowing and gingery fur a-glisten in the light of the moon.

"Hello, Mr. Coyote," I said then, wondering why I wasn't afraid.

"Hello, Miss Poppy—" he answered, but by that time he had changed again, and what stood there, despite the long nose and sardonic eyes, was a very good-looking young man...

By the time I got back to my bed dawn was on its way. Tonight I'm going to meet him again, and I don't know if I'll ever go home. Coyote says it's time to change things once more, time folks stopped being afraid of the Guardians and looking back to the time Before. He's got a lot to teach me, and I think I'm ready to learn.

And I can guarantee that something will always be happening when Coyote is around.

EARTH'S SONG

by Laura J. Underwood

Laura J. Underwood is the author of numerous tales of fantastic fiction who lives, writes, works and occasionally hikes the mist-covered mountains of East Tennessee where she was born and raised. She shares her domicile with a Cairn Terrier named Rowdy Lass and a harp named Glynnanis. Her stories to date have appeared in several volumes of SWORD AND SORCERESS as well as Marion Zimmer Bradley's FANTASY Magazine, *OF UNICORNS AND SPACE STATIONS, TALE SPINNER,* Appalachian Heritage, *NEW MILLENNIUM WRITINGS (forthcoming), and ADVENTURES OF SWORD & SORCERY.*

I am looking forward to meeting her in person at this year's Fantasy Worlds Festival, for she has promised to attend.
   —MZB

The woman at the center of the tavern brawl was more than equal in height to any man in the room. Six armored brutes challenged her currently, while the rest of the customers crouched in corners, urging their male comrades on with loud catcalls and hoots. Anwyn Baldomyre had given up trying to be heard above the chaos after a tankard smashed into the wall too close to his head for comfort. He decided that under a stout table was the safest haven for himself and his magic harp, and Glynnanis was inclined to agree. This, the harper begrudgingly reminded himself, was why he hated large Lamborian towns.

Whoever trained the loam-haired woman to battle ways should have been proud. The six men were outnumbered by her skill alone. She had yet to draw steel, making do with her wooden staff. Two men sat on the floor shaking their heads, and with a quick snap of her pole she left the third one retching from a crack to the groin that had every man in the tavern groaning in sympathy. She quickly lashed at the fourth, who fell and took down the fifth in his attempt to avoid the staff's aim for his head.

The sixth, however, seized advantage of that moment to raise a chair behind her back.

"Look out!" Anwyn cried.

She barely turned in time to duck the sweep of the chair. The thick oak staff spun in her hands, catching the man in the nose. A spurt of blood rushed down the front of his jerkin. He stumbled back, clutching his nose with a howl. Brown eyes set in a handsome face flashed Anwyn a wink and a smile before the woman walked calmly towards the tavern door. She disappeared into the night in a swirl of earth tones.

"Curse the hellcat!" one of the fallen groaned. "May the Black Wind rot her and the goddess she serves!"

Anwyn was creeping out from under the table with the rest of the locals when he caught sight of the dark look aimed in his direction by one of the aggressors.

"And may it rot the one that warned her as well!" the man snarled. "Fetch me that harper!"

Never short on common sense, Anwyn knew his welcome here was at an end. He seized his possessions and bolted for the door, barely eluding the hands that attempted to snag his cloak as he threw it about his own shoulders and raced out into the night. In moments, he could hear the thunder of feet on boards and cobbles as the few of the six who were able to move with any comfort came after the harper.

Lords and Ladies! he thought, shaking long tendrils of red hair from his silver eyes. He ran down the streets of Allynford, seeking a safe haven while praying the town watch did not notice his flight. If he could just get to a place of concealment, he could sing his Gate Song and get out of the sprawling township and back to the safety of the open road. Alas, his pursuers were bent on vengeance and determined not to lose sight of their quarry. He was much slighter of build than the smallest of them, and knew he had no advantages in a fight—the curse of being the youngest and favorite son of a gamekeeper with an open heart and mind. Flight always had more appeal in these cases.

Anwyn saw an alley and ducked into it, hoping for sanctuary, but the men had obviously seen him enter it and one shouted orders to cut him off. He ran its length, casting back over one shoulder when hands seized him, covered his mouth, and jerked him through a doorway into darkness. He clutched Glynnanis close as he was shoved against the wall and held there by an incredible strength. The harp's cry of warning rang too late in his head. There was a strong odor of damp earth in his nose as a voice hissed, "Be silent, or we both shall have cause to regret it!"

Anwyn froze. It was a woman's voice, but in this dark he could only hear and smell and feel her powerful presence tinged by magic...and trembled with uncertain fear for what it meant.

Boots pounded past the closed door. He heard shouts of "Split up and search! He can't have gone far!" that knotted his stomach with terror. Long moments passed before the pressure relaxed, allowing him to stand on his own. Slowly, he stretched one hand, hoping to find the door and escape.

"Be at peace, harper," she said in her breathy warm voice. "You did me a favor. I returned it. You have no reason to fear harm from me."

Anwyn held his place. "What do you want from me?"

She let out a slow breath. "Come, I know a place where they might not think to look for either of us," she said.

He frowned, uncertain if it would he wise to go with her, for the sense of magic was strong. *Glynnanis?* he thought. *Why does she feel like a mage?*

"I'm not sure, but I think it must be something the battle wench carries," the harp replied.

So she wasn't a mage, Anwyn was relieved to know. His encounters with others born with the mark of silver or grey eyes were not always pleasant. And it meant she could not hear the harp's rude remark.

A door opened, and Anwyn made out the silhouette of a woman peering out, street torches casting their rusty highlights on her dark hair. She stepped through the gap, signaling that all was clear and leaving him to follow on his own. And as he stepped into the alley, there was a moment when he thought to go the other way...

At least until the distant ring of a familiar voice cursed the night. Safety, he reflected, might be better sought in her company, considering her skill. Having grown up with a family of sisters who wore armor and were better than he with a blade, he was not going to argue any points of chivalry. He bolted after the woman, catching up with her at the corner.

She led him through the streets as though knowing her way, making him all the more curious.

"Just who are you?" Anwyn asked.

"You can call me Nessa," she said and stopped at the edge of the main square. There were very few folk about. With a cautious glance at their surroundings, she started across the expanse towards a tavern on the other side. "And what name shall I call you, harper?"

"Anwyn," he said.

She stopped before the door of a tavern, pushing it open and letting him enter first. Here, the locals barely took notice of the harper or his tall warrior companion. Most of them seemed just as eager not to he noticed themselves, drawing back into the shadows and hiding their faces in their tankards. Nessa chose a booth that afforded her privacy and a view of the door. She seated herself, pushing back her cloak to reveal leather armor over a padded tunic and tartan trews. The breastplate was marked with symbols that Anwyn recognized as the mark of the element earth. Silently, without asking, the tavernkeeper brought two short ales to the table and returned to his bar to continue the chore of wiping out the mugs.

She is known here, the harper thought.

"Drink up," she said. "It's on the house. You are in the company of a Temple Guardian."

"You're a Temple Guardian?" he repeated. In Lamboria, women warriors, though not lacking, were rare.

"Aye," she said, sounding amused. "I serve the Earth Mother's Altar."

"And those men who attacked you?"

"Thieves," Nessa said. "Four nights ago, they came to the Temple in the dark. They numbered ten at the time, and while four of them dared to engage me in battle and lost, the others broke into the Earth Mother's Nave and stole a stone box hidden within an altar we call the Mother's Womb."

"What was in the box?" Anwyn asked.

"Just this," she said and reached into a pouch on her hip. "This is why they are after me. I caught up with them and took it back before they could give it to Lord Bres."

She drew forth an object the size of a fist in a leather bag and placed it on the table between them. With a glance at the rest of the room, she slowly opened the bag, pushing it down to create a nest.

Within the folds lay a stone like none Anwyn had ever seen. It swirled brown, gold and amber, earthy colors convulsing inside a crystal sphere. Cautiously, he reached out to touch it, and as he did, he felt a deep thrum, like the lowest string on a harp being stroked. It throbbed with an eerie life. He closed his eyes and felt a rich song entwining itself in his soul, nearly bringing him to tears of joy...

Until his wrist was snagged and jerked back, breaking his contact and sending needles of pain shooting up his arm. Nessa pulled up the leather to hide the stone with her free hand, never relinquishing her grasp on him. Her eyes were dark with anger.

"What did you do?" she insisted.

"Nothing," he said. "It sounded...beautiful."

"You can hear its song?" she said. "Then you are one of the mage folk, and I have let you near a sacred object of the Great Mother herself..."

"But I'm not a real mage," Anwyn said. "I have not made my sacrifice..." He was regretting now that he had followed her, for her grasp on his wrist was hurting. He had seen evidence of her strength. If she broke his hand... "Look, I can't help being what I am, but I've no desire to take what does not belong to me. My father was an honest man who never tolerated thievery from any of his offspring..."

She let go as abruptly as she had grabbed him, drawing back and frowning. "Honest or not, I should never have shown you this," she said, touching the pouch. "You will covet its song as Lord Bres does now."

"Lord Bres?" Anwyn said. "Just who is he?"

She sighed and studied him for a moment, and he sought to keep his face as open as possible. "Just where are you from, harper, that you do not know the name of Lord Bres?"

"Nymbaria, in Thuathynboria," he said.

Her dark brows rose in disbelief. "Thuathyn?" she marveled. "I thought your kind were just stories like the faery folk my father used to tell me about."

"Hardly," Anwyn said.

Nessa shook her head. "Well, then," she said. "Lord Bres is as you are, harper, a man with silvery eyes who holds nearly all of Allynford prisoner by the small jewels. No man or woman refuses what he desires. Even the Duke of this town is under Lord Bres's thrall. Only those who serve the Temple of the Four still defy him. We are the last of his enemies, and all that stand between him and the good folks among whom he would spread his wickedness."

"And he covets this stone," Anwyn said, cautiously gesturing towards the sack still resting between them.

"Aye," she said. "And would kill to possess it."

"Why?"

"Because any man who possesses this stone will have power over Earth."

Anwyn frowned. "But a mage doesn't need such an object to control the elements," he said. "I have not even made my sacrifice, and yet I possess the power to control the elements with certain spell songs I have learned."

"You do not understand. It would give him power over Earth...over the Avatar of the Great Mother herself!"

Anwyn's eyes flashed down at the stone encased in leather. Earth? The Avatar of the Great Mother. Lords and Ladies, this was not a stone to control the elements...but an elemental stone! "It's a heartstone!" he said.

"A what?" Nessa said with a frown.

"This is a heartstone," Anwyn said. "This Avatar you call Earth must be an elemental wraith, and by possessing this stone, Lord Bres would have the power to bend that wraith to his will. And once he was able to do that, there would be no one to stop him from destroying the Temple of the Four. The sooner you return this to your Temple, the better!" Anwyn recoiled as though the bag held a serpent. His encounters with elemental wraiths were even worse than with other mages. He wanted nothing to do with such a creature, avatar or not!

"And that is what I am sworn to prevent, but even now, Lord Bres has men guarding the streets leading to the Temple, in search of me," Nessa said. "I have tried every way I know to get there, but his men hound me. That inn where you helped me used to hold a secret entrance to the Temple in its cellars, but I arrived to find Lord Bres had sealed that path and left his henchmen to trap me. I dare say, it will not be long before he seeks me out again..."

Her words barely fell from her lips when the door to the tavern slammed against the wall. A swarm of bodies rushed through the gap, swords and crossbows drawn. "Don't anyone move," an angry voice shouted at the room.

Nessa pushed the sack towards Anwyn. "I will believe you are an honest man, harper, and give this into your trust," she said. "Take it to the Temple of the Four and let it be returned to the Mother's Womb."

"But I don't know where your temple is," he protested.

"On the High Court Road," she said.

"But..."

"Go!" she hissed and exploded out of the booth, drawing sword and staff. With a terrifying howl, she threw herself on the crowd at the door just as a man in a rich blue cloak was stepping into the tavern. Anwyn got a glimpse of pale grey eyes set in a handsome face under long black hair before the armored men threw themselves into his path to protect him.

Nessa shrieked like a fury as she lay into their numbers. The quarters were too close to make crossbows serviceable, which she put to her advantage. Two men were on the floor, and she was striking down the third when she looked at Anwyn and shouted, "Go!"

That distraction was her folly. The armored men swarmed her in mass before his startled stare, taking her kicking and screaming to the floor. Some of their numbers broke rank to surge at the harper as well. He froze, wanting desperately to help her, but uncertain as to how.

"Let's go!" Glynnanis sang.

The harp's song broke Anwyn from his fright. He called his Gate Song, thinking of the road down in the forest below Allynford, and sang the notes out loud. He saw angry grey eyes go wide, their owner charging forward with his men, before darkness surrounded Anwyn and slung him through a weightless, airless void. Solid ground appeared under his feet, and the harper dropped to his knees. The dark gave way to night sky and starlight and the scattered silhouettes of trees. For a moment, Anwyn stayed where he was, gasping for breath. The sudden rush of using that spell sometimes left him dizzy.

"Come on, we'd better go," Glynnanis said.

"I can't," Anwyn said, looking at the weighty sack in his hands. He could barely sense the stone's song through the thick leather, and it sent feathers brushing his nerves. "I have to return this to the Temple of the Four. It's the least I can do, having fled like a coward and left poor Nessa to die..."

"And how do you propose to do that?" Glynnanis insisted.

"You've used the Gate Song and must sleep before you can use it again."

Anwyn shrugged, peering at the distant glitter of torches visible beyond the trees. "I was hoping you'd have a suggestion.. "

"What I would suggest," the harp grumbled, *"is that we get away from here now, because I'm starting to feel some vibrations that might not bode well for either of us..."*

Anwyn lurched to his feet as a great surge of magic tingled his skin. *Lord and Ladies, I'm a fool as well as a coward!* he thought grimly as he bolted off the road and into the thicket of trees. *Lord Bres is a mage, and will need little effort to follow my clumsy trail!* Anwyn had learned long ago from Rhystar and his own experience that magic left traces, and though normal men could not track it, a mage like Bres would have no difficulty following another with silver eyes.

Anwyn was hardly into the copse before he heard a crackle like lightning and felt static as the magic swelled. He flung himself behind an ancient oak, crouching in the moss and loam amid a snarl of roots. The voices of angry men filled the air. One of them cursed, followed by the smack of a fist on flesh, and snarled, "Vicious hellcat! Do that again and I'll rip your heart out!"

Anwyn ventured a glance around the bole of the tree and spotted Nessa, bound and gagged, staggering to right herself. "By the Four," he muttered. *What now?*

"Harper," a man called. "I know you're here. Come out and we shall talk."

Anwyn squinted at the one who spoke. A tall figure wrapped in brilliant blue. Narrowed grey eyes scanned the sides of the road. The harper quickly drew back, recalling Rhystar's warning that mage eyes could often see what mortal eyes could not. There was no doubt in Anwyn's mind that the peacock cloak was worn by Lord Bres.

"Come now, harper," Lord Bres called. "I know what you are, and I know what you have, and I should tell you I do not intend to leave here without it."

Footsteps rustled the underbrush near the roadside, the sound of men searching the thicket. Anwyn hunched down, unsure of what to do.

"We can bargain, harper," Lord Bres said. "I am a reasonable man and would gladly trade this warrior's life for what you hold."

Nessa grumbled epithets and threats even Anwyn could hear through her gag. He imagined she was struggling like a wild cat.

"Surely you owe no loyalty to this Temple of the Four," Lord Bres continued. "You are a stranger to these parts, a mage like myself. Our kind should always deal reasonably with one another."

Lords and Ladies! Anwyn wished Rhystar were here. The great mage of Far Reach would know how to deal with this mess.

"Come, harper," Lord Bres said. "I'll give you to the count of ten to show yourself freely. If not, I'll cut this warrior wench's throat and come after you myself."

Come after me yourself? Anwyn thought. He did not understand why Lord Bres had not done so by now!

"One..."

Glynnanis, what should I do? Anwyn thought frantically.

"Two..."

Anwyn's heart thundered when the harp made no reply. "Three..."

Of course, Glynnanis's voice would give me away!

"Four..."

He should have moved deeper into the woods when he had the chance. *But, he'll kill Nessa!*

"Five..."

Anwyn brought his heels under him, intending to rise and surrender in hopes of buying their lives, but in the dark, he stumbled on a root and fell to his knees, dropping the sack.

"Six..."

The stone rolled out of the sack, and where it touched the soil, the ground beneath began to glow. Its earthy song reached into Anwyn's soul.

"Seven..."

Unwittingly, he reached out with both hands and seized the stone. Its primal song flowed softly through every fiber of his being. The life within it surged around him. The very earth seemed to groan.

"Eight..."

"What do you will of me, harper mage?" a woman's voice sang to his soul.

"Nine..."

Save her! Please save the Guardian! he cried with his mind, still clutching the stone.

"Ten!" Bres shouted. "Kill her!"

Anwyn could not truly say what happened for several moments. The earth song continued to throb in every part of him, and yet the world beyond his inner senses was wrapped in wool. He was aware of something moving through him, some presence he could not visibly perceive. And of a power as ancient and strong as the world itself. There seemed to be nothing in his field of vision, save the glow of the sphere clutched in his hands.

And then he heard it, the muffled screams of men in terror and pain. The night rang with the wretched sounds of death. The air around him thickened with the dank odor of rich loam, suffocatingly sweet. Power rushed around him, making him one with the earth and the song. The screams died to whimpers, then nothing. Silence veiled the world, except for the low thrum of the song..

"Anwyn, let go before it consumes you!" Glynnanis's voice rang sharp and clear.

Anwyn gasped and jerked his hands away from the stone. The earth song faded and the sphere lost its brilliance. He sank back, staring in horror.

"What have I done?" he whispered.

"Anwyn?" Nessa's voice was full of concern. "Are you all right?" He turned to find Nessa crouched just at the edge of the tree. "What happened?" he asked, noting her clothes were splattered with mud.

"I was about to ask you the same question," Nessa said, one eyebrow rising. "One minute, I was standing on a dry dirt road, about to have my throat cut, and the next, I'm watching a sea of mud reach out to suck every last man into the ground." She shuddered and wiped mud from her hands.

"Lord Bres?"

"Gone with the rest," Nessa said. "Just what did you do?"

"I didn't... I mean..." He felt himself trembling. "I only asked her to help you..."

"Asked who?"

"The... Avatar."

"By the Four," Nessa said and sat down, her face growing pale. "How did you summon her?"

"The heartstone," he said, nodding towards the sphere that now looked as dull as a riverstone. Had it lost its power? He reached for it, and the earth song gently hummed. "You'd better take this back to the Temple of the Four," he said, quickly catching up the leather sack and pushing the stone into it with the hem of his cloak, unwilling to touch it with his hands. He thrust the sack into Nessa's care.

"The gates of Allynford are kept locked from dark to dawn, so we'll have to find a generous farm hold for the night. There are several near the walls." She eyed her burden with a hint of respect. "And there are still the guards Lord Bres loosed about the Temple, though I doubt they'll be much trouble once they realize he is gone."

"I'm sure you'll manage," Anwyn said.

"Aye, I will at that," Nessa said. She pulled herself to her feet, dusting soil from the knees of her trews in spite of the great quantity splattering her armor. "Are you coming?"

"If you don't mind, I'd just as soon stay here awhile," he said.

"Suit yourself, harper Anwyn," she said and grinned. "Oh, and thank you. I now owe you my life."

"Not really," Anwyn said. "The Avatar saved you. I merely asked for her help."

"I doubt she would have given it to one undeserving," Nessa said and shrugged. Hooking the sack to her belt, she glanced about at the world. "Then may you find peace of mind and good fortune on your journey." She stepped back onto the road, trudging towards the outcrop of farm holds scattered like mushrooms around the township walls.

Anwyn stayed where he was, drawing his cloak tight about him and nestling himself against the ancient tree.

"I think she likes you," Glynnanis said. *"Of course, she's not your type."*

Anwyn shook his head. "She reminds me far too much of my sisters," he said with a faint smile. "They used to push me around and tease me more than my brothers did."

"Did all your sisters wear armor?" Glynnanis quipped.

"All save the two who wed and gladly gave up their swords to raise their families," Anwyn replied with a long sigh and glanced off at the distant lights of Allynford. Its silhouette against the night did remind him a little of Nymbaria Hold, and the resemblance sent a rush of longing into him. He missed his family just now. Perhaps tomorrow, he would gate back to visit them before returning to Lamboria to continue his journey.

As if knowing his heart needed soothing, the ground beneath him grew warm as a mother's embrace. Softly, he heard the faint hum of the earth song offering comfort to his weary soul.

INGREDIENTS

by Lawrence Watt-Evans

Lawrence Watt-Evans is the author of more than two dozen books and a hundred short stories—science fiction, fantasy, horror, humor, etc.— including the Hugo-winning story "Why I Left Harry's All-Night Hamburgers", the ETHSHAR fantasy series, and most recently the Tor novel TOUCHED BY THE GODS. He was president of the Horror Writers Association from 1994 to 1996, has scripted comic books for Marvel, Dark Horse, and Tekno Comix, and has meddled in various other things best left alone. He's been happily married for more than twenty years and has two kids and a cat.
    —MZB

Irillon watched, fascinated and appalled, as Therindallo was dragged up onto the scaffold. He wasn't struggling, but that was obviously because he had already been severely beaten; his hair was matted with blood.

She frowned at that—partly from her natural human sympathy, but also wondering whether that might cause her any difficulty. She needed both blood and hair, but they were supposed to be separate—and she was fairly sure she needed the blood to be liquid, not clotted.

Finding herself thinking so callously about human blood troubled her. There were times, ever since she began her apprenticeship, when she had serious reservations about this whole wizardry business, and this was one of those times. In fact, this was perhaps the most extreme yet. She had always known that wizards required a variety of odd ingredients for their spells, and even that some of them were not just odd but loathsome, but until now she had not really given much thought to just what that meant—not until her master, Ethtallion the Mage, had told her what she was to fetch this time.

In the past eighteen months since becoming Ethtallion's apprentice she had gathered ash from the hearth, had helped catch spiders, had ground up those spiders once they were properly dried out, had bought roosters' toes from the local farmers, had collected her own tears and drawn her own blood when asked, and none of that had been especially unpleasant—not that drawing blood had been *fun,* but it was not really dreadful.

Collecting the blood and hair of an executed criminal, and a piece of the scaffold he died on, was an entirely different matter—especially since the "criminal" in question was being beheaded for a crime Irillon herself was equally guilty of. Therindallo's "treason" was swearing fealty to the King of the Isle, rather than the King of the Coast, and Irillon of the Isle, like all her family, also took the Islander side in Tintallion's civil war.

She could hardly admit that here in the royal seat of Tintallion of the Coast, though—she would be arrested immediately, or perhaps simply killed on the spot. At the thought she glanced nervously at her neighbors in the small, sullen crowd gathered in the plaza below the walls of Coast Castle.

They didn't look very enthusiastic about the proceedings but they were making no move to protest, either; the only visible movements were stamping and huddling against the cold. Irillon pulled her own cloak tight, and suddenly found herself shivering uncontrollably. She turned her attention back to the scaffold, trying to distract herself.

The guardsmen threw Therindallo on the block and buckled a strap across his shoulders; the executioner stepped forward and raised his axe. Then he paused, waiting, for no reason Irillon could see.

An official in royal livery stepped forward, fumbling with his coat; he pulled out a paper and began to read aloud.

It was a short speech that basically said King Serulinor was the rightful ruler of Tintallion and that he was having Therindallo's head chopped off for not agreeing. A good many words were wasted reciting Serulinor's alleged titles and grievances, and rejecting his cousin's claim to the throne; Irillon's attention wandered, and she found herself glancing up at the overcast sky, wondering whether it was going to snow again.

She hoped not; she had walked almost ten leagues through the snow to get here, and the walk back would be quite bad enough without the weather gods adding any further depth to what was already on the ground.

Then the official finished reading, rolled up his message, and tucked it in his sleeve, and the executioner's axe fell without any further ceremony, so suddenly that Irillon didn't quite see it happen.

INGREDIENTS

Blood splashed, a really amazing quantity of blood, and Therindallo's head dropped into the waiting basket. The executioner knew his job, and had needed only a single stroke.

Gasps and a smothered squeal came from the audience. Irillon gagged at the sight of the headless body, then swallowed hard, trying to tell herself that at least it was quick, and Therindallo couldn't have suffered much. It was over—and now she needed to get Therindallo's blood and hair, and a piece of the scaffold.

Two of the guards were dragging the body away, though, and a third followed, carrying the basket. The executioner was climbing down one set of steps, the official down the other, and the little crowd was already dispersing.

Irillon blinked in surprise and almost called out; she had somehow assumed that the body would be left there, where she could reach it. She hesitated, trying to think what she should do, and a moment later she was standing alone in the plaza, her feet sinking in muddy slush.

The scaffold was still there, at any rate; she finally collected her wits sufficiently to walk up to it, draw her belt knife, and pry a few splinters from the edge of the platform.

She looked over at the bloodstains that spread out from the block, and hurried around to the side, fishing a vial from her belt-pouch. There she stooped and peered underneath.

Yes! Blood was still dripping through the cracks between planks. She collected several drops, then sealed the vial and tucked it away. For good measure she pried up a few more splinters, this time choosing damp, stained ones.

"Hai!" a man's voice shouted. "Get away from there!" He spoke with a Coastal accent.

Irillon looked up, startled, and saw a guard coming toward her, one hand reaching to grab. She turned and ran, heedless of direction, out of the plaza and into the narrow ways of the surrounding town. She heard a few heavy footsteps behind her at first, but after a moment's desperate flight through the winding streets she paused, back pressed against a cold stone wall, looking and listening, and could make out no signs of pursuit.

She was panting from fear and exertion, and she gasped and swallowed, trying to catch her breath. Then she looked down at her hands.

Her knife—her *athame,* her wizard's dagger—was in one hand; the other clutched a little bundle of bloody splinters. A vial half-full of Therindallo's blood was in her pouch.

That was two of the three ingredients she had come for; now she needed some of his hair.

But the guards had taken Therindallo's head away with them, in that basket—how could she ever find it, to cut a lock of hair?

She could scarcely walk openly into the castle looking for it; she was an Islander, and if the guards questioned her her accent would almost certainly give her away—she could try to disguise it, but she doubted her ability to convince anyone.

And if she were recognized as an Islander, she would get much *too* close a look at that scaffold.

It was such a shame that the king's father had been a twin, and that the wetnurse had lost track of which boy was the older; if that hadn't happened this stupid war would never have begun, and Irillon could have gone anywhere in Tintallion in relative safety. If only the Coastal King's line would die out, so the rightful king could assert his authority...

But that wasn't going to happen. Serulinor had a daughter. No son as yet, but a daughter would do to continue the feud. And Buramikin had a son, so the Islander line would also last at least another generation.

And people like Irillon would have to choose one side, and be in constant danger from the other any time they left their homes.

She had caught her breath now; she sheathed her knife, and wrapped the splinters in a handkerchief before tucking them away in her pouch.

That severed head was somewhere back in the castle. She had to go back. She couldn't go back to Ethtallion without that hair! He had already complained bitterly about her ineptitude, cursing his decision to take her on as an apprentice; if she went home without what he had sent her for he might well cast her out completely.

And while she did already know seven spells, she couldn't imagine making a living from those seven. The only one that had any obvious commercial value was the Dismal Itch, and an entire career of imposing and removing such a trivial curse had no appeal at all.

She adjusted her scarf, turning it over in hopes the guard who had chased her off wouldn't recognize her, and slogged back toward the plaza.

At least Tintallion of the Coast wasn't big enough to get really lost in, as she had on her one visit to Ethshar of the Rocks—she could catch a glimpse of the castle's central tower from almost any intersection, and use that as a guide. She arrived safely back at the square without incident.

Four big men were tearing down the scaffold; if she had waited any longer than she had she would never have been able to get a piece of it. She let her breath out in a cloud at the sight.

Then she looked at the castle, trying to imagine how she might get in. The gates, twenty feet to the right of the vanishing scaffold, were closed, the portcullis down. The walls were cold, featureless stone, thirty feet high, topped with elaborate battlements...

And on those battlements two soldiers were setting a pike into place, with Therindallo's head impaled upon the pike.

Irillon had heard of people putting heads on pikes as a warning to others, but she had never seen it done before; she blinked, and swallowed bile.

It was truly disgusting. Therindallo's mouth hung hideously open, and something dark was oozing down the pikeshaft.

On the other hand, now she knew where she could get the hair she needed. And she even knew how. The pike was set leaning out over the castle wall, for better display—all she needed to do was stand directly below it, then use Tracel's Levitation to rise straight up until she could reach out and cut a lock of hair.

But she would, of course, have to wait until the guards left. She leaned back against the wooden corner of a nearby shop, rubbing her hands together to warm them, and watched.

The pike was in place and left unattended within a minute or two; the scaffold was cleared away in perhaps a quarter of an hour. The guards ambled away—except for one, who stood by the gate, looking bored.

Irillon frowned, shuffling her feet to warm them and clear away the slush; was he going to stay there?

Apparently he was. She watched, shivering, hoping he would doze off, or step away for a moment.

If he did step away, she realized, he might not be gone for long. She would need to act quickly when the opportunity arose. Tracel's

Levitation took four or five minutes to prepare—she couldn't afford to waste a second.

She opened her pouch and rummaged through it. She had brought the ingredients for all the spells she knew—tannis root for the Dismal Itch, dust for Felshen's First Hypnotic Spell, a whistle and tiny tray for the Spell of Prismatic Pyrotechnics, and so on. For the Levitation she needed a rooster's toe, an empty vial, a raindrop caught in midair, and her *athame*. She found them all, then stuffed everything else back.

Someone brushed past her, bundled up against the cold, and hurried across the plaza. That reminded her that it wasn't just the guard she needed to avoid; it was *anyone* in this hostile town. Fortunately, the gloomy cold and damp seemed to be keeping almost everyone inside.

With the ingredients in her hand she watched the guard; he didn't seem to have noticed her presence at all. He was staring dully straight ahead, at the next street over from the corner where she stood.

All the same, she decided she had stood in one place long enough; it might be suspicious, and besides, the cold wasn't as bad when she was moving. She began strolling along, looking in the shop windows, as if she were simply bored.

She was actually watching the reflections in the windows more than looking at the goods displayed, but she hoped no one would notice.

She had been wandering aimlessly back and forth, staying always in sight of the gate and its guard, for what seemed like hours, when at last the guard shifted uneasily, turned, and trotted out of sight down an alley, one hand tugging at his kilt.

Irillon dashed across the square, her hands already busy with the spell's preparatory gestures. She mumbled the incantation quickly as she ran.

She came to a stop with her nose to the castle wall, beside the gate and below the pike, still chanting. She dipped the raindrop up with the cock's toe, performed the necessary ritual gestures, transferred the drop to the empty vial, then closed the vial and tapped it with her *athame*.

At that tap she felt suddenly light; she tucked everything but her knife away and spoke the final word, and rose from the muddy ground.

A moment later she stopped herself, hanging unsupported thirty feet in the air, just a foot or two from poor Therindallo's ruined face. He looked much worse close up, but she refused to let herself think about that as she grabbed a hank of his hair and began sawing it free.

Seconds later, with her knife sheathed and the hair safely stuffed into yet another vial, she spoke the word that would trigger her descent.

Only then did she remember to look down.

The guard was back at his post, but now he had his sword drawn and was staring up at her.

There was nothing she could do, though; she was sinking slowly downward, like a pebble in oil, and there was no way to restore the spell before she touched ground.

Desperately, she drew her knife again and tried to think what she could do.

She was a girl of fourteen, not large for her age, armed with a belt-knife; he was a burly guardsman with a sword. She couldn't fight him fairly.

She was a wizard's apprentice, and knew just seven spells. She couldn't use Tracel's Levitation again in time to be any help; the Dismal Itch would just annoy him; and Fendel's Elementary Protection wouldn't stop cold iron, such as a sword. The Spell of Prismatic Pyrotechnics or the Sanguinary Deception or the Spell of the Spinning Coin wouldn't do any good here at all.

That left Felshen's First Hypnotic as her only chance; if she could daze the guard with it she might be able to escape before he recovered. She reached for her pouch...

But not in time; the guardsman stepped forward and grabbed her ankle before she could get the flap open. She yelped, startled, and tried to wrench free, but could not escape, and as the Levitation continued to fade she tumbled backward until she was lying on her back in the snow, one leg raised, the guardsman gripping the ankle tightly with one hand, and pointing his sword at her chest with the other.

"I think you need to speak to the captain," the guard said, not unkindly.

Irillon, flustered but not so distraught as to forget her Islander accent, didn't reply at all.

A few moments later she was inside the castle, being escorted into a small, wonderfully warm room; guardsmen gripped both her arms, and her knife had been carefully taken away. A fire burned cheerily on the hearth at one end of the room, while armor and weapons adorned the other walls. Much of the floor space was taken up by a heavy wooden table, its surface strewn with rolls of paper; on the far side of that table sat another guardsman, but this one was older and more elegantly attired, with rings on his fingers and a golden band about his right arm.

He looked up. "What's this?" he asked.

The right-hand guard explained, "She was stealing hair from the piked head over the gate. She flew up there and back."

The seated guardsman leaned back in his chair. "Flew?"

"Yes, sir," the guard replied.

"Just the hair? Not the whole head?"

"Just hair."

"Then she's not a relative trying to give it a proper pyre." The guard shrugged.

The seated man looked Irillon in the eye. "I'm Captain Alderamon," he said. "Who are you?"

Irillon swallowed and said nothing.

Alderamon waited a moment, giving her time to change her mind, then sighed.

"You're a thief," he said. "Thieves we punish. If you flew, though, you might be a magician, and magicians we treat more respectfully. Now, thieves might be mute, I suppose, or deaf, but a wizard or a theurgist or a demonologist can't be, because then he couldn't recite incantations. I don't know for certain about witches or warlocks, or all the other sorts of magician, but I never *met* one who couldn't speak. Let me ask again—who are you?"

She looked at him, at his unyielding face, and realized that if she remained silent she would be treated as a common thief. While that would probably mean flogging or imprisonment rather than beheadlng, it still wasn't anything she cared to experience. Islander accent or not, she had to speak.

"I'm Irillon of... Irillon the Apprentice," she said, trying to imitate the captain's accent.

"Apprentice what? Who's your master?"

"Apprentice to Ethtallion the Mage. I'm a wizard."

INGREDIENTS

"I thought so. Only a wizard would have any immediate use for a dead man's hair." He leaned forward, elbows on the table. "Irillon, we don't want any trouble with the Wizards' Guild, but you *were* caught stealing. Can you *prove* you're a wizard's apprentice?"

"Yes," Irillon said. "If you give me back my knife I can show you a spell. And there's a spell on me that will tell my master if I'm harmed..."

"The Spell of the Spinning Coin, I suppose?" Alderamon interrupted.

"Yes," Irillon admitted, startled that a non-wizard had ever heard of it. She had certainly never heard of it before her apprenticeship.

"So if your heart stops, the coin will stop spinning. I've had it explained to me before. We certainly don't want *that.* Now, what spell can you demonstrate? Something harmless, please!"

"Ah...the Spell of Prismatic Pyrotechnics?"

Alderamon nodded, and a moment later Irillon had the spell ready. She blew on the silver whistle, and a shower of sparks in a hundred different hues sprang up from the little silver tray, exploding in tiny bursts of color.

"Very pretty," Alderamon acknowledged. "And it would seem you are indeed a wizard's apprentice. Now, in that case, why were you stealing that hair, rather than buying it?"

Irillon blinked in surprise.

"Buying it?" she said.

"Of course."

"Ethtallion...my master just said to fetch the ingredients..."

"And he didn't mention that we sell them?" Alderamon sighed. "Well, we do. I told you, we don't want any trouble with the Wizards' Guild. That means we don't try to withhold ingredients wizards need for their spells—but that doesn't mean we'll just give them away! You don't give away your spells, do you?"

Irillon stared at him in amazed silence.

"Wizardry has been around for centuries, Irillon," the captain said. "In all that time, naturally we've found arrangements that are comfortable for everyone. What sort of fools would we be if we didn't know wizards use hair and blood and bone, and pieces of scaffold, and fireplace ash, and dragon's scales, and a thousand other things? And what would be gained by either denying wizards those ingredients, or giving them away for free?"

Irillon still couldn't think of anything to say.

"Now, do you have coins, or will we need to work out an exchange?"

"Uh...how much...I have some..."

And the dickering began.

In the end, Irillon paid seven bits in silver—all she had with her—and placed the Dismal Itch on two guardsmen who had been involved in a drunken brawl, promising to remove it again in three days. In exchange, she kept the blood, hair, and splinters she had already collected, and was allowed to depart freely.

Captain Alderamon escorted her to the castle gate. There he patted her on the shoulder and said quietly, "Here you go, girl, safe and sound—but take my advice and don't come back here. I told you we didn't want any trouble with the Wizards' Guild, and we don't, but next time might be different. Don't come here again."

Irillon, greatly relieved that her mission appeared to be a success and made bold thereby, looked up at him. "Why not?" she asked.

Alderamon grimaced. "Do you really need to ask? Your imitation of a Coastal accent is *terrible.*"

Then he pushed her out the gate and turned away.

LOST MOON

by India Edghill

India Edghill's interest in fantasy can be blamed squarely on her father, who read her THE WIZARD OF OZ, THE FIVE CHILDREN AND IT, and ALF'S BUTTON before she was old enough to object. Later she discovered Andrew Lang's multi-colored fairy books, Edward Eager, and the fact that Persian cats make the best paperweights. She has sold stories to CATFANTASTIC IV, Marion Zimmer Bradley's FANTASY Magazine, The Magazine of Fantasy and Science Fiction, and the Datlow/Windling Fairy Tales anthology (#5). She and her cats own too many books on far too many subjects. She has written an as-yet-unpublished novel about Queen Michal of Israel, and is currently at work of another historical novel.
—MZB

The quest to restore something that is lost is one of the most ancient stories. The modern reader brings to such a story a particular collection of expectations about the object searched for and how it is found, but at the risk of sounding pretentious, think "Lost Moon" is a story about confounding the subtext of expectation. This version is set in a timeless fantasy world that is at the same time familiar and peculiarly other, and the question is, what is it that really has been lost, and what is it that the young heroine finds?
—Rosemary Edghill

On nights when the moon was full, Tira danced at midnight in the old apple orchard behind her father's farmhouse. On those three nights she lay awake in her clean narrow bed until the rest of her family slept and the house itself seemed to dream. When the silence spread through the house until her own heartbeat sounded loud within her ears, Tira slipped from her bed to curl upon her windowsill and watch the full moon rise.

She watched as the bright moon gently rose into the sky, turning its ebon black to deepest blue and overwhelming the cold diamond brilliance of the stars with her glowing light. And at midnight, when the moon's silver disc rode high in the heavens and roofs and roads and wheatfields reflected moonlight like rough mirrors, Tira slipped from her room and down the narrow stairs, moving silently as a sigh to lift the latch on the kitchen door.

Then she walked through the moon-bright night, through the kitchen-yard to the gate that separated farm from orchard. The gate was almost as old as the orchard, its wood time-dark even in full moonlight. But it always opened easily to Tira's touch, admitting her into the half-wild place it guarded.

In the orchard a thin path ran through the twisted trees; a path worn through the long grass by Tira's bare feet, for she had danced with the moon since she was a child. Since the night silver light across her face had woken her from black nightmare and she had peered fearfully out her window to see moonlight dancing among the ancient apple trees. Moon-called, she had run out of the house to try and catch the moonbeams in her small hands.

The next morning she had been found asleep under the massive tangled apple tree in the center of the old orchard. Her feet were grass-stained and the hem of her nightdress soaked with dew, and her fists were clenched over nothing. The moonbeams in her hands had vanished at moonset.

When shaken and questioned, Tira told her angrily fearful mother that she had had a nightmare; it was decided that the child must have walked in her sleep. In future months Tira took care never again to worry her mother. Moonlit nights were too precious to lose.

Since that long-ago night, Tira had danced with the full bright moon each month. And during the dark nights between, the memory of those midnights danced silver in her eyes.

No one knew the moon and her moods better than Tira. Each month she watched fading moonlight as the bright moon waned; endured three long black nights as the moon rose dark. But after the dark came the rising light, until the moon shone full and bright once more.

Today Tira had been restless, her fingers clumsy on her household tasks, for her mind and heart were elsewhere. Tonight the moon rose full at sunset.

And as the sun fell in the west, Tira stood by the pen where she was supposed to be feeding the young pigs and watched for the full moon to rise in the darkening east—first with anticipation and then, as the sky melted from day's blue into night, with an odd dread.

For no moon rose.

Tira stared and waited, shivering in the chill night air, until her eldest sister called crossly from the doorway that Tira must come lay the table for supper. With great care, Tira poured the remaining slops into the piglets' trough and walked towards the house. At the half-open door she stopped and once more searched the darkening heavens.

At the rim of the western horizon, day fled in a splendor of fire and rose. Above the treetops to the east, stars burned cold in a black silk sky.

But in all the wide night sky, the dancing moon was nowhere to be seen.

Tira waited through three black nights, searching the sky in vain. But the moon did not rise. And by the time a fortnight had passed, it was clear that the bright moon was gone, and only dark nights remained.

No one knew what had happened to the moon, although there were wild guesses enough to fill a fortune-teller's bowl. The missing moon was a curse, plain enough; the land had been hexed by goblins or blighted by trolls. Gypsies had netted the moon and melted it down into silver coin. A dragon had gobbled up the moon, and would soon start on the local maidens.

But after the first shock of the moon's loss passed, and nothing else untoward occurred to trouble them, others grew accustomed to moonless nights and endless dark.

But Tira did not. The lost moon shone in her eyes; her blood beat faster on nights when the bright moon should have risen and poured silver moonlight over the black world. On those empty nights Tira haunted the orchard, a human ghost shadowing the dark beneath the twisted trees.

But she could not dance in darkness.

Spring passed, and summer too, and by the evening that autumn's chill first bit the air, it seemed to Tira that all but she had long forgotten there had ever been a full bright moon shining in the midnight sky. On the night the full hunter's moon should have risen but did not, Tira flung herself upon the frost-rimed grass beneath the oldest apple tree and wept in black despair.

And when she had cried so long her eyes ached, Tira lay and stared up through the apple tree's interlaced branches into the empty night sky. No moon; no bright moon ever again...

"*No.*" Tira's voice, hoarse from an hour's weeping, echoed through the trees like a rasping sigh. *No, I will not let her be lost to me. There must be something I can do.* And that was when Tira remembered the witch who lived on the other side of the wood.

The house held no hint that within its walls, it contained a witch and her magic. In fact, the witch's house looked very much like all the other houses Tira had ever seen—save that its yard seemed tidier than most, and that even in autumn, white roses bloomed beside its green-painted door.

There was one difference, an ominous one. No welcome-lantern hung above that rose-framed door.

But a fire's warm light gleamed between the chinks of the shutters protecting the house from the dangers of night air. A fire meant someone sat beside its comforting flames.

Telling herself firmly she had nothing to fear—save bruises if her father came to hear of this—Tira raised her hand and knocked upon the witch's door.

Tira didn't know what the witch would be like. But she had fashioned an image in her mind from fairy tales and gossip of an elderly white-haired dame, bent and wrinkled by long years and harsh magics.

The woman who answered Tira's knock was neither bent nor wrinkled. She was full-bodied and tall, and her mass of fire-red hair was piled high upon her head and skewered into place with green glass pins. Wisps of hair escaped the pins' confinement to dance like willful flames about her neck and cheeks. She was, perhaps, as old as Tira's mother and looked far less worn by care.

"Oh," she said, "it's you."

Unsure how to respond, Tira opted for the truth. "I've come to see the—the witch."

"You're looking at her," the fire-haired woman told Tira. "Now what are you staring at, girl? Has my face turned green?"

Tira shook her head.

"Of course it hasn't." There was a pause, then the witch added meaningfully, "I'm sure your good mother taught you better manners than this."

Flushing, Tira sketched a curtsy. "Oh, she did," she assured the witch. "And—"

"And if she knew you were here, she wouldn't like it at all, so don't bother concocting a tale about how she sent you here for some idiotic potion or other. If she wanted something of me, she'd have come herself, as is proper." The witch eyed Tira keenly, and Tira's face reddened. "So you've come for yourself, and at your age, too. Well, if it's a love charm, my girl, you can turn right 'round and march yourself back home. You're too young for that nonsense."

"It's not a love charm," Tira said hastily, "and it's not for me—well, not *just* for me, but nobody else seems to care, and—"

"And I think," said the witch, stepping back and opening the door wide, "that you may come in, if you like. And you may ask your favor of me. And after that, we'll see."

Rather to Tira's surprise, the witch's cottage looked no different than any other well-kept house. True, bunches of herbs hung drying above the fireplace, but where else would one dry herbs, after all? A cat coiled upon the hearth, but the animal was a mere brown tabby, plump and placid and prosaic as a loaf of bread. Tira was faintly disappointed; she'd expected better—or worse—of a witch's house.

"Now," said the witch, crossing her arms and staring sternly down at Tira, "what brought you here, and at this time of night, too? You ought to be asleep in your bed." The witch sounded quite as censorious as Tira's own mother.

"I—I came—" To Tira's mortification, she sounded like a squeaking mouse; she stopped, trying to summon persuasive words.

"Perhaps you'd better go home," suggested the witch hopefully.

"No!" Tira drew a deep breath and pressed on. "The moon's gone."

"I've noticed," said the witch.

"I want the moon back," Tira said.

"Well," said the witch, "it's about time someone bothered to do something about that. Out of the mouths of babes, they say."

"I'm not a babe," Tira protested before she thought. But as no supernatural punishment was inflicted upon her for her temerity, Tira gained confidence enough to ask, "Will you tell me what happened? Why is the moon gone?"

The witch seemed to consider for a moment, then said, "Humans aren't the only shortsighted creatures cluttering up the Lands, you know."

Tira didn't know, but the witch's tone had been caustic enough to etch glass, and Tira hesitated to provoke her further. "Oh," Tira said at last, and the witch seemed to relent somewhat.

"There's a good many afraid of the dark, as you know—oh, don't bother to deny it. Well, there are just as many afraid of the light, and with more reason."

"Oh," Tira said again, and then dared ask, "Are you afraid—"

"I fear neither. The world needs both, not that you can make some folk understand simple fact." The witch sounded both irritated and long-suffering; she sighed, and went on, "A dark of the moon without a full-bright one for balance is just plain unnatural. I don't like things that aren't natural."

Tira considered this, and asked, "If you don't like the moon being gone, why haven't you done something about it?"

"Because I can't."

"But why not? You're a—"

"Witch," the woman prompted helpfully, as Tira hesitated over the word. "Perhaps I am, but that doesn't mean I can whistle and have the world dance."

"Oh," said Tira.

"Disappointed? Well, there are rules, you know, and a price for everything. I can neither advise nor interfere, only wait to be asked." The witch wrapped a shawl snugly around her shoulders and nodded to the stool beside the hearth. "Sit down, girl, and ask your favor. And be careful how you ask it, and that's all the advice you'll get from me."

Tira sat gingerly upon the smooth-polished wooden stool, keeping her back straight and folding her hands in her lap. The witch sat cross-legged on the braided rug before the fire, beside the dozing tabby cat.

"Odd how things turn out," the witch remarked, stroking the cat, which purred in an absent-minded way. "I'd expected half the village here long since about the moon. But no; half a year goes by without any more gumption out of them than you'd find in a peck of turnips. And finally what do I get? A slip of a girl mousing up to my front door."

"I think," said Tira, choosing her words with care, "that everyone else just got used to the moon being gone and the nights always dark."

The witch bent and muttered something close to the tabby cat's ear. To Tira, it sounded as if the witch had simply said *"People,"* in an exasperated tone, but surely that couldn't be right. Doubtless, thought Tira, the witch was asking her familiar's advice and aid. The tabby cat yawned, showing a rose-pink tongue and sharp white teeth.

The witch shook her head, and for a moment Tira wondered if the witch's precariously-pinned hair would fall loose. But the green glass pins held the flaming tresses securely; only a few tendrils skittered across the witch's cheeks. "I suppose you're right, girl—it's amazing what people will get used to, especially if the remedy's difficult of achievement."

Correctly interpreting this to mean that finding the missing moon would be arduous, Tira hastened to assure the witch that she didn't care how difficult the task might be.

"Or how dangerous?" the witch asked, continuing her idle stroking of the sleepy-eyed cat.

"Or how dangerous." Tira thought of the endless black nights without even the hope of moonlight and shivered.

"So you're not afraid?"

"Yes," Tira said, "but not as afraid as I am of the dark nights."

"Dark of the moon's all very well," said the red-haired witch, "and so's her sister, but one without the other's unnatural. So ask and pay, and get what you've asked and paid for."

I never thought of payment! Tira knew from the old tales told by the fireside that a witch must be paid with something of value. Tira owned only one thing of value: the chain of silver links she wore around her neck. Moon-metal, given to a moon child, and her only jewel. But it was all Tira had to offer, and so she lifted her hands and unclasped the silver chain from around her neck.

"I can give you this." With a pang for her loss, Tira tilted her hand and the silver chain slithered from her palm to coil in the witch's cupped hand.

"Well," said the witch, running her fingers over the silver chain's delicate links, "I see you know how to pay for what you want, child." The witch rose and went to the table, where she dropped Tira's chain into the balance of a scale. To Tira's surprise, the scale's balance sank down as if the little chain were thick lead instead of thin silver. The witch smiled.

"Well paid; now ask and receive what you ask. But I grant only what you ask, so think well before you ask it."

"I want to see the Moon," Tira said, "and I want the shining moon back in the night sky."

Sighing, the witch shook her head. "Sloppy," she said. "You'll learn." Then she went on, in a brisk, no-nonsense tone, "Very well, I shall give you the means to obtain what you have asked and paid for." The witch scooped the silver chain out of the scale and dropped it to coil in Tira's lap.

"Keep your silver; as payment, I wish you to complete a task for me."

"What is that?" Tira asked, wary.

"When you have seen what you wish and done what you must, you are to sew a sampler with your own hands, and when it is well-sewn down to the last stitch, you are to hang it over your bed and read it aloud every night before you say your prayers."

"Very well," Tira agreed, glad the task was no more arduous than embroidery. "What is this sampler to say?"

"'Be careful what you ask for'," the witch said, "'for what you ask may be granted.' Now take what I'll give you and listen to what I'll tell you, and don't come blaming me for what happens when you do it."

Three midnights later, on a night when the moon should have been shining against the sky, Tira slunk out of the house once again. Silent as a weasel, she ran through black shadows down the path to the apple orchard. With each step her heart pounded and with each breath she gasped with fear; without the moon, the night was very dark.

Beneath the trees, it was darker still. Tira felt her cautious way through the trees to the center of the orchard. When the blackness became too frightening, she closed her eyes and felt her way along, praying for the courage to take each step. Where the oldest apple trees grew, Tira stopped, and pulled the talisman the witch had given her from her apron pocket. She rubbed its silver surface with the corner of her apron, and then set the small round mirror upon the cold hard ground as she had been instructed.

Now I will see the moon.

Tira waited, growing colder and more frightened with each heartbeat. Around her, shadows clustered like ravens, ominous and chill. Above her, leafless branches entwined, black web against a midnight sky. On the ground before her, the witch's mirror shone like a black moon...

The night wind rose and the night shadows wavered like dark flames. And then a woman stepped down out of the dark night sky.

She had night-black skin and night-black hair and eyes like midnight shadows. The mirror before her feet reflected sparks like bright stars.

I have failed, Tira thought, and so spoke before she weighed her words. "Who are you and why have you come here?"

The night-woman smiled. "You called me down, and so I came."

"No I didn't; I called the moon."

"*I* am the moon." The dark lady's voice sighed, a night-wind's whisper.

"No you're not. The moon is bright and full of silver light."

"Yes, that too. You speak of my sister, the Bright Moon."

Tira stared, and remembered half-a-year ago, when there had been a moon travelling the sky. A moon that had waxed and waned, and then vanished for three dark nights....

"You are the Dark Moon," Tira said, and thought with despair, *The Dark Moon, and I wanted to see the Bright. That is what the witch meant about taking care what I asked. I should have asked to see the Bright Moon. I have wasted my wish—*

Despairing, Tira cried out, "Where is the Bright Moon? Where have you hidden her?" Tira looked up into the black night sky, and then at the Dark Lady standing before her.

"That is not my doing. Why should I banish my sister from the night?"

"Because you were jealous," Tira whispered. "Because she is bright and shining and you are only darkness."

To Tira's surprise, the Dark Moon only laughed, and stars flared in her midnight hair. "And so you think no one loves me? Perhaps you do not, but there are many who love me well—yes, who love me better than they love my bright sister. I offer rest to the weary, sanctuary to the hunted."

"Then where is the Bright Moon?"

"I do not know. I know only that she wished to walk the land for a time, to see the world for herself. But when it was time for her to return, she did not. Now the days grow short and the nights long; soon it will be winter, and the nights longer still."

Thinking of long winter months with no moon to brighten the hard cold nights, Tira shivered. "She must come back," Tira said despairingly.

"Yes, but she has not. My sister is lost and I cannot find her." In the twilight gloom a dark gleam streaked the Dark Moon's cheek: a shadow, or a tear.

Tira stared into the Dark Moon's nightshadow eyes. "Could I find her?"

"Perhaps—if you are willing to risk the dark to find her."

"I will risk anything to have her back," Tira said.

"You must seek my sister where I cannot," the Dark Moon said, "across the land she chose to walk."

"But where shall I look?" Tira asked.

"Her light calls your heart. Surely you will know where to seek her."

But I don't! Tira cried silently.

"And I can give you this," said the Dark Lady, and when Tira held out her cupped hands something round and cool fell into the hollow of her hand. She looked and saw a stone black and fulgent as the Dark Moon herself.

"It is a moonstone," the Dark Moon said. "Look upon it when all is darkest, and it will light your way."

Curious, Tira stared into the black moonstone's midnight heart. And when she lifted her head again, the Dark Moon had vanished. Only night's shadows remained beneath the apple trees. Tira closed her fingers over the dark moonstone and walked swiftly back through the old orchard to the house.

Uncertain where to begin, Tira started upon her search for the Bright Moon by climbing the oldest apple tree in the old orchard. She clung to its topmost branches and gazed across the night-dark land—looked past the farmyard, and past the old apple orchard, and past the road that led to the hills beyond her father's farm. Far across the meadows beyond the dusty road lay a swamp, an unchancy maze of bog and thickets, its secrets guarded by hidden quagmires and tangles of wild thorns. Once the full moon's light had gleamed upon the waters of the swamp, turning its peril into a shimmering lure. Without that reflected moonglow, the swamp was only a blacker stain on the fields of night...

Suddenly Tira stiffened, and stared harder at the distant swamp. Was that a glimmer there, an odd flicker of light deep within the ghost forest's dead and dying trees?

She could not be sure; seven sleepless nights had left her too drained for certainties. Rubbing her hot eyes, Tira looked again. The shadow of light had vanished. Had the silver gleam ever been there, or had her own desire mocked her with illusion?

Tira looked up, seeking the Dark Moon's presence. "Was it moonlight?" she asked, but saw no answer in the starlit sky. This question she must answer for herself.

The untamed swamp was even less pleasant to travel than Tira had feared. Murky water oozed from too-soft ground; long-dead trees, their branches sharply bare, stood guard over the half-drowned land. Even by day, the swamp was unwholesome, avoided by all with any sense. By moon-dark night, the swamp became a malignant quagmire, a snare even for those wary and wise in the patterns of its shadowed maze.

Tira was neither wise nor wary, merely stubbornly determined. For after half-a-year's mourning, she had at last seen moonlight. No matter that that light had been no more than a flicker, a blink of foxfire deep within the swamp's foul depths. No matter how difficult the task, Tira swore she would search the swamp's bogs and fens until she found the Bright Moon it held imprisoned.

A simple vow to make; a harsh vow to fulfill. The swamp tricked her, lured her in with glows of foxfires and fireflies; beguiled her farther and farther into its lethal web. As the night slowly passed and midnight pressed upon Tira's bones, she realized she was lost beyond hope.

Behind her lay the chimera's-nest of the swamp through which she had wandered for so many dark hours. Before her a mass of briars barred her way. Black sky above; black thickets ahead; black fen behind. Never before had Tira been so shrouded in black velvet darkness. Fear throbbed through her blood, its cold beat urging her to run until she ran free of the feral swamp and its midnight perils.

But to run would only lead her deeper into the clutches of endless darkness. And who knew in what Land she might emerge, if she ever escaped at all?

All is darkness. This is when all is darkest— With a trembling hand, Tira reached deep into her pocket and closed her fingers around the black moonstone that been the Dark Moon's gift. Careful not to drop the precious stone, Tira cupped the moondark gem in her hands and waited, holding her breath.

At first the Dark Moon's gift lay cool and quiet within her grasp. Then, as Tira stared, the moonstone shimmered, and began, slowly and faintly, to glow. The new light was cool as moonlight; like moonlight, it silvered Tira's hands and cast a gentle glow over the earth around her. At last the stone glowed luminous as moonlight, and Tira saw where her wandering steps had brought her.

She had come to the very heart of the swamp, and before her lay a pool. The pool brooded dark and featureless, its banks ringed by long-drowned trees. Thorn-bushes enshrouded the dead trees and sank keen-barbed vines down into the pool's depths.

And deep within those tenebrous depths, as if mirroring the moonstone's glow, Tira saw a flicker of light.

Ignoring the fear that whispered over her chilled skin, Tira leaned far out over the pool, seeking the source of that feeble glow. At first she saw nothing, and then, far below the smooth black surface of the water, her eyes followed a stray gleam of light. And for the first time in half a year, Tira gazed upon the Bright Moon.

But a Bright Moon caged behind briars; a silver radiance trapped within a thorn-studded snarl of vines.

And there was no one to free the Bright Moon from that tangled prison but Tira.

Tira stared down into the pool's black water. Those thorny spines were fang-long and knife-sharp, and the water was very dark and very deep. For a heartbeat, fear whispered, *Forget this, you cannot do it. Go back.* For a breath, Tira hesitated, her hand poised over the chill smooth surface of the pool.

Then the night wind soughed through the trees, as if the Dark Moon sighed for her lost sister and the Bright Moon for her lost freedom. And as the small wind faded, leaving silence behind it, Tira slid her hand into the water.

The swamp water clung to her hand, flowed oddly warm over her cold skin. As she reached down to the thorn-trapped light, Tira thought of serpents, and snapping lizards, and fought the urge to yank her hand free of the clinging water.

There are no snapping lizards, she told herself firmly, *and serpents are more fearful than fearsome.*

Nevertheless, when something slick and supple stroked her hand, Tira uttered a faint shriek, like a dying mouse, and tried to snatch her hand back into the night air. But even as she pulled back, thorns pricked her fingers, and Tira somehow knew that if she failed now, she would get no second chance. Closing her eyes, she lunged forward, shoving her hand through thorns that ripped her flesh, releasing blood that warmed the water circling her questing fingers. And then her torn fingers closed over something cool and soft, and Tira knew she had touched the imprisoned moon.

But how to free that bright lady from her thorn-bound trap? Tira tugged, but the snarl of briars refused to release their prisoner. Again Tira tried, and again failed to move the thorny vines. And then Tira knew that if the Bright Moon were ever again to ride the night, Tira herself must enter that dark water and unbind each tangled knot.

The water was cold as well as dark, and the bog deeper than Tira had thought. Beneath her feet the bottom squelched and slid, and barbed vines clutched her knees and ankles as if seeking to drag her down into the muck below. Gritting her teeth against the water's chill and the thorns' keen grip, Tira sank beneath the surface of the pool.

Once surrounded by the dark water, Tira forced herself to open her eyes, and was rewarded by the sight of moonlight glowing in the liquid dusk. Black briars caged the Bright Moon; chained her white wrists and wove through her shining hair. Freeing the Bright Moon would be neither easy nor swift. Grimly conscious of the water's menace, Tira grabbed the briars and pulled herself closer to the trapped Moon. Then, taking infinite care, Tira began to untangle the keen-thorned briars prisoning the Bright Moon.

Long before she had the last bramble unknotted, Tira's body pleaded for air. But Tira refused to abandon her task, fearing that if she paused to take even one breath, the thorned vines would wrap themselves about their prisoner once more.

Her fingers bled and her heart pounded against her breast and by the time she pulled the last thorn from the last strand of moonsilver hair she could see only blackness before her eyes. But then light flashed past her, and Tira knew she had succeeded. The Bright Moon was free at last.

When Tira splashed and sprawled her way out of the frigid pool, she saw the Bright Moon standing upon the muddy bank, her radiance icing the briars and turning the drowned trees to silver ghosts. "You're back," Tira gasped, shoving wet hair out of her eyes. "Oh, you're back."

"I have you to thank for it, brave child." Like her sister's, the Bright Moon's voice was clear and soft. She seemed cooler than her dark sister, her silver light more brilliant than Tira had expected.

"I had to find you," Tira said.

"And you did." With that, the Bright Moon smiled and began to move away from Tira, heading into the trackless swamp. Moonglow washed over wood and water, turned blackness into silvered radiance as the Bright Moon passed by.

"Wait," Tira said, and when the Bright Moon paused and turned back, "I lost my way in this swamp, and cannot find my path home again."

"Oh," said the Bright Moon, apparently startled by this plea. Then she smiled and danced off, beckoning to Tira. "I am not afraid of darkness," the Bright Moon called. "Come, and I will light your way."

The journey back through the swamp took the last strength Tira still possessed. But at last Tira and the Bright Moon came to the place where the soft mud dried to hard earth, and the swamp's cat-tails yielded to wild meadow. There they stopped and Tira savored the solid ground beneath her cold wet feet.

Beside Tira, the Bright Moon stretched, as if reaching for a handful of night stars, and shook out her glowing hair. "Oh, see the sky—and my sister waiting for me. They must have missed me, all those nights I lay prisoned beneath the water and the briars."

"We all missed you," Tira said, and fingered the moonstone resting in her deepest pocket. The Bright Moon was plainly eager to rise into the night sky and be gone; but Tira knew she must ask the question that had tormented her for half a year. "Wait, please. Before you return to the sky, tell me how you came to be buried there, in the swamp pool."

"Why, I wished to come down and walk about upon the earth," said the Bright Moon, as if puzzled that Tira needed to ask. "I yearned to see the land as itself, not as my moon-mirror. I did not know there were creatures who loathed my light, and who wished me harm."

The Bright Moon shuddered and silver radiance rippled upon the meadow grass. "Horrid things seized me and dragged me into the depths of the swamp and prisoned me far beneath the water, hidden from the sight of those who might seek me. I cannot say how many nights I lay captive there, bound by thorns, my light buried deep in darkness—"

"Half a year," Tira said. "I counted every dark night; you were gone for half a year."

"So long? Then I must return to the sky at once." But as the Bright Moon began to rise, she paused between earth and sky to smile one last time at Tira. "You were very clever and very brave, and I am very grateful."

Some response was called for; Tira curtsied, and thanked the Moon for her kind words. "But it was the witch's charm and the Dark Moon's talisman that found you, Bright Lady."

"But it was your own feet that took you into the dark swamp, and your own hands that freed me from the bog," the Bright Moon said. "And it was your own heart that found me." She had risen higher into the sky, luminous as a pearl against the fading night.

"Come and dance with me," she called down.

"I will," Tira promised, even as the Bright Lady shimmered into a silver crescent, a slender crown adorning the rose-gold dawn. Tira smiled, and added, for herself alone, "But I have a task I must complete before I dance again by moonlight."

That night Tira once more watched at her bedroom window, gazing over the treetops to the far horizon. The dying day stained the western sky crimson; on the borderland between sunset and twilight, the Bright Moon rose for the first time in half a year of dark nights.

And in that magic moment called twilight, Tira could clearly see that the Bright Moon held the Dark Lady in the arc of her silver arms.

Smiling, Tira gently touched the black moonstone hanging upon the silver chain around her neck. Then she settled herself upon the wide window-ledge, and began setting the first stitches in the witch's sampler.

REHABILITATION

by Syne Mitchell

I live in the rain-drenched mountains east of Seattle with my husband and three cats. Writing science fiction and fantasy is the only avocation I've stuck to over the years. Other occupations I've pursued include: nuclear physicist, bead seller, high school teacher, and technical writer.

"Rehabilitation" grew out of my first attempts to interview people for story details. Initially, I worried that I wouldn't be able to locate people with the specialized knowledge that I required—or that they wouldn't have time to talk to me. But then I lucked into meeting people with exactly the information I need and who were amazingly gracious in sharing their time and expertise.

I would like to thank the following people who helped me research this story: Jacki Bricker and Carol Bufi for details about the Seattle Aquarium, Robert Reeder for Gaelic translations, and Mike Keiper for explaining 911 procedures. Their help was invaluable; any misinformation is my own invention.

—Syne Mitchell

Marie unlocked the loading-bay door of the Seattle Aquarium and descended into the concrete stairwell.

She groaned. Another shift as an intermittent, filling in at all hours for staff biologists. Would she ever get a permanent position? Would she last that long?

The tang of brine and ozone hit her on the third step. Marie straight-armed the fire door at the base of the stairs and entered one of the oddly shaped workrooms the public never saw.

Bob, the night supervisor, strolled up as she clocked in. He was a wide, lumbering Polynesian man.

"Any special instructions?" she asked.

"We acquired a harbor seal." He waved his maglight in the direction of the rooftop stairs. "A rehab job. Some idiot hit her with his motor boat. Didn't even stop. Two sea-kayakers found her on the beach near Anacortes."

"What's her condition?"

"Stable. There are gashes along her right side, but nearly closed.

They're nothing like the bone-deep gouges described by Fish and Wildlife's report." He shook his head. "Someone down there must have been smoking dope yesterday. She looks viable to me. I don't know why they pulled her from the wild." He shrugged, a great heaving of flesh. "Just stay with her between rounds, make sure she's not bleeding." He pointed to a set of phone numbers posted on the stainless steel refrigerator. "If her wounds reopen, call Joel and the vet."

"I'm surprised Joel isn't camped out here."

"Susan ordered him home. She wants him fresh for the television crews tomorrow." He sketched a banner headline in the air, "Seattle Aquarium saves wounded seal. A little something to spur public interest ...and donations."

Marie's chest tightened. Full-time biologists made the decisions, published research papers, were interviewed by television crews. Her job was hardly worth the name. An on-call temporary with a biology degree. She grabbed her windbreaker off its hook. "Show me the new arrival."

Bob and Marie stomped their hiking boots in a low bucket of disinfectant and climbed up the staircase to the roof.

It was cold outside; the last few days of March still clung to winter. The roof was lit by the twinkling of city lights from the skyscrapers that rose, cliff-like, behind them. Beyond the edges of the roof was the glistening black water of Puget Sound.

Bob and Marie squeezed by a rack of wire cages and walked onto the rooftop. A green fiberglass tub, ten feet in diameter, sat under the sky.

Bob flicked a switch. A sleek body flashed in the halogen glow, pale white freckled with tan. A whiskered face popped out of the water, oversized brown eyes winced in the sudden light. Her cat's face was slender and delicate. Her ears were tiny whorls.

"Isn't she beautiful," Bob breathed.

There was something more than mere appreciation in his voice. His expression was wistful and tender.

The seal's eyes glanced from Marie to Bob, snorted, then slid back into the water; barely a ripple marked her passing.

"I didn't see the wound," Marie said.

"It's on her right side." Bob spoke without looking at Marie. "From her flipper to the base of her tail."

They watched the water, but the seal didn't resurface.

Bob sighed, his round face creasing with regret. "I don't think she likes me."

Marie smiled wryly. "You better not let Joel catch you anthropomorphizing the mammals. He'd read you the riot act."

Bob pursed his lips, staring at the tub. "Maybe." He shrugged. "Either way, she's all yours. I'm for home and bed."

He left and she was alone in the aquarium.

Marie did her rounds. She crawled over convoluted snarls of tubing and squeezed through tightly-packed rows of tanks to check water flows. Her ears pricked for a change in the sound of a pump or a persistent dripping. She peered into tanks to make sure nothing was leaking, dying, or giving birth.

She paused to watch moon jellies pulse in the research tanks, their gentle perambulations like slow-motion ballet. Tiny nauplii, left over from a previous feeding, jittered between tentacles. They glowed like stars where she passed the beam of her flashlight.

Marie finished her rounds and typed a summary report into the computerized log. Time to check on the new arrival; make sure her wounds hadn't reopened.

As she stepped onto the roof, the hair on Marie's back and neck prickled.

A naked human crept across the rooftop towards the pier. White skin reflected the city lights. Its right arm dragged something limp and wet.

Something the size and shape of a harbor seal.

Panic clenched Marie's chest. This couldn't be happening. Not on her shift.

"Stop!" Marie shouted. She flicked on the worklight over the seal's tank. The sudden brightness blinded her. She searched the tank with watering eyes.

Empty.

A wet trail snaked from the tank to the intruder. In the halogen glow, Marie now saw the figure's burden, not a seal—a harbor seal's pelt.

He'd killed the new seal.

Outrage sluiced away fear. Marie couldn't believe her widening eyes. "You monster!" She dashed across the rooftop.

The intruder turned toward her and froze. She was small, barely four feet. Her breasts were mere ripples on the swell of her chest. Only a black triangle of pubic hair marked her as woman, not child.

The woman dropped the pelt and bolted.

Even with a head start, her short legs were no match for Marie's long stride. Marie tackled her at the edge of the roof.

The woman barked in pain as her hip slammed against the concrete railing. She flailed and bit Marie's arm. Needle-sharp teeth drew blood.

Marie pounded the woman's head away, grabbed her right arm and wrenched it behind her back.

Holding her captive with one hand, Marie scanned the rooftop.

Marie's adrenaline was wearing off and she was scared. This tiny woman couldn't have killed and skinned a harbor seal. She must have accomplices.

"Cuidich rium," the woman wailed as Marie pushed her through the rooftop door.

Marie seated her captive on a molded-plastic chair near the coffee pot then duct-taped her wrists and ankles together.

Keeping an eye on the woman, Marie opened the first-aid cabinet and pulled out bandages and antibiotic ointment. She stripped off her jacket and inspected her arm. The gash looked more like a knife cut than a bite.

The woman watched Marie dress the wound. Soulful dark eyes followed her every move.

Any other time, Marie would have pitied the woman. But she had killed, or helped kill, the new harbor seal. A hurt, defenseless animal. Marie's eyes narrowed.

How had she gotten onto the roof? And why break into the aquarium to kill? Harbor seal pelts weren't that valuable. Marie looked at the woman's nakedness. Was it a bizarre cult ritual? Was the woman insane?

She picked up the pelt and shook it in the woman's face, "Why did you do this?"

The woman looked at the seal skin and her eyes teared over. She raised her sharp-pointed face to Marie and said, *"Feumaidh mi a'tilleadh gu mhuir."*

"Speak English," Marie said.

The woman blinked and licked her lips. *"Cuidich rium."*

No answers there. Whatever was going on was beyond Marie's

control. There must be others outside. The self-locking fire door to the roof protected her, but vandals could jump down through the netting and destroy the bird exhibit, or trash the salmon pens. Marie picked up the phone and dialed 911.

A man's voice said, "Seattle Police. What is the nature of your emergency?"

Marie tucked the receiver into her shoulder and picked up the seal pelt, examining it as she spoke. Her probing fingers found scarring along its side, probably from a boat's propeller—but it was an old wound, nearly healed.

"There's been a break-in at the aquarium. They're still outside." She smoothed the empty skin against her thighs. It was still warm. "A seal's been—"

There was no blood.

No blood on the pelt. If it had been skinned, it should be dripping. But it, and the woman, were clean.

"Ma'am?" the phone voice asked. "You still there?"

The woman's pale skin was unmarred by any stain, save for a smattering of tan freckles on her back and shoulders. Marie's gaze traveled along her ribs. Scars. Pink and recently healed. The spiraling cuts looked like something she'd seen on manatees while working in Florida ...like cuts made by a boat's propeller.

"Ma'am? I am sending a unit to your location. The police will—"

"No! Don't," Marie said. "I—I made a mistake." Her voice was unconvincing. She hung up before the 911 operator could ask more questions.

Marie examined the pelt closely. There were no entry nor exit wounds. Only a set of recently healed cuts that helixed up the creature's ribs. Marie touched the ridges on the pelt, then the scars on the woman's ribs.

They were the same.

The woman nodded vigorously and wriggled in her bonds. Marie bit her lower lip. It was impossible. This woman couldn't somehow...be the seal?

But Marie's scientific mind couldn't ignore the facts. Her hands held a perfectly empty—and perfectly intact—harbor-seal skin. There was no logical way it could have been removed.

The same wounds, in the same location, on the seal and the woman. Surely that was too much for coincidence? Now that she looked closer, tan patches on the harbor seal's pelt matched clusters of freckles on the woman's shoulders and back.

And where was the seal's corpse? Either it had been thrown into the ocean or...it was sitting in front of her.

"What are you?" she whispered.

The woman glanced from Marie to the pelt. *"Cuidach rium,"* she softly replied.

Marie stared at her features: the pointed chin, the tiny whorled ears, the wide, lipless mouth.

A crazy excitement jolted through Marie. This was the kind of discovery that could make a biologist's career. If she had proof of intelligent aquatic races, there would be no limit to the funding she could raise, the publicity, the scientific acclaim. She could break free of part-time jobs and write her own ticket. Full-time staff biologist—no—head biologist. Anywhere. She could work at Monterey, where the real money was.

She glanced around the dimly-lit workroom. Did Joel know? No. If he did, he'd be here now, director's orders or not. This was too valuable a specimen to leave unguarded.

Marie smiled a private triumph. The glow of a wondrous secret that only she knew. How best to use that knowledge?

Over the humming of pumps and the gurgle of water, came the sound of scratching at the door to the roof.

Another one...like her?

The captive struggled fiercely in her bonds, calling out. The chair she was on toppled and she wriggled on the floor.

The scratching turned into a pounding. Then a man's voice, high and pure, shouted behind the door, the same strange language the woman used.

The phone rang. A jangling of bells that made Marie jump. She jerked up the phone. "Seattle Aquarium. Marie Glover speaking."

A familiar voice spoke. "We received a 911 call from this number. Do you have an emergency?"

The woman thrashed against the concrete floor, screaming and crying.

Marie's heart pounded in her chest. Trying to keep her voice level, she said, "No. There's no emergency. Things are just a little hectic right now. I have to go."

"Ma'am, are you the person who placed the call?"

"Yes—yes."

The woman heaved against her bonds. The molded-plastic chair was tangled with her limbs. She crashed to the concrete floor. Each time she rose, the awkward metal-and-plastic brought her down. Her motions were like a netted seal struggling to reach the surf.

Marie burned with shame. She remembered preteen years assisting a wildlife rehabilitator. The first lesson: do no harm. The goal: safe release back into the wild. This creature was wild and unwounded. Keeping her here, captive, was wrong.

"Ma'am. Is someone there preventing you from talking freely?"
"Yes—No! Of course not."

The woman crawled. The chair's weight shifted and ensnared her arms. She smacked face-first into the floor.

"I have to go." Marie slammed down the phone.

She lifted the woman up and put her back on the chair. Her cheek was already purpling. Tears streamed down the woman's face.

The phone jangled again. Marie reached over and ripped the plug from the wall.

The man still pounded on the rooftop door. Each blow like the beat of a panicked heart.

Marie covered her face with her hands. How had her career ambitions carried her so far from her original goal? She'd become a biologist to understand and preserve wild populations, not exploit them.

She looked at the woman she had captured: her bruised face, the tears. Here was something rich and rare. And what had been Marie's reaction? She'd hog-tied it and planned to use it to further her career.

Shame constricted Marie's chest and she tasted bile. It had to stop here. She had to change the direction of her life...but how? Sirens howled in the distance, dopplering towards them. Whatever decision she made, it would have to be quick.

If she hesitated, the woman and her accomplices would be captured. Would the authorities believe her story about the seal-woman? Probably not. The naked babbling woman would become a permanent resident of Harborview's psychiatric ward. But worse if the authorities did believe. Profiteers would capture creatures like her for display and rich men's pets. Biologists would hound them.

Something hot and wet seeped down Marie's cheeks. She picked up a fillet knife and walked to the woman.

Her enormous brown eyes grew impossibly huge and she thrashed harder, trying to escape.

"All right," Marie cooed. "It's going to be all right."

She slipped the knife between the woman's wrists then ankle, cutting the duct tape.

Shakily, the woman stood. She called over her shoulder and the pounding on the doors stopped.

The woman rubbed her wrists and eyed the pelt on the table behind Marie. Their gazes met. In the woman's liquid eyes, Marie saw a question and a need—freedom.

"Cuidich rium," the woman asked, stretching out her hands for the pelt.

Sirens howled down the street outside. The police would be here within minutes.

If a marine mammal disappeared on her shift, she'd be fired. No other aquarium would hire her. Fish and Wildlife would pull her rehabilitator's license. She might never work with animals again.

The woman's entire body expressed longing, pleading, arms stretched forward. *"Cuidich rium."*

Marie sighed explosively. "What's my career against your life?" She pressed the pelt into the woman's hands.

The smile on the woman's face transformed it from sharp strangeness to elvin beauty. Dark eyes twinkled over a wide thin-lipped mouth and pointed chin.

The sirens were just outside the loading-bay door.

Marie made a shooing gesture with her hands.

The woman shook out the seal skin. She slipped one slender foot into the mouth opening. It stretched impossibly, more like latex than leather. Her thin hips wriggled in, her feet filling out the back flippers.

A pounding on the loading-bay door of the aquarium, then, "Open up, it's the police."

White shoulders slid into the seal skin, the woman's collarbone melted into the shape of a seal's shoulders.

Marie wiped the handle of the fillet knife and put it on the table.

Only the woman's head remained. The seal skin crept over her head, as if by osmotic pressure, until only her deep brown eyes remained, looking out from a seal's face. The seal-woman murmured, *"Tapadh leibh."*

"You're welcome," Marie whispered. She ran up the stairs and opened the rooftop door. "Now go."

The harbor seal galumphed up the stairs behind her.

A policeman kicked on the steel-reinforced front door.

Four other harbor seals met the new arrival at the top of the stairs. They touched noses and whuffled deeply. Then, as one, they looked at Marie. Their unblinking gaze fixed her in the door. Marie wrapped her arms around herself to block the chill.

The sky was illuminated by reflected city light and false dawn. It shined off the black wavelets in Puget Sound.

"Go," Marie gestured with her head, "go quickly."

The seal-woman barked once. The seals slipped over the edge of the concrete roof and thumped on the pier below.

Marie rushed to the edge just in time to see the last pale form slip over the edge of the dock.

They were gone. And they had taken her career with them. Marie didn't regret it. She was exhilarated. She'd seen something wondrous—and had the strength to release it.

The feeling lasted all the way down the stairs.

Back in the workroom, the policeman's pounding snapped her back to reality.

She pressed the intercom to the loading dock. "I'll buzz you in."

Four policemen tromped down the loading-bay stairs and into the room. Guns out, they scanned the area. "Are you the woman who called 911?" one asked.

Marie took a deep breath. "Yes. The intruders are gone. They took one of the harbor seals with them." She glanced at the dangling phone cord. "Do you have a phone in your car? I need to call my supervisor and the biologist in charge of marine mammals."

Twenty minutes later, the police had swept the aquarium. Marie sat by the coffee pot, giving her statement for the fifth time.

Joel arrived first, hair uncombed and wearing jeans over a red union suit that Marie suspected was his pajamas. His pale blue eyes were bloodshot and suspicious. He surveyed the cops, then asked her, "What the hell happened?" He grabbed Marie by the shoulders and shook. "How could you let someone break in here?" His voice raised both in pitch and volume. "It was your responsibility to protect—"

One of cops put a restraining hand on Joel's elbow. "Easy now.

She did the best she could. We found five sets of footprints outside." He pointed to the overturned chair and duct tape. "She caught one and called 911 before his buddies came along and yanked the phone out of the wall."

Marie said nothing, silently blessing the cop's interpretation of events.

Joel glowered, but he didn't argue.

The cop said, "We need to get some information from you about the animal that was stolen." He led Joel away.

Bob showed up a few minutes later. He was wearing the same clothes he'd left in, as if he'd stayed up all night. His breath whispered of gin. "I hear the new arrival is gone," he said calmly, taking a seat next to Marie.

Marie tried to smile, the strain of the night's events frayed it at the edges. "I suppose I'll be fired."

Bob stared at the door leading to the roof. "The director won't be happy about having to call KCTV and cancel the human-interest story, and there are people on the staff who will crucify you." He stood up and pulled her after him. "Let's go see how bad the damage is."

A spattering of fingerprint dust decorated the edge of the green tub that had housed the seal-woman.

Across Puget Sound, a golden-pink dawn illuminated the Olympic mountains. The morning was crisp and damp. Marie guessed it would warm into a glorious afternoon.

She looked down at the slapping waves. No dark eyes stared back at her.

Bob roused her from reverie with a hand on her shoulder. "Joel's going to burn a lot of boat fuel out there looking for her. You should have told the cops she was killed."

Marie looked up at him, surprised.

He smiled distantly at the waves. There was disappointment, or regret, etched between his eyes. "You're a brave woman, Marie. She didn't belong here. But, I couldn't do...what you did."

"Thank you," she said, and stared down at her laced fingers. A moment of silence passed between them.

"It's not my decision," Bob said, finally, "but I'm going to recommend that the head biologist keep you on." He squeezed her shoulder with an engulfing hand, then turned and headed down the stairs.

A lone kingfisher dove into the salmon run, hunting breakfast. Behind Marie the city was waking up; traffic noises and the patter of early-morning panhandlers filtered up from the boardwalk.

In front of her were the fretful waters of the sound. She watched waves turn blue-green in the growing light.

Something broke the water's surface for a moment; probably a porpoise, but perhaps a seal.

Marie smiled. Losing this job wouldn't be the end of her life. Or even her career. A new urge pushed her to go back to school for a master's degree—maybe specialize in coastal-mammal research.

The seas were filled with many secrets. And she had a lifetime to explore.

THE ACCURSED VILLA

by Cynthia L. Ward

Cynthia Ward was born in Oklahoma and has lived in Maine, Spain, Germany, and the San Francisco Bay Area. After attending Clarion West 92, she moved to Seattle with her husband. She has sold stories to SWORD AND SORCERESS *(Vols. 8, 9, 11, 14, & 15),* THE ULTIMATE DRAGON, TAPESTRIES *(a* MAGIC: THE GATHERING *anthology),* NEW AMAZONS, BLOOD MUSE, 365 SCARY STORIES: A HORROR STORY A DAY, DESIRE BURN: WOMEN'S STORIES FROM THE DARK SIDE OF PASSION, Asimov's, Galaxy, Tomorrow, Absolute Magnitude, *and many other magazines and anthologies. She writes the monthly "Market Maven" market-news column for* Speculations *writing magazine. She is currently working on an SF mystery novel.*
—MZB

Lady Kiona woke in darkness to a pounding headache and a crushing weight. Gravel prickled her face, and a stone pressed painfully into her throat. A coppery reek filled her nostrils. She tried to rise. The weight held her down, and a terrible pain lanced through her left leg. Kiona groaned, and memory returned. She wasn't a soldier, but she'd been in a battle. A cavalryman had cut her leg to the bone; she'd succeeded in parrying his next blow, but his deflected sword had struck her horse in the gut. The mortally wounded mount had screamed and reared, throwing Kiona from the saddle; the impact with the ground had knocked her senseless. After that, she realized, a body had fallen on top of her, hiding her from enemy eyes. She shivered, wondering if the Esphanese soldiers had heard her waking groan.

Lady Kiona was part of the Thalarian diplomatic delegation, sent to parley with the Esphanese to prevent a border war. Kiona was twenty years old, and this was to be her first treaty-talk. The diplomats traveled with a white-robed priestess of Justice, under the white banner of truce; despite these sacred signs of peace, they were attacked by Esphanese troops. An honor guard of Thalarian cavalry accompanied the diplomats; but surprise and superior numbers gave the treacherous Esphanese an insurmountable advantage.

The Thalarian soldiers formed a ring around the five diplomats, and the diplomats formed a ring around the unarmed priestess of Justice. Brave but badly outnumbered, the Thalarian soldiers were soon slaughtered; and Lady Kiona and the other diplomats found themselves fighting the Esphanese. The high-born diplomats were not soldiers, but they were trained in the art of the sword. However, they had no armor. They did not last long.

Now Kiona lay motionless beneath a corpse, listening for the clash of combat. She heard only her own harsh breathing. She held her breath, and heard only the croaking of crows. If any Esphanese were near, they were keeping as quiet as she.

She struggled to move the corpse. It must be a diplomat's body, for it wore no armor; but still Kiona found its weight a terrible burden. She was exhausted, and every movement sharpened the pain in head and leg. But she dared not fling the body aside, lest a foe notice. She must shift the body with dreadful slowness. When she'd moved it enough to raise her face from the dirt, she realized the stone that had pressed into her throat was actually her necklace's ruby-set pendant, which was the disguised sheath of a tiny knife. She drew a deep breath and kept shifting the body, slowly—so slowly, she thought she would die of old age before she won free.

She lost her grip and the body slid abruptly off her back, exposing her to the setting sun and whatever foes might be about. She turned her head, ignoring its brutal ache to look swiftly in every direction. Had the enemy seen her?

Kiona lay in a vast field of corpses. Nothing moved nearby save crows and vultures. But the carrion-birds weren't the only living things in sight. At the far end of the battlefield, men moved black against the blood-red sunset. They were examining the fallen. A sword swung down, flashing red in the light; it rose again, red this time with blood. Laughter and shouts came clearly to Kiona across the battlefield, but she didn't need to hear the words to know these survivors spoke Esphanese. They were enemy soldiers, seeking wounded comrades to help and wounded foes to slay. Kiona dared not rise; they'd spot her instantly.

She began to crawl away from the Esphanese.

The body she'd pushed off her back was blocking her way. She froze, recognized the priestess, Leva. The priestesses of Justice did not bear or use weapons; everyone knew that. Yet Leva's death had not been an accident. Her body bore dozens of sword wounds.

The priestesses of Justice were the most powerful clerics in the South, for they served the Goddess who had power over all deities as well as all humans. Justice weighed the souls of the dead in Her balance, deciding who would gain Paradise and who would return to the world, reincarnated in a new life. The living were judged by Her priestesses, whom She granted the power of Truth-Hearing. No mortal—even a king—could raise his hand against the priestesses of Justice. They were sacrosanct. Yet the Esphanese had butchered the priestess Leva.

Kiona shook off her horror and crept around Leva's body. She moved slowly, and not only because she wanted to avoid detection. As she crawled, sharp stones gouged her flesh, and her long skirt repeatedly entangled her legs. Every move sent agony shooting through her left leg like a flaming arrow. Her left foot wouldn't brace against the earth to push her forward. Her skull throbbed like a blacksmith's anvil. Her neck bowed under the weight of her gold necklace and the ornate sheath masquerading as a pendant. All Thalarian diplomats wore a small knife disguised as jewelry; it allowed the self-defense of suicide if a foreign lord turned to treachery and attempted to torture information or concessions out of the diplomat. Kiona left the three-inch blade sheathed. She didn't want to die. She wanted to bring word of the Esphanese betrayal to her king.

But she feared she would fail. The deep sword-slash in her calf was still bleeding; it might drain her fatally. Exhausted by battle, she was wearied further by crawling around piles of bodies. Sometimes she recognized a body, and had to spend precious seconds choking down grief so she could keep moving. She tried to avoid the pools of blood, but still mud smeared her hands and her linen traveling gown. When she crossed a dry patch of earth, dust rose, making her fear discovery. The dust irritated her eyes and coated her face and lips. It tasted bitter.

Distantly, Kiona wondered why this vast field was bare dirt, without cottages, crops, or herds. The rest of the borderlands were equally dry and difficult to farm, yet they were covered with wheat and vegetable fields, olive groves, and goat herds. This field was uncultivated.

Kiona glanced over her shoulder. The Esphanese soldiers were numerous and fast-moving. They'd already crossed half the battlefield. She tried to increase her speed. Agony wrenched her leg, darkening her vision for a moment. She couldn't crawl any faster than an injured beetle. Sweat poured down her face, cutting tracks through the dust. The voices grew louder; the enemy drew closer. Kiona wanted to go east, away from the sun and the Esphanese, into the deepening dusk; but her way was blocked by a stirring soldier in Esphanese armor, who might see her and try to kill her, or summon his able-bodied fellows to cut her down. She turned south.

She saw a clump of oak trees not a hundred yards away. The unexpected sight sent her hopes rising like the morning sun. She might find shelter in that grove!

As she drew near the trees, she heard a shout in Esphanese. "Look! A Thalarian noblewoman still lives!"

"Kill her!"

The cries were bloodthirsty as a striking hawk's, and quickly followed by the thump of heavy footsteps as the armored soldiers ran toward Kiona. She didn't glance back. Oh gods, why had they discovered her now, when the trees were so *close?*

No point in caution now. Kiona pulled her uninjured right leg underneath her and started to rise. She glimpsed the sagging outlines of a ruined villa in the shadow of the oaks.

Her left leg folded. She fell, restraining a scream of agony. She struggled again to stand. She couldn't. The sword-cut in her calf had crippled her.

Kiona reached for her sword, and found the scabbard empty. She'd lost her sword when the horse threw her. She had only the dagger on her belt and the knife in her pendant. She was on a battlefield; she should be able to find a sword. If she couldn't, she was doomed. She shook her head. Whether or not she found a sword, she was doomed. She resumed crawling. She would find a place in the villa to put her back, a corner in which she would sell her life dearly. She would take as many of the treacherous Esphanese with her as she could, and rejoice when Justice weighed their treacherous souls and flung them back to earth to suffer a hundred miserable reincarnations as punishment.

The enemy soldiers began shouting again.

"The accursed villa!"

"Let her go!"

"Run!"

Kiona spoke Esphanese like a native, but she couldn't believe her ears. She looked over her shoulder. The soldiers had stopped their advance. They were staring into the grove; as she watched in amazement, they turned and ran away from her.

Kiona crawled into the grove. She didn't know why they were fleeing, and she didn't care. She cared only that they stayed away from the villa, and therefore her.

Despite the shadows lying over the villa, Lady Kiona recognized its construction as dating to the Dhontish Empire, which had fallen two hundred years ago. After vanquishing their Dhontish overlords, the people of Thalaria and Esphan had resumed their ancient border wars. This villa was within the disputed territory, so Kiona was surprised it still stood. Indeed, it looked whole. Why had she thought it ruined? Exhaustion and the evening shadows must have fooled her eyes.

She realized the villa was intact because the soldiers of both kingdoms must fear it. Doubtless they believed it infested by soul-eating ghouls. Kiona felt contempt. Soldiers were, as her parents and her fellow diplomats had told her, as ignorant and superstitious as peasants. Soul-eaters didn't exist. Only the Goddess Justice had power over the soul.

As Kiona crawled toward the villa door, she saw that the wall bore a mosaic mural. Though many of the small tiles were missing, the images were clear. The mosaic showed fair-haired, fair-skinned men and women enjoying food and wine and love, which had always been popular subjects in Dhontish art; but it also showed them enjoying the torture of slaves or captives. Kiona shivered, though she knew the mosaic was at least two centuries old, created in the decadent last days of the Dhontish Empire.

The Empire had fallen after a thousand-year reign, rotted from within by corruption and attacked on all sides by its subject nations. The Dhonts were long gone, and the villa was shelter from the superstitious, murderous Esphanese. Kiona crawled onto the doorstep. She raised an arm and pushed. The door swung silently inward.

Into the doorway stepped a stunningly beautiful young woman. She said, "I thought this door was locked and warded."

She held a clay lamp. Its light gleamed on her gold-bordered green silk tunic and her tight-curled black hair, and made her dark skin glow like polished bronze. Her eyes were a startling blue. She was Thalarian, but had spoken Dhontish. She must be high-born; only nobles spoke the ancient tongue, which served as the language of the Thalarian and Esphanese courts.

The woman glanced down and saw Kiona on the doorstep. Her puzzled expression changed to surprise. "Who are y—" She fell silent, her eyes widening. "You're injured!"

"Ravenna, *who* are you talking to?"

A tall, lean, dark-eyed man appeared in the doorway. He wore a plain tunic of gray silk. He was as curly-haired as Ravenna, but paler, olive-skinned; despite his old-fashioned Dhontish name, Tarvis was obviously Esphanese. *Enemy.* Kiona expected him to produce a sword and strike off her head.

Ravenna pointed at Kiona and said, "Help her into the villa, Tarvis."

He looked at Ravenna curiously. "Why?"

"What do you mean? We must help her, beloved! The lady will bleed to death or take a fever if we don't."

Tarvis looked utterly astonished. Then he said, "You're right, Ravenna, we can help her." He sounded surprised. "I'm no wizard, but I know something about herbs."

"We'll save her life," Ravenna declared. Her face was transfigured by an oddly intense expression. "Oh, my love, how long has it *been* since we've seen another person?"

"Forever and a night," Tarvis said.

Kiona stared at them in confusion. Surely they'd seen the battle outside their grove—

"Lady, can you walk?" Tarvis asked, leaning over Kiona. "No, obviously you can't," he realized. "Let's see if you can stand with assistance—" He crouched on her left and extended an arm. "May I offer you a hand?"

Was this more Esphanese treachery? If it were, Kiona realized, he wouldn't bother with courtesy; he'd just capture or kill her. She nodded permission. Tarvis slipped his arm under hers. His flesh was warm and hard-muscled.

He initiated formal introductions. "Lady, I am Tarvis." He didn't give a title; was he not high-born? He was certainly courtly enough. And his comportment made it clear he was no servant. "And she is

Lady Ravenna."

Kiona reciprocated. "I am Lady Kiona of Sedarria." She named her mother's homeland, a kingdom not at war with Esphan.

Tarvis rose slowly, helping Kiona stand. Carefully, he turned and started walking down a narrow hallway, his arm around her back, supporting her weight as she lurched forward. Her left leg was useless, foot dragging limply. Despairing, she realized she would never again walk unaided. The tendon in her calf had been severed.

Lady Ravenna went before them, lighting the way. "Tarvis and I will have to hide you, Lady Kiona," she said quietly. "I cannot say what Lord Borkalu will do if he finds you; but if he does, you will wish we had killed you."

Kiona froze. Borkalu was a Dhontish name, but popular with the Esphanese nobility. Was this Lord Borkalu working with the Esphanese officials who had ordered the massacre of the Thalarian diplomats? How could he not be? The slaughter had taken place practically on his doorstep. No wonder Lady Ravenna had feared he'd hurt Kiona!

Kiona turned to flee. She'd forgotten her crippling wound. She would have fallen if Tarvis hadn't caught her.

"My Lady," he whispered urgently, "you have nothing to fear. Only be quiet, and you will be safe."

"Indeed, Lady Kiona, you have nothing to fear," Ravenna murmured. "Borkalu won't matter after tonight."

A curious smile flitted across her face as she looked over her shoulder at Tarvis, and he gave her back the same odd smile.

Tarvis and Kiona followed Ravenna into a large, well-lit room furnished with a marble table and marble couches. Kiona stared at the silver plates and goblets, at gilded cressets and an entire wall sheathed in lapis lazuli. She was amazed to see such wealth carelessly displayed in the disputed territory between Thalaria and Esphan.

The room had several doors. Tarvis turned Kiona to face the nearest door.

"My dears!" a new voice boomed from a different doorway, speaking flawless Dhontish. "Who is our guest?"

Like the voice, the man was powerful and indolent. He also looked like a classic Dhont, with his white skin, blue eyes, hawk's-beak nose, and straight golden hair. His gold-embroidered blue silk tunic was cut in the classic Dhontish pattern, and a half-cape draped his left shoulder Dhont-style. Kiona had seen other throwbacks who resembled the Dhontish men who had ravished the women of Thalaria and Esphan; but she had never before seen a throwback who affected Imperial garb.

Was this Lord Borkalu, who Ravenna thought would hurt her in ways too terrible to name? *Gods defend me!*

The yellow-haired man approached, as lazily graceful as a leopard. "Ravenna, my darling wife," he murmured, "did you think I wouldn't sense a new soul in our happy home?"

Ravenna looked stricken.

The big man turned slightly. "My sweet brother," he said, touching Tarvis's cheek. "Have you found a new mistress?" Tarvis's body went rigid.

Ravenna cried, "Tarvis! Borkalu!"

This man *was* Lord Borkalu. Kiona began to shake. "Remember you are brothers," Ravenna said, "and be civilized before our guest."

"Half-brothers only, my love." Borkalu's eyes widened in mock surprise. "Don't you remember Tarvis is a slave's bastard?"

Kiona stared at Borkalu. Thalaria and Esphan had both outlawed slavery after overthrowing their Dhontish overlords two hundred years ago. Servants and peasants were free. Was Borkalu crazy, to see them as possessions?

He must be crazy. He lived in a villa decorated with a foul mural celebrating torture.

Kiona's shaking grew violent. The Esphanese soldiers had been right to flee the grove. It was home to a *madman.*

"Don't worry, wife, we will talk like civilized men," Borkalu assured Ravenna. He faced Tarvis. "Now, do not deny it, brother," he said. "You are sleeping with my wife."

"No!" Ravenna screamed.

"That's not true!" Tarvis shouted.

"Oh, what liars," Borkalu said calmly, and pulled Kiona away from Tarvis. "Brother, I will keep your new wench for myself." Tarvis swung a fist at Borkalu.

Borkalu kept his hands locked on Kiona's upper arms as he sidestepped the blow and kicked Tarvis behind the knee, knocking him down. Then Borkalu released Kiona's left arm for a second to slap his wife. The clay lamp fell from Ravenna's hand and shattered on the marble floor. Blood appeared on her lips.

Kiona stared at Borkalu in shock. The man was past his youth, yet he'd moved as fast as the best swordsman she'd ever seen. And his hands gripped her arms painfully; inescapably. He had a madman's strength.

He studied Kiona. Then he gave his wife an unfriendly smile and announced, "The chit is pretty, for a Thalarian. I will enjoy her tonight."

"Husband!" Ravenna's voice held angry scorn.

Borkalu's reply was equally scathing. "You *dare* talk thus to me, faithless bitch? Would you like me to skin you alive?"

Fear transformed Ravenna's face. "I meant no offense, husband," she whispered. "I wished only to say that the woman is badly injured. And you are a wizard—"

"I am a mage," Borkalu said. "Do not forget it."

A mage? Kiona's mind reeled. The mages had been the most powerful wizards of the Dhontish Empire. But they had died with the Empire. There were still wizards, but they were weaker than mages. And they were rare. The Thalarian government had only two, and had seen no reason to send one on a diplomatic mission. The Esphanese had included no wizard with the troop sent to massacre the Thalarian diplomats.

Borkalu was far gone in madness, to think himself a mage. "Husband," Ravenna said. "The woman is covered in blood. She is crippled. You must heal her!"

"I don't believe what I'm hearing," Borkalu said. "Ravenna, the most selfish of women, is asking for something for somebody else."

Tarvis had regained his feet. His nose was bloody. "Lord Borkalu," he said, "the lady *crawled* to your door. She needs help—"

"You also want to help her, Tarvis?" Borkalu exclaimed. "I am astonished! You're just like Ravenna. You've never thought of anyone but yourself in your life."

"Please, husband, help her," Ravenna implored.

"Tarvis, hold her," Borkalu ordered, and shoved Kiona into Tarvis's arms. Then Borkalu pulled the dagger from her belt and began to raise her skirt. Kiona's terror doubled. She struggled desperately, but couldn't escape Tarvis's embrace.

Borkalu raised the blood-soaked skirt only high enough to expose her calves. "Gods," he swore, "someone's half cut off this chit's

THE ACCURSED VILLA

leg." He glanced at the table, laden with enough food for a feast, but set with places for only three people. "And dinner's waiting."

He cut the linen with Kiona's dagger, widening the sword-slash so her wound stayed visible when he let go of her skirt. He tossed her dagger across the room and began a spell. He wove a complex series of gestures and muttered in a voice too low for Kiona to understand, though she caught an occasional word of archaic Dhontish. When the spell ended, he pointed at Kiona's chest. Golden light burst from his fingertip. She stiffened, sure that Borkalu had decided to dispose of her before dinner.

The golden light surrounded her. The agony in her head and leg vanished. She looked at her leg. Her skin was smooth and whole. Her foot moved in response to her will.

"You're healed, chit," Borkalu said. "Now join me for dinner. You'll need all your strength for what I have in mind!"

He wrenched Kiona away from Tarvis and flung her onto the nearest of the three marble couches surrounding the table. The impact knocked the breath from her lungs. As she lay stunned, he stretched out beside her, pinning her right arm beneath his body. He slipped his left arm around her shoulders, closed his right hand on her free wrist, and hooked a muscular leg over her thighs, trapping her on the cold stone couch.

He glared at his wife and brother. "What are you two gaping at? You'll need to feed us. Pour my wine."

Tarvis went to the table and raised the open wine bottle. Borkalu kissed the side of Kiona's neck. She tried to twist away from his lips, but she couldn't move far. His yellow hair tickled her as he kissed the hollow of her throat. Over his head she watched Tarvis pour red wine into a silver goblet, and knew she could expect no more help from Tarvis or Ravenna.

Tarvis put the goblet on the table by Borkalu's couch. "Your wine, my lord brother."

Borkalu raised his head. An irritable expression crossed his face. "Can't you see my hands are occupied?" he demanded. "You must serve us, little brother." He turned a mock-tender smile on Kiona. "Let my new love have the first sip."

Tarvis's eyes widened and he almost spoke. He gazed at Ravenna. Ravenna looked upset.

Kiona remembered Tarvis helping her walk in the hallway,

warning her to be quiet for her own safety, and Ravenna cryptically remarking, *Borkalu won't matter after tonight.*

"You lazy, insolent son of a slave!" Borkalu snarled at Tarvis, releasing Kiona's wrist and snatching the goblet off the table. "Drink, my new lady," he said, and brought the goblet to Kiona's lips.

Kiona's hand swept up and struck the goblet. It flew from Borkalu's hand and rang on the floor. Wine spread like blood on the white marble. Tarvis moaned. Ravenna gasped. Borkalu yelled, "You ungrateful—"

Kiona said, "The wine is poisoned!"

Borkalu's eyes swept over his wife and half-brother. Their faces twisted in terror, and they turned to flee. The wizard's face crimsoned with rage, and he opened his mouth and raised his hand to strike them dead.

"Be silent, wizard!" Kiona cried. "One word, one gesture, and I kill you! *No* spell is faster than a knife at the throat."

She pressed just hard enough enough to cut Borkalu's skin. Borkalu's face went pale as spoilt milk.

When Borkalu had turned his wrathful attention on his wife and brother, Kiona had raised her free hand to her necklace and flicked a pair of tiny latches on its pendant; the bottom of the pendant had fallen into her palm as the three-inch steel blade slid free. Three inches seemed a toy's size; but a knife this small, double-edged and sharp-pointed, could piece the heart or sever the windpipe as successfully as any sword.

She dared not look away from Borkalu as she shouted, "Halt!" The fleeing footsteps slid into silence. "Come back here, you two, or I release the wizard to spell-slay you!"

She heard the steps resume, hesitantly returning.

She spoke again. "Let go of me, wizard."

Borkalu took his arm from her shoulders and his leg from her thighs. He raised his body slightly and she slipped her left arm free. He never took his eyes off her hand at his throat.

Kiona glanced up. "Tarvis, Lady Ravenna, I want you to bind and gag the wizard. I have no wish to spend the rest of my life lying here with a blade against Borkalu's throat."

"Why bind him?" Ravenna demanded passionately. *"Kill* him!"

"You two tried to keep me safe from Borkalu," Kiona said, "so I saved you from him. But I won't kill him, or let you kill him. I was crippled. Only a wizard could restore movement to my leg. Borkalu did. He healed me, and I will not hurt him if I can avoid it. I will not offend the Goddess Justice by rewarding good with evil."

She glanced up at Ravenna and Tarvis. She gasped. Their faces were changing, the skin sagging into wrinkles and the black hair turning white. Terrified, Kiona looked at Borkalu, wondering how the wizard had cast a spell when he couldn't speak or move. She found the same dreadful change had overtaken him.

She looked up again to find Tarvis and Ravenna gazing into each other's wrinkled faces. They looked a hundred years old. Yet smiles blossomed on their faces—inexplicable smiles of great joy.

"May all the gods bless you, Lady Kiona!" Tarvis cried.

"We know not how you've done it," Ravenna said, "but you've *freed* us from our curse!"

The lovers did not stop smiling until the wrinkled skin cracked and flaked off their skulls. Their bones fell clattering to the floor and burst into powder. And Borkalu turned to dust beside Kiona.

With a horrified cry, she leaped to her feet.

And discovered the villa in ruins. The roof was gone, the lapis lazuli wall cracked and collapsing. Dust shrouded the couches and table and suddenly-bare plates; cobwebs filled the corners with darkness. The cressets had burned out. The light came from above, from the morning sun—

But Kiona had entered the villa at sunset. She hadn't been in the villa an hour. It *couldn't* be morning!

Kiona ran out of the villa.

The sun remained in the eastern sky.

Kiona fled to the edge of the grove, and froze. A figure moved upon the battlefield, leading a horse. Kiona suppressed a groan of dismay. An enemy soldier kept watch over the battlefield. She was trapped in the grove of the accursed villa.

No! The figure wore a white robe. This was a priestess of Justice.

Kiona walked onto the battlefield. She staggered. Her leg was healed, but she was exhausted.

"Who is there?" called the priestess.

"Priestess, I am Lady Kiona, a Thalarian diplomat."

"I am called Zara." The priestess approached the grove, leading her roan horse. She was a short, slight woman with close-cropped gray hair and ascetic features. "When a priestess of Justice dies of violence," she said, "all her sister-priestesses sense it. Since I was close, I felt where she died. I came here, and found a battlefield. Did you see the battle?"

"Yes, Priestess."

"Lady Kiona, you look about to collapse," Zara said. "Seat yourself on that fallen tree and tell me what happened here. And remember that Justice has blessed all Her priestesses with the power of Truth-Hearing."

Sinking down on the prone oak, Kiona told Zara about the battle, and waking afterward to find the priestess Leva dead, deliberately butchered.

When Kiona fell silent, the priestess did not speak for several moments, only stared at Kiona piercingly. Kiona had not lied, and she had told everything she could remember about the battle; but as the silence stretched between them, she felt fear seep into her heart. Did Zara sense she hadn't mentioned the accursed villa and the strange events that had transpired within? But they had nothing to do with the battle!

"You speak the truth," Zara declared. Relief poured through Kiona, dizzying as strong wine. "The Esphanese soldiers massacred people traveling under the peace-banner and executed a priestess of Justice. The Goddess will not let the soldiers or their commanders get away with such knavery."

"All praise to the Goddess!" Kiona said fervently.

"You spoke the truth, Lady Kiona," the priestess said, "but you didn't finish. Tell me how you came to be the battle's only Thalarian survivor."

Lady Kiona described her escape from the battlefield, and the puzzling retreat of her pursuers, and her terrifying, mystifying night in the villa.

When she was done, the priestess said, "You don't know about the villa?" Startled, Kiona shook her head. Zara sighed. "It's true soul-eaters don't exist, but that is no reason to scorn the common people. You high-borns are so arrogant you don't know what every peasant child does, that the Dhontish villa on the border is—was— under the Goddess's curse.

"The curse was a judgment on the three who lived in the villa. Borkalu had been a war-mage and his half-brother Tarvis a cavalry commander in the Dhontish army, but they committed atrocities so shocking, the hardened generals sent them into early retirement. Borkalu married a part-Thalarian woman, Lady Ravenna, and returned to his homeland. Both he and his bride took lovers. She liked to play her lovers against one another. Scores of men fought to the death over her."

"Ravenna and Tarvis were as evil as Borkalu, yet I never guessed it," Kiona said. She felt ill.

"All three were more evil than you will ever know," the priestess said. "Lord Borkalu eventually tired of Lady Ravenna's lethal adulteries, and of being shunned by his peers. He took his wife to the distant villa she had inherited. Tarvis accompanied them. Here the three entertained themselves by fatal torture of slaves; and Ravenna took Tarvis for her lover. This adultery was too deep a betrayal; Borkalu decided to torture his wife and brother to death. Unaware of his intention, they acted first. However, the poison Tarvis concocted did not kill Borkalu instantly, as they'd expected. Tarvis's herb-lore, secretly studied, was incomplete. Borkalu had time to cast a death-spell.

"They found themselves standing together before Justice. The Goddess had never seen three more thoroughly cruel and selfish humans, and She refused to weigh their souls in Her balance. Instead, She sent them back to the mortal world, condemned to eternal life—of a sort. Every night they lived again, only to reenact their triple murder. They were doomed to die their agonizing deaths over and over, until they freed themselves from Her curse. But She did not tell them what they must do to end the curse, because they had to act out of sincere motives. Otherwise, their souls would have learned nothing."

Zara laid a hand on Kiona's shoulder. "The Goddess did not tell them," Zara said, "but She told Her priestesses, and now I tell you: She required each of the three to perform an unselfish act, and receive charitable treatment in return."

Kiona stared.

"Ravenna and Tarvis offered you shelter and assistance with no ulterior motive," the priestess said. "Borkalu healed you though it gained him nothing, and might even have been to his loss—after all, a cripple couldn't run away from him. And because they each helped you, you spared their lives. Your unselfish act joined with theirs to free them from their curse."

"Oh, Goddess," Kiona whispered in astonishment and awe.

The priestess held her hand above Kiona's head in the ancient gesture of benediction. "The Goddess blesses you for your just action," Zara told Kiona, "and She does not forget."

Zara took Kiona's hands and drew her to her feet. "Mount my horse, Lady Kiona," said Zara, "and we will be away from here before the Esphanese can discover us. We must bring word of the massacre to the king of Thalaria."

"We will," Kiona vowed, "and I will help the king and the Goddess repay the Esphanese for their treachery!"

AS THREE TO ONE
by Dorothy J. Heydt

Dorothy J. Heydt still has one husband, two or three kids, four or five cats, entirely too many computers, and Chronic Fatigue Syndrome. She thinks you ought to know that Baron Bodo's quotation about three to one was originally attributed to an Earthfellow named Napoleon Buonaparte. She has contributed regularly to Marion Zimmer Bradley's FANTASY Magazine *and to the Darkover and SWORD AND SORCERESS anthologies.*

I first met Dorothea of Paravel (as she was styled) in the early days of the Society for Creative Anachronism, where she was attempting to keep an ongoing history of the SCA; she worked as a medical secretary at Kaiser Health Plan, where the doctors appreciated her accuracy and literacy.

Later she married Hal von Ravn, an SCA knight who was famous for an ongoing set of challenge matches involving horrible puns about eggs and yolks and friars.

These days, I occasionally run into Dorothy's daughter Meg, who works at one of the best Berkeley fabric stores and teaches workshops about historic costume; Meg's bio notes that she's been in the SCA all her life, which is literally true.

Dorothy's always had writing talent and a good imagination, so I'm surprised none of her books has hit the best-seller list. Yet. Her recent novel A POINT OF HONOR (DAW, 1998) has been getting favorable comment from its readers, so maybe she's finally on her way.
—REH

And the moral of the tale is, Valmai told herself, don't buy the pig in the poke, or the cat in the bag, or the horse without looking at his teeth. The Prince of Almora had hired her to command a century in the defense of Huffsford at his eastern border against Ulvaeus and his mages and his unnatural armies. She had ridden out expecting to find a hundred rough native troops, and found a hundred shivering farmers with spades and hayforks and their hearts in their boots.

The place stank of fear. After walking through the near-deserted town, empty of any scent of life, to descend the bank into the water-meadow was like wading out into a sewer—and the laundries were not open for business. All the noncombatants had been sent away west, days ago—young children, women with child or giving suck, the feeble elders—and *these* were the best Huffsford had to send into battle. They sat or lay on the short grass, one by one or in little groups. Few spoke. Many hid their faces.

And what more could she expect, after all? They weren't soldiers; they'd had no training; to them a fight meant two or three young hotheads punching each other's noses behind the alehouse of an evening. Nothing in their lives had readied them for a day when they would have to stand, billhooks and pitchforks in hand, shoulder to shoulder—if none of them broke and ran—against an army of gangers.

It was the fear of being recruited, of course, that frightened them so deeply. Fall in battle against an ordinary foe, you were worms' meat. Fall to undead gangers, you'd soon find yourself fighting again, against your own people. None of the Prince's mages were prepared to say whether you would realize it, know who you had been and what you had become.

It was true what the fellow had said—who had said it? probably Baron Bodo; he had said practically everything in his long life—"in combat, the moral is to the physical as three to one." These were strong young people, with muscle enough to put up a fight—but unless Valmai could put the heart back into them, they wouldn't lift a hand even in defense of their homes.

Gods, Valmai said, *I shall do the best I can with this material, such as it is. Afterwards, we shall discuss this at greater length. Wherever we happen to be.*

"We've got, what, about an hour before sunset?" she said to the man beside her. "I'd better look the place over. The river's that way, right?"

"Yes, Captain," the man said, she would remember his name in a moment. "Among the trees there. And on the other side another water-meadow, it's where the river spills out in the winter floods. Then it slopes up again to the plains." Kember, that was his name, son to the town headman, left in reluctant command till Valmai came.

Little enough traffic there'd been this spring, but the wheel-ruts still showed faintly through the green grass. Valmai and Kember followed them through the trees to the water's edge. The river was about a bowshot in width. Nodding irises, their blossoms a brilliant blue, marked a path through the shallow water to the other side.

"Any other places near here where you could get across?"

"I'm afraid so." Kember, no fool, realized why this was bad news. "About a quarter-mile downstream there's a big shallow place. And a few shallow patches upstream. You can tell where the shallow water is; the blue-flags grow there."

Valmai considered this. "Hmmmm. Are there any particularly deep places? A bottomless pit with a strong undertow would be ideal."

Kember forced a smile. "I dare say it would, Captain. There's nothing like that around here, just the younglings' swimming-hole. Nice and deep, safe to dive in, but no undertow."

"Upstream from here, or down?"

"Downstream. Right before the other ford; it's a good place for fishing, too, if you can keep the children out. Captain, you're smiling. What have I said?"

"Later," Valmai said, and splashed across the ford to the eastern bank. She followed the wheel-ruts up the bank till she reached the plains. Tough, close-nibbled turf covered them, good sheep country, but the sheep had all been sent west before the advancing troops could reach them.

"How far away are they?" Kember asked.

"Don't know yet. When I left the capital, the Prince's mages were sending out birds that reported the enemy some five days' march from the river. And that was four days ago."

"So we could see them here as early as tomorrow."

"We might." The sun had disappeared behind the trees, and the shadow was pouring over them, but there would be some daylight left on the other side of the river. "One more thing. Where's a good tall tree? You grew up here; you must know where the good climbers are."

"Yes, Captain. In fact, this one here—" He led her to a tall horn-oak, its bark rough under the hand. "There's a place high up on this one where a limb broke in my dad's time and there's a clear view eastward."

Valmai swarmed up the trunk and found the stub of the broken limb; it gave a good foothold and a fine view of nearly ten miles of grassland, flat as a calm sea: empty but for the faint track of the road, little-used since the snows melted and the war began. Good. She dropped through the branches and landed with a thump at Kember's feet. "No sign of 'em. We'll post a sentry tomorrow."

"What if they attack tonight?"

"Well, now, they never have, not that anyone's told of. They can't see in the dark any better than we can."

Kendrick stared. "They can't?"

"Of course not. I see I need to make a speech to you and your folk. It's full moon tomorrow night, though, isn't it. 'Trust in the gods and tie up your camel,' as they say. Let's post the sentry tonight. Good thinking, Kember. See to it, will you?"

"Yes, Captain." They splashed back through the river, blue-flags brushing against their knees. "I'll find three or four wide-awake lads, to climb the tree by turns and keep company at the foot. And whistle like a woodlark if they see anything."

"Do you have woodlarks in this part of the country?"

"No, Captain."

Back at the water-meadow, Valmai mounted a haywagon and called for attention. Slowly, the pallid faces turned toward her. "Move up! I've got some things to say, and then I've got an errand for you before the light goes." Squinting, she held up her hand to the west: two fingersbreadth between the sun and the horizon meant half an hour of daylight.

"Now then. Tomorrow or maybe the next day, as you know, the army of Ulvaeus will get here, and you will have to fight them. As you also know, most of them are gangers. What you don't seem to know is that there are ways of fighting gangers, and I'm here to tell you about 'em."

This appeared to be news to practically everyone. Eyes widened.

"How do you make a ganger in the first place?" she began rhetorically. "You need one corpse and one amulet. *He's* got to have his arms and legs and head, somewhere to hand, and *it's* got to have the proper spells on it. String the amulet around his neck, and all the detached bits and pieces latch on where they belong and he gets up and does what you tell him to."

Kember was moving among the people, speaking to a long-legged youngster here and there. They followed in his wake and clustered together near the meadow's edge: three, four of them.

"The problem with a ganger, of course, is—" she shrugged—"you can't kill him. Slice off his head, he picks it up and puts it back. Cut off his arms and legs, tear out his guts, the same. That's the one thing he's got over you. He can't do anything he couldn't do before, except resist death.

"He can't see in the dark. Does that surprise you? He can't fly; he's no stronger, no better a fighter than he was before; he's no *smarter* than he was before—and probably a lot less so. The wits seem to be the first things to go."

The people were sitting up straighter now, paying attention. A young man and woman practically at Valmai's feet glanced at one another, held each other's hands.

"So never mind killing him, how do you take him out of the battle?" She paused. "First, as ought to be plain enough, you can take his amulet away. Get it off his neck—or break it—and he's dead meat again. Trouble is, it's hard to get that close without his doing something to *you* first.

"In the south they had a company with some very good archers. One of them—he'd made his living winning fancy competitions—had some crescent-shaped arrowheads, mounted 'em horns forward, the inside edge sharpened. He could cut the amulet cord right off the enemy's neck. Any archers here? No?

"Well, this is sheep country: how many of you are shepherds? How good are you with a sling?"

Several hands went up. "Well, now, a slingstone doesn't hurt a ganger any, won't even bruise him; but if you can hit the amulet, you'll break it—they're only baked clay—and that will drop him.

"And the only trouble with that is that they all carry spare amulets on them. Ulvaeus's mages made a mold, and his thralls press clay into it and turn 'em out by the hundreds. But it slows them down nicely; and if you take out the one in front, the one behind is likely to trip over him. Yes, Kember, what is it?"

"I have the sentries ready. Should they go now, or wait?"

"Let 'em wait; I don't have much more to say. Suppose you're not a slinger or a prizewinning archer," she went on. "What can you do? Well, you can cut his head off, if you're strong enough.

"Even a ganger's not much use without a head; he can't fight without it because he can't see or hear without it. Of course, he'll try at once to take it away from you and put it back. If you can keep it, though, you've put him out of action, and if you keep him out long enough he'll decay enough that the amulet won't work any more. Takes about a day and a night. In one place the fighting came into the town and the people had very good luck throwing the heads up onto the rooftops.

"Or if the fighting here comes up to the riverbank, anything you drop into the water will float downstream at least as far as the swimming-hole. The bodies will try to crawl after their heads, which should keep them busy till you can get around to them—or until the amulets fall from their headless necks. In which case you can take your time."

There was some nervous laughter, and people shifted where they sat, alert enough now to realize their backsides were going to sleep.

"But I've saved the best for the last," Valmai said, and took a bundle from her back: long and narrow, it reached from her shoulder nearly to the ground. She unwrapped it and showed them a dozen long wooden sticks with sharp splintery ends. "What's the traditional way to lay an undead lich? One without an amulet, one that's had the enchantment laid directly on him? What do all the old tales say? You bury him with a wooden stake through his heart. If the heart isn't whole, no magic can make the body move. The stake simply keeps the heart from growing back together. And, yes, an arrow through the heart works too—till someone pulls it out.

"Well. Imagine I'm standing on your riverbank tomorrow, and here comes a ganger straight for me." She took one of the sticks, held it point-forward like a lance. "He's been dead for months. His flesh is getting a little soft. His clothing is going to rags. Armor? He never had any. So I let him get within my range, and I go *POKE—*" she thrust into the air—"I've pierced his heart and he drops. Now watch." She took the tip of the stake with her left hand, a span below the point, and broke it away. "I've broken it off in the wound. I take a moment, if I've got a moment, to step on it, drive it further in. Now *he's* got a stake through his heart that will be very hard for his ganger comrades, with their tiny wits, to pull out. And *I've* got a fresh point on my stake, to stab with again—or if it isn't quite sharp enough, a few strokes of a knife will fix that. This is spicewood, by the way; it splinters nicely; cedar or copperholm will do too, or any softwood. It does have to be dry, to break properly. If there's a carpenter's shop in town—"

"There is and I've got the key," a young woman called. "We'll see what we've got that splinters."

"One more thing," Valmai said. "The worst thing about fighting gangers is the fear that you may suddenly join them." Ah, now she had their undivided attention. "I invite you to think about this: the same stake that takes out a ganger can keep you or me from becoming one. If I get my throat cut tomorrow, say, Kember here takes his stake and drives it into my heart." (He'd have to cut the straps to her breastplate first, but never mind that.) "He can go back into battle, leaving me where I fall, knowing all the amulets in the world can't make me rise up against him.

"We say in the army, 'Bare is brotherless back,' and that goes double for us now. I advise each one of you to pick out a partner, one to whom you can swear, 'If you fall, I'll see to it you stay safely dead,' and one who can do the same for you." All across the meadow pairs of eyes met, hands clasped for bargains sealed. The young couple at her feet gripped hands tightly, and the woman bent her head to her man's shoulder.

"Now we're almost out of daylight. Those who can sleep tonight, do. The rest, I've got some work to do once the moon rises. I want dry brushwood and digging tools, whatever you can find, right here." She pointed to the ground at her feet, under the haywagon. The young couple looked startled. "I'll explain later what it's for. That's all."

She jumped down from the haywagon, and the people began getting up from their seats on the grass—and, yes, their morale seemed to have risen to the two-to-one level at least. Pity she couldn't give them time to practice, raise their confidence further. Some went to seek brushwood; others turned toward the town in search of supper and bed. Valmai followed them; Kember had spoken of stew at the alehouse, and she had not eaten since daybreak. As she climbed the bank, she found a heavy-set man climbing beside her, legs bowed from long hours in the saddle, his dark jerkin embroidered in a northern style. "Captain, I wanted to speak to you," he said.

"Speak," she said, not pausing in her march toward the alehouse, and beckoning him to follow.

"My name's Andvar," he said. "I don't live here; I was visiting my kin when this blew up. I live in the north, in cattle country, and to catch the wild cattle we use this." They had reached the alehouse door, and Valmai paused to look at what he held up before her: three cords, knotted together at the near end, each of the far ends tied round a small stone.

"This is a balbo," he said. "You hold it by one cord and swing it around your head to work up speed, and loose it at the cow's legs. The cords wrap round her hocks and she drops. But it'll work on two-leggers just as well."

Valmai nodded slowly. "Come inside and let's eat. Do you have any more of those?"

"Not on me, but I can make more." They found places at the table, and small loaves and bowls of stew were set before them. "All they are is cords and stones, which I can find as soon as the sun's up."

"How long does it take to learn the thing?"

Andvar shrugged. "Several days, I would have said. I know, we don't have several days. But you were talking about how a slingstone's no use unless it hits the amulet dead on, and I thought a slinger, who's already got an eye and arm used to throwing—"

Valmai swallowed a mouthful of bread. "—Might pick it up faster. Good. Try it. Talk to Kember, have him send some slingers your way." She applied herself to her food, wondering if she should try one of the things herself. No, better to use her crossbow at a distance, put a few quarrels through a few breastbones, and switch to spicewood slivers for close work.

When she had eaten she left the alehouse and returned to the water-meadow. The moon was just rising above the trees, and people were gathering with piles of brushwood, with hoes and mattocks. Valmai collected their attention.

"Suppose you didn't live here," she said. "How would you know where the ford was?"

Some looked puzzled, one muttered something about wheel-ruts, and then a tall burly woman shouted, "The blue-flags!"

"Right," Valmai said. "Because they like to grow with their feet wet, but their heads have to reach the air, they show you where the shallow water is. We're going to move them. Come along."

The river water sparkled under the moon, broken into ripples by fifty pairs of feet. Under Valmai's direction they stretched a rope across the water, just downstream of the ford. They let the brushwood drift up against it, tucking in loose twigs here and there. It would float for a while, and bear the weight of the blue-flags uprooted from bank and ford.

AS THREE TO ONE

By midnight a blue-flowered path curved away from the shore, arced gracefully and returned to the shore opposite. "How deep is it under there?" Valmai asked.

"Seven, eight feet," Kember said. "Can those things swim?"

"Not if they couldn't before," Valmai reminded him, "which is to say, probably not. They may float, though. You folk," she added, "go and sleep now, if you can. If you can't, go downstream to the other ford, below the swimming hole, dig up the flags there. If you can't find some deceptive place for them, then cast 'em downstream, let 'em mark somebody else's ford. You've done a good night's work."

"What now?" Kember asked.

"Now, sleep for me, and for you if you can, and I'd surely advise it. We'll be up again at dawn, gathering sticks and stones."

"Right. There's a bed for you in my house, my dad's house that is, opposite the square, with the crownbuck's antlers over the door."

Valmai thanked him and began to climb the bank. Bed, that word sweeter than gold, let alone love; at this time of year she might get all of five hours' sleep between midnight and dawn. The night airs were gentle on her skin, and a woodlark was singing—

Oh, hells, a woodlark where no woodlark ought to be. She turned back toward the river, Kember at her heels, hearing feet landing with a thump on the riverbank, splashing through what was left of the ford.

"There's only one," the dripping young man said as he ran up from the bank. "On horseback, coming straight this way; I think he's following the old wagon-ruts."

"And my bow's still tied to my saddle," Valmai muttered. "Where are those splinters?" She took a fistful from the haywagon and headed for the water. "Everyone, grab something and hide among the trees. This might be quick."

On the far bank the moon shone like silver over the grass. On the horizon a little dot moved, swelled, became a single rider on a hard-driven horse. Slowly, not to draw attention, Valmai slid down against the nearest trunk, squatted on her haunches. If he came this way—

He was almost upon her before she moved: a little man's shape atop a tall horse, its eyes white and staring, its nostrils flared; his eyes were sunken and he seemed not to breathe at all. Valmai stood up almost under the horse's nose, and it reared; she dodged its hooves, stick at the ready. As the horse descended, she raised her splinter and let the ganger's own momentum drive it smoothly up into his heart. He fell, snapping the stick off squarely at the skin: she'd have to give it a new point.

The townspeople were cheering under their breath. *(There you go, m'lord Baron,* she thought: *there's your three.)* "Well, yes, that's the way it's *supposed* to go," Valmai said, bowing right and left like a juggler. "It's not always that simple, but you get the idea. Somebody catch the horse: it's probably drugged, so be careful. You others, get the body across the river and under at least a thin layer of earth so the scent doesn't travel. Wait a minute." She took the amulet from the corpse's neck, and found another in the pouch at its waist. "Now I'm off to bed; I'll see you at dawn."

"Captain, I want to talk to you." A woman's voice this time, the young woman who had sat at her feet while she spoke from the haywagon. Valmai shrugged and signed her to follow.

"I'm Brenna," she said, pattering along after Valmai, three paces to her two. "Kolim the baker's wife."

"If he baked the bread I ate this evening, he's good," Valmai answered politely.

"He is good," Brenna said. "He's good, and quiet, and innocent. He's not the kind of man that makes a fighter."

Valmai raised up in her mind the image of Kolim sitting beside his wife that evening: tall, rangy, with broad shoulders and a stubborn jaw and arms heavy with muscle, and considered that perhaps they hadn't been wedded that long. "He may surprise us, when day comes."

"He'll be *killed,* when day comes. He's *not* a fighter. Why did the Prince bid us raise a hundred fighters? If he'd only said, 'raise whoever's best-fitted,' they would have sent Kolim away."

"I've been in places where, in like case, they'd have sent all the women away, even the fit ones, and kept all the men, even the old and ill. Surely this is a better way: Kolim will go to battle with the best, the most dedicated comrade to guard his back."

"You won't send him away?"

"I have no authority to send away, only to lead into battle. Your town council chose your century before I ever got here."

"If he dies—" Brenna ran up ahead of Valmai at the headman's crowned door, blocked her way, fists clenched. "If he dies, I promise to live just five minutes longer, so I can put my splinter through your throat."

"Tomorrow, when it's over," Valmai said, "if we're still in the same world, we'll discuss it. Meanwhile, to bed with you, and get some rest; those are your captain's orders, soldier; get moving."

"If he dies, you die," Brenna repeated, and stalked away.

Valmai heaved a weary sigh and pushed the door open. Not that she couldn't count on warding off a green recruit's rage-blinded attack; but an extra complication was not what she needed tonight.

Gods, a fresh straw-tick, sheets that smelled of sweet herbs, warm blankets. She lasted long enough to pull off one boot, maybe two, before falling into darkness.

In the hour before dawn, when (so men say) the veil between this world and the next wears thin, and the truth seeps outward in strange shapes, Valmai dreamt. Baron Bodo sat beside her, that crafty old man, peering out of his single eye as he did from the wall-painting at the Academy. "The magical," he told her earnestly, "is to the physical as three to one."

"Yes, but—" Valmai began, and the old man raised his hand and pointed into the distance. "See there."

She looked, and saw a pair of ugly dream-monsters, venomous and spiny; and one walked on many legs, and the other seemed to have no legs at all, but floated like gossamer from weed to weed in the autumn winds. Valmai had a cord in her hand with a weight at its end, and she whirled it and cast it and watched it wrap about the two beasts, drawing them closer together till there was only one left: they had run together like two raindrops. The remaining monster had no legs, and it was too heavy to float about, and now it would be an easy task to kill it—

And something cried out, and she drifted up out of the dream saying, "This means something, in dream-reasoning—"

"Captain," said Kember again.

"Hush a moment," Valmai said, "if I could cut their legs out from under them, and it's moral or maybe magical. Is it dawn?"

"It's full daybreak," Kember said. "At dawn there was still nothing on the horizon, so I let you sleep a little longer. We've been gathering splinters."

"Just as well. I dreamed—Curse! it was something important!

What was it I said?"

Kember repeated what she had said, keeping his face politely grave.

"Oh. Well, it must mean something, or I think it must. What did I do with—" her hand searched her pouch and brought out the two amulets, unglazed baked clay marked with the spidery characters of the spell.

"That northerner's collected stones and cords," Kember went on, "and he's made a great heap of his balbo things, and people are out practicing with 'em. He was right, the slingers are picking up the skill faster than anyone else."

"Good. Remind 'em a ganger can't get at you if his feet are hobbled and his fellows are walking over him."

"Yes, Captain. Breakfast's at the alehouse."

So Valmai belted on her shortsword, went and got small beer and more of Kolim's bread, and pondered the two amulets that lay on the table before her. Oval, flat, the size of one's ear; exactly alike so far as she could tell, with the same marks, the same meaningless dents around the edges, because they had been formed in the same mold. The markings meant nothing to Valmai, who had never studied magic.

She picked up one at random, brought it closer to her eye Gods! What? she could've sworn the *other* had moved, slithered a span's distance across the table toward Valmai's brisket. The hairs rose on the back of her neck. And in that moment a chorus of shouts broke out in the street outside, and one shrill scream. Valmai's arm jerked, the amulet went flying; without looking after it she drew her sword and ran for the door. More shouts, and the hoarse bubbling cry that was the only sound that could come from a ganger's slack throat.

Ten paces from her it lay, a sharp splinter protruding from its chest. A woman leaned on the splinter to drive it in further, broke it off flush, and stepped on the stub, all according to orders. "Right," Valmai said, and stepped over the softening body. Kember sat on the doorstep of the house opposite, his shirt stained with blood. Gangers don't bleed.

"Captain," he said softly as she reached him, "if I die, you'll see to it—"

"It's a promise," she said, "but I don't think you're dying just yet. Came near, though." The knife-wound along his shoulder was long and bled freely, but it was shallow. "It aimed for your throat, I'll bet, and missed."

"Just."

"How'd it get this far without your scouts seeing it?"

"I think it forded further north. It came into town from the north. Funny." He grimaced and reached up gingerly to feel of his shoulder. "Just as it struck, the amulet around its neck jerked sideways and the cord broke. The stroke went awry and it fell. Captain, you're smiling; have I said something useful?"

"I think, I think so. You!" Valmai pointed at an onlooker. "Get him bandaged. You, set more sentries to north and south, in case they try that again. You, you, and you, get this buried so they can't smell it. Only first let me—" she found six amulets in the ganger's pouch, and the other in the street, but it was broken.

Inside, the amulet she'd thrown against the wall had broken too, but the other had slid only six or eight feet and was intact. She stuck it in the pouch with the rest and went in search of Andvar.

An hour's practice taught them the trick worked best if only one amulet, not three, flew with the balbo, lest the motions cancel each other out. Best, in fact, to loop the amulet through its own cord where the three balbo-cords joined, and hold the amulet with one stone in your hand while winding up, and let all fly together.

They also learned that the other amulets would not move unless the balbo came within fifteen feet of them. Never mind, it was still a gain, and they had learned all at the cost of only one amulet broken: the ground in the water-meadow was soft. And overhead came the call of the woodlark.

This time it was no scout, the youngster reported, but a company on the march, five hundred at least, maybe a hundred on horseback. Valmai spaced out her people: a line of splinterers shoulder-to-shoulder in front of the trees, others waiting here and there at water's edge, a dozen sent to guard the southern ford. She set Andvar and his balbo slingers before all, well spaced out, and last of all she wound up her crossbow and placed herself behind Andvar's right elbow, far enough removed that his balbo would not strike her and she could shoot clear of him.

"Captain, when do we start?" That was the slinger on Valmai's other side.

"Andvar, what do you think?"

The man looked dubious. "Well, with the regular balbo you want to trip up the ones in front so the others will trip over them. But the special ones should go over their heads, to fly as far as possible. Two regulars first, maybe?"

"It's your call."

"All right, two plain first, then the special, over their heads. And then as you please, I guess."

"At Andvar's command," Valmai said, and the slingers looked toward her and back to him.

The ganger army came on at a brisk walk, the horse only a little ahead of the foot. Behind Valmai's back she heard the soft-footed thump of the last sentry dropping from the tree to join the splinterers on the riverbank.

The gangers were coming near, their forward lines in good order, the frightened horses kept in check by the gods knew what alchemy. "I'll—" Andvar began, and his voice cracked. "I'll count to five. One plain balbo each, throw on 'five.' One—" Six sets of stones began winding through the air, whirring softly like locusts: oh, good, no one was hitting himself with an ill-aimed stone. "Five!" Andvar shouted and the six balbos flew over the grass, wrapped themselves about the horses' legs. Valmai heard a bone snap, and a shrill scream. Six horses went down, and the others milled and reared behind them.

Behind them, the second rank regathered itself and began to push through. Valmai chose one that had made its way through the turmoil, raised her crossbow and spitted the rider through the breastbone with the wooden shaft. The ganger toppled and the horse reared and turned away. Valmai rewound her crossbow, judging that she had time for one more shot. The gangers were now very near.

Andvar loosed his second volley of balbos. Again they took out six horses—no, seven, by the gods, one insanely lucky balbo had wrapped itself about the forelegs of two close-pacing horses and brought them both down.

Andvar was sweating now, glancing between the turmoil a scant bowshot away and Valmai where she stood behind him. "At your command, Andvar," she said.

He nodded and muttered, "Might as well. Special balbos!" he cried aloud. "Hold 'em by one stone and the amulet. One—"

The gangers moved close. Valmai could make out individual

AS THREE TO ONE

faces now, dull-eyed and marked with many wounds. Wait! that fellow in the center, in red on a white horse, that one was alive still! Valmai raised her crossbow and loosed her bolt straight into the rider's throat, and he fell under his horse's hooves. *Well done, wench,* she told herself, *that may have been the only brains they had.* She set her crossbow against the tree—too close now for another shot—and picked up a handful of splinters.

"—Five!" Andvar shouted, and six balbos ceased to whirl and roared over the heads of the enemy like three-headed death sprites, singing as they flew.

The cords and thongs that held the amulets, Valmai decided later, must have been old and worn, soaked with the dead sweat of the wearers and exposed to all winds and weathers. Most of them snapped and loosed their amulets into the air. Gangers crumpled like flowers in the frost.

But there were more to come up from behind, and now they were close enough for splinter work. Valmai got one of the last riders and was nearly crushed under the hooves of his panicky mount. From somewhere nearby she heard Andvar shout, "Hold your balbos! Wait for fallen amulets!" and then it was all mud, blood, and confusion for the next quarter hour.

Once she paused long enough to watch two fresh balbos, amulets in tow, go sailing into the enemy to the confusion of that many more gangers. Another time she saw a ganger with its hands around Brenna's throat—and Kolim, sharp-pointed stake like a spear in his hands, roaring to the rescue. She saw Andvar fall with a sword through his guts, and herself stepped over to give him his quietus and a wooden shaft of safety through his heart. The enemy were growing thin; in fact, there seemed to be no more of them, only the survivors of Huffsford, and a few bewildered horses, and the dust.

It was becoming quiet again, broken only by the sounds of feet splashing through the ford or a wondering, "Gods, I'm still alive." Little splinters were stuck under Valmai's nails, painful and likely to fester; she pulled them free with her teeth and sucked at her fingertips. And through the dust came Kolim and Brenna, dragging between them a limp body dressed in glittering armor. "Captain, is this one still alive, can you tell? I hit him over the head, but Brenna thinks he's still breathing." Gods! Ulvaeus—?

Not Ulvaeus, but one of his captains, and he was still breathing: a valuable prize. When he woke he retched and cursed and could not stand. Valmai had him locked inside an empty smokehouse with a cot, water, and a chamberpot.

Kember was still alive, now bleeding from the other shoulder too. He had thrown the splinterers of the rear guard now here, now there, taking out the gangers that had made it through the front ranks; scarcely any that had drifted down to the southern ford had been in any shape to fight.

Of the Huffsford century, twelve had died. The survivors cheered and wept by turns as they impaled and buried the dead.

And the sun was only halfway up the sky. "I've got dough to punch down," said Kolim, and went away to do it. Brenna, trailing behind him, avoided Valmai's eye. She'd catch her up and say "I told you so" later.

"Now what?" Kember said.

"Now, back to your old lives," Valmai said, "unless some of you want to come to the capital and join up. You, maybe? You'd make a fine sergeant, with a bit of training." But Kember only shook his head and laughed.

"It's back to the capital for me in any case," she said, "with the tidings about the balbos, and the prisoner. But then, he's not fit to travel yet, so I can afford to spend a few days here."

"We'll be happy to make you welcome," Kember said. "Bed and board are at your disposal. Captain, you're smiling. Did I say something?"

"Not yet," Valmai assured him. "But you will."

THE HIGH ALTAR

by Dave Smeds

Dave Smeds, a Nebula Award finalist, is the author of several books including the novels THE SORCERY WITHIN, THE SCHEMES OF DRAGONS, and, in 1998, X-MEN: THE LAW OF THE JUNGLE. His short fiction has appeared in five volumes of SWORD AND SORCERESS, as well as in RETURN TO AVALON, THE SHIMMERING DOOR, ENCHANTED FORESTS, Realms of Fantasy, Asimov's, F&SF, and numerous anthologies, with contributions to SIRENS AND OTHER DAEMON LOVERS (HarperPrism, 1998) and PROM NIGHT (DAW, 1999) due out soon.
—MZB

One of Dave's friends tells us, "Some writers—some very good writers—wait and hope and pray for inspiration. If and when that inspiration hits, the ideas come, the words flow, the story unfolds.

"Dave Smeds always has great ideas. He hunts them down, he culls them, he husbands them, he builds them from scratch. Dave's words always flow. With language as his medium, he crafts his ideas into seamless, evocative prose. As for how it all unfolds... I've long admired Dave's ability to simply sit down with a specific story in mind, and in short order (and with deceptive ease), produce something brilliant. If a tale well told is a sign the muse has struck, then Dave is surely among the most inspired of writers."
—Risa Aratyr (author of HUNTER OF THE LIGHT, HarperPrism, 1995, a novel of a mythic ancient Ireland)

The rich, wet scent of reeds and duck grass rose into the breeze. Burrow's nephew Rye rushed ahead to the edge of the bluff and skidded to a stop, exclaiming reverently. Burrow joined him in gazing down at the wide, lazy curves of flowing water. He did not have to wonder at the youth's amazement. Here was more water than Rye had ever seen in one place—all the snowmelt and runoff and upwellings of springs from the Mountains of the Sunset, sweeping across the Land of the Grasses and dividing it into the northern and southern plains.

Burrow inhaled until he thought his chest would burst. The moisture in the air tempered the grittiness that coated the insides of his lungs. He lifted his hand and tousled Rye's hair. "Well, boy, is it all you expected?"

Rye shook his head. "No. It is more, Uncle. How can there be so much water here, when there is so little in our meadows?"

Burrow's face tightened around his eyes. "Ah," he murmured sadly, "that is exactly it. You see for yourself how far the balance has tipped. Come. Let us go down."

Rye danced down the path in the side of the bluff, adroit as a meadow buck. Burrow followed more sedately. He was far from the greybeard that Rye had expected when he arrived at the Great Crossroads, three nights past. Rye's mother was not yet done with her childbearing years, and Burrow was her younger brother. Still, a shaman had to conduct himself with a certain measure of dignity.

They forged through the riot of cattails and brambles at the base of the bluff, a marsh sustained by the fertile strand of alluvium on this side of the open water. From time to time their feet collapsed through the lattice of old reeds. Floodwater seeped into the hollows, drenching their toes.

Burrow grunted. He pointed to the willows half submerged in the current farther out. "That's the true river's edge."

The afternoon glare dimmed as a towering billow of cloud glided between them and the sun. A behemoth of vapor, as thickly flocked as the animals Rye's father herded across the rangelands of his home in the south. It passed, carrying every drop onward toward the mountains.

Burrow looked back down just in time to see Rye reach out and press the mat of reeds near his feet. Water filled his cupped hands.

Rye did not drink. He rinsed the grime from his face, sighing at the cool caress of liquid. Burrow understood. His nephew had had a quota of water to drink throughout the drought. But enough to spare for washing—that he had not had in a season and more.

"Listen," Burrow said. His heart butterflied against his throat. In the reeds nearby, a frog had started to chirp.

"I hear it," the youth whispered.

"Come evening, you will hear a chorus between his kind and the crickets that can lull a wolf gone rabid."

Hearing just one soothed the ache in the shaman's heart. It took him back to the long seasons when he was younger than Rye, when the meadows grew lush with feed for the herds, and frogs croaked along the pools and watering holes throughout the plains. It

THE HIGH ALTAR

reminded him of long walks from range to range, his mother and father at his side, the heart of the southern plains his playground.

Now he was here, at the Great Crossroads, a high shaman now, his only true link to those days the arrival of a sister's son he'd not seen since infancy, the music of frogs calling back a simpler, treasured time.

Burrow knelt near the clump of reeds from which the noise emerged. The croaking ceased. "Now, apprentice," he told Rye, "watch how I do this. I will expect you to be able to do it yourself two summers hence."

The man leaned nearer the clump. "Don't be afraid," he murmured to the unseen frog. He began to chant.

The fine hairs on the back of Burrow's neck rose up as the magic swept into him. He didn't know the original meaning of the words sloughing off his own tongue, but he knew their power. It was his ability to harness this sorcery that had lifted him from his life as a herder. What was new was the observation of his new pupil—perhaps his successor, if his nephew's spark of the talent could be nurtured into a flame.

The chant exuded images of peace, pleas of friendship. The words shaped into lures no frog could resist: promises of insects hopping onto its outstretched tongue of their own choice. A fine, eager mate. The ability to banish herons, muskrats, and rival frogs with no more than a single bellow from its vocal pouch.

Hop. A tiny, striped frog appeared on a tall reed, slowly bending it over with its weight. Burrow reached out his hand. The frog leaped from its teetering perch into the offered palm.

"A noble specimen," Burrow declared. He opened his belt pouch. The frog hopped within and did not struggle while the shaman pulled the laces snug.

"Must we take him from his home?" Rye asked.

"In seasons such as this, we all must make sacrifices," the shaman replied seriously. He gently patted the pouch. "Even the young and the small."

That night, the clans gathered around the bonfires. The Great Crossroads seldom housed so many tents. The turf of the council circle had long since been trampled to dust. The meat of a full dozen sage bison emerged from the cooking pits and yet was barely enough to provide all comers with their ritual serving. For all his experience and study of the history of his people, Burrow had never imagined the Land of the Grasses contained so many people, for in normal times families followed their beasts hither and yon until the nearest neighbor's tent was two days' walk over the horizon.

The shaman kept a grip on his apprentice. The youth would have otherwise been squeezed to the fringes of the pack by those jostling forward to hear the decree of the steward of the plains.

"Our meadows are brown," the elder announced. Though everyone could see that fact with their own eyes, a pall fell over their countenances to hear the revered one admit it so flatly. "Our herds dwindle from lack of grazing. The clouds hold back their bounty, giving it to the mountains. The river and its tributaries cannot sustain us, for they do not bless the wide reaches of earth that lie between them as the rain would do."

The people had no choice but to confront the arid truth of what he said.

"We know why we suffer so," the old man continued. "The mountain god calls the clouds to him. He hoards what is ours.

"You have asked me why I do not send an emissary to treat with him, and until now, I could only tell you that the clans had no one who could succeed at that task. Now, at last, we are ready." The elder raised his shepherd's crook. The ceremonial tent of antelope and ermine was opened. Out stepped a robust daughter of the plains. A woman, but not long since a girl.

Burrow blinked. Lark little resembled the mischievous juvenile who had trained under him these past few years. She was draped in a weave of cashmere so fine and thin it seemed to belong to the breeze. Around her neck hung a necklace of seashells, that rarest of treasure here so far from the ocean. Burrow was reminded of his own adolescence, when his female cousin Thistledown transformed overnight from his rough-and-tumble playfriend into a bride leaving with her new husband over the downs to Long Meadow.

Rye was Burrow's pupil now. Lark had become something beyond that.

"Sing for us, my child," the steward called.

Lark took three steps to the center of the circle and opened her mouth. As Burrow had done that afternoon, she sang in words unknown to scribes. But with each note she struck or held or

THE HIGH ALTAR

dismissed, the audience was leashed and brought to a dreamlike place where they understood her.

Burrow closed his eyes and gave in to the spell. Even the common folk would be swayed by her voice, but he, with his gift, knew its message better than most.

The song brimmed with sounds beyond Lark's single, human voice. Burrow heard the melody of the singer's namesake, the meadowlark, and then that of other birds. Frogs chirped. Bees hummed. Stalks of wild barley and oats rustled in the wind.

The shaman's eyes brimmed with tears. This was the song of the Land of the Grasses. Anyone who had spent their lives on these plains could not help but cast away any thought and attend entirely to the music, and be reminded of home.

When it ended, no one spoke. They savored the memory, not wishing their murmurs and coughs to quell the echo. An owl hooted in the direction of the river. The wind rustled the tent flaps. These noises had been part of the song, too, and they provided a sort of bridge back from the realm of magic, back to their mundane world of dust and desiccated fodder.

The steward smiled. "Blessed is our singer," he intoned, his utterance dissolving the last of the enchantment. "Let us feast. We have long awaited this moment."

Lark was led away into the crowd. Small children reached out to touch her. She beamed and stroked their wrists, their faces. Soon she was lost from view among the milling bodies. Burrow was left standing in an open space by the ritual tent with his nephew.

"What now?" Rye asked.

Burrow bent his head down and fixed his eyes on his toes. "She will be treated to a night in the sweat lodge by the river. The smoke will be sweetened with moth brush incense. Her sisters will wash and anoint her. She will be fed her favorite foods. The hope is that, in the morning when we leave for the high mountains, she will be light of spirit and remember all that is best about the lowlands. A worthy plan."

"To what part of the mountains will you go? How will you find the mountain god? It is said he has many altars."

Burrow frowned. "We must go all the way to Mount Stone, to the high altar. Where he is most likely to hear us."

"And will he?" Rye asked.

"He must," the shaman replied. "This is the one purpose I have trained Lark for. She is as ready as I can make her."

The youth leaned closer. "But is she ready? Is her talent rich enough?"

Burrow met his nephew's gaze. "The steward has declared it."

Rye nodded. "The steward had no choice. He had to give the people hope. But I am to be your apprentice, and I must know how to judge. The song I heard tonight—is that enough? Is she strong?"

"You are a clever lad," Burrow replied. "I will answer you honestly, but you are not to repeat my words. Lark is not all I had hoped for. She is a marvel when it comes to charming snakes from their holes or hawks from the thermals, but catching the ear of a god requires more than that.

"Picture this," the shaman continued, shaping his hands like a mountain peak. "The god is as one with the granite heart of his domain. Like a drunkard, he dotes on the soft touch of raindrops and snowflakes upon his vast, immobile body. It is all he cares about. He has no idea his greed has grown so extreme that he deprives the lowlands of its share of the clouds' treasure. I fear that only the greatest of voices will succeed in reminding him we exist."

"Lark is not the equal of singers of the past?"

"No. But that is no reason to surrender. No one knows precisely how much power is needed. I only know that no other has come forward in this generation who possesses half of Lark's gift. We have no choice but to send her. The drought will be the end of us if it lasts another season."

"I want to go with you, Uncle," Rye said. "I want to hear her try."

Burrow shook his head. "The journey is long and arduous. Tall you may be, but you are less than a month gone from your mother's campfire. I fret enough over Lark. You must stay here, so that I can go forth knowing that one of my charges is safe."

Rye scuffed at the woefully dry sod, unable to hide his disappointment.

At the point in the hills where scrub brush gave way to towering evergreens, Burrow's guide stopped and pointed at the trail.

Burrow knelt down. He frowned at the huge feline paw prints in the dirt.

"Tiger," the guide said. As did all the rugged hillmen whenever they spoke of one of the many dangers of their territory, he smiled.

"Will it bother so large a party?" Burrow asked, gesturing back at the men, women, and animals that followed, single-file, along the side of the gorge.

"It could," the man admitted. "They weigh more than you and I put together, and they fear nothing. But look." He traced his forefinger along the quail tracks that covered those of the huge cat. "He left these marks more than a day ago. By now he could be two mountains away. Their hunting ranges are vast."

The man chuckled. Burrow shivered.

However, they saw no further traces of the tiger. The day ran its course. Burrow collapsed gratefully as they struck camp at one of the few flat parcels of ground they had encountered since early morning. Though he was a good, strong walker, his legs ached from the constant incline.

The guide, a man Burrow's age named Root, set his aides to building the fire immediately. For, as the hillman had pointed out more than once, few beasts cared to approach open flames. Fire was the mountain god's gift to mankind, a means of rescue from both predators and cold weather.

Burrow's head ached at the challenges and dangers of the Mountains of the Sunset. Tiger. Cave ape. Bear. Twice that day their way had taken them past precipices where one wrong step would have caused them to plunge to their deaths. Still ahead were the rocky upper slopes, slick from the storms and prone to avalanches. Lowlanders did not belong here.

The shaman watched Root. Here, ironically, was the worst danger of all. The hillmen were not always friends to the plainsmen, and yet Burrow's party was entirely dependent on their good will.

Root was looking at Lark. The young woman was strolling around the campsite, relieving some of the stiffness left from riding her mount all day. All the others had walked, but she was pampered. Her hair was not limp with the sweat of hiking. Her face was not gritty with the dust of the trail, because she had been perched high.

She was beautiful. Burrow had long treasured her as a prized student and potential heroine of her people, but now he couldn't help but also gaze at her as a man admires a woman. He knew this was how Root viewed her as well.

"She would make a fine bride for my son," Root commented.

"She is sturdy, like the land."

"Then tell your son to court her," Burrow replied. "But I beg of you, do not keep her from her destination. She could not learn to love a man who doomed her people."

Root coughed. "I have not forgotten our bargain. Have no fear, I will take you to Mount Stone."

And he did. They knifed their way through more deep gorges and over treeless ridges and came to the divide of the continent. A weathered, especially rocky slope loomed ahead. All around, the terrain thrust upward into an overcast sky.

Root and his tribesmen stopped and made camp in the saddle of meadow at the base of a final, massive cone of granite and scree.

"There has never been a god as deaf as ours," Root said, nodding upward. "You've come far. I hope your journey is not wasted."

For the seventh time in as many days, Lark left her companions waiting on the flat, boulder-strewn crown of Mount Stone. The highest point of all lay ahead, a thick crag of rock jutting another bird-flutter above the rest of the peak. Carved steps led up to a hewn slab etched with runes. The high altar.

She was surprised to see a wisp of moly nettle growing from a fissure beside the chiseled stair. The peak was so high the air here never truly seemed to fill her lungs. Plants did not thrive here, even with the snows gone for a few brief months. How had she missed seeing the weed on her previous climbs up the stair? Perhaps the rain on her eyelashes had distracted her.

Today, the rain held back. As she reached the top, she could finally see the full vista around her. More than ever, she knew it as a place for a god to dwell, not small, mortal creatures such as she. Peering eastward beneath the canopy of grey clouds, she could actually see the plains, dim in a haze of dust. Lark trembled.

Drizzle began to mat her hair. She had to proceed quickly, before true drops began to fall, and distracted the god once more from her song.

She opened her mouth and let the notes pour over her weary vocal cords. She had tried and tried all week, to no effect. This time felt no different. Three movements into the song, she halted. She dropped her chin to her chest, admitting defeat.

For the first time, she heard the echo of her voice returning from

THE HIGH ALTAR

the palisades of cliff on the far side of the valley to the west. Every previous occasion, the raindrops had muffled the effect, but the drizzle was not yet strong enough to do so.

She lifted her head. How sweet the music was. To hear the echo was almost like being a member of her own audience. That last sustained note—that was the keening of a prairie wolf, proclaiming the nobility of its pack.

She listened. No longer absorbed by her own need to make song, she heard a whisper of another voice. It chanted of rain and hail and snow massaging smooth the hard, sharp features of the high peaks. It held an undeniable confidence and potency as it summoned the storms.

"How beautiful," Lark murmured.

As the song she was listening to reached a natural pause, she replied with a snippet of melody of her own, warm with the cadence and rhythm of the Land of the Grasses.

The mountain song dimmed. Lark sensed "ears" turn toward her. She sang again, fully this time.

Before she came down from the altar, the drizzle had ceased and the clouds were parting.

As the expedition neared home, a lookout spotted them and ran toward the Great Crossroads to announce their imminent return. Within an hour a dozen welcomers appeared atop a knoll. Burrow recognized one of them as his nephew, and waved.

Rye nearly tripped as he scrambled down the slope. He arrived breathless at Burrow's side.

After a long hug, Burrow held the youth at arm's length to regard him. "You've grown a thumb's width just since I've been gone!"

Rye nodded. "I sprouted with the rain. Like the grass." He pointed at the new shoots poking up through the mud.

The green blanket upon the land was only one of many signs of the mission's success, from the clean freshness of the air to the mud caking the travelers' footwear and lower garments. It had rained three times since the party had left the foothills less than a fortnight past. Great, slow-passing tempests full of grape-sized raindrops, the sort of summer deluges the Land of the Grasses was known for. Feet and hooves were heavy with the burden, but the walkers stepped lightly as they rounded the knoll and witnessed another hundred of their friends and relatives rushing from the tents to meet them.

The steward of the land, slowed by his age, arrived later than some, but no less enthusiastically. "Well met, my friend," the leader told the shaman. "Were there any casualties?" For a moment, fright sparked in his pupils. The expedition had consisted of a score of tribespeople and nine large gelded sage bison to carry the supplies. Only seven people had returned with Burrow, and only four of the bison. Among the missing was the steward's youngest son.

"We lost only two pack animals. All our people are alive and well," Burrow replied happily. "We left them safe on the slopes of Mount Stone. With Lark."

It was the next day, after the celebration, after Burrow had enjoyed the luxury of the steam lodge and a wash in the river, that his nephew finally voiced the question that had been threatening to burst from him every moment since the return.

"When can I go?" Rye asked. "When can I see the high altar for myself?"

Burrow chuckled. "You've scarcely begun your apprenticeship and already you're finding ways to escape from your lessons?"

"It's not that," Rye protested.

"I know," the shaman answered gently. "You're merely young, and find waiting the most difficult and constant part of your whole existence. You will have your wish soon enough. We will send pilgrims at least twice a year to take the place of those who wait in the mountains, keeping our singer company. I will see that you have your turn."

He could tell that Rye found small satisfaction in that promise. The next such expedition would not leave until spring.

"Try to be content," Burrow said. "Your sacrifice is nothing compared with that of Lark."

The youth blushed. "I didn't mean to say that it was. She—"

"Yes?"

Rye took on a solemnity beyond his years. "Is there no hope of her returning? Must she truly live the rest of her life there?"

The shaman sighed. "I fear so. The god must hear the song often or he will forget us again. Lark must not stray more than a few days' hike from the vicinity of an altar until we can send another singer to replace her."

"Then let us hope we can do so."

THE HIGH ALTAR

"Yes," Burrow said, "let us hope. It can happen. But our last singer remained in the Mountains of the Sunset for two generations, and died of old age before Lark came along. Perhaps the next adept will turn up in only five years, but it could again be half a century. I may have trained the last I will live to see. The next may well be your responsibility to teach."

Rye shuddered as if a locust was crawling up his spine. "How does one do that? Teach a person thus and take her to live far from home, perhaps never to return?"

"I could not imagine how until I saw the meadows dry out and our herds dwindle. It is a thing you learn to do because you must. Which I am sure is how Lark found the courage to fulfill her part."

"Is bravery enough?" Rye wondered aloud. "What of the song of the wildflowers, of the sod? She will never hear our land's music again for herself. Will her memories be enough to sustain her message?"

"In that I was able to help her," the shaman replied. "I have given her a token."

At the high camp near the foot of Mount Stone, Lark emerged from the lodge her companions had repaired—the summer home of her predecessor. The afternoon was cooling rapidly now that the sun was hidden behind the western palisades. The valley would not actually grow dark for hours yet. This bright, peaceful, extended twilight pleased her. There was nothing like it in the plains. It was something she had gained, replacing a sliver of all she had lost.

The sky was blue overhead. No clouds. The god was behaving himself. At week's end, she would climb to the peak again, and sing.

She wandered down to the stream, sat beside a hot spring, and slipped off her fur boots and her leggings. She dipped her toes where the upsurges mingled with the chill runoff from the peaks. The pool was just the right temperature—hot enough to soak away the aches of climbing steep paths, but not so steamy as to boil her flesh. Looking up again at the immense sky, she decided she could be happy here. What young woman of all her people had such a grand purpose to her life?

But was she happy yet, in this first season of her exile? She swished her bare feet in the pool, and knew that she was not. That would have to come bit by bit.

She reached into her satchel and removed a small, carved stone reliquary. She lifted the lid.

Within the box sat a small, striped frog. It chirped in greeting. Lark stroked it, admiring its sleek, healthy body. She checked compulsively to be sure that yes, the magic of the reliquary remained active, providing the amphibian with a warm, safe haven in which it could survive the frigid winter. A glow surrounded the receptacle. Within a few seconds a gnat floated by and was pulled into the radiance. The frog snapped it up. It was getting fat from all the insects that had fallen to the snare in recent days.

The frog began to ribbit. Lark closed her eyes and listened. She was pulled into daydreams of meadows, of herds, of rivers flowing lazily across the Land of the Grasses. She thought of being a little girl, playing in the mud. She remembered the chorus of hundreds of little croakers, sharing the range with her.

The mountain god had its serenader. The singer had her own.

ONE DRINK BEFORE YOU GO

by Michael Spence

Michael Spence grew up in the shadow of two prominent educational institutions: one, a major university founded by Thomas Jefferson; the other, a nearby private school whose students included my secretary, Elisabeth Waters. They became friends, and he introduced her to science fiction. Separated by college in different states, grad school in different time zones, and her moving to California after finishing her Master's degree, they didn't see each other for twenty years.

They met again at the Worldcon in San Antonio in 1997, by which time Elisabeth had become a writer and a Life member of the Science Fiction and Fantasy Writers of America (although if you had asked anyone who knew them when they were 17 which of them was more likely to do that, the answer would have been Michael).

Michael lives in Texas and is working towards a Ph.D. in systematic theology. His dissertation is currently entitled "Author- and Reader-based Hermeneutics for Imaginative Literature as an Aid to Analyzing Popular World-views, with a Focus on the Fiction of Harlan Ellison."

In addition to this story, he and Elisabeth have just sold a story to me for SWORD & SORCERESS XVI, which will be out from DAW Books in 1999.
—MZB

"May I offer you a cup of our finest wine before you go, Your Majesty?" asked the widowed innkeeper.

The barbarian king, who had already conquered half of her country and was now on his way to the capital to finish the job, had rousted her and her staff out of bed well before dawn to feed his army. Now, seated at her best private table, he glared up at her suspiciously from beneath black eyebrows like thunderclouds. "As I said, I've heard of you. And not just because they tell me you serve the finest roast *kradlik*-beast between my kingdom and the sea. Although you do," he said, his expression lightening. "This is superb." He looked down at his nearly emptied plate and his grease-smeared hands. "Good thing Cresennica now *is* my kingdom. Or will be, in another two days. We can leave out all that 'between' business."

He resumed his train of thought, and the glare returned. "No, I've also heard about your love philtres. Too many young boys in my army boasted about crossing the border and procuring something from you that guaranteed them the favors of women who had spurned them. And they thought that made them men." He snorted, took another bite of the roast, and continued around it, "As if flooring a girl with a drink did anything other than tell the world how loathsome one must be without it.

"No, my hostess. You are a fine cook, my wizards tell me you've not bespelled the food, and I'm not sorry I brought my soldiers here. But I do not think I care to have you give me drink. Our own ale will serve me well, thank you." Suiting the action to the words, he took another swallow from the cup beside him.

"I understand completely, Your Majesty," she replied with a small bow, her voice still somewhat husky from her forced early rising. Then she bent toward him, lowering her voice to a conspiratorial whisper. "Confidentially, I agree with you. My potions bring in the extra money that keeps the inn running; it seems man does not live by roast *kradlik* alone. But I wouldn't think of using one myself. My Grigorio *chose* to love me, because of something his unenchanted mind saw in me; and for that reason I considered his love all the more precious." *But fifteen years ago he went to war,* she thought, with a touch of bitterness, *where you, Your Majesty, killed him by your own hand. And here you are, in my hands. Oh, how I miss him still! And you can do nothing now to hurt me any more than you have already done.*

"Having known such love, why should I ever settle for another man's infatuation—especially if I created it myself? That is," she went on, matter-of-factly, "assuming I could find someone who would want to even look at me now. Oh, you needn't say it: I could tell by the way your eyes darted away when you first saw me. You weren't the first to do that, and you'll not be the last.

"So, if you will accept my word, I freely give it. I have supplied your soldiers with enough provisions to last several days, and I have not mixed any potions or other magical preparations with them. What your men have is good food, plain and simple. Your wizards will confirm it. And I tell you that you need not fear my wine either."

The invader looked at her, considering. Finally he said, "Very well. I'll taste your wine. But only," he added, his mouth twisting into a calculating smile, "if you will drink it with me."

"Of course," she answered smoothly. "I offer you even further surety: Please feel free to select any of the cups on the sideboard over there, so you will know they've not been tampered with. And," she added quietly, sadly, "you can always look upon me as you leave. If suddenly I am beautiful in your eyes, you will know to have your wizards check you for the love potions we spoke of."

He nodded, his smile becoming a fraction—but only that—more cordial. "I shall." He rose, strode over to the other side of the room, and returned to the table carrying two goblets, which she filled with wine while he sat down again. She waited for him to choose one, and then, still standing, lifted the other.

"A toast, Your Majesty? To your new conquest: may you live long and rule Cresennica well." As he watched, she took a long, leisurely draught of the wine, allowing every drop to delight her senses as it went down.

He watched until she had finished her goblet, then sniffed the wine and found it pleasing. He drank, with obvious enjoyment.

Noticing the lightening sky through the window, he quickly said, "We must go." He finished the last few bites of his meal and called out orders. As the soldiers made their exit, she accompanied him to the door.

Outside, the rising sun had barely cleared the mountain ridge behind them. In its light the early morning mists slowly dissipated to reveal the valley spread out below them, already beginning to glow with the deep green of an early summer dawn. From somewhere down there came the bleat of a sheep, and in response to the versicle a mockingbird announced the new day's beginning. The king took in the panorama for a minute and then said quietly, "Do you know, I never realized how beautiful a land could be. I've seen many territories—and taken them—but this is the first time I've actually had to stop and observe. You are blessed here."

She smiled. "My Grigorio always said so."

He unhitched his horse, then mounted and joined the others. As the army prepared to ride off, the king turned in his saddle and saw her standing on the doorstep. "For your hospitality I thank you, lady," he called to her. "You are a remarkable woman."

She smiled back at him. "My Grigorio always said so."

He turned again and waved his men forward, and they followed him down the mountain road toward the highway to the capital.

As she watched him go, a sudden dizziness swept over her and her knees almost gave way. She managed to catch herself upon the door frame, then turned, stumbled back into the dining room, and sat down heavily on one of the benches, placing her forehead down upon crossed arms. *Finally,* she told herself. *Finally I can rest.*

One of the serving people saw her and, alarmed, hastened to her side to offer assistance. She waved him away and again put her head down. A moment's respite, and then, exhausted or no, she would get up to help with the cleaning.

And then, perhaps, she might claim several hours' sleep. She had earned it. They all had. The dining room would simply have to open later in the day.

No, she never would take one of her "love potions." Really, when you thought about it, what love was to be found there? And yet if she more accurately called them "lust potions" or "obsession elixirs," the market for them would shrink dramatically.

But a true love potion—ah, now *there* was something to contemplate. She thought of the barbarian king, riding to seize his new throne. The doctored wine would do its work, and he would eventually become a just, compassionate ruler. He already had the strength to make justice and compassion speak firmly; and on the doorstep she had seen the smallest hint of an emerging empathy. She would be patient until it grew to be a mountain.

Of herself she thought not at all. She already loved her land and its people beyond measure. What more was there to add?

WASHERWOMAN

by Steven Piziks

Steven Piziks is an English teacher who lives in southern Michigan with his wife and son. He plays the folk harp, dabbles in professional oral storytelling, and spends more time online than is probably good for him. His fiction has appeared in SWORD AND SORCERESS, Marion Zimmer Bradley's FANTASY Magazine, *and* DID YOU SAY CHICKS?! (the sequel to CHICKS IN CHAINMAIL). *His science fiction novel* IN THE COMPANY OF MIND *is scheduled for November 1998 release by Baen Books.*

He tells us, "The idea for 'Washerwoman' has been wandering around inside my head for several years, and I used this anthology as an excuse to make myself finish it. I would like to dedicate this story to Sam Junilla, who came up with the ending one day in creative writing class when I mentioned I was stuck. Teachers do indeed learn from their students."
—MZB

Dan Fitzpatrick let his red washing bag thump to the tile floor with a sound of dismay. This couldn't be happening. Not at two o'clock in the morning.

Leaving his bag where it had landed, Dan wandered through the launderette in disbelief. No one was in sight, but the place thrummed with activity. Soapy water churned madly in front-loading washing machines and the top-loaders hummed in monotonous harmonies while brightly colored clothes danced in the dryer windows. Mounds of dirty washing obscured the floor. Every single machine was full.

Dan's heart sank. His job interview at the hospital was set for ten a.m. and he hadn't noticed until almost midnight that every dress shirt he owned was dirty. In Ireland that would've been a problem, but not here in America. Much as he liked to grumble about the American obsession with making money, he had to admit that twenty-four-hour grocers and launderettes were extremely convenient for night-owls like himself.

Until now, at any rate.

The sickly-sweet smell of fabric softener filled Dan's nose as he threaded his way between white machines and blue folding tables. He wasn't particularly tall or muscular—the American obsession with bodybuilding still mystified him—but he had the trademark Irish red hair and green eyes, which meant his friends sometimes teased him about pots of gold. The sight of this impossibly busy launderette, however, was more amazing that anything you'd find at the end of a rainbow. Dan was so astounded that he didn't notice the woman until he almost bumped into her.

"Hi!" she snapped without turning around. "Watch yerself!"

Dan jumped back and smothered a yelp. The woman wore a white dress and was slightly plump. Black hair sat in a limp bun on her head and the skin on her neck was sickly pale. She was standing in front of a folding table piled so high with clothes, it seemed to Dan that a sudden noise might start an avalanche.

"Sorry," Dan said. "Uh—are all these clothes yours, then?"

"They are not," the woman replied, still not turning around. She was folding clothes with swift, deft movements. "I'm just washin' them. And before ye ask, I can't be givin' up a single machine. I need every one."

Cold unease stole over Dan. Gooseflesh rose on his arms and neck, though he couldn't say why. "Ye're Irish," he said, purposefully strengthening what the Americans called his accent, though anyone with half an ear could tell who were the real manglers of his native tongue. "Look, all I need is—"

The woman turned to stare at him. Her eyes were pale and flat as bone and the front of her skirt was drenched in scarlet blood. Cold air washed over Dan and his mouth went dry. A strangled sound escaped his throat.

"All ye need is what?" she asked.

Dan tried to look away, tried to tear his eyes away and run. But he couldn't move. The woman hung before him like a bloody shroud. Her eyes bore into him for a long, horrible moment. Then she turned back to her folding.

Dan fled. He bolted from the launderette and pounded up the lamp-lit sidewalk. Four blocks flew by before he paused to lean against the cool steel of a lamppost and catch his breath. He crossed himself with shaking hands and a fervor he hadn't felt in years. Thank heaven he had gotten out of there. All that blood! And her eyes—cold and lifeless, like a dead fish.

Then he remembered. He had left his washing bag on the floor. His shirts. The interview.

WASHERWOMAN

Dan crossed himself again. *Sweet Mary,* he thought. *I can't go back there.*

Except the orderly job was his last chance. Unless Dan found a job soon, he was going to have to swallow his pride and write Uncle Rory for money to fly home on. Uncle Rory would understand—he always understood—but Dan didn't *want* him to understand, was tired of him always understanding. Dan, however, doubted the hospital would hire him if he showed up in a wrinkled polo shirt and smelly socks. Taking a deep breath, he forced himself to turn and stride briskly back to the launderette.

What're you so scared about? he scolded himself. *She just had a red stain on her dress, that's all. Besides, she's a fellow Irishman. Turn on the old charm and surely she'll be letting you have one wee washer.*

But his pounding heart and frantic breathing belied his calm thoughts. Tension gripped his stomach and he had to force his feet to keep moving.

The launderette was still loud with humming machinery. One of the washers lurched in place like a loose tooth before going still, a yellow light winking for attention on the console. Heart still pounding, Dan took up his washing bag from the floor where he had left it and made himself walk back to the woman's folding table.

"One of your washers is unbalanced," he heard himself say.

The pale woman whirled on him, a pair of blue jeans in her hands. The red stain on her dress glistened fresh and wet. Her horrible pale eyes met his, but this time Dan thought of Uncle Rory's understanding smile and he stood his ground.

"Look," he continued, lapsing into his normal accent, one that sounded less like a leprechaun, "I have a job interview tomorrow and need a single washer. Do you suppose there's just one to spare?"

The woman looked at him a moment longer. When Dan didn't try to turn and flee, she turned away and shrugged. "There isn't, and it's sorry I am about that."

"Are you all right?" Dan asked. "I mean—" He gestured awkwardly at her skirts.

"I'm not right at all, young man." She cracked the blue jeans like a whip and folded them neatly in half. "I've been dead for almost fifteen years."

Dan blinked. He must have misheard. "Dead?"

"Aye."

"So you're a ghost, then?"

He had meant the question as a joke, but the woman simply picked up a red t-shirt and nodded. "Aye."

Dan snorted. "That's a good one. A ghost that does...does..." He trailed off and stared at the woman. His washing bag thumped to the floor again as his fingers suddenly lost their strength.

"A ghost that does washing?" The woman folded the shirt and selected a pair of khaki slacks. "Aye."

Memories rose in Dan's mind. He remembered sitting on his mother's lap before she died. He remembered the musical tone of her voice as she told him fascinating tales of strange creatures, of phookas and selkies and redcaps and washerwomen who died in childbirth.

"The *bean nighe,*" he whispered, pronouncing it *ben nyah.* "Sweet Mother Mary."

"She won't be helping me," the woman said, still folding. "I've asked."

Dan swallowed dryly. Except for her pale skin and flat eyes, the woman didn't look much like a ghost. "All these clothes belong to dead people?"

"They do not." A washer stopped spinning and the woman promptly emptied the wet contents into a washing cart, dumped in another load from the piles on the floor, and wheeled the cart over to a dryer. "These belong to people whose lives will end tonight."

Dan looked around at mounds and mounds of clothes. "Jesus."

"He won't be helping me either."

"I thought the *bean nighe* washed clothes in streams and such," he said inanely.

"Now why would I use a stream in death when I had a washing machine in life?"

I can't believe this, Dan thought. *It's two o'clock in the morning and I'm talking to an Irish ghost in an American launderette.* An extractor came to a halt with a *thump* and the woman began pulling wads of damp clothes from the silvery basket inside.

"Listen," Dan said as respectfully as he could. "Could I just do one wee load? If I'm not getting this job tomorrow, I'll—"

"Sorry, boy-o," the woman interrupted, still pulling clothes from the extractor. "I'm on a schedule. The bomb's set to go off in less than two hours, and I need to have all this washed by then."

Dan's stomach clenched as if someone had hit it with a sledgehammer. Another memory slid sharp into his mind, cold and sharp. He was fourteen again back in Dublin. The doorbell rang. Uncle Rory and a policeman were waiting outside. Uncle Rory's face was wet, as if the cold wind blowing off the ocean had rained twin tracks of salt water down his cheeks. In the kitchen behind Dan, the radio was already reporting the latest IRA bombing. Names of the victims were being withheld pending notification of the families.

"A bomb?" Dan croaked.

"And what do you think could cause this many people to die all at once?" She wheeled the washing cart to a dryer, which stopped just as she reached it, and unloaded the crisp, warm clothes. A pair of baby-sized overalls tumbled onto the folding table. Dan swallowed hard and glanced around. His eye fell on a pay phone in the corner.

"A bomb where?" he asked, edging sideways.

"At the hotel up the street. A certain diplomat is staying there in secret with his latest mistress, but I suppose it isn't as great a secret as he thinks." The *bean nighe* paused to wipe a trickle of sweat from her face, and Dan, sidling closer to the phone, wondered why a ghost would perspire.

"If you're going to call the police," she said, "you'd better be doing it quick."

Dan halted and blinked. "How did you know I was going to call the police?"

"I have the uniforms of two demolitions officers in machine twenty-seven." She sighed and jingled her dress. "One of them is fated to make a tiny slip, and *boom,* I land in an all-night launderette with a pocket full of quarters. And ye can forget calling the hotel—they won't be able to evacuate in time."

Dan folded his arms. "I won't call anyone, then. Not even the police."

"Which means someone else will." The woman wheeled the overflowing cart back to her table. "If there's one thing I've learned, laddie-buck, it's that ye can't twist the tail of fate."

Dan watched her go, unable to respond. He was seized with a sudden urge to ring Uncle Rory, to tell him what was going on. But even if Dan could afford an overseas call, and even if Uncle Rory believed Dan's story, there wasn't much the man could do from

Ireland.

Another pair of baby overalls landed on the *bean nighe's* folding table. These were blue, and the words *I love my grandma* were printed on the front. Dan bit his lip. You couldn't get away from the bombs, could you? Not even if you ran all the way to America. Ireland might have the IRA, but America had its own troublesome people. Some of them rented trucks and drove to Oklahoma.

Dan looked at the baby overalls again. The people who planted bombs didn't even know the names of the people they killed. The victims were just anonymous sets of clothing to be folded and buried in washing room baskets.

The *bean nighe* dropped a yellow sun dress and a man's denim shirt on top of the overalls. Dan wondered if somewhere, ten years ago, a ghost in a launderette had washed his mother's favorite red blouse and his father's soft corduroy trousers, folded them neatly, and gone on to the next load.

"Am I going to die, then?" Dan asked abruptly.

The *bean nighe* stopped her folding and gave him a long look. "We all die, boy-o. That's why I'm here. But if ye mean are ye going to die in the explosion, the answer is no. Ye could be sitting right next to the bomb and somehow ye'd survive. Part of the rules—the people who see the likes of me aren't fated to die anytime soon."

She turned back to her work again. Dan glanced at his watch and saw it was nearly two-thirty. Time was leaking away like water from a bad tap. Another urge to run seized him. Why should he hang around? The *bean nighe* had said you can't twist the tail of fate, and she would know. All he could do was put as much distance between himself and the bomb so he wouldn't have to hear the explosion and the screams that followed.

But memories of his parents kept creeping back into his head. Dan tried to push them away without success. He remembered the way his mother sang wherever she went, and he could still smell the lilac candles she loved. He remembered the way his father carried Dan on his shoulders as they walked to mass. He felt the dirt on both their hands when they came in from working in the garden, smelling of green grass and rare Irish sunshine. The coroner had said their deaths had been instantaneous, but how could the man know for sure? What had their screams sounded like? Would the baby whose overalls said he loved his grandmother scream as they had?

Could Dan outrun that sound?

The *bean nighe* unloaded another washer. Dan set his jaw and strode past her. At the back of the launderette, he found a locked door. Three swift kicks later, it was open.

"Hi!" the washerwoman shouted from her table. "What do ye think ye're doing?"

The concrete-floored room behind the door was dimly lit and smelled of old soap. A bank of electrical boxes occupied one wall. Dan reached for the big switch on the first.

A cold hand closed on Dan's wrist. He yelped and jumped back but the hand didn't let go. The *bean nighe* was standing beside him.

"None of that, now," she admonished. Her fingers bit into his wrist like a bony icicle and tiny drops of blood from her skirt spattered the floor. "I don't want to be washing clothes in the sink." She released him and Dan massaged life back into his skin.

"Every minute I delay you," he said levelly, "the better."

The *bean nighe* sighed. "It won't change anything. Look, laddie, there's no call to be angry at me. I'm not the one who planted the bomb."

Dan glanced down at the woman's bloody dress. He took a deep breath to brace himself and lunged. His hand flashed into the *bean nighe's* pocket and came up with a handful of quarters. They were slick with cold blood. Vomit and bile rose in Dan's throat and he backed away, scarlet drops trailing from his hand.

"Try finishing your bloody washing now," he snarled.

"Oh, laddie." The *bean nighe* reached into her pocket and produced a handful of quarters equal to his own. "Maybe ye didn't know—I joined the fair folk on the day I died. Money is easy for us to come by. Now stop being daft and come out of this dark little room. The washing will get done—it always does."

She turned and walked back into the launderette. Dan didn't know what else he could do but follow. The *bean nighe* loaded yet another washer and went back to her folding table. There were only two piles of dirty clothes left. Several washers and dryers stood empty. Dan could do his washing if he wanted, but now it didn't seem important. He felt suddenly exhausted. He had run all the way to America to get away from the bombs, from the memory of his parents, but both haunted him even here.

Dan slid to the floor next to his own washing bag and leaned against a washing machine. Its sloshing hum throbbed in his bones. After a while he noticed his hand was cramping up. He looked down. His fingers were still clenched around the handful of quarters he had stolen from the *bean nighe*. He set them on the floor with a clink and noticed some of the *bean nighe's* blood had smeared his polo shirt and jeans.

Dan looked down at his clothes, then at his red washing hag, then over at the pale woman. The *bean nighe,* doomed to wash the clothes of those about to die. Dan's heart began to pound. What if...?

He checked his watch. Quarter of three. Probably less than an hour before the bomb went off. The *bean nighe's* work was almost done.

Quietly, Dan got up, opened his washing bag, and took out a wrinkled t-shirt and a pair of gym shorts. They smelled a bit, but not intolerably. Swiftly he kicked off his shoes, stripped off his bloody jeans and polo, and donned the shorts and t-shirt. The *bean nighe* was still working at her table, her back to him. Dan emptied his washing bag and mixed his own clothes into the final pile on the floor. Then he snatched up the empty bag and went back to his spot on the floor next to the washing machine. Dan leaned back against it and closed his eyes, letting his earlier exhaustion wash over him. The tile was chilly on his legs but the washer thrummed a soothing lullaby at his back. A moment later he fell asleep.

Dan opened his eyes with a start. Yellow sunlight slanted through windows at the front of the launderette. He got up and looked around. The place was deserted, the machines empty and silent. No clothes, no baskets, no *bean nighe*.

Something crunched beneath Dan's foot and he glanced down. A pile of dry leaves lay on the floor where he had dropped the *bean nighe's* quarters.

Heart pounding, Dan checked his watch. Eight o'clock. He dashed out to the street. Normal traffic noises greeted his ears, and there were people out and about as normal. There were no police cars, no ambulances, no fire trucks. No explosion. Three news vans occupied parking spaces in front of a brick hotel up the street, and a reporter was speaking urgently into her microphone. Dan couldn't hear what she was saying, but he could guess. Chalk up another success to the New York bomb squad. The truly amazing thing was that Dan had slept through what had probably been an impressive commotion. Perhaps the *bean nighe* had had something to do with that.

A woman wearing a yellow sun dress emerged from the hotel. With her was a man in a blue denim shirt. He was carrying a baby whose overalls said *I love my grandma.* A grin slid across Dan's face and he ducked back into the launderette.

He picked up his washing bag and checked the *bean nighe's* folding table, expecting it to be empty. It wasn't. His clothes, washed and folded, were stacked there in a neat pile.

Dan's grin widened. He had been right. Anyone who caught sight of the *bean nighe* wasn't slated for death anytime soon, but she, who only washed the clothes of those about to die, had accidentally washed Dan's. Apparently not even fate could handle a paradox.

Whistling a cheery tune, Dan started putting the clothes into his bag. If he hurried, he could still cadge a shower and make the hospital job interview. He had a good feeling about this one, as if fate were on his side. Then he gasped and dropped a pair of socks.

With trembling hands, he picked up the red cotton blouse and pair of soft brown corduroys which had been lying at the bottom of the pile. Their familiarity made his heart swell. Dan Fitzpatrick held them to his chest for a long time as fresh, cleansing tears washed his face. After a while he wiped his eyes and gently deposited blouse and trousers in his bag. Maybe he could live with the memories after all.

Dan slung his washing over his shoulder and trotted out to the sidewalk. The *bean nighe* had been right—you couldn't twist the tail of fate.

But surely you could send it through the wringer.

CHANGE-CHILD

by Elisabeth Waters

Elisabeth Waters sold her first story to me about twenty years ago. She also lives here on the premises. She has been here at Greenwalls for about eighteen years, starting out with a sleeping bag on our library floor and a share of the tuna fish and rice. And she still likes tuna fish!
She has developed into a fine writer and has written several novels, although only one of them has appeared under her own name. Her first novel, CHANGING FATE, won the Gryphon Award in 1989 and was published by DAW Books in 1994. For years people have been asking her when she's going to write a sequel, and, while this story doesn't quite qualify, it's a start. She is planning to start work on a proper sequel to CHANGING FATE this summer, during her annual two-week vacation, but she says that this story is more likely to be part of book three, if she ever gets that far.
—MZB

Druscilla frowned as she looked down at the cradle where she had left her infant daughter sleeping. "Briam, do you have Zora with you? She's not in her cradle."

Her husband came in from the balcony, lute in hand. "No, I haven't seen her since you put her down for her nap." He looked down at the pile of white fur currently occupying the cradle. "I see that Fluffy decided to join her."

Druscilla sighed. "I certainly haven't been able to keep that cat away from her. But that doesn't tell us where Zora is."

"She *can* crawl," Briam pointed out.

"Crawl, yes," Druscilla agreed, "but I don't think she could have climbed out of the cradle without falling, and one of us would have heard that." She looked pointedly at the lute in his hand and added, "At least *I* would have."

Briam smiled sweetly. "I know I tend to get lost in my music—Goddess knows it always drove my poor sister to distraction—but I think I've improved enough that I would have noticed my own daughter crawling past me, so I don't think she came that way. Where were you?"

"Sewing in the courtyard," Druscilla said, "which means she didn't go that way either. And it's odd that she got out without waking Fluffy."

Briam's eyes widened, and he set down his lute and looked more closely at the cradle. "Maybe she didn't."

"What do you mean?"

"There are two cats here."

"That's impossible!" Druscilla protested. "We have only one white cat." She took another look. Two apparently identical cats were curled so close together that they looked at a glance like a single animal.

Briam looked at her pale face and quickly helped her to a chair. "I wish Akila were here," he said, chewing on his lower lip. "This is much more her sort of thing than mine."

"What is?" Druscilla asked faintly.

"Shape-changing." Briam said the term tentatively, as if he expected Druscilla to start screaming.

Considering the attitude Druscilla had held towards shape-changers when they had first met, she could understand his caution. But contact with his sister Akila had broadened Druscilla's horizons quite a bit. Besides, at the moment she felt numb with shock.

"Your sister is the changer," she pointed out. "You're not. Both of you told me that when we married."

"It's true," Briam assured her quickly. "I can't change, and I tried very hard to learn when Akila and I were children."

"But you think that our daughter is a changer?"

"We don't have two identical white cats," Briam pointed out. "And Akila and I *are* twins. I don't think she knew how to change when she was only eight months old, though."

"When did she start changing?"

"The day we were playing on a shed roof and she fell off," Briam said. "We were three at the time. She was an eagle before she hit the ground."

"I can see why that would be a reasonable response," Druscilla said. "But what do we do with an eight-month-old baby who turns into a cat?—assuming that's what's happened here. How do we even tell them apart?"

Briam frowned in concentration for a moment, then his face cleared. "Pick them up."

"Are you saying I can tell by maternal instinct?" Druscilla picked up one pile of fur, which hung limply in her arms and mewed softly in protest. "This one certainly feels like a cat to me."

"Then it's the other one," Briam said with certainty.

"How do you know?" Druscilla asked, picking up the second cat. She gasped, nearly dropping it. Looking at the cradle, she saw that it had been lying on Zora's clothing.

"Zora weighs more than a cat," Briam said. "She can't change her weight much—at her age, probably not at all. Akila explained it to me once; in order to fly, she had to become a bigger bird with a larger wingspan as she grew. Zora probably can't fly at all yet."

"I certainly hope not!" Druscilla cradled her fur-covered daughter in her arms. "How do we make her change back?"

Briam shrugged. "I don't think we can."

"Briam, there are things I am not prepared to tolerate from my daughter. I am raising a human being, *not* a cat!"

"I'll send a messenger to Akila," Briam said. "Maybe she'll have some ideas. But I've never heard of any way to force changers to change against their will."

"So we simply have to make her want to change," Druscilla said. "That, I can do." She walked into the courtyard at the center of the house, still carrying Zora, with Briam trailing anxiously behind them.

"Dru, what are you doing?"

Druscilla knelt at the edge of the pool in the center of the courtyard. "Motivation." She dipped the cat into the pool, being careful to keep the head above water.

Seconds later she held a wet crying baby in her arms. Making soothing noises, she carried her daughter back to her room and dressed her in clean clothing. "She's either going to get over this trick soon," she informed Briam, "or she's going to be the most frequently-bathed baby in the kingdom."

Briam looked fondly at his wife and daughter. "I've always been in awe of your capabilities, but I didn't expect you to cope so well with this—not that I expected our child to be a changer," he added hastily.

"Neither did I," Druscilla said, "but she's our daughter, and we'll manage. After all, there's more than one way to skin a cat."

THE WHITE FALCON

by Heather Rose Jones

Heather Rose Jones says, "I am 40 years old and working on what I hope is the last year of a Ph.D. in Linguistics at UC Berkeley (specializing in Medieval Welsh). In addition to the handful of fantasy short stories I've sold, my publications include an eclectic mix of historic onomastics, song-books, and immuno-cytochemistry research. Like everyone else, I have several novels (mostly lesbian historic romances) in various stages of completion, but that part is on hold until the dissertation is finished. My hobbies include gardening, music, the SCA, and learning dead Indo-European languages."

She's forgotten to mention the SCA awards she's received: Order of the Laurel (excellence in the arts); Order of the Pelican (excellence in organizational assistance); and more. Heather is talented at everything she does, from embroidery to songwriting to studying the history of people's names.

I sold Heather her first PC in my pre-MZBFM days, and we got slightly acquainted. Later, when I needed an assistant at MZBFM, I heard Heather was job hunting so I hired her. And thence she came to join Cindy and Raul's writing group. I found she was better than I was at pointing out what's wrong with a story, so I still encourage her to stop by the office even though she's no longer working here.

Marion and I chose her story to end this volume because it's both vivid and powerful. It's the kind of story that will make you want to sit quietly and savor it for a few minutes after you finish the last page.
   —REH

The innkeeper had long practice in sizing up guests quickly. You got an odd lot here, just outside the city gates—the ones who had missed the curfew, or preferred the cheaper prices. It had become almost a game to see if he could guess their crafts and stations before they so much as spoke. Now this group...the twitchy, nervous-looking man who was handing the horses off to the stable boy could be anything, but he would be the servant, not the master. He had the look of a man who would carry out orders well—not through any competence or sense of duty, but because he hadn't the wit to look beyond the task.

The other man—he would be a professional soldier. There was no mistaking the swagger of a man who lived off plunder, tricked out in finery made for another, and who had gotten what he held by his own hand. And it wasn't too hard to guess where he had been fighting last, given the troubles in the land. The innkeeper took a mental inventory of the current guests. A soldier from the levies would cause few problems—only wanting to serve his time and go home—but this type looked for trouble. But perhaps his employer would keep a tight hand on him. That would be ...the lady?

Now here was a puzzle. The cloak that enveloped her was ragged beyond road-wear, and it was more than the journey that seemed to weigh on her. But her calm authority and quiet confidence belonged in a noble hall ...or at the head of an army. Here was a woman who could lead men to the ends of the earth, whether for her own sake or for whatever banner she took up. If these two were the best she could command these days, the innkeeper guessed that it had not always been so.

On impulse, he bowed lower to her than was his usual custom. "How may I serve my lady?"

She nodded to acknowledge his greeting and a sad, wry half-smile touched her mouth. But she said no word as she turned to the swaggerer, and the innkeeper heard the chink of metal beneath her cloak as she moved.

The other pushed her roughly to one side and stood before the innkeeper, his hands on his hips and a scowl on his face. "We'll have a room for the night—a private one that locks. And dinner for two—something cheap."

The innkeeper looked back and forth between the two in confusion, then shrugged and turned to lead them within. He gestured at the pegs by the fire where cloaks were hanging to dry. This time it was more affronted courtesy than simple impulse that led him to assist the woman with hers—as if she had indeed been a great lady—while the men tossed theirs at the pegs. The soldier scowled again and jerked her away by one arm, snarling, "Keep away from her!"

Again came the chink of metal, and this time he could see the cause: the short chain fastening the cuffs on her wrists. Now the innkeeper could only stand and gape as the soldier shoved her onto a bench in the corner and unlocked one cuff to clamp it around an ornamental railing.

"Hey, you can't do that," he protested, recovering himself with difficulty.

The soldier shot him a warning glance, but the woman, misunderstanding him—perhaps deliberately—answered in a low, rich voice with just a hint of amusement, "Have no fear that I will damage your property. He only chains me to show that he can."

At her last words, the soldier gave her a sharp, backhanded blow across the face, saying, "You speak when I give you leave!"

In response, she only stared at him, the effect marred by the blood on her mouth, but he was the first to look away.

The blacksmith was a neighbor, and a regular evening customer at the inn. There had been a time when he had had a wife to cook for him, and family at his hearth in the evenings. But fever had taken the wife, and the wars had taken the family. He wasn't the sort to care for spending time alone with his memories, so he took his dinner at the inn most nights. When he first laid eyes on the woman, he felt only a mild annoyance: she was sitting in his usual corner. But then he took in the colors and martial cut of her garments, and his face darkened in something too tired for anger and too impersonal for hate. He spat on the floor in her direction and turned to call for his dinner.

"Marron! What's your wife got on the fire tonight?"

Faralha was a harper from Leuin—the west country—where all the troubles were. Two years past she had fled here to the city to escape the fighting and to try to find a living once more. The living was scanty, for though Leuinori folk in exile were still hungry for the songs of home, they had little money to spare for harpers. So she slept in a shed where some of her countrymen kept a stable, and mostly sang for the Doruni, the easterners, as she did in Marron's inn. But those were different songs than she used to sing. The land here did not listen, and her tunes were no more than the piping of the blackbird.

She slipped in through the kitchen, knowing Marron would allow her a bite on credit before she began, so she heard the kitchen folks whispering about the lady in chains before she went out to see for herself. And when she saw, she knew the colors of that tattered coat, and the cut of those boots, and knew where this lady was from. And then she looked at her face, and though she had never seen her before, Faralha knew who the lady must be. They knew too—the soldiers who chained her like a circus bear—though the other folk at the inn had not guessed yet. All the hope and light drained out of her world, and Faralha knew a curious, ringing lightness where her heart had been. It left her feeling freer than she ever had before in her life: what could anything she did matter now?

Faralha settled herself in her usual place near the fire. Not so near as to put the harp out of tune, but near enough to keep her fingers from stiffening. And first she played a soft air from her own country, one she often played to begin. She glanced up briefly at the lady and was rewarded with another of her faint smiles. Then she moved into a tune the people here knew as an old country dance, one with strange changes and an almost marchlike beat. But in her land there were words to it, and she sang them in the tongue in which they had first been sung to her. It was an old story, the one of the king—or sometimes the queen—who slept under the hill, who would return when fate seemed darkest. *Still with us, still with us, she will return.* The refrain whispered in the corners of the inn. Then Faralha did what she had never before dared and turned the lyrics to the tongue of this land of exile.

She will come riding all on a white stallion,
Still with us, still with us, she will return,
Then we will cast off the chains they lay on,
Still with us, still with us, she will return.

The blacksmith looked up sharply from his dinner and frowned at her. Faralha threw her head back and closed her eyes as she began the new verse, the one that they had started singing only five years before.

High in the heavens I see a white falcon,
Still with us, still with us, she will return,
Shining in sunlight and wearing a gold crown,
Still with us, still with us, she will return,
Harry the hounds over hillside and mountain,
Still with us, still with us, she will return,
This is our land and so it will remain,
Still with us, still with us, she has returned.

Her fingers kept on singing though her voice could not, and her own tears blinded her to what her song had stirred up. For the lady wept too, though silently, as one might at remembering a departed

THE WHITE FALCON

loved one, and she fingered the remnants of silver stitching on her breast that had once been an embroidered falcon. The blacksmith was not the only one who stared at her in dawning understanding, and a few of those others made the sign against evil. But the swaggering soldier turned crimson with rage and crossed the room in three quick strides to box the harper's ears and send her sprawling across the hearth.

"Be silent with your traitor's songs or I'll silence you myself."

She scrambled out of his way, trying to protect her instrument. The lady had stood, straining against bonds less visible than her chains. But it was Marron, the innkeeper, who smoothed the tension, taking the soldier cajolingly by the sleeve and thrusting a pitcher of ale into his hand.

"Your dinner is ready as we speak, sir. See, my daughter is bringing it to your table. Let the girl be. She sings what she chooses and if you don't like it, you can keep your coins in your pocket."

The man let himself be led back to the table and started in eagerly on the stew and bread. Marron coughed loudly to get his attention, and he looked up in annoyance.

"What about her?" the innkeeper asked, nodding at the lady. "What about her?" the soldier echoed.

"About dinner..." He faltered as the soldier laughed loudly.

"I'll be rid of her tomorrow. Why should I waste good money feeding her anymore? She won't starve to death in one night." At the look on Marron's face he sneered and looked around to address all the patrons. "You've got it so soft here, you can afford to be self-righteous. If you spent a day—just one day—out there on the border, that'd drive out any pity you're feeling. They're wolves in human flesh. And you let them come here and set up their dens at the very walls of the city and think they've changed into lap dogs like that one." He pointed at Faralha. "You'll learn different some dark night when they turn on you like they did on the people of Alar-Nessa. Have you even heard of Alar-Nessa?"

"Aye!" growled the blacksmith.

"Then look to your own backs, and leave her to me."

After that, the blacksmith stared at the lady for a long time, with a scowl twisting his face, and his mind lost in thought until Marron came bringing his dinner.

When the harper's song ceased, the merchant slowly unclenched his fingers from around the shattered cup he had been holding and looked in distant surprise at the blood where it had cut his palm. How could the music still affect him so, after all these years? He had left that behind—left it behind with the other things of his childhood. He looked around guiltily to see if anyone had noticed the strength of his reaction.

The songs rarely crept into his memory any more. And when they did, he could think of it all as a child's dream...that once he had sung to the land and it had sung back to him. That wasn't real—not real like six wagonloads of goods headed for a buyer in the city. Not real like the children who waited for him within the city walls: well fed, rosy-cheeked children who were dressed in unpatched clothing, a son who was nearly a man.

Songs were a fine dream, but they didn't bring buyers to the market. At least not any more. And when the year had been bad, they didn't pay the taxes on the goods you hadn't even sold. And when you rose up against the lords in their stone keeps—keeps built with the very money they had squeezed from you—songs were a poor substitute for arrows and good swords.

Who could blame him if he had headed east? Who could blame him if he wanted more for his children-to-be than the scraps he had grown up on? And here he was, with a prosperous business and a fine wife—a wife who had brought him respectability and a house in the better part of town, not in the ragged village outside the walls where later-come Leuinori scraped and starved, just as they had at home. Who could blame him if he shed even his name, as he had his western clothes and speech?

He wiped his hand surreptitiously on a kerchief and dropped the shards of the cup under the table. Why couldn't they let it rest? Let it go? He had seen a dog by the roadside the other day, run down by a cart. It had dragged itself to the edge of the road and lay there whining softly in the hot sun. From time to time it would try to stand, but the hind legs lay useless and limp. And he had done the merciful thing and killed it before moving on. There was a time to call an end and give up the struggle.

He looked over in the corner where *she* was sitting. Their eyes met, and to the merchant her gaze spoke of recognition and accusation. She knew him for what he was. And she could reveal it here in front of everyone. She had but to stand and point and name his clan, and everything he had built, had worked for, would come tumbling down. The times were too tense. You could not live where he lived, deal what he dealt, go where he went, and be known as Leuinori. His wife would be mocked and his children spat upon. He looked away again and tried to calm his racing heart.

The old stonemason had helped Faralha up from the floor, and clucked over the new scratch on her harp, and slipped a bit of coin—though he had little to spare—into her hand. "I never knew that was one of the Old Songs," he said, settling her back in her place. "My grandmother used to sing something to that tune, but I never knew what it meant."

"Your grandmother was Leuinori?" the harper asked.

"Well, I don't know about that. She never said one way or the other that I recall. But she was always singing something, and some of it was in some strange language or other. Do you know "The Fairy Ring", then? Or "Ardoal's Voyage"? I love songs about the old legends."

Faralha shook her head, trying not to show her disdain. "Those are Doruni songs. Some court poet wrote them in the old king's time."

"Is that so?" the old man wondered. "I would have thought them as old as the rocks."

One of his friends joined them then, laughing good-naturedly at the old man's astonishment. "Half the 'Leuinori" songs you hear on the streets these days were written by some rhymester at court. It's all the rage now. Last winter they had a masque with everyone dressed up like someone out of the old stories. My niece works in the kitchens up there and snuck a peek at some of it."

The harper held her tongue only by virtue of long practice. They meant no harm, but neither did they care for her feelings in the matter. What was it to them if the singer of this year's fashion was feasted at court while those who sang the true songs starved?

"Sing one of yours, then," the stonemason asked her. "One of the Old Songs about magic."

Faralha shrugged and checked the tuning of the strings. She'd give them a Leuinan song, but it would be all the same to them which it was. She'd save the Old Songs for those who knew the difference.

The merchant found himself trembling like a leaf in the wind, and his eyes kept moving back to the lady's face, whether he would or no. Then the harper started again: a quiet traveling song—one you sang to your horse on the road. And without realizing he did it, the merchant's mouth shaped the words—words he had known in his childhood as he had known his own name. The lady saw it and smiled, and that broke the spell. He stood so abruptly that his stool crashed to the floor. Fear chilled to hate in his heart, and he hurled himself out of the common room and up the stairs to the sleeping chambers. But even the dark and silence would not banish the echo of that music.

Marron looked nervously over at the soldier as he emerged from the kitchen carrying a laden platter. Then, steeling himself, he walked to the lady's corner and set it before her. She looked up at him in surprise, an unspoken question on her lips. But before either of them said a word, her jailer was on his feet with a cry of outrage.

"I told you to keep away from her! And I said she was to have no food."

The innkeeper wiped his hands on his apron and moved back a step. "No, sir. You said that you would not pay for her food. Someone else has."

"Beef? You're feeding her beef and you fed us that stinking gruel?"

Marron backed up another step. "I fed you what you paid for, and I'm feeding her what was bought for her." He looked around as if for support. "Surely you can't complain about that."

The soldier, too, looked around, but his gaze was accusing. "Who did this?" Only silence answered him. "Who spent good coin to feed this dog of a traitor?" he roared. Then his eyes fell on Faralha and he dragged her up by the neck of her gown. "You!" She twisted in his grasp but could not break free. Finally she glared at him defiantly and said, "Would that I could! I would give all that I have, to my very life, for the *Lohanor*. But I cannot give what is not mine, and I haven't the coin to buy her even a crust of bread."

"I don't believe you," he said, slapping her casually with his free hand. He raised it back for a second blow and was surprised when his wrist was seized in a grip of iron. He let the harper fall from his grasp and turned to face the blacksmith.

"You're a bit too free with your fists for my taste," the big man said quietly.

"What business is it of yours?" Now *he* was the one who squirmed in a grip he could not break. "Are you some Leuinlover?"

The blacksmith's eyes narrowed. "I lost a brother at Alar-Nessa, and a son at Qarnfeld. But that's nothing to do with this girl, and I won't have you beating her for something she never did."

"How do you know what she did or not?"

The blacksmith released his wrist and said flatly, "Because I paid for the woman's dinner." There was a stunned silence in the room. "And I'll pay for her bed, too. Marron, give her your best room and I'll pay the charge."

The soldier looked from one to the other with no understanding in his face. But there was no answer he could make, so he shrugged and went back to his own table.

The lady had watched it all with detached curiosity. Now she caught the blacksmith's eye and beckoned him near. He took no step closer, but neither did he turn away. With a flicker of eyes in her jailer's direction, she said softly, "Thank you for the dinner." His face was like stone, as if daring her to guess his reasons. "I'm sorry that you lost your son."

"You're sorry," he hissed back at her.

"I know how you feel," she continued, as though he hadn't spoken. "You see, I have lost five thousand sons and daughters to this war. And every one of them I loved as you loved your son." She looked as if she would have said more, but the soldier shot her a warning look and she fell silent, returning him the wry, almost amused smile that seemed to drive him to fury.

"You won't think it's so funny tomorrow," he spat. "Let's see you laugh at the gallows."

She chuckled. "I've been laughing at the gallows for the last ten years."

From somewhere in the room there was a muffled laugh, and the soldier looked around to spot the culprit. It had begun to dawn on him that he was playing the fool for these people. Every time she jerked *his* chain, she gathered more sympathy. And he was clever enough to see what was happening, but not enough to know what to do about it. He muttered an oath aimed at the others in general, then growled at his partner, "Keep an eye on her," and strode out into the yard.

Faralha had retrieved her harp and readjusted its tuning. "What would you hear, Lady?" she asked, settling herself again by the fire.

"Sing me 'The Dark Lass of Linerth', and 'The Hazel Pool', and 'Nellan Argues with Her Cow.' Those were always my favorites as a girl."

Faralha gaped at her in surprise. "Lady, I haven't the heart for such merry tunes tonight."

"If not tonight, when will I hear them again? Child, there will be time enough for tears after I'm dead. Don't rush me to the grave."

The harper swallowed heavily and looked away. Then she set her fingers to the strings and began the tune for the tale of courting gone hilariously awry in the village of Linerth. By the time she began the second verse, the song had worked its charm and the cloud had lifted from her heart. Even the other customers—though they could not follow the words—were absently tapping their toes and fingers and chattering of lighter matters. The quick dance meters of "The Hazel Pool" even had Marron's daughter out jigging with her pitcher as she passed around refilling cups. Faralha began the next strain, then paused.

"I need another voice—will you be Nellan or the cow?"

The lady laughed, but then a shadow passed over her face and she said, "You'll have to be both, I'm afraid. It was part of my bargain with them...that I would not sing."

"Not ...not sing?"

"How did it happen," the blacksmith broke in abruptly, "that you came into the power of a man like *that*. I had heard better of you."

Faralha bristled on her lady's behalf, but the woman only sighed and the entire room hushed in expectation of a tale.

"It was after the battle at Istern, when we knew there would be no victory—nor even terms. We sang down the mist to cover our retreat and slipped into the hills. I'm sure you've heard that part of the tale by now. And there I released my captains from their oaths and sent my people home, to try to take up their lives again if they could.

"We had left our pursuers wandering blindly by the sea, but every army has its stragglers—in this case, deliberate stragglers perhaps, who had had no taste for the battle we were fleeing. When we came to the pass at Anaq, they blocked our way and would have held it against us.

"Oh, we could have fought our way through—there were no more than a dozen of them—but not before the fog lifted and the main army could chase us again. Some could have climbed the peaks and gone around, but not all, and not the wounded. And there was no going back.

"But I saw that these were men who fought for their own gain, and I pointed out that there was no profit to them in standing against us, except what they would have earned from the main battle itself. But if they would stand off and let the army pass through, I would trade myself for that passage. They took the bargain, but they had no mind to share me with the regular army. These two were set to bring me here—to the king himself—to claim their reward. That is the whole of the tale. And because it made no difference, I agreed to their terms: that I would allow myself to be bound, and swore not to attempt escape or harm against them, and they forbade me to sing, because they feared sorcery and would not take my word on that matter."

"How could you?" Faralha asked, through a voice halfway between sorrow and rage. "Every one of us would have willingly died for you. How could you throw that away?"

"What would their lives have bought me? Where could I go?"

Faralha said, in the tongue that only the two of them understood, "You could ride back to the Hill and wait for the next time."

She smiled her sad smile and shook her head, replying in the same tongue, "The next one will not be me. This falcon has made her flight and hit short of the mark. There is no second cast."

The harper scrambled to her feet and shouted angrily, "They will parade you through the streets and hang your head on the city gate and boast that they have slain the *Lohanor*. And there will be no 'next time'!" Then she whirled and ran from the inn.

The lady looked around at the crowd, who stirred uneasily at being left out of the exchange. "It seems we will have no more music tonight. My apologies for that."

As the noise slowly returned to normal, the blacksmith came over to sit across from the lady. She waited for him to speak first, finishing her dinner hungrily, in the best thanks she knew how to give. But when she had finished and he still sat in silence, she asked, "Why?"

He would not answer her at first, though the struggle showed clearly on his face. Then he said, "My son was home on leave the month before he died."

She waited, sensing that the tale would come in its own time.

"Do you know what he said to me, the night before he marched away? The last thing he ever said to me?" He searched her face as if expecting an answer, but she only waited. "He said, 'They tell us we are fighting a great evil, but no one fights as these people do except from love and desperation.' And then he looked around, as if he thought someone might be listening, and he said, 'I have seen their *Lohanor,* and—God help me—if I were free, I would fight for her too.' And I hated you then. It was not enough that you had stolen his life, but you had stolen his heart as well."

"And now?"

He looked down at his hands. "And now...I have seen what he saw." And then, abruptly, he pushed away from the table without meeting her eyes and left the inn without a word.

The soldier came back, in no better mood than before, and called for the innkeeper to show them their rooms as he unchained the lady from her bench. He made a great fuss of demanding that he be given the only keys to the rooms, and when they had been shown them, he dismissed Marron and glared at him until he went downstairs again. He looked around the well-appointed chamber that the blacksmith's money had bought, then pushed the lady down the hallway to the smaller room and locked her to the bedframe before returning to share the better room with his comrade. Exhaustion sent the lady to sleep almost before she heard the key turn in the door.

The merchant rose at dawn, not so much eager to get his wagons through the city gates before the streets clogged, but eager simply to get away from the inn. However much he justified his own actions in his mind, his heart still whispered 'traitor'. No. Let all those useless hopes and dreams fade away until the songs were no more than pretty music and the *Lohanor* was a fairy tale for children. He had done what he had to do—there had never really been a choice. But the music still whispered in his ears, and he could not explain away the tears that fought past his control.

The sun streaming through the window onto her face woke the lady at last. She opened her eyes to stare at the ceiling, noting incuriously that the angle meant it was nearly noon. Odd, that no one had come for her yet, but it hurt too much to wonder, to question...to care. Her only thought was, *Please, let it be over soon.*

After what seemed a long time, there was a tentative tap on the door, then a more authoritative knock.

"I cannot reach the door," she called out. "And if I could, I have no key."

There was silence at the door for a while, then the sound of heavy footsteps in the hall and a key in the lock. The innkeeper stared in surprise to see her there.

She schooled her face to its sad, wry grin. "My companions thought they would take advantage of the smith's generosity." She nodded toward the ring in his hand. "I seem to recall they asked to have the only keys..."

"And do you think I'd be such a fool not to have spares? But I haven't a spare for those," he said, pointing to the manacles that bound her to the bedstead, "so you'll have to wait until I roust your friends out."

He disappeared back down the hallway. She heard him pounding at another door in the distance, then the rattle of keys, followed by a confused din of shouting and coughing.

Some time passed before anyone came to enlighten her. It was the innkeeper's daughter, pale and shaking and carrying a small black key.

"Dead!" she exclaimed as she unlocked the chain from the bed. "They're dead, both of them! Someone dumped sleepwort down the chimney, then stopped it up."

The lady rose and followed her down the hall. They had thrown the windows open, and someone had gone up on the roof and unplugged the flue. A faint, sweet odor lingered in the room, but it hadn't been that that killed them—the herb had only kept them from waking while the smoke did its work. The two men lay side by side on the bed as if asleep, except for the fine layer of soot that covered everything.

"She did it! She killed them!" someone shouted from the crowd that filled the room, pointing at the lady where she stood in the doorway.

"And how could I have done that," she asked, "with me chained to a post and the room locked as well? And what would it profit me to kill them?"

The accuser gaped at her a moment. "Why, to escape, of course!"

She laughed in outright astonishment. "And so I killed them, locked myself back in my room—somehow returning all the keys to their possession—and waited until now, rather than stealing a horse in the night and being halfway to the Fleth? Don't be a fool." It was the closest thing she had shown to anger in the time she had been there.

"Sorcery!" someone muttered.

"No one else would have reason to kill them," another said. "Send for the city guard."

"No!" she protested frantically, seeing where this would lead.

She looked around to Marron and held out her hands. "I swore that I would surrender myself to the king of my own will. Let me do that—not be dragged before him by the guards as if I were a common criminal!" Marron hesitated and she continued, "I had no part in these deaths. I give you my word on that. Will you let me finish this journey in peace?"

He shifted his stance and sized up the mood of the crowd. "It isn't that I doubt you or anything," he said slowly, "and God knows, if you *had* done it, it isn't as if they could do anything worse to you. But if it wasn't you, you see, we need to know who it was. I don't like the thought of a murderer hanging about my place. Why would anyone else want to kill them?"

"Who knew that they were in this room?" she countered. The room quieted as the meaning of her question sank in. "Did anyone know they had switched rooms with me? You didn't," she said, turning to Marron. "Did anyone?" When the silence had begun to fray, she said, "Shouldn't the question be, why would anyone want to kill me?"

That question stumped them. Who would kill a dead woman? As they pondered the riddle, Marron herded them out of the chamber and down into the common room.

Somehow, no one found it strange when the lady took charge of matters and began questioning the guests. It was what Marron had noticed in her at the first: the natural habit of command lay so easily on her shoulders that it would be impossible to take offense. Afterward, they talked openly of sorcery, for all she did was ask simple questions and watch your eyes as you answered. And with most, she nodded and dismissed them after that, but those who had tried to dissemble found themselves queried more sharply until she was satisfied.

But no answer emerged. No one had seen or heard anything, or turned up any reason why the deed might have been done. Marron had sent out messengers to call in the locals who had been there just for the evening. "Of course, there were three travelers who left early this morning," he added. "It could have been any of them. The two heading up north are long gone, but the fellow with the wagons lives right in town. He showed up after they closed the gates yesterday. I could have him fetched."

The lady brought him to mind—the one who had mouthed the words of the Leuinal song. Had he thought to kill her lest she betray him? But if it had been him, he had brought about his own betrayal by the deed. She shook her head. "Leave him be for now."

They brought the blacksmith in, grumbling at being taken from his forge. But though he still would not meet the lady's eyes, neither did he show any surprise that she still lived. And they brought the old stonemason in, who spat on the floor when he heard of the deaths and said he had no tears for the likes of them. And finally there was only Faralha left to come, who had to be searched out in the corner where she slept most of the day away.

They heard the harper's voice, tight with emotion, as she approached the door. "What happened? What do you want with me?" She stepped through the doorway and blinked a moment in the darkness of the common room, then Marron stepped from between her and the lady. Faralha's face went pasty white. She swayed and clutched a table edge to keep from falling. "No," she whispered, almost too softly to hear. The lady stood and went to her, and Faralha sank to her knees before her, face buried in her hands and sobs shaking her thin shoulders.

"Why?" the lady asked, though she suspected the answer.

The harper looked up and struggled to find her voice. "To steal their victory. To leave us our dreams. To take you out of their hands before they could make a sordid circus of your death!" She clenched her hands into fists. "I will not ask your forgiveness for trying, only for failing."

The lady shook her head. "I will forgive you for trying, but I will not forgive you for killing two others in my place."

Faralha looked around wildly and realized the most notable absence in the crowd. "But then you are free!"

"No! It was never these chains that bound me, but my own word.

No one can free me from that." She took Faralha by the arm and raised her up. "Today—as I swore in exchange for my people's lives—I will walk into the king's court and deliver myself into his hands. And you will be my herald, and sing the *Allohan* before me. That is your penance."

"Please, no..."

The lady's voice lowered. "Must I go alone, then?" she asked. And for the first time, her mask of calm acceptance began to slip. "Be there with me, until the end. Sing to me."

The harper gulped and nodded.

The lady looked around the room. "Then if you are satisfied, we will leave you." But when she would have gone to the door, Marron blocked her path. "There's no need for haste. It's nearly evening and the gates will be closing. Tomorrow will be soon enough. Rest another day. We can find you a bath and some fresh clothes—or would you go before the king in rags and filth?"

A ghost of the wry smile returned. "That is how most of my countrymen have entered this land."

And then the blacksmith faced her again and moved to unlock the heavy chains from her wrists. She moved to protest, but he said, "Tomorrow, if you insist, you can be chained again, but for one night you can do without."

She stared around at the small crowd that remained. In their faces she saw a familiar look. Somehow, in a single day, she had moved from being their enemy to being the Queen Under the Hill. They loved her. If she lifted her hand, they would follow her. If she spoke the right words, and sang to their hearts, they would even die for her. The burden was far heavier than the one the smith had removed. Though she wished nothing more than to have the whole matter done with, she let herself be persuaded. And while water was being heated, and her clothes whisked away, and a dozen other preparations made, Faralha slipped off on errands of her own.

The morning was gray and misty with the sort of summer fog that would burn off soon with little warning. The lady had stayed wakeful until the early hours, but at last had slipped into a few hours of sleep. Now she woke, rising in her borrowed shift, to find a suit of clothes laid out at the foot of the bed. *Could such a thing be done in one night? she* wondered. *And how many needles did they find to work this?* She lifted the quilted coat, with the pattern taken from her old torn garment, down to the falcon badge stitched on the breast. And a clean shirt and hose, and her old boots cleaned and polished. A shiver went through her as she put the garments on.

And then she went down into the courtyard. The blacksmith came out toward her from a knot of waiting people. Almost shyly, he held out a pair of delicate silver bracelets, linked by a silver chain. She put them on, thinking that the stories would make much of that. Would they say no baser metal could have bound her? And then Faralha came from the stable, leading a white mare, who the day before had been pulling a vegetable cart. But now she had been brushed until her coat gleamed like moonlight.

The lady mounted, and Faralha led her through the city gates and along the streets toward the plaza before the palace, chanting the plaintive strains of the *Allohan.* Echoes came from every alleyway and shadow that they passed—Leuinori exiles forming that invisible layer on which every city stands. They took up the chant until the whole city seemed filled with the sound of the ancient tongue. And then they stood before the palace gates, with the eerie music swelling around them, and the harper proclaimed in a loud voice that the *Lohanor* had come to give herself into the king's hands. And as she spoke, the fog parted, and a shaft of sunlight lit the rider on the white horse, and high overhead the lady heard the sound of a falcon screaming.

For the first time since the pass at Anaq, the journey seemed not an ending, but a beginning.

ABOUT MARION ZIMMER BRADLEY

Marion Zimmer was born in Albany, New York, on June 3, 1930, and married Robert Alden Bradley in 1949. Mrs. Bradley received her B.A. in 1964 from Hardin Simmons University in Abilene, Texas, then did graduate work at the University of California, Berkeley, from 1965-67.

She was a science fiction/fantasy fan from her middle teens and made her first professional sale to *Vortex Science Fiction* in 1952. She wrote everything from science fiction to Gothics, but is probably best known for her Darkover novels. In addition to her novels, Mrs. Bradley edited many magazines, amateur and professional, including *Marion Zimmer Bradley's FANTASY Magazine*, which she started in 1988. She also edited an annual anthology called SWORD AND SORCERESS for DAW Books.

Over the years she turned more to fantasy. She wrote a novel of the women in the Arthurian legends—Morgan Le Fay, the Lady of the Lake, and others—entitled MISTS OF AVALON, which made the *New York Times* bestseller list both in hardcover and trade paperback, and she also wrote THE FIREBRAND, a novel about the women of the Trojan War.

She died in Berkeley, California on September 25, 1999, four days after suffering a major heart attack. For more information, see her website: www.mzbworks.com.

Made in the USA
San Bernardino, CA
10 January 2014